Plzeň
(Pilsen)
Horažďowitz
Strakonitz
Czechoslov
Lin
Salzburg
W
E
S
MY Book
Barbara Galbreath

DETROIT
PUBLIC
LIBRARY

DETROIT PUBLIC LIBRARY
3 5674 00648520 6

THE WORKS OF

ERNST LOTHAR

A WOMAN IS WITNESS, *A Paris Diary*

THE WARLORD, *A Novel*

LONELY PEOPLE, *Stories*

POWER OVER MEN, *An Epic Trilogy*

THE TRIUMPH OF DECENCY, *Stories*

CHILDREN, *Stories*

THE FIGHT FOR THE HEART, *A Novel*

THE CLAIRVOYANT, *A Novel*

LITTLE FRIEND, *A Novel*

THE LOOM OF JUSTICE, *A Novel*

MARRIAGE, *A Novel*

OH WORLD, *Essays*

AUSTRIAN ESSAYS

ROMANCE IN F-MAJOR, *A Novel*

THE RIGHTS OF MEN, *A Cycle of Novels*

Beneath Another Sun

BY ERNST LOTHAR

DOUBLEDAY, DORAN & CO., INC., GARDEN CITY, N. Y., 1943

PRINTED AT THE *Country Life Press*, GARDEN CITY, N. Y., U. S. A.

Translated by Barrows Mussey

To

Countess G. S. P.

A great woman in Czechoslovakia

Exilioque domos et dulcia
limina mutant
Atque alio patriam quaerunt
sub sole iacentem.

And for exile they change their homes
and pleasant thresholds
And seek a country lying
beneath another sun.

VERGIL, *Georgics* II, 511, 512

Foreword

THIS IS A NOVEL only to the extent that people and destinies are portrayed as if they were figments of the storyteller's imagination.

But such is not the case.

On the contrary, the people and destinies of this book obey the storyteller only where he is no more than the interpreter of their thoughts and feelings.

That which makes them think, feel, and act is prescribed not by him but by history; it is based on documents and trustworthy reports.

Except for slight disguises, connections, and interpretations, it is a transcription of today's great witchcraft trial.

For no novelist's imagination can even approach the unthinkable course of history since the rise of Hitler. And so I felt that I should confine myself to chronicling an age that sets the universe at naught and holding up to future generations a mirror in which they will look with the blank astonishment natural to those who have overcome and almost forgotten the New Middle Ages, thanks to Nature's kindly gift of a flagging memory.

ERNST LOTHAR

Colorado Springs, Summer, 1942

Contents

PART ONE

Where you belong . . .

Chapter 1

FOR THE TWENTIETH TIME the old man in the green Loden hat gazed along the station platform, shading his eyes with his hand against the dazzling late-afternoon sun. It was a firm, heavy hand that showed no sign of age; the veins scarcely stood out, and the hand did not tremble. Nor would old Mumelter's figure have given any hint of the ninety-one years he had spent in Bozen. Unbowed, broad-shouldered if rather haggard, he was moving with the impatient stride of a man who could still walk upright unsupported.

"You simply can't depend on anything any more!" he said savagely; there was not a puff of smoke to indicate the approach of the express. "This is really a sin and a shame! The accursed train is three quarters of an hour late already—and why? No one can tell you! Never a train arrives on time hereabouts any more, nor the mail; the wood is green, the Calville apples are all frozen. A devil of a way to go on!"

"Don't go getting excited again, Grandfather!" said the girl at his side, but she laughed as she spoke. Riccarda Mumelter had been keeping house for the old man and her two brothers for years, owing to the death of her parents in quick and mysterious succession during the fifth winter of the occupation of South Tirol. She was laughing now because she knew how her grandfather loved to get excited. He positively blossomed out when he discovered anything that, by comparison with the days before 1918, put the Austrian regime in a better light; these differences he pursued like a butterfly collector and impaled them triumphantly on the pin of his wrath the moment he could lay hold of them. Although it was July of 1939, and he had had more than twenty years to get used to the new order of things, any attempt to reform him was perfectly hopeless. Time, which had scarcely impaired his physique, had also passed him by in this respect.

He had not accepted the fact that South Tirol no longer belonged to Austria and was being Italianized from year to year and from hour to hour under increased pressure and with redoubled craft. Old Mumelter never accepted history when it was vile in his eyes; and his eyes, still good enough for delicate wood carving, were keen.

"Ridiculous!" he said in his gruff South Tirolean German. "I say things the way they are!"

The porters, elderly men and all of Austrian birth, who were sitting on their baggage trucks, likewise awaiting the train, nodded to him and called: *"Gruess Gott,* Herr Mumelter!" This was not only a greeting but a recognition of the fact that old Mumelter was a privileged character who could afford the luxury of such public grumbling.

Others, who felt just as he did, never spoke except privately and in terror of the Italian prefect. Old Mumelter, on the other hand, did not subdue his language under any circumstances, and the authorities, who otherwise took severe and cruel action if anyone ventured the slightest disapproval of Italian rule, winked with both eyes.

Why? The head of the Bozen police, Conte Mestrozzi, had specially impressed it on his subordinates: "Just don't make any martyrs, signori! How long has old Mumelter left to live? A year or two if he's lucky. So let's let him spend those two years walking around as a living symbol of the fact that we magnanimously tolerate the views of our opponents!" But the head of the police had been mistaken. At that time old Mumelter was eighty-three. Now he was past ninety-one. And still savagely excoriating everything Italian.

The sun was lower now. It was beginning to set the mountains ablaze, particularly the wild, jagged, snow-covered Rosengarten. It would have been a superb sight if it had not at the same time kindled the metal letters of the station sign, which infuriatingly bore the name *Bolzano* instead of the century-old *Bozen*. Whenever he saw the hated name the old man spat, and this did, after all, try the patience of the authorities too far. The passing *carabinière* who was on station duty warned in Italian: *"Sputare prohibito!"* Whereupon the old man took out his handkerchief and carefully spat into that.

"Heavens above, Grandfather, you are a trial!" said his laughing granddaughter. She was in glorious humor, for her favorite brother was coming home at last. She did hope he would arrive soon, not simply because the old man was impatient and the special gala dinner might suffer from delay, nor entirely because Andreas' homecoming would give a new center and a fresh gaiety to the orphaned household.

The reason was Sepp, the youngest of the three children, who had promised to sneak out in good time from the Avant Guardia roll call that afternoon and be at the station promptly. It was miraculous enough that Grandfather had not noticed his absence long since and asked, "Where's that brat Sepp?" Then Riccarda could have done nothing but reply that he, like all the other young lads of Bozen, had had to go to the Avant Guardia; for lying was something she could not do.

She felt a physical aversion to people who lied, and in this, as in many other ways, she was intolerant. She was not beautiful, which she knew; but she was, without knowing it, attractive. Her black eyes and her firm, catlike body were part of this attraction, and so was her voice, which was resonant though husky. She slipped her arm under the old man's.

Just then he halted and asked: "What's wrong with Sepp, anyway? Doesn't he think Andre's coming is important enough to bother with?"

The girl, with a vague, "Probably he's still busy," tried to divert the storm.

But old Mumelter persisted: "What could he be busy about, the donkey? His business isn't as important as all that!"

Oh, the old man was not one to give up his authority! Although his late son's children were not children by any means—Andreas was nearly twenty-five, Riccarda was twenty-one, Sepp was going on eighteen—he ruled the house; and now that the eldest grandson was pursuing his studies abroad, Grandfather's sway was absolute. He soon wormed it out of Riccarda that Sepp was at another of those damned Youth meetings that the Italians were poisoning the younger generation with. What did they learn at the Avant Guardia, anyway? Deadly sins! In the first place, that they were not Austrians but Italians, devil take them all! Then, that you had to give obedience not to your parents or relatives or anyone else reasonable or worthy of respect, but to the Fascisti. God damn them! And, finally, that the Church was unnecessary, and piety was ridiculous. The old man turned purple with rage when he thought of it. And yet he had forbidden his grandson not once but a hundred times to attend or have anything to do with those thugs. Ninety-one-year-old Numelter was in such a fury that he yelled so as to be heard the length of the platform: "A dirty young whelp if ever I saw one!"

This is a fine how-do-you-do, thought Riccarda; *he's quite capable of spoiling the whole party.* She was fond of her grandfather beyond question and respected his opinion. But she thought it downright wrong of him to force his opinion on all of them. It always produced a contrary effect on the self-willed Sepp in particular, who had, furthermore, a childish fondness for uniforms and was highly sensitive to slights.

"Grandfather," she begged, resolved not to provoke the long-overdue clash at the very moment when all should have been harmony, "couldn't you ask the stationmaster how much later it's likely to be? The chickens'll be burned in the oven."

The old man shrugged his tall shoulders contemptuously. "There isn't any stationmaster here any more! Nothing but a *Capo di Stazione,* and all he'll tell you is a hatful of lies!"

Just then the noise of the expected train was heard, and a few moments later Andreas Mumelter was getting off.

He kissed his grandfather's hand and kissed his sister on both cheeks.

"Late, what?" he asked.

He was tall and broad, good-looking and high-spirited. His was one of those faces that can be read, and which to read is a pleasure. Over his forehead (which was not particularly high, but broad and open) hung obstinate hair that had evidently just been tamed with a pat of the hand; below it were brown eyes, not so large and dark as his sister's, but lively and inquiring. The cheeks, upper lip, and chin were clean-shaven, tanned by the sun. The special point of his face was the mouth. It was full, sharply chiseled, and dominant. Perhaps this was due to Andreas' habit of sticking out his lower lip past his upper lip when he was studying something or thinking.

He wore this expression now as he listened to his sister, who told him in a few words—here, too, the Mumelters were typical South Tiroleans, sparing of talk—the news of the last few days. Veronika, the old servant, had started to leave in high dudgeon day before yesterday, goodness knew why, but had changed her mind and stayed on; Andreas' room was repapered, and she hoped he'd like it; Foxy, the bitch, had had pups, seven of them, and five were given away and two had been kept. He noticed that something was amiss, and as he stooped for his suitcase he asked her in an undertone: "Something wrong with Sepp?"

She started to reply, but the old man inquired suspiciously: "What are you two whispering about?"

They stood before the station in the evening sun, and Andreas' heart swelled. Three years he had been away. Berlin and Munich were worth seeing, no doubt. But here, this was lovely. What air! How he had missed the mountain air in the cities! It had a smell, a taste; it was cool; you breathed it, and there was strength in your lungs. And the light! All that light those last years—gray in the morning, wan in the evening; the only brightness was electric. Here, on the other hand, the sky was radiant, gentian-blue, and the glacier atop the red Rosengarten shone snow-white, and the fantastic saddle of the Schlern was golden, and the Wassermauerpromenade was laurel-green. It was wonderful to be at home again, with a training that no one need be ashamed of, with an academic degree that promised a future. That very Monday he would look up the man who was building the viaduct over the Talfer, and if nothing came of that, he might still get the place with the Virgl railway that had been half promised him in case he should get his diploma as a mechanical engineer. That was in his suitcase, and with it drawings that he really ought to show to a military expert. His future was in his bag, and before him was Bozen, the loveliest city he knew. His future was here.

"Hotel Bristol!" "Hotel Laurin!" "Hotel Mondschein!" "Hotel Greif!" cried the runners lined up before the station, the moment they caught sight of the first arrivals coming out. As there was no answer, they dutifully translated into Italian: *"Albergo Griffone! Albergo Luna!"*

"Hold your tongues!" growled the old man, walking quickly toward them. Buttonholing the runner from the Hotel Greif, he went on: "What does this mean, Vincenz? In the first place you know us. And in the second place you're not going to blackguard the old established Hotel Greif into any nonsensical *Albergo Griffone!* Now don't forget!"

Only now did the men with the gold-edged caps realize that they had far overreached themselves in their professional zeal. Imagine taking the Mumelters for strangers!

"Blockheads!" the old man shouted after them as he started home with his grandchildren, scorning taxis and trams. It was not far to the Silbergasse, where they lived; they had only to go through the city park and across the Waltherplatz; and Andreas, carrying his suitcase, told about the last examination as they went. He had got four questions out of five in building construction, five out of five in machine construction, oral and written both. Not too bad, was it?

Accordingly, by way of congratulation, the grandfather offered his grandson a drink in the garden of the Hotel Greif on the Waltherplatz, while Riccarda went on to look after the roast chickens. The old man declared he was not averse to a glass of red wine, and the two sat down at one of the tables that stood outdoors between green, ivy-covered walls near the gray, weathered corner of the low building. The hour was too late for afternoon coffee and too early for supper, and so there were few other guests. The Terlaner having been brought, sampled, and pronounced drinkable, therefore, the old man was able to get at the real purpose of his generosity. From the moment his grandson had stepped off the train, one question had been burning on old Mumelter's thin lips. With conditions as uncertain as they were, he had not dared write; yet everything depended on this question. And so he asked it, wiping the wine from his white mustache with the back of his hand: "How's the business?"

What he meant was obvious. The business of South Tirol, the only thing he still existed and endured life for. He thought it was high time for the Third Reich, whence his grandson had just come, to take the South Tirolean business in hand and restore the rights of the outraged land at last. Not that he could be very enthusiastic about the Nazis, this old wood carver who had given the wooden model of the Innsbruck tomb of Maximilian to his Emperor in 1898, and received for it the Imperial and Royal Silver Cross of Merit with the Crown, which he still wore on special occasions. "His" Emperor, now and always, was Francis Joseph I of Austria-Hungary; and, like Francis Joseph (who had died in 1916), he still wore round, short-trimmed imperial side whiskers. He had been, no, he still was an Austrian to the marrow, and the only songs he knew were *"Gott erhalte, Gott beschuetze unsern Kaiser, unser Land,"* and *"Zu Mantua in Banden Andreas Hofer lag."* But in 1918, after the last war, when the Austrian delegation at St. Germain had to accept the demands of the American President Wilson, the world ceased to exist for old Mumelter.

"Just imagine," he used to say fiercely as often as anyone would listen, "a man without the slightest notion of what we are, where we are, or what we're like, an American who can't speak a word of German, who doesn't know anything except by hearsay and from Italian lies, simply announces one fine day: 'You South Tiroleans, you have ceased to be what you've been for thirteen hundred years. Overnight you're part of Italy, not Austria. Your country isn't called South Tirol any more, but Alto Adige; anyone who says South Tirol is to be punished; you aren't to speak German, but Italian; your children are to go to Italian kindergartens and schools; the priests won't preach to you any more; you've got to forget Andreas Hofer, Haspinger, and Speckbacher, whom you used to be proud of, and instead you've got to put up monuments to the deserter and traitor Cesare Battisti; people will spit in your deputies' faces; they'll kill your teachers; your good, honest, old German names will be butchered—Figl the wax chandler is going to be called Vigili, Goller the baker Golli, and Count Sarntheim will actually be Sarentino.' Just imagine that, if you can!"

The cut made by St. Germain between North and South Tirol still ached like an inflamed wound. His eyes, in search of help, had long rested on the new German Austria. Good God, what had become of the great, powerful, Imperial Austria with her fifty-four millions that he had known and served? Nothing but this tiny country, German Austria, without strength or vitality, governed by the red Social Democrats—bah! Still, that tiny land of seven millions had lost South Tirol but kept North Tirol. Therefore, the old man hoped, she would not rest until she recovered the whole Tirol; for anyone knew that North Tirol and South Tirol belonged together like fingers of one hand. If you chopped off two, the other three were good for nothing! And so he had been looking across the ridiculous Brenner frontier to the Austrian brethren, year in and year out, waiting to see what they would do. But the brethren did nothing at all; they ought to be ashamed! And when Hitler had swallowed them, body and bones, a year before, they had simply let themselves be devoured, just like that, the whipped dogs, without so much as chirping! *But be that as it may,* the old man had thought—and countless others in that country thought like him—*the Anschluss has at least one good feature. Now that Hitler has swallowed the new Austria, there is nothing to prevent him from swallowing us too; then we would at least be together, a united Tirol; we could speak German and live and die as we have always done. If Hitler helps us now, I'm willing to say "Heil Hitler!" too, even though anything we hear or see of the Nazis hereabouts isn't particularly enchanting. Of course he's bound to help us,* Mumelter reasoned further, *because what is it he wants in the world? The liberation of German-speaking minorities—that's what he's fighting for. He has already liberated the Sudeten Germans, and he wants to free the Danzigers; aren't we German South Tiroleans worth more than all the Sudeten Germans and Danzigers put together? We gave Andreas Hofer to the world, Walther von der Vogelweide, and the Songs of the Nibelungs and of Gudrun, Michael Pacher of Brunneck, Defregger and Egger-Lienz, and the most beautiful Gothic architecture you can find in Europe; obviously our hour of liberation must come, and the sooner the better. Holy Trinity,* he prayed, *let me live to see the day! Let me see the Fascisti haul down their tricolor, and the Tirolean eagle flying over the country, and let me hear the "Andreas Hofer Lied" sung here in Bozen and yonder in Meran and Klausen and Brixen, everywhere—all the way up to the Brenner Pass, where they've put that ridiculous frontier.*

His hand trembled a little as he put the vital question to his grandson, who had been in Berlin and Munich and Vienna, and so, naturally, must know: "How's the business?"

But the grandson thought otherwise. When he had gone to Germany in 1936 to study, because there was no technical academy in South Tirol, he had thought as his grandfather did, to a hair. Not now. No, now he didn't feel like the old man and most of those in the country; he was unspeakably glad to be back. And he was positively ecstatic to think that he would never again have anything to do with the Third Reich. *In spite of everything, we're incomparably better off under the Italians,* he had learned to think.

But, lest he blurt anything out too suddenly, he merely said: "I haven't really heard anything new."

This vexed and disappointed the old man beyond measure. Hadn't his grandson called on the people and organizations he was supposed to call on—the Schillerbund at Innsbruck, the Alpine Club in Munich, the Catholic Young Men's Associations in Vienna?

Oh yes, Andreas had done all that.

"And," the old man persisted, "how far have they got? What does Hitler intend to do?" At one of the tables along the outside wall of the Hotel Greif, farthest away from the two Mumelters, who were sitting only a few yards from the Walther von der Vogelweide monument, a man's head bobbed up from behind a copy of the *Corriere della Sera*. The man, a baldhead with a close-clipped mustache, reached for the *Popolo di Roma,* which lay with other Italian papers on the table at his left, and presumably in so doing he noticed the two wine drinkers.

"Buona sera," he called loudly across the empty tables. *"Come sta, Signor Mumeltro?"*

"My name is Mumelter!" replied the old man contemptuously, and then, making introductions: "This man's name is the same, because he's my grandson! That's Signor Poschacher, Andreas." Jerking his thumb over his shoulder, he added aloud: "I'd like to bet that you'll never guess what that gentleman's business is. Would you believe it? He—he in person—puts out the only German paper we still have. The silly rag is called *Dolomiten*—I don't know whether you ever saw it abroad. Well, destiny in the Alto Adige sometimes plays pranks, and makes Signor Poschacher the head of a German newspaper." Calling for the waiter to pay the score, he added: "You're tied up somehow with Negrelli, the head of the Roman press section, who had the predecessor of your *Dolomiten,* the *Alpenzeitung,* published here, aren't you? A marvelous sheet, I tell you, Andreas, which praised everything Italian to the skies and chucked everything German in the muck—just like the high-principled *Dolomiten*. Isn't that right, Signor Poschacher?" Turning to the waiter: "We had three fourths of a liter of the old vintage," and in the same breath, hardly less loud, to Andreas: "He's bribed, the scoundrel!"

The editor of the German paper shrugged his shoulders with a smile and remarked in heavily accented German: "I'm happy to see that Signor Mumeltro is still in the best of humor. Just arrived, young man?"

"Yes, the young man has just arrived and is just leaving!" replied the old man gruffly. The two got up and walked past the Walther monument, whose coats of arms—the old man pointed to them without a word—had been repainted in the Italian colors during Andreas' absence. The square, Lord have mercy, was now called the Piazza Vittorio Emmanuele, after the Nutcracker King, whom you could hardly do more than laugh at. The old man cast down his eyes as he passed the shameful street sign, and it was probably due only to the presence of his grandson that he did not spit on the ground below it now.

They walked in silence down part of the stone colonnade and came to the Silbergasse, whose seventh house on the right was the Mumelter family dwelling; according to an inscription carved in the stone over the doorway it had been built in 1703 by Pangratz Xaver Mumelter, "renovated" in 1812 by Johann Xaver Mumelter, and "provided with a colonnade" in 1854 by Severin Mumelter, imperial and royal reserve lieutenant in the Imperial Rifle Regiment No. 1. In the colonnade, a stone arcade with pointed arches, shadowy and pleasantly cool, was the office of the firm—handed down from generation to generation—which had existed since the reign of Empress Maria Theresia, with branches in the Oetz and upper Inn valleys and now bearing the name of United Tirolean Wood-carving Shops, Christoph Mumelter's Heirs. Laurenz, the ninety-one-year-old, was the last of his trade, since it had been the Lord's will that his only son, the wood carver Thomas Mumelter, should die young, and his descendants had entered upon other careers.

The old man had therefore only one hope left: that Riccarda would marry a man who had the skill and sense for sculpture in wood and didn't think himself too good (as those two toplofty young lads Andreas and Sepp did) to carve the many saints and few laymen who were worthy of it, along with various animals, in stone pine and larch wood, and sell them to America for dollars, now that there was no domestic market left for self-respecting crafts. He had often thought that while it might be President Wilson's fault that they had to live like foreigners in their own country, at least the Americans had tried to patch up the cruel blunder by buying what he and those like him produced with such skill.

When they reached home, which was on the second floor, the table was already set and there were guests present. These were the two Malettis, brother and sister, friends of Riccarda's and Sepp's, and tolerated by the old man even though they had lived here for only fifteen years and had moved here with their father, a doctor from the Trentino, which had also once belonged to Austria. Just as Veronika, the old servant who had just given notice but had stayed after all, and whose wrinkled face smiled broadly upon the returned prodigal, was serving the clear soup with the round yellowish dumplings in it, the setting sun achieved a masterpiece, sending a superb Alpine afterglow through the window to the little company—the light that magically bathed the glaciers before darkness briefly reddened the linen and the thin, white-whiskered face of the old man, who had risen to say grace.

"Our Father in Heaven, bless this food to our use," he began, after he and the others with him had crossed themselves over brow and breast; in a murmur he asked the blessing of Heaven upon the meal and those who were to enjoy it. Just then the front door was slammed noisily, running steps echoed up the stone stairs, and a moment later Sepp, the youngest, yanked open the door.

He had been forgetful or careless enough not to take off his Avant Guardia uniform, but rushed in wearing his black cap with the black tassel, the red scarf, black shirt, black pumps, and black stockings to welcome his brother. "Hello, old boy!" he loudly interrupted the last words of the grace, then froze, crossed himself like the others, and did not venture, until afterward, with a shy glance at the old man, to come over and shake hands with Andreas.

"You're late," said his grandfather curtly. Carefully tying his napkin around his neck, he ordered: "Go take off that carnival costume, and then come back in like a decent human being!" He said this quite regardless of the presence of the two Malettis, who acted as if they were busy with their plates. You had to expect such things in the Mumelter family, and put a good face on them—that is, act as if you did not take the old man seriously because of his complete senility.

But this time Sepp's touchy dignity was too deeply affronted. He would show his elder brother and the guests that he was no small boy to be barked at! He did not move, but stood as before.

"Well?" asked the old man, and the veins above his eyes swelled.

"Grandfather, I won't be yelled at," said the lad, growing pale with anger in his turn.

"Sepp!" cried Riccarda imploringly.

But with a quick gesture the old man cut off this intervention.

"Oh," he said. "You won't be yelled at by your grandfather. But at the Avant Guardia, where they taught it to you, you'll let yourself be yelled at there, eh? There you'll snap to attention and hold your tongue when they order you to dance to their tune! You won't be yelled at, won't you, you whippersnapper? And I suppose you won't learn that it's a piece of rascality, damned rascality, for you to put on this silly masquerade and act as if you were one of them! Who are you trying to fool? Do you think they'll believe you're one of them? The devil they will! They'll simply laugh at you, going and coming; to them you're a *porco Austriaco,* no matter if your shirt's black ten times over! But no, you shine up to them; you're ready to choke with awe when that scoundrel, the subprefect, gives you a civil look. All right, go to the devil, go on associating with that scum and dragging your name in the mud——"

"Grandfather," Sepp interrupted, trembling all over, "I will not endure having you unjustly——"

At this the old man in turn broke in, with absolutely terrifying violence: "Silence! This instant! Do you hear?" And with arm outstretched he pointed to the door.

Riccarda and Andreas made imploring signs to the youngest to do as the old man bade him. Sepp obeyed, his face absolutely bloodless.

"The soup's getting cold," said the old man when he had gone, and began spooning it up. When Sepp came back after changing and sat down at the foot of the table, the old man did not so much as glance at him. He went on spooning his soup.

The soup was good, the dumplings melted like butter on your tongue, and the Ueber-Etscher that was poured next was better yet. It was made from muscatel grapes; it sparkled blood-red in the cut-glass goblets and ran down your throat, as the old man used to say, like chill fire. Then came the spring chickens with cucumber salad and new potatoes, and finally Salzburger Nockerl, as sweet and light as downy foam. Amazing how the old man could still eat and drink despite his years and his anger; counting the glass he had taken at the Greif, this made three, without the slightest sign of wavering. His face was just a little redder, and he breathed just a trifle faster. But after dinner he lit his china pipe (bearing bright-colored half-length portraits of Emperor Francis Joseph and Crown Prince Rudolph) with hands that obeyed him; and when he rose to go into the living room and sit down in the stiff armchair by the window, he walked as erect as ever.

"You've come back to us, then," he said to Andreas, concluding the conversation that had distracted attention from Sepp during dinner and finally absorbed them all, "a loyal Fascist, and no doubt Prefect Mastromattei and Mussolini will have reason to rejoice in you!" This was his judgment of what the newcomer had said, partly on his own account and partly to justify his younger brother. Although his grandfather spoke in a jesting tone, Andreas could feel all too well the bitter; almost contemptuous disappointment behind it.

He replied: "You put it one-sidedly. I didn't say I was for the Fascists—forgive me, Roberto and Elena—I simply said I was not for the Nazis."

He walked to and fro, smoking. "Perhaps I didn't make myself quite clear," he admitted.

"No! You certainly didn't," said the old man promptly, drinking the black coffee that Riccarda had poured for him without sugar or cream. Reproachfully he repeated: "You did not. After all, everything can't have changed overnight in a sensible mind like yours. When you left here, we agreed that there was no help except to have Germany make us German again. There hasn't been anything to show a change of heart in our correspondence since then. Consequently, something must have happened to you to make you suddenly see things altogether differently, I take it?"

Andreas paced to and fro; the happiness and excitement of homecoming made him more loquacious than usual.

He's extraordinarily good-looking, thought Elena, the sixteen-year-old daughter of the Trient doctor, who was said to have moved here because he wanted no further part in the fanatical persecution of Germans at Trient. *He's handsomer than anyone I know,* she admitted to herself. *But he's much older than I am—worse luck!* She sat down where she could watch his every movement and where he could not help seeing her whenever he looked at his grandfather.

"Yes," he said, ceasing to walk up and down, and coming to a sudden halt. "Something happened that changed me. I'll tell you about it." His lips opened; he hesitated. His eyes gleamed. He said nothing. *He's irresistible,* thought Elena.

"Well," said the old man, "we're waiting."

"It was like this," the grandson began. He looked at no one; not at the old man, not at his sister, who glanced occasionally at Roberto Maletti, who in turn never took his eyes off her; not at Sepp, who gazed admiringly past his grandfather toward the eldest grandson; he had nothing and nobody before his eyes, not even the long-lost, glorious range of mountains, now paling swiftly from purple light into shadow. All he saw was the unspeakable thing that he wanted to put into words; seeing it within arm's reach before him, he felt the same roar in his ears that once already had been the automatic reaction of his blood to an excess of loathing.

"I had my second examination behind me," he began haltingly, "about—wait a minute—about a year and a half ago, in March of 1938, in Berlin. What I'm about to tell you is the reason why I left Berlin for Munich. I thought Munich would be different. That was idiotic of me."

He was not a good speaker. As he talked, or rather as he struggled for one word after the other, with that absent, inward-looking expression, his lower lip pushed out beyond the upper, Elena could feel him exerting an influence, indeed a fascination such as she had never known before. He had said nothing, but still the shadow of what he was about to tell haunted the pleasant room. The walls with their gold-framed family portraits, the heavy yellow curtains, the tables with their velvet runners and lace centerpieces, the glass cases with the heirloom china, all lost their harmlessness, and—so it seemed to Elena—became unfamiliar, gray, and menacing.

"The thing is," Andreas began for a third time, "that Hitler marched into Austria, as you know, on March 11, 1938. That was a Thursday. No, Friday. I'd passed my examination on Thursday, and so I was in wonderful spirits because of that and because of the invasion. Austria German would mean South Tirol, too, of course, and a couple of us South Tiroleans who were living in Berlin at the time had agreed to meet and celebrate in our usual resort, Heinz's Restaurant in the Dorotheenstrasse. There were seventeen or eighteen of us, and we'd had several drinks and done a lot of singing when a man came into our private room and asked: 'Is any one of you gentlemen a doctor?'

"Three of us were doctors, Goller, Karl Sottriner from Brixen, and Kastlunger from Klausen, and they spoke up.

"'Which of you can speak English?' asked the man, whom we originally took for an employee of the restaurant.

"I was the only one.

"'I need one of the doctors and the gentleman who can speak English,' said the man. 'Please come with me; it's important.'

"Heinz's Restaurant is on the ground floor. The man who had fetched us led Kastlunger and me upstairs to the sixth story of the same building. There were two doors on that floor. The man opened the one on the right, which bore a visiting card: 'Dr. Hans Klein, Chief Correspondent of the *Neues Wiener Journal.*' The man showed us into a room with one bed. On the bed, fully dressed, lay a girl of about twelve. Her face, turned toward us, was white; her eyes were shut.

"'Please examine her,' said the man to Kastlunger.

"The child looked like a corpse. At the foot of the bed, equally motionless, her face to the floor, lay an elderly woman.

"'She's just shamming—she's as sound as a bell!' said the man, brushing the prostrate figure with the toe of his heavy shoe.

"'What are you doing there?' I asked.

"'You can see perfectly well what I'm doing,' the man answered. 'I don't care for play acting by hysterical women!' He bent over and tried to sit the woman up, unsuccessfully. 'I'll be damned!' he roared. 'When I went out five minutes ago you were perfectly chipper, talking away merrily in English. Kindly don't try any of your tricks here, do you understand?' Then he turned to me. 'Talk to her in English. I'm perfectly sure she understands German splendidly, but English may revive her a little. Her name is Miss Mary F. Smith, and she's the governess of this Jew brat here, who, naturally, would have to have an English governess. When we fetched her parents, the damned kid began to raise such a hysterical row that we clipped her one. And the old Englishwoman made herself rather troublesome, too, so we also calmed her down. But she's a foreigner, after all, and we don't want any nuisance with her. So you tell her she can go wherever she likes. The sooner the better!'

"Meanwhile, Kastlunger had been examining the child. 'Fainted,' he said, got water, and after a few moments the girl came to, without opening her eyes. But you could hear her breathing. Then he turned his attention to the Englishwoman, which took rather longer; when he sat her up against an armchair, a broad ribbon of blood came in sight, running down her left cheek to her throat. Her peaked, haggard, bird-like face looked ghastly.

"The man remarked: 'I suppose when I went for the doctor the miss took a drop too much of her native whisky and came to some harm!' "

Standing at the end of the room between the windows, Andreas ran his fingers through his hair. His eyes were wide open, looking nowhere.

"Imagine the scene, can you?" he asked, as his grandfather often did, conjuring up the scene that he had not been able to forget. "Two unconscious people. A child, both of whose parents have just been taken away—incidentally, the father died three months afterward in the Dachau concentration camp—and an elderly person trying to console the distracted child, and knocked down with a truncheon or a whip. They both recover consciousness. Almost at the same instant both remember what has happened. The child begins to cry, and the old person, scarcely knowing what she does, says in English: 'Don't cry, dear! Don't cry. Everything will turn out all right!' The man who brought us roars at her: 'What did you just say?' I answer for her: 'She told the child everything would come out all right.'

"At this the man turned to me. 'Nobody asked you! And what makes the lady so optimistic—will you kindly ask her that?'

"I looked at him. 'No, I won't ask her that,' I told him. Meanwhile, the deathly sad, hunted eyes of the child on the bed traveled from one to another.

" 'I didn't know there were Jews in South Tirol,' the man said insolently to me.

" 'No,' I said, 'but there are South Tiroleans, and they don't take orders!'

"Kastlunger said nothing except, 'Right.'

"Well, the man hadn't been expecting this. 'Interesting,' he said, casually showing the Gestapo badge that we'd been ready for long since. 'We've always been assured that you South Tiroleans were whining for us to free you!'

"Kastlunger is much more violent-tempered than I am. He drew himself up to his full height in front of the man and said in a resounding voice, 'Just you remember something, you. The South Tiroleans don't whine, and if you say anything of the sort again, I'll——'

"I had trouble in holding him back. 'Let's go,' I warned him. 'We aren't needed here any more.'

"But the old Englishwoman hastily grabbed my hand. 'Please don't go, sir! Please stay! He'll kill the child! Please!'

"So we stayed. Again the man wanted to know what she'd said. I translated: 'She's afraid of you.' He lit a cigarette. 'Not quite so optimistic any more, then?' he asked her, and turned abruptly to the child. 'Jew brat, come on! You're going along. The old dame can go to blazes. Tell her that!' The last was for me.

"He grabbed the child by the wrist. She was a sickly, pale, city child.

" 'Get up!' he ordered.

"The child resisted. She hung on with both hands to the brass rods behind her, without a word. The veins in her forehead stood out.

" 'For God's sake,' said the Englishwoman in awkward German, 'don't hurt the child! I'm responsible. She's such a sweet child, and never did anyone any harm. In her midyear examinations she had nothing but good marks—except in mathematics—I mean—— Let me go away with the child! I promise you I'll look after the child! I have a little something saved up. I promise you,' she repeated imploringly and senselessly as the man knocked the girl, still clinging fast, off the bed. She was barefoot. 'I've got to put on my shoes and stockings,' she said. Those were the first words she had spoken.

" 'You can manage without, too, I expect, gracious young lady,' jeered the man.

"But the elderly governess did what she must have done often before—brought the child's shoes and stockings and started to help her put them on. The man brushed her away with a gesture.

" 'The Jew brat can put on her own dirty stockings! Interesting, by the way, to discover that you understand German perfectly, I see?'

"At this the child, remaining barefoot, made a supreme exertion to say: 'I'm not Jewish. I'm a Protestant!'

"The Englishwoman nodded eagerly. 'Yes, she certainly is!' she agreed.

" 'And Papa?' asked the man with a look of contempt such as I had never before seen on a human face. 'And your esteemed Mama? Both Protestant too? Papa, whose valued father was a kosher butcher in Vienna, and your esteemed Mama, whose sweet-smelling maiden name was Veilchenblüh—all pure Protestants?' His patience giving out, he drove the girl toward the door with a second blow. 'Thank you, gentlemen,' he said to us. At the door he turned. 'Just to keep our South Tirolean friends up to date and prevent atrocity stories, I may say that the surprise commando to which I belong arrested and removed that Jewish rabble for shady dealings by order of Reichsführer Himmler, and left me behind to render assistance when these two put on their sham faint.'

"That was what he actually said: 'assistance.' Nobody prevented him either from using the word or from turning to go with an expression of indescribable contempt. He was still holding the child by the wrist.

"'Please! Please! Please!' said the old Englishwoman in German, clasping her hands in utter despair.

"This was too much for Kastlunger. 'Leave her here, the girl!' he said evenly.

"'I'd advise you not to meddle in this,' the man declared, one hand on the knob. 'Oranienburg is a nice playground. And although it's a place for men I'll manage it to get her a separate admission.' He grinned ambiguously, then added: 'Anyway, she can play falling in faints there as often as she likes.' Oranienburg is the concentration camp near Berlin.

"'Will I see my father and mother there?' the child asked in a faint voice.

"'No. They won't be that well off,' was the answer.

"When the Englishwoman heard the word 'Oranienburg,' she flung herself fiercely upon the man from behind, faster than I can say it, and although she was as old and thin as a leaf, he swayed for a moment, letting go of the knob. But before we could stop him he gave the woman a kick with his heavy boot that knocked her groaning to the floor. Kastlunger helped her up, while I—— Now there's the question. What did I do? Did I kill the fellow? Did I at least thrash him within an inch of his life? Nothing of the sort. I stood there and watched. I stood there thinking: *Ought you to risk interfering with the Gestapo?* While I was thinking these splendid thoughts, there was a quick, shrill, not very loud scream. The child had got away from the man at the moment when he opened the door; she rushed into the bathroom, locked the door after her, and when we found her she was lying flat—not in the bathroom. She was lying on the pavement of the Dorotheenstrasse; she had jumped out, to run away or to die, I don't know which. She was dead. She lay barefoot on the pavement; her mouth, nose, and open eyes were unharmed, but her forehead and the back of her head were a bloody mass. Kastlunger closed her eyes, and I didn't even do that. Her name was Agnes. That was her name. She had all good marks except in mathematics. And she was eleven and three quarters."

No one spoke when Andreas finished. He himself said nothing. Not until the old man addressed him again to ask: "Have you heard anything of the affair since?" did he answer: "Constantly. I hear of it constantly. Every night. I hear that quick, shrill, not very loud scream of a girl not yet twelve, who would rather jump out of the window than stay where it was prohibited to help children. And where grown people docilely obeyed the rule. Yes indeed, I hear it all the time." There was a bitterness, a shame in his voice that hurt Elena intensely. The man there between the windows was in deadly earnest. His words were charged with reproach, of himself, but also, Elena felt, of the others.

"And that changed your attitude toward our cause?" the old man asked. You could not tell from the tone of his question whether he found this comprehensible or not.

"Yes," said the grandson, "that." And, after a breath: "I don't want anything to do with a country where you are forced to look on at crimes every day and thus become guilty yourself."

Shortly afterward the company wished one another good night. The Malettis said they had an enjoyable evening. When Elena shook hands with the new arrival, she could feel his cold sweat.

He went up to the second floor; there was the room he had had since boyhood. Here in this room, from which there was little to be seen beyond the sign and gable of Gemaassmer the baker across the way and a bit of sky now studded with stars, he had been four years old when his native land became Italian; he could still remember very well the march of the Black Shirts; here he had been a schoolboy when both his parents died, and the house grew silent and dark;

here he had become a man. The old, torn wallpaper with the faded rose pattern was gone; Riccarda had replaced it with a pretty, bright new one without a pattern.

As always, old Veronika brought him a stone jug of fresh drinking water before he went to sleep.

"What's this that Riccarda tells me," he asked, sitting on his bed, "Vroni, you were going to leave us?"

The maid poured out a glass. "Yes, young master," she said—for to her Andreas the man was still young Master Andreas, whom she had known and held in her lap when he was Andreas the baby and Andreas the boy. "It's on account of the old gentleman. He's really more than a person can stand. You might think now, mightn't you, young master, that an old man like him would be quieter and have better sense? I can see it happening to me. But the old gentleman—— A regular devil, pardon me for saying so. 'Have you clean forgotten, Herr Mumelter,' I asked him the other day, 'what you promised me when the young gentleman's sainted parents, heavenly Mary rest them, died one after another?' Why, if the old gentleman doesn't go and pretend he doesn't remember at all! 'What do you mean, promised you?' he had the impertinence to ask me, begging your pardon, young master. I told him, all right! 'Don't you remember, sir,' I asked him, 'that I was the first to find the poor young lady' —your mother, young master—'with the gas pipe in her mouth three weeks after Herr Thomas Mumelter's death? And how you promised me at the time: "Vroni, if you don't say anything, you'll be taken care of here for the rest of your life?"' She just couldn't stand it, your mother, without your father, young master, and it's true enough, the old gentleman's right when he says a woman with children mustn't do such things, it's a mortal sin, and may Holy Mary forgive her! Yes, he's probably right about that. But you know, young master, even so I don't think he understands. He doesn't understand anything at all about love—he's too rough, with your permission, and he doesn't know much about good living, either—he's too saving for that. He won't allow himself anything, the old gentleman, nor anyone else either. I'd really like to know who he would allow anything. 'That's what you promised me then, Herr Mumelter,' I said to him, 'and how did you keep your promise? By yelling at me like a dog—I wouldn't yell at Foxy the way you did at me!' And why? Because in ironing a shirt—I tell you, young master, it was an old, no-good shirt—I scorched it a little. 'This is too much,' I said, before bed at night, so that nobody else in the house would hear, 'I'm full up to here!' and I was going to leave, after twenty-seven years. But in the morning, when I woke up, I finally changed my mind after all. One gets set in one's ways, young master, and when one's old one doesn't like to change. Am I right?"

"Yes," said Andreas. "Perfectly right. Good night!" And he turned out the light and lay there in the narrow bed of his boyhood.

The good air was easier to breathe. *Home at last!* he thought gratefully, saying his paternoster. Before he fell asleep he saw the woman who had been his mother with the gas pipe in her mouth; she had died an unnatural death in this house. He could scarcely remember her and his father. The unnatural death had been carefully kept from the children. Grippe, they said, to the children and to the city. This was the first time he had heard what his mother died of. *But why does one call it an unnatural death?* he wondered with tired eyes. It was such a natural death when you could endure an unnatural life no longer.

He was almost asleep when a quick, shrill, not very loud scream made him start up. The child was lying on the pavement; he could see that her eyes were open, looking for help. But no one helped. A natural death.

The bell of the parish church struck eleven, such mighty strokes that he shot up again from his half slumber. He took a drink of the fresh, ice-cold water that the old servant had put out for him. His blood ran cooler then. High time for sleep, he told himself. Have I come back to hear old wives' tales, and to tell them? He could see the bit of sky with the stars from where he lay. *Lovely to be home again,* he thought. *Tomorrow we start the future!*

He forgot that the next day was a Sunday.

Chapter 2

It was five in the morning when the old man rose from slumber. An alarm clock on a wooden bench beside his iron bed startled him out of a deep, sound sleep. On weekdays, when he slept until six and woke up promptly of his own accord, he needed no alarm clock—only on Sundays. But then he had to wake up the household for Mass, which he was obliged to do in person now that old Veronika had grown undependable. In spite of his age Laurenz Mumelter looked down with disdain on old people, as if he did not feel that he was one of them and indeed incomparably older.

He pulled up the green shades before his two bedroom windows and opened them wide. The morning air cooled his face; it can be pretty hot at Bozen in summer, and unless all the indications were wrong, this was going to be one of the hot days. The old man cocked a weather eye at the sky, which was beginning to turn from a bluish haze into a cloudless blue above the arcades. The city was quiet, enjoying its Sunday sleep, although Sundays were the very days when a decent Bozner had to be earliest up and about. Since 1925 there had been none but Italian Masses, and you didn't live to be ninety-one to worship God in a strange tongue. No sir, that was something the rulers at Rome could never accomplish—make a Mumelter say his prayers in Italian. And so there was nothing for it but to attend six-o'clock morning Mass, the only one allowed to be held in German. Naturally the wily Italian prefect had counted on its being far too early—with sleep particularly tempting on Sunday mornings, too much so—to rout more than a few pious old zealots out of bed. But here again the prefect was wrong, very! For not Grandfather alone but hundreds of German Bozners got up at crack of dawn Sunday after Sunday, woke their wives, children, and grandchildren, and were in the parish church at the stroke of six to hear God's word in the tongue they had learned it in as children.

And so fifteen minutes later—the old man was not long about washing from head to foot in the cold water from the Eisack and putting on the black Sunday best laid out the evening before—he knocked at his grandsons' doors, and then roused Veronika too. For it was her duty to make the family coffee before their departure and fetch the fresh half-moon rolls and the Sunday ham. The old man could scarcely enjoy either one now that the baker was called a *panificio* and the butcher shop a *marcelleria;* the only comfort was that the two entwined pretzels on the German bakers' signs still remained as the mark of the guild that they had represented since the time of Emperor Maximilian.

Andreas started up in a flash, hearing the knock and dreaming something that he could not remember when he awoke, but that was connected with the unexpected noise. Only gradually did he realize that it was the almost forgotten Sunday-morning knock of his grandfather, meaning simply a hasty breakfast and a yet hastier walk to church. He almost laughed aloud as he in turn poured jugs of cold water over his naked body, refreshing himself for the day's work, which today could still consist of sheer idleness. *Tomorrow, though,* he thought, rubbing down chest and arms with one of the rough towels that the young Mumelters had had to use since childhood, *serious business begins.* He had all kinds of changes in mind, which so far he had wisely kept to himself. But with all due respect, this matter of Grandfather could not possibly go on; he got in the way of everything you did. Though Andreas had not talked about it to Sepp or Riccarda, he was sure of this much: under present conditions there was no future here for any of the three. If it hadn't been for Grandfather and his stiff neck, Sepp would long since have had a scholarship at a university; Riccarda (who, judging by last night, seemed fond of young Maletti) might already have been married, *and I,* he thought, *would probably have the job with the Virgl railway in my pocket. You don't have to go around being a rebel all the time to prove how devoted to your country you are. There's something almost pathological about doing nothing but grumble and swear for twenty-one years. Granted, the Italians have behaved like swine to us, and have not kept one, not so much as one, of all the solemn promises they made. But since we have to live here—wrong, since we want to, and can, live only here and nowhere else, as I have learned from my own bitter experiences by three years in which I almost burst with homesickness—for God's sake, some way has got to be found! Better the Italians than the Nazis! Grandfather will have to recognize this in the end, and it's high time he took it in.*

Strange that in his reflections the grandson did not consider the possibility which had predominated years before in the mind of the police prefect—that there was no counting on or arguing with so aged a man. On the contrary. For Andreas, for his brother and sister, for Veronika, and for all those who knew him well, it was simply impossible to imagine the old man no longer a part of life. It did not seem to occur to anybody that someday, today or tomorrow, he might be robbed of his power to object and contradict because he would be lying dead in his iron bedstead.

Half an hour later the family had taken their seats in the parish church, and the early Mass was about to begin. There sat the worshipers in the nave and left transept, as they had done since time immemorial in this superb Gothic church, built by Schussenried. For four hundred and eighty-two years the two red marble lions had guarded the portals that the city families had passed through to the Lord's Supper on countless workdays and holidays. The sun was not yet high enough to pick out the faces in the prevailing twilight, only partially relieved by the altar lights. But these were the faces of the same Tiroleans whose fathers, grandfathers, great-grandfathers, and remote ancestors had knelt on these same stone flags and leaned back comfortably on the same wooden benches when the priest in the high pulpit began to expound the virtues and vices of the world. The pews still bore the old names on shiny, oval brass plates, engraved in the metal and beyond removal by prefect or decree; the persons who answered to those names today, and to whom the so-called hereditary seats had passed down through generation after generation, were all present.

In the seats of Thomas Tieffenthaler, who was master of the guild of vintners in 1574, sat Urban Tieffenthaler, his wife and two sons; the hereditary seat with the name of the baker Jakob Platter, who acquired it in 1577, was occupied in 1939 by the veterinarian Jakob Platter; the family of Georg Paechl, on whom Bozen citizenship had been bestowed in 1580, was represented by Konrad and Rudolf Paechl, who continued in the Rainerstrasse their hereditary trade of making silver "good-luck rings"; in the pew for which Michael Lochner, the teacher, had paid eight silver thalers in 1581 prayed Creszenz Lochner, the lawyer's widow, who had given and buried three sons for Austria in the World War; Clemens Hoermann, whose name first appeared in Bozen on his opening a quarry at the present Wassermauerpromenade in 1582, even now had numerous descendants. They consisted of the cemetery superintendent, Jakob Hoermann, his wife Christine, his sons Peter, Felix, and Caspar, and his grandmother, Anna Hoermann, née Kerschpamer; all six sat in the left transept next to the altar painting in which Lazzarini, a pupil of Tizian, had captured an Ascension in deep colors that were gradually conjured out of the twilight by the morning sun; next to them was Dr. Faider, an ear specialist, a descendant of the stonemason Michael Faider, who had adorned the high, square tower of this parish church with an open gallery in 1585; the very old Frau Malfertheiner behind him, the last of her name, traced her origin back to Johann Malfertheiner, who discovered a cure for the murrain in the Groedner valley in 1589 and moved from there to Bozen as a blacksmith; the pew of Urban Roell, master of the guild of butchers about 1592, was occupied now by Barbara and Elfriede Roell, both of them widows of direct descendants from Urban Roell.

With the name of Leonhard Schgraffer the seventeenth century was reached, for it was not until 1601 that a man of this name established the inn still existing on the Waltherplatz under the name of Hotel Schgraffer. The surviving couple were named Hanns and Emma Schgraffer. Next came the descendants of the families of Am Orth, Adam Entleuthner, Anton Berger, Zacharias an der Lan, Valentin Dorffner, Anton an der Lan; Zacharias an der Lan the Younger, who saved the burning city from destruction in 1627, being mayor at the time, by opening the sluices in the Eisack and having the water carried to the scene of the fire in wine casks; he personally assisted in this, and was burned up. To this day there was a Melchior Auer, and he sat in the hereditary seat of Melchior Auer, town clerk and author of the book on the Peace of Westphalia published in 1649; Jakob Eppurger, Felix Kerschpamer, Christian Perathoner, masters of guilds all three, had progeny of the same name; then, pew by pew, followed the leading Bozen families of the eighteenth century. Johannes Web, Anton Hueber, Josef Anton Tschudaeth, Johann Josef Fenner von Fennperg, Pangraz Xaver Mumelter. This is where we encounter the name of Mumelter, and here, in the third row of the nave, his descendants had still their seats, immediately next to the descendants of Johann Gustav Leiterperges, the fruit-grower, whose daughter Virginia had married Pangraz Xaver Mumelter in 1751.

After hereditary seat 194, the last in the third row, formerly the property of Karl Ferdinand Innkofler, an apothecary, who had fought in 1809, and whose place was occupied now by the pensioned Imperial and Royal Colonel Adolf Innkofler, the fourth center row remained entirely vacant. That is, it had neither occupants nor brass plates to indicate the hereditary pews; and for this there was a reason.

In that pew, on Maundy Thursday, 1809, sat Andreas Hofer, Johann Speckbacher, and Peter Mahr, who heard Mass and took Holy Communion. This pew introduced the younger generation and the twentieth century, and had been left empty for all time out of reverence. None of the Bozners had ever ventured to sit there, and even the present generation could feel the imminent wrath of God when a couple of airy, scornful Fascists chanced to do so.

Behind the fourth row, in the fifth, sixth, seventh, and eighth, and in the left transept as far as the ninth row, sat those whose forefathers had fought with and for the men who had occupied the fourth row while praying for the liberation of the Tirol a hundred and thirty years before. Compared with those in the very front they were recent families. But compared with those who ruled Bozen now they were patricians.

The organist started to play, and the congregation rose. There must have been a thousand or more. The early light coming brighter and brighter through the stained-glass window, and casting a shifting radiance from the altar upon the devout, picked out their faces ever more plainly. One who had seen the sight often might perhaps not be surprised; but a person watching for the first time could not help being struck by the look of the thousand. The Austrian poet Grillparzer said: "All Tiroleans have the same face." You realized that the saying was true as you scanned these thousand different faces; they belonged to graybeards, men, mothers, brides, children, and they were all one face, one and the same. The clear, frank eyes and foreheads, the firmness, the deep lines even in the young faces, the thick eyebrows meeting over a nose as sharp as a knife, all were perfectly alike, as if this species of man had grown and been shaped upon one pattern. There was the same seeing and listening, the same slow taciturnity. Years of suffering had stamped that look and those scars on these faces, even the youngest, yet without leaving any touch of querulousness. On the contrary. The deep-dug lines around mouths and on brows were furrows of defiance. Here they stood, bearded or smooth-shaven, with heads bowed, praying. They knelt and repeated the prayers in a murmur, the Aves and litanies and Amens aloud. Then they sat down in the hereditary pews of their forefathers, and leaned back at ease to hear the sermon. They rested frank and searching eyes on the preacher.

He was the pastor, Canon Gemaassmer, a descendant of the miller and baker Albrecht Sepp Gemaassmer, hereditary pew sixth row number 604, purchased in 1824, occupied today by the unmarried seventy-three-year-old Fräulein Eulalia Gemaassmer, the sister of the pastor who was delivering the sermon. He was a man in his mid-sixties and looked exactly like the congregation to which he spoke. He began by praising those present for attending the Sunday-morning services in such numbers and asked that they continue to do so. For, he said, it was not only God's word that they came to hear that would strengthen and support them; it was the words of their mother tongue that they came to hear, and that they must preserve and cherish as a sacred possession.

"The mother tongue," he said, "has not been received by anyone singly, but by all; it is one of the dearest possessions that the earth has in its gift. One's mother tongue is the speech of heart and mind, in which the whole soul finds expression for thought, feeling, and mood. It has become so completely entwined with our whole spiritual life that any attack on it seems an attempt to tear away part of the soul of the people.

"Every individual," he went on, "has a sacred and inviolable right to his mother tongue. The rights of nature are the same for all men; let everyone ask himself whether he would not feel any attack on his mother tongue as an injustice crying to Heaven!

"Yes, my devout listeners," he said, "every one of you has felt this flagrant wrong deep down within himself when an attempt has been made to send your children to Italian kindergartens and schools, to take away your mother tongue. I say attempt! For that which is part of oneself cannot be taken away; it grows up and down with us, upward into life and downward to the grave. As a man is born, so he remains; the forces of civilization and schooling and faith can bring no decisive change. As a man is born, with firm hands or gentle, with his eyes turned outward upon the world or inward upon his own little corner, with love or hatred, rejoicing in power or in service, humble or doubting, with a spirit of good or evil, willing or obstinate, so he remains. That is the root he grows from. If it is pulled up, his being perishes—good or evil, but still his being. And the roots cannot be moved; the roots must remain. Ask the wine growers among you whether they transplant vines. Ask the fruitgrowers among you whether they transplant trees. They will tell you that one cannot transplant from the sun into the shade, nor from the shade into the sun. And not even from sun into sun, or from shade into shade. For the sun is different in different places, and so is the shade; where a vine has grown and borne grapes, and where a tree has grown and borne fruit, there the vine and the tree must stay. The roots must remain.

"Language, my devout listeners, is just such a root, going deep down into the soil of all existence. One's native land is just such a root, from which one's whole being grows, and the roots must remain. As you go home from here, most of you will pass by the monument to our great Walther von der Vogelweide. Many, many hundred years ago, in the thirteenth century, he sang:

"Where you belong
There stay and die.

"He knew even then that nothing else was possible but this: where a man is born and where he dwells, and likes to dwell, there must he live and die. No one must touch the root, and he who does must die. If you look around you here in this holy parish church, you will see the empty memorial pew in your midst; it reminds you of our greatest man, Andreas Hofer, who dared to defy Napoleon and defend our land even from him. Andreas Hofer said and wrote: 'There is no such thing as two homelands. There is only one. Into that one, your own, you are born, so inseparably that you cannot but hold fast there through trouble and death. You are born into your homeland, and you die into it.' "

The priest went on speaking, in his native Tirolean dialect, so simply that all could understand. He said that the words of these two laymen, the medieval minnesinger and Napoleon's adversary, had been sanctioned by the Church and quoted in the papal bull called *Tua patria.*

Although Andreas was no lover of sermons and had applied the words "born doubting" to himself, still he pricked up his ears. The preacher in the high Gothic pulpit was quite right. There was no such thing as two homelands. But why did he not draw from it the one conclusion that possibly could be drawn? Surely anyone who lived in a threatened homeland must do the precise opposite of what the militant priest and his own obstinate grandfather wanted, which was to destroy and throw away all pleasure in one's native land for sheer truculence and contrariness! *Isn't it bliss to be here?* he thought. *If I go out now and take the few steps to the bridge over the Talfer instead of passing by the Walther monument, as His Reverence advises me, I shall have before my eyes not the author of an outworn inscription, but the blue, everlasting range of the Mendel and the Eppen highlands. And I can turn around and put the Rosengarten and the jagged Schlern in front of me. Ten paces more, and the Ritten and the green vineyards will rise between the Talfer and the green Eisack, no matter whether the Eisack be called Eisack or Isarco. With every step I take I shall see a land of dreams; whether its mountains and rivers go by Italian or German names makes no difference at all: they are mountains and green rivers, the clearest and most beautiful on earth. What was it the canon said, or was it Andreas Hofer? This is the country I was born into. I was born into the most magnificent country on earth. I, Andreas Mumelter, say so! You could hunt the world over and not find the equal of what I see here—high mountains and orchards as far as the eye can see, vineyards and laurel forests, everlasting ice and shining sun, mountain torrents and blue lakes like mirrors. If only the pastor and Grandfather and my valued countrymen were a little more sensible, they would say this was so wonderful that it was worth any sacrifice! Our forefathers did not have to make that sacrifice; the country fell into their laps like the apples that thrive here as they do nowhere else. We, on the other hand, have got to make the sacrifice in order to keep our glorious country. Nothing could be more simple.*

As the organ swelled after the benediction, the churchgoers left the building. Usually old Mumelter would stop at the monument to Peter Mahr, the fighter for Andreas Hofer, which stood opposite the old parsonage, for a Sunday chat with friends. He did not do so today, but accompanied his eldest grandson to the east side of the cathedral, which was flanked by the churchyard.

As they went, he said: "I was watching you inside there. I didn't like the look of your face. In fact, I don't like your whole way. What's on your mind?"

The young man, being thus asked straight out, found himself breathless. He said, "I'll tell you later."

"Tell me now," insisted his grandfather. "But read this."

Entering the churchyard, he led Andreas to a proclamation affixed to the inside of the gate. It read:

"Decree of the Prefect of Bozen. On and after September 30, all epitaphs must be exclusively in the Italian language. UMBERTO RICCI."

"Did you read it?" asked the old man.

His grandson nodded.

"Understand it?" asked the old man.

"Naturally," was the reply.

The old man stared mutely at his grandson for a moment. Then he said, "Do you think it's natural for you to put Italian words on my tombstone? In that case there's only one thing for me to do. I'll have to make sure I peg out before the thirtieth of September. Because I don't mean to be buried in Italian."

This was the first time Andreas had ever heard his grandfather speak of dying. His throat was parched. He replied, "You're right, Grandfather."

But the old man's eyes and ears were too good. He mistrusted the answer. And so as the other people began to arrive he turned on his heel and left his grandson standing there.

Andreas debated whether to follow him. He did not. He could see it was useless; the man's mind could not be changed. No matter what Andreas might say to him he would think it stupid or cowardly. After a moment's hesitation the young man went over to the west side wall of the cemetery, where his parents were buried. Thence he left the quiet spot through the gateway giving on the Eisackstrasse.

He had no objective except to walk around his own city and feel that he was there. He wanted to resume possession of it all. But he could not shake off the thought of his grandfather and the sermon. *This cult of the past,* he thought. *What's gone is gone; you can't set the clock back by whole generations.*

Have they actually renamed the Laubengasse Via dei Portici? he interrupted himself. *And the Obstmarkt Mercato delle frutta?*

Yet even so, this still isn't Andreas Hofer's day any more! We were brought up to worship Andreas Hofer, he admitted to himself softly, *yet to be impartial—and one should be, for goodness' sake—one must admit that the Andreas Hofer legend suited the year 1809; but it doesn't suit the year 1939! In those days a patriotic innkeeper, unques-*

tionably a wonderful man, could send around "circulating notes" through the country, patriarchally asking the "shooting people" individually "to do him the favor and have the kindness" to chase the enemy out of the country with old muskets and scythes and sickles and flails—and "many thanks in advance!" But today you can't operate with flails, nor with patriarchal simplicity either. You can't stand up against machine guns with scythes, or bombers with sickles. And a few thousand ridiculously armed peasants aren't enough. Not even a hundred thousand. That's as plain as the sun yonder over the Schlern, or as the idiotic idea of turning the Talfermauerpromenade into a Lungo Talvera. What's the use, then, of constantly displaying Andreas Hofer to us as the *Tirolean? None at all. In the history of our region we had a very brave and highly estimable man; all well and good. But for the present day there is no conclusion, not even the most trifling, to be drawn from it. And if Hofer were to come back to us today, I'm afraid he would be a helpless, if not a comic, figure. Naïve people are comic. Does anyone suppose for a minute that Mussolini can be fought with naïveté?*

It's really a maddening piece of stupidity for them to call the Virgl the Virgolo, he thought, returning through the Kapuzinergasse and noticing the sign that pointed to the cable railway up the Virgl mountain. But the annoying inscription gave him the notion of walking that way. *Well, and something follows from that,* he continued his reflections. *Instead of pursuing a practical, realistic policy, they're still guided by their emotions, like Hofer. But they can't turn the Virgolo back into the Virgl that way. The few capable political figures we had here are dead or in exile: sharp-witted old Mayor Perathoner is buried beside my parents; Dr. Reut-Nicolussi, who has the brains to help us, is a refugee in America; Pastor Delug and Canon Psenner, who not only used to preach but knew what they were preaching, have been prevented from opening their mouths. And here we are, forsaken on every hand, amusing ourselves with all this sentimental trash!*

Meanwhile, having crossed the Eisack Bridge—they called it the Ponte di Isarco now—he found himself before the little station whence the cable railway ascended to the Virgl lookout. Here there was a newsstand, and the old woman who kept it, recognizing him, slipped three picture post cards into his hand along with the German newspaper, *Dolomiten.* "Proscribed," said the first card, which showed a Tirolean family emigrating. First came an old man with an Andreas Hofer beard, carrying the statue of the Saviour; women loaded with monstrous burdens followed him. They were going down the mountain, defiant-eyed and stooping under their load. The second card was entitled "South Tirol." On it was the Tirolean eagle, and underneath a chained Tirolean in Hofer costume of white shirt, green suspenders, leather shorts, and white knee socks. With a supreme effort he was bursting his shackles. The inscription underneath said:

We would be free as our fathers were.
Sooner death than live enslaved!

The third card was also entitled "South Tirol." Here a Fascist, dagger in hand, was leaning against a cliff, with an iron boot on the bare neck of his victim, who was savagely clenching his fists. Caption: "Don't forget!"

"Lovely cards, aren't they, Herr Mumelter?" whispered the old woman, proud of her wares. And, seeing someone approaching: "Did you have a good time in the Reich?"

Actually he felt like tearing up the cards and throwing them at her feet, so bitterly was he struck by this palpable nonsense. But he counted out the required centesimi, put the cards in his breast pocket, and said, "Magnificent, Frau Fingeis."

He was not in the mood for further conversation; instead, so as to be alone, he got into a car of the cable train that stood ready for departure. It was the first train in the morning, and entirely empty. He was still furious during the four-minute trip to the summit. *Why, they're digging our graves for us!* muttered the lone passenger into the hum of the iron cables. *No! Something's got to be done about this!*

He was at the lookout. "It's going to be hot today," said the conductor to him in Italian, and when he replied, *"Si, molto caldo!"* the man, with a positively pleased and flattered expression, opened the car door for the gentleman with the German paper.

Andreas left behind him the Hotel Weinegg and the Kohlerhof above it, and climbed to the ruin of Haselburg Castle, which towered over the cliff on the edge of a sheer drop. It was a minute or two after eight. The bells of the parish church, the churches of St. Oswald and St. John in Bozen, and the parish church in Gries had just struck the hour, and down below the day was beginning with the Sunday parade of the Avant Guardia. Was Sepp in it? his elder brother wondered. Again he was about to tear up the colored post cards that annoyed him so, and once again he did not.

He went the familiar few paces behind the castle to a jutting rock scarcely big enough for two people side by side. From where he now stood he enjoyed a magnificent distant view. The Dolomites spread to their full extent before him, with the slender Geisler peaks in the foreground, the wildly carved Schlern, the majestic Rosengarten, and the bold, baroque Latemar; farther back, in the morning haze, but still visible with every ridge and height and crag, the rocky cathedrals of the Cimone della Pala; next to it the Weisshorn and the Schwarzhorn like a gigantic bull's head with two towering horns; in the south the Adamello, a dense white cloud with rosy edges; then the fiery Presanella, the long, airy ridge of the Mendel, and the Ortler range, glacier-covered peak after glacier-covered peak like sentinels unapproachably guarding the horizon.

He gave himself up with his whole soul to this sublime outlook. Then stones slipped away under his feet; he lost his balance, and for a single second he knew the feeling: *this is my death*. Something iron halted his descent at the last moment. He saw then that it was a hook driven into the jutting rock for God knows what reason; but he gave thanks for the mysterious reason as he leaned against the ruined wall, recovering his breath. At that moment singing voices were heard, apparently belonging to people who had ascended not by the cable railway but by the footpath from the Eisack Bridge by way of Haslach. They were singing in German. A moment later they came in sight, and someone said to Andreas with immeasurable delight: "Why, Herr Mumelter—this *is* a surprise!"

Andreas, who had just recovered from a still greater one, and had no fondness for surprises in general, put on a wooden face. Then he recognized Elena Maletti. Her brother Roberto was not among the lads and girls who now surrounded him, evidently on their way to great things, for they were carrying not only Kodaks but a Leica, a phonograph, a radio, and quantities of provender.

"If we'd known you were going up, too, we'd have joined you," said Elena. "Why didn't you tell us anything about it last night?"

He forced himself to answer: "Because I didn't know."

"Or did you happen to hear me telephoning to Riccarda at quarter of six this morning?" the girl inquired, with a sudden flash of dizzy hope.

Andreas replied matter-of-factly: "No."

"Aha," said Elena, disappointed yet blissful at seeing before her very eyes the man she had been thinking of incessantly ever since yesterday. Naturally enough, the others did not share her enthusiasm, and after the girl had managed a hasty introduction they began urging departure. Their goal was the Long Wall, almost fifteen hundred feet higher.

Elena, however, had already reached her goal, or at least what her sixteen-year-old brain, bewildered by wakefulness, the rapid climb, and this electrifying encounter took to be such.

In a flash she made a plan. Either Andreas would join them, which she considered improbable and would not particularly have welcomed, or else he would stay here; in that case she would pretend to follow the others, and come back quickly under some pretext. She had no ulterior thoughts—that is to say, at the moment she was thinking of nothing at all except how she could manage to stay near him.

She went to work adroitly enough. For Andreas, as expected, declined her offer to join the climb. Accordingly, with the natural dramatic talent of Italians even when they speak German and are from the Trentino, she said, "We're awfully sorry. Well, good-by, Herr Mumelter. Have a good Sunday."

"Gruess Gott," said Andreas bluntly. Then, feeling that it was rather too blunt, he managed a "Same to you!" To his mind this disposed of the matter, and he occupied himself exclusively with the fact that by rights he ought now to be lying down below, just as little Agnes had lain, a bloody mass. *But I have my shoes on,* he thought with an illogicality that struck him. *It is now eight-seventeen; my last moment was therefore at eight-thirteen.* Illogicality, which ordinarily horrified him, did not disturb him in the least today; he took positive pleasure in dwelling on the thought that he was one of the few people who had survived their last moment. *For,* he told himself, *anyone that slips and falls there*—he looked at the providential iron hook and was dizzy at the mere thought—*is a dead man.*

The sudden danger and his incredible escape had thrown him off his mental balance; this was a favoring circumstance that the scheming Elena had not counted on. But when she reappeared after a bare quarter hour he had had time to take stock of the good luck he had just enjoyed. So he asked cheerfully: "What is it? Did you forget something?"

On the contrary, aside from herself she had brought several things along. One, one of the picnic baskets; two, the portable phonograph; three, a radio disguised as a suitcase; of these numbers one and three were her property. And as she did not know whether Andreas might be a lover of blues and tangoes—she hoped he was—she had made sure by inducing her friend Bianca to lend her the phonograph. Piled high and breathing quickly, she put the things down and seated herself beside them in the morning sun, which was growing steadily warmer.

"Seriously, what goes on?" Andreas inquired in his own characteristic matter-of-fact, precise, and naïve fashion (although he would have defended himself manfully if anyone had thought of calling him naïve). But naïve he was, despite his acuteness and the mistrustfulness natural to him as to most of his countrymen. "Andreas," his sister had once said of him, "is positively the classical example of a man you can take in." And indeed if you make up your mind to it and he was unprepared, you could make him believe whatever you liked. This was due partly to his aversion for asking questions or answering them—in other words, to a sort of inertia, and partly to a dependability so ingrained that he never dreamed of doubting others at first. It was only when his suspicions were aroused that matters changed, though in that case they altered so completely that the person in question could never again make it good.

At first, then, he did not suspect that Elena had made up her mind to spend a Sunday with him, but took at face value her excuse that the others were coming in a while, and she thought the walk to the Long Wall was too tiresome. "Besides," the girl was honest and determined enough to admit, "I'd much rather be with you."

Here, too, he felt at a disadvantage. Flattery—this was how he privately described any expression of friendliness toward himself—filled him with instant confusion. This was why he found it so difficult to deal with women. He could not flatter people himself—he would sooner have bitten his tongue off. And accepting flattery was perhaps even more repugnant to him, because you never knew what to say in return. That any young man of his age should be—a few brief adventures aside—so shy and inexperienced as he in such matters was hard to believe. It was the case, nevertheless, and he positively congratulated himself upon replying to this flattery: "The pleasure is mine, Fräulein Elena."

Having gone this far, he thought it suitable to say, "Fräulein," which at least made it somewhat more formal.

Elena, on the other hand, had no inhibitions. She said, "That's good! But don't call me Fräulein. Last night you called me Elena! I do like to hear you say Elena."

Goodness, he thought, *now a person should be able to think up some more flattery.* For he had felt that his "The pleasure is mine, Fräulein Elena," was a perfect piece of flattery in itself.

So he answered: "What difference does it make whether I call you Fräulein or not?"

There it is, she thought, *he's laughing at me—how I did dread his treating me like a child!* And she cursed the difference in their ages, which made her a mere chit to him, although she knew herself to be well past that stage.

"Are the others coming soon?" he inquired. He felt ill at ease, and would have been heartily glad of reinforcements.

Mistakenly regarding the question as encouragement, she said, her face lighting up: "Oh, not for a long time! We've got lots of time! May I give you cognac? Or would you rather have wine? Or do you want something to eat? Or do you think it's too early?" she added, abashed at his hesitation. "It's only half past eight."

Right, he thought, reminded, *it's half past eight. Seventeen minutes ago was my last moment, which I survived.*

"Cognac and wine," he declared, therefore, suddenly overwhelmed by the feeling that it was indescribably marvelous to be not lying dead below, but up here in the sunny grass and sweet-scented thyme, being a mechanical engineer with a diploma, back at home after three long years that had been harder than he would ever admit. The emotion of being alive swept over him afresh, multiplied by the altitude.

"First cognac, then wine," he decided again, like a pasha.

She had already filled his glass, without taking one for herself, since she did not care for either wine or cognac, and the raspberry soda, which she adored, had unfortunately been forgotten. But it was an indescribable delight to wait on him and watch him drink from one of the glasses that usually stood on the sideboard at home.

"Grand!" he said, draining his glass. "Is it French?"

"I think so," she said, embarrassed at her ignorance. But she looked at the label, and it was, in fact, Cordial Médoc. "Is that a good brand?" she inquired, thankful that he had liked it.

"One of the very best," he observed soberly, and soberly he inquired: "Where did you get it from?" He did not realize that her father, Dr. Maletti, had the reputation of being a heavy drinker.

Elena, feeling that this, too, was a drawback in their relationship, said evasively: "I got it from Papa." For she had simply taken one of the innumerable bottles from Papa's cellar, as she did for every picnic. Oddly enough the boys all liked the bitter stuff, or at least boasted that they did. But of course with a grown-up gentleman like Andreas it was different. He was used to drinking such things; he wouldn't boast.

"That's what I call a generous papa," he acknowledged.

"Yes," she said, and in order to get away from this ticklish subject as quickly as possible, she added: "Another glass?"

"Another glass," he repeated. He took it and drank it.

"And now a glass of wine, Herr Mumelter?"

"Why, this is impossible!" he declared. "You don't want me to call you Fräulein Elena, and then you call me Herr Mumelter."

Quite carried away, her smile radiant with sheer delight, she replied, "May I say Herr Andreas?"

He shook his head. "Andreas."

She turned red at first, and then, the blood streaming to her heart, she paled. "Yes, Andreas," she said, relishing saying the name like a fairy-tale gift. To redouble the pleasure she asked: "A glass of wine, Andreas?"

"Don't hurry me, Elena. Another glass of cognac," he decided.

His saying "Elena" made her catch her breath. Her hands were so unsteady that she spilled a few drops, which he noticed.

"Oho!" he said, starting to get up. "Careful! Wait, I'll do it myself."

She would not let him. "I do like being able to wait on you, Andreas," she said.

He gave her a sidelong, mistrustful look, thrusting out his lower lip. Flattery.

But her eyes were so clear that he was no longer quite sure it was flattery.

She handed him his third glass, and he drank it in slow, luxurious little sips.

She's very pretty, he decided to admit. Too bad the whole crowd is coming right away. He saved up the last sip awhile, for he was determined it should be the last.

If only she had known what he was thinking now! She wanted nothing else in the world, and was racking her brain to think what she could do to make him think what he was already thinking anyway.

"Don't you want anything, Elena?" he asked.

The "Elena" delighted her. "Oh yes. I'll eat a bit of chocolate," she said. She considered whether she dared allow herself the pleasure of adding "Andreas." But she decided the occasion was too trifling. After all, you could hardly say, "I'll eat a bit of chocolate, Andreas." So she refrained, contenting herself with the sweetness of a bar of milk chocolate.

For a while they said nothing.

"Your forehead is getting red in the sun, Andreas," she ventured at last. Sun and Andreas—that was all right.

It was true; his forehead was burning, and his cheeks as well; his skin seemed to be stretched taut, with a pleasant sensation in every pore, as he lay stretched out full length. *Flattery from everywhere,* he thought, but he was not so mistrustful now.

"Can't you do something so that your party won't stay here too long?" he inquired.

Had she heard aright? She was just setting the bottles out of the sun into the shade of the larch tree that stood on the edge of the cliff. Leaving the bottles to their own devices, she ran over and asked him: "What?" She wanted to be perfectly sure.

"I mean," he explained unemotionally, blinking up at her against the strong sun, "couldn't they have their picnic somewhere else? Instead of right here?" He looked up the line of her legs; it was not his fault; she was standing that way.

Now she fell to her knees with delight. "Oh, they aren't coming at all!" she said.

"They—what?" he inquired.

"Aren't coming at all, Andreas," she repeated, feeling justified this time in adding the name, which gave her a delicious shiver every time she said it.

"How so?" he asked, still not understanding.

"Because that was all a fraud before," she admitted doubtfully. And after a second's reflection: "Do you mind, Andreas?" She saw that he did not; she saw it so plainly that she sat down close beside him, near the cranberry bushes with the still unripe berries. Her heart was pounding in her throat; he was the first man who had ever meant anything to her—no, that was a pitifully inadequate phrase. She was so head over heels in love with him that she would have done anything he asked. If he had said: "Jump off that cliff!"—Heaven knows she would have done it.

"Why are you looking down there, Elena?" he asked, following her glance.

"Oh, just looking," she said.

"Did you know that by rights I'd fallen down there? Just before you came. It's a regular miracle that the rescue party isn't carrying me into the morgue at this moment. Actually!" He said this with no particular purpose in view—simply told her because it was running through his head. But since she was so close to him, he had a good view of her face. He saw, therefore, that she had not only startled, but turned pale.

"What?" she asked tonelessly.

Flattery? he thought, and his heart leaped. Was she startling and turning pale from flattery? Good God, she really meant it!

"Elena!" he said.

His tone made her turn pale again, so completely was it transformed. This, too, was like a fairy-tale gift. If only he would say it again! Just, just like that—with the unspoken overtone!

"Elena!" he said again. Just like that.

She sprang up and went toward him. From the cranberry bushes to him was four steps, or five at most. Through the cranberries, through the thyme. She took the first step through the cranberries. The second through the thyme. The third, the fourth, the fifth.

There were six. There was one still to be taken. But she stopped, because her heart was pounding too hard, and she had to catch her breath. Then she took it, the sixth step, treading on the thyme, which smelled but the sweeter.

"Andreas?" she said. It was a question, and she wanted an answer. She was young enough to believe there was such a thing as an answer to this question, a third fairy-tale gift.

It was hers.

If she lived to be a hundred, this would always be the divine moment of her existence—standing there, half stooping down to him, asking him, and having him answer: "Elena!"

Then he kissed her, or was it she who kissed him? She fell into his arms, which he closed about her as he lay there. Ridiculous, perfectly absurd, that people called this kissing! It was heaven on earth. She was perfectly breathless with bliss, and inexpressibly honored that he, so much her elder, a full-grown mechanical engineer, should find a sixteen-year-old worthy of his kisses when the lads of her own age and slightly older treated her as if she were not worth bothering with and quite beyond the pale. Would he tell her in so many words that he loved her? Call her darling? If he did, she would be too happy to bear it.

He kissed her, held her away, kept pulling her back to him; but he did not say what she wanted to hear. How could he, since it was not true? Even if he was a little tipsy—with the altitude, the joy of being alive, the wine—still he would tell the truth. It was glorious to live and to hold the young creature in his arms; he could have asked nothing better. "Say something," he was wishing in his turn, but lending no significance to the wish.

He wants me to say it first, she thought; and, often as she had read what she was supposed to say, and heard it on the stage and in the pictures, it paralyzed her throat.

"Wait—wait, darling," she began. The "darling" cost some effort, but she felt she had brought it off. "Wait—I believe I'll have a drink after all. Another glass for you, darling?" She had actually managed to say it again, offering him a drink solely for that purpose, and although it seemed foolhardy and mad to her, still she felt sure that all this was only a beginning. Now he would say darling, too, and tell her he loved her, and would ask of her something that she was damnably afraid of. But she would not say no; she would do it. First she would take a drink, not the bitter, burning cognac, but a glass of wine to drive away her fears.

Although he was reluctant to let her go, she stood up and took the six steps to the picnic basket, where she poured out two full glasses; she came back the six steps far, far slower than before, balancing both glasses, but not spilling a single drop. She handed him his and drank hers at a draught. It tasted, as wine always did to her, rather queer and unfriendly.

She put both glasses somewhere or other, for his arm was stretched out to her, and now she would say it, now before she kissed him.

She said it.

It came with difficulty from her lips; she was terribly bashful; but once it was said: "I love you," and fate, as she supposed, was thus decided, she grew bolder. She bent her head back, so that instead of kissing her he could answer. Now he would say, "I love you too!"

Perhaps he might say "Elena." Perhaps he would not say it until afterward, when she had given him what he demanded?

Now her life would be settled, she felt. That is to say, of course it had been settled already!

For a moment Andreas thought, *Shall I say I love her?* But he rejected this possibility with a vigorous shake of the head. That would really be too silly! She was too old not to laugh at such a "declaration." How long had he known her? Three quarters of an hour, for the previous evening did not count. If his face had not been reddened by the sun, it would have been by embarrassment at the thought of straining her credulity so far.

So he said: "Marvelous here, isn't it?"

She nodded, a shade disappointed. Had she failed to do or say something?

"Wait," she said, forgetting the "darling" in her confusion, "I'll start the phonograph, shall I?"

"If you like," he conceded.

She played her favorite records. "Ramona"; *"Wien, Wien, nur du allein."*

"Vienna, Vienna, no other town Shall ever call my dreams its own," she sang, kneeling by the phonograph. She had a pleasant soprano voice, and sang easily, like all Italians.

"Why don't you say anything?" she asked when it was over. "Didn't you hear me say I loved you?"

The wine began to trouble her. *I shouldn't have drunk anything,* she thought, experiencing a slight stupor that made her unsure of herself.

He was feeling the wine, too, after the three glasses of cognac. And the sun. And the elevation. And the joy of being alive. He tried to sit up, but had to use his right arm to help support himself. He laughed. Before, on that cliff yonder, he had not wanted to be dizzy; now in the green meadow he did everything to make himself so. Wasn't life funny? He laughed. He was a little, and deliciously, tipsy: there sat Elena, who kissed and sang so nicely; he could see her quite distinctly, and that yellow thing there was a butterfly.

He was not too drunk to catch it—by no means. It was true that he would hardly like to stand on his feet at the moment. Ha! ha! his legs were being contrary: but just the same we should have that little butterfly in a moment! He waited until the yellow creature came to rest for an instant with fluttering wings on one of the shrubs of thyme, and sure enough, he nabbed it with the lightning snatch of his cupped hand that had stayed with him from boyhood.

"Look!" he said triumphantly.

Again Elena nodded, even more disappointed than before. She got up too; her dizziness was gone, and she could see clearly. This time she scarcely took a moment for the six strides; she knew the way now. When she was beside him she looked into his eyes and asked: "Darling, why don't you say it?"

Something in her eyes frightened him. He did not stop to think about it, his head in an agreeable whirl. But he thought himself particularly clever and secretly patted himself on the back for asking her to go on playing the phonograph. "Wind up the radio again," he said, not noticing that he had said radio instead of phonograph, and letting the yellow butterfly go.

"Yes, of course," she said.

Obediently and literally she did what he asked; instead of stumbling over the little word "again," she turned on the suitcase radio—apparently he hadn't liked the phonograph music. The radio, too, gave out music, then a few spoken words, then more music as she went on dialing to find music he would like.

Meanwhile, he had lain down again; with his head resting on his arm he watched the little butterfly approach the yawning depth that he had so recently escaped. Light, graceful, happy in its freedom, it floated over him and vanished.

"What's that?" he asked as Elena, looking for better music, caught a few more spoken words. They were in Italian.

". . . Represents a solution to the German minority problem in the Alto Adige which cannot but be described as ideal. This minority, embracing scarcely 200,000 Germans, or rather persons of German tongue, is thus . . ."

A voice sang in German: "I rest at ease in the tall green grass"—Brahms's "Feldeinsamkeit." *Right you are!* thought Andreas in his delicious befuddlement, broken by a few spoken words.

"In the orbs of Heaven gloriously entwined . . ." He joined in the song. Then suddenly he sat up.

"What was that?" he asked, for another wrong figure had been given. Damn it, there were not "scarcely 200,000," but more—at least 220,000 Austrians and Germans in South Tirol!

"Would you turn on the news again?" he asked.

Elena looked at him helplessly. She had been enjoying his lying there singing in his deep voice. So that was the music he wanted! Unfortunately she did not know the song. "I thought you wanted that music—darling?" she asked, but obediently spun the knob.

"And as Greece and Turkey in 1932 solved one of Europe's knottiest postwar minorities problems by transplanting 1,400,000 people back to their native soil, so the Axis has solved the South Tirolean problem with yet greater statesmanship and foresight. The substance of the agreement, reached after negotiations between Undersecretary of State Giulio Nitti and the Prefect of Bolzano, Giuseppe Mastromattei for Italy, on the one side, and S.S. leader Himmler and Gauleiter Bohle for Germany, on the other side, is as follows:

"1. All German citizens resident in South Tirol must return to the Reich forthwith.

"2. Those residents of South Tirol who were subjects of the Austro-Hungarian Monarchy before the annexation of South Tirol to the Kingdom of Italy, and who became Italian through the annexation, are also advised to return to the Reich. These former Austro-Hungarians have, however, the right to make a free and uninfluenced decision in a plebiscite whose details will be announced.

"3. Former Austro-Hungarians who do not wish to re-emigrate, but to remain in Italy, have not, however, the right to choose the place where they will reside in the future. The Royal Italian Government will decide this matter in the individual cases.

"4. The evacuation of South Tirol by the German-speaking minority has been put in charge of S.S. leader Heinrich Himmler.

"We will now give the time signal. It is exactly fifteen minutes after nine o'clock."

Elena, too, had listened more and more attentively as the announcer went on. When Andreas stood up and came toward her to stare fixedly down at the little suitcase that was spreading the mellifluous words through the sunlit stillness, she knew he had not come to her.

"Further bulletins at 12:45 P.M." The news ended. Then came the broadcast of Sunday Mass in the Bozen parish church—the regular Italian Mass.

"Shut it off!" said Andreas roughly as the organ began to hum.

Was the sun behind a cloud? It was gray. Did this chill come from the wind? It was cold. The thyme had no scent. The mountains looked different. Everything looked different.

"I've got to get down," said Andreas to the girl.

She could feel that for him she no longer existed. *I've lost my chance,* she saw, and could not help thinking more about this than about what she had heard.

"I suppose we'll simply vote for Italy," she suggested uncertainly, hoping to say what he would like to hear.

"Yes," he said. "Freely and without influence."

"Yes," she agreed, not noticing the biting irony.

"You probably want to meet your party, don't you?" he said.

When was it that he kissed me? she thought. *A year ago? Five years ago? Did that strange man kiss me?*

He grew more and more unfamiliar to her from moment to moment. He stood and looked, with his lower lip protruding. He did not see her. For a moment he looked at the cliff over which the yellow butterfly had been wafted away immemorial ages ago; then he held out his hand to her.

"I hope we'll be seeing each other soon?" he asked, taking the little timetable of the Virgl railway out of his pocket. The next train left in forty-six minutes.

Never in her life had she been so lonely.

"Can't I ride down with you?" she asked slowly.

"Why, of course," he returned with a casualness that tore her in two.

And already he had turned and started down. She walked behind him; the path was narrow. But in the cable railway they sat face to face. This time, too, the train was almost empty. He looked at her, but she knew perfectly well that he was not seeing her. His face was pale in spite of the sunburn.

"Herr Mumelter," she said, for the whole trip lasted only four minutes, and two were already gone. She dared not even say "Herr Andreas," let alone "Andreas," to this strange man. *And long, long ago I was calling him darling!* she thought.

"Yes?" he asked, not seeing her.

"Nothing," she said.

"Yes," he repeated. "It's too bad. But we'll have to be thinking about more important things, shan't we?"

She still had fifteen seconds with the strange man whom she had called darling.

"Be good," he said, with a faint, faint touch in his voice of the tenderness he had shown long ago.

"Mhm," she said.

Then her time was up.

Chapter 3

THE TWENTY-FOUR MEN were gathered in a so-called "extra room" at the Hotel Schgraffer. There was not much time to waste; alarming reports kept coming in, and every hour brought a new one. While at first, with the false optimism that takes hold of a good many thoughtful persons faced with news of disaster, people had tried to believe that Sunday's radio bulletin had not been authentic, but had come from some foreign propaganda station, proof to the contrary had gradually piled up. Pastor Gemaassmer, who held the chair among the twenty-four Bozen citizens who had gathered as "The Council," counted them off.

From the prefect, he admitted, it had been impossible so far to obtain either a confirmation or a denial, and the Italian papers were as bare of the slightest hint as the German ones. On the other hand, official "emigration bureaus" had been opened this morning in Bozen and in the near-by health resort of Meran, and the purpose could obviously be nothing but the emigration of the German South Tiroleans. And perhaps more, the head of these Italian bureaus was not an Italian, but the German S.S. Storm-band leader, Dr. Luig!

"Actually?" asked Herr von Fennperg, who belonged to the false optimists, and, like everyone else, knew the reputation Dr. Luig had come to enjoy here. "Where did you learn that, Your Reverence?"

Pastor Gemaassmer, a man whose speech was as short and compact as his peasant figure, replied: "From him himself," and went on to the next alarming point.

"This morning," he reported, "I had an interview with a man known, I might almost say notorious, to you, Antonio Udacher, the Nazi leader here. He told me—— Wait a minute, I took it down, and I'll read it to you word for word.

" 'The two Axis partners are fully agreed that all German citizens living here in South Tirol must leave the country as soon as possible. Former Austrians, who became Italian through the Treaty of St. Germain—that's our situation, and includes about 220,000 or 230,000 of us—have the right to say whether they will remain Italians or be repatriated.' "

"Well, then!" interrupted another optimist, the furniture dealer Johann Josef Traxl. "That obviously means that there won't be any change at all for us former Austrians. If we say we'll stay Italians, everything will be in order."

"Unfortunately that isn't what it means," contradicted the pastor, and one might have known from the first by looking at his face that he had little hope to hold out. "I won't even touch upon the difficulties of conscience that this so-called right of option involves us in. We never wanted to be Italians, as you know very well. But, absurd as it sounds, that isn't the important point any more. For the benefit of those among you who may suppose, as Herr Traxl does, that they have only to vote for Italy, and then they and their families can go on living in their old Bozen houses, pursuing their occupations and bringing up their children here, even though in Italian schools, Herr Udacher declared triumphantly to me—I quote: 'Those who choose Italy can no longer count on the interest and protection of the Third Reich.' As you may imagine, I asked him what he meant. Here is his answer: 'It is absolutely at the discretion of the Italian government to do whatever it pleases with the former Austrians who decide for Italy.'

"'And what will it please?' I asked him. Whereupon he shrugged his shoulders meaningly and remarked, 'The Italians regard Ethiopia as a land of milk and honey.' You can probably draw your own conclusions from that."

The moderately large ground-floor room, stuffy with the heat of July and the pipe and cigar smoke, was filled with a pregnant silence. To avoid being heard outside, it had been necessary to keep the windows closed. The twenty-four men, hastily elected the day before, and representing the former Austrians in the prefecture of Bozen—the false optimists among them included—had a feeling that the very air they breathed was cut off.

"We'll simply have to make representations in Rome!" Dr. von Hueber, a lawyer, finally ventured to say.

His words seemed to fall like pebbles into an abyss.

"Do you happen to have another tried-and-true representative of our interests at hand like your bosom friend Radio von Radiis?" asked Dr. Faider, the ear specialist, bitterly, bringing to mind a late Meran deputy who had obediently said yes in the Roman Chamber to every order that Mussolini gave.

"Preposterous," contradicted the lawyer with a look of consternation.

Another helpless pause. The priest was about to say something. But old Mumelter asked for the floor.

He stood erect, his china pipe in one hand, the other hand leaning heavily on the table top.

"Tell me, you men," he said, speaking with a strong Tirolean accent. "I keep hearing talk about repatriation—is that the word the

Axis powers are using, Your Reverence?" he interrupted himself. And when the priest nodded: "Then I'd like to know what they mean by repatriation. If," he answered himself, "it means the same as return home, or resumption of citizenship at home, then in our case it must be the most impudent fraud imaginable. Repatriation? Yes, you men, but where is our home, our *patria?* It's right here. In Bozen. In Meran. In Brixen. In Klausen. In Stubai. In Kalten. In Alt- and Neu-Praggs. In Toblach. In Innichen. It's in the South Tirol! It's right here, and right here it has been for more than thirteen hundred years. In those thirteen hundred years we and our forefathers, with God's help, have made the country what it is today. A beautiful land. A marvelous land. A fertile, industrious, pious, rich land. In our case, then, repatriation could only mean that South Tiroleans living abroad, in the Canary Islands for all I know, or in the Never-Never Land, who have become foreigners, God knows why, could come back home here and be South Tiroleans again. Is that what it means, Your Reverence?" he inquired with the tenacity and truculence of old age.

"No, of course not, Mumelter," answered the priest through the smoke, the heat, the breathlessness.

"Then," replied the speaker, nodding disdainfully, "I want to object to the expression 'of course.' It is very peculiar what people here regard as a matter of course"—this with a glance at his grandson. "Because there could not possibly be anything less so, or more unnatural, than to offer us a repatriation that ought, if I know enough Latin, to be called an expatriation. Because that's what it is. It follows, as plain as day, that we have just one question to ask ourselves, and that is: Do we want to go abroad? Even if, as I take for granted, they were to transport us to North Tirol and settle us there, it would still be abroad to us. Men! To us everything is foreign that isn't our own country here."

Another silence, longer and more profound than before. No one had the heart to answer this man who was talking, at ninety-one years of age, about staying or going. He waited for his answer, still standing erect and looking from one to another.

Finally the priest said: "It isn't by any means certain, Mumelter, that they want us in North Tirol. I had more of a feeling that they were thinking about sending us to East Prussia or Moravia."

You could hear the twenty-four breathing, so perfect was the immobility that followed upon these words. The old man sat down without a sound. His heavy, sinewy hand still gripped the table top. His sharp eyes went from one to another of those who sat there with him.

From the dental technician Peter Entleuthner to Konrad Sturz, proprietor of the candied-fruit shop in the Dr. Streitergasse; to Jakob Hoermann, the cemetery superintendent; to Jakob Kerschpamer, the saddler; to Dr. Hanns von Hueber, the lawyer; to Andreas Mumelter, to his grandson; to Michael Auer, the optician; to Felix Feigenputz, who worked at Schenker's Bank and Travel Bureau; to Eugen Lanser von Moor, the fruitgrower; to the brothers Konrad and Rudolf Paechl, proprietors of the lucky-ring shop in the Rainerstrasse; to the pastor's brother, the baker Karl Valentin Gemaassmer; to Helmuth Anton Tschudaeth, the teacher; to Christian Robert Fenner von Fennperg, the fruitgrower; to the proprietor of the Apotheke zum Engel Mariae in the Kapuzinergasse, Kaspar Tolloy; to Dr. Johann Mayrhofer, the general practitioner; to Johann Josef Traxl, the furniture dealer; to Josef Franz Doerfel zu Steyerheimb, the fruitgrower; to Urban Tieffenthaler, the jeweler on Holy Trinity Square; to Dr. Hans Steger, another general practitioner; to Caspar Simmerl, a fruitgrower, and to Johannes Gemaassmer, pastor and prebendary of the parish church.

You twenty-three! his eyes said. *You men of our country—did you hear that? Help us!* his eyes said, and his firm hands began to tremble.

Voices and footsteps grew loud outside, approaching at great speed. Shouts could be heard: *"Ein Volk, Ein Reich, Ein Führer!"* As the twenty-four stared into the smoke from their pipes and cigars, their ears were assaulted with it: "One people, one realm, one leader!"

Again. And again.

Apparently this was one of the strictly prohibited night parades that the local Nazis had held now and then during the previous few years, and not a few of the German Bozners had toyed with the idea that it might be desirable to belong to one nation, one realm, and one leader. Even a few of those present had thought so, and perhaps still did. Herr Feigenputz, for example. Dr. von

Hueber. Herr Tolloy. Their eyes lighted up as the shouts and the marching footsteps came closer.

"They're even venturing out into the open now!" said Tieffenthaler, the jeweler, bitterly. "And of course the prefect doesn't mind, because he'll be rid of the shouters soon enough anyway. They'll all emigrate!"

"Well, it's the only sensible way, the only way worthy of a German!" cried Herr Feigenputz, whereupon Dr. von Hueber, Herr Tolloy, and also Herr von Fenner nodded their agreement.

"I say, Herr Feigenputz." Tschudaeth, the teacher, turned to him. "If you don't mind? We aren't Germans. We're Austrians!"

"I don't see any difference at all." Tolloy, the apothecary, came to Herr Feigenputz's support. "We Austrians have always felt as Germans, and always shall."

"That," objected the teacher indignantly, "is one of the greatest frauds there is! If you had the slightest glimmering of our Austrian history, you'd know that nothing has ever connected the Austrians with the Germans, and in spite of all the Anschluss business nothing connects them now. The Austrians and the Germans have just one resemblance: they speak German. But so do the Swiss speak German, and they feel as Swiss! And the Americans speak English and don't consider themselves Englishmen. We aren't German—I want that clear. Thank God we have different blood, a different history, a different civilization, and different feelings! A true Austrian has as much in common with a German as Mozart has with Wagner! And that has always been so—it isn't only *now* that the Germans bear more resemblance to the Huns than to any other people. Long before Hitler we loathed everything German and hated every Prussian as our hereditary enemy. And it was the Bavarians whom we fought and beat under Andreas Hofer." Angrily he shook his lean head until the long hair whirled over his face. "It's high time to stop talking about our Germanness to us. We Austrians are not Germans, and, damn it, we needn't worry our heads about what is or isn't worthy of a German! Instead, let's decide what's worthy of an Austrian. That's what we're here for!"

A murmur of approval and several "Bravo, Tschudaeth!" followed this outburst, and Andreas was about to ask for the floor when the door opened without a knock, and a man wearing a swastika arm band came in.

"Heil Hitler!" he said, hooking his left thumb in the belt of his Storm Troop uniform and raising his right arm. It was Herr Udacher, the Nazi leader and Gauleiter in the district of the Bozen prefecture.

Three or four of those present replied with a Hitler salute. The others said, "Good evening." Or they said nothing at all, like old Mumelter.

"Having a session?" asked the newcomer, pulling up a chair for himself between Herr Tolloy and Herr Feigenputz without waiting to be asked. On the Waltherplatz outside, the shouts swelled sharply and rhythmically: *"Ein Volk, Ein Reich, Ein Führer!"*

And in answer, like gunfire: *"Sieg, Heil! Sieg, Heil!"*

"Fellow Germans!" said Herr Udacher in the midst of the tumult, jumping up, "the hour has struck! I presume you have met here to discuss your future. Fellow Germans, there is nothing to discuss! The die is cast—in your favor, thanks to the wisdom and magnanimity of our Führer! Only a few days ago not one of you would have dreamed that the hour of liberation was so near. Yet now it is here! The brotherly arms of the Third Reich are open wide to you all, and your return home there after long years of sorrow and suffering will be the return of a son almost given up for lost!"

Someone interrupted: "Tell me, Herr Udacher, are we the brothers or the sons of the Third Reich now? I'm a little mixed up about the relationship."

It was Hoermann, the cemetery superintendent, who made this biting remark, and for the first time in that apprehensive evening a hint of a smile was to be seen on the lips of the company.

"Sieg, Heil!" came the whiplash words from outside.

The saber cut on the cheek of Antonio Udacher, the former university duellist, reddened. "You have a peculiar sense of humor, fellow German," he replied sharply.

But the cemetery superintendent, whose long association with the dead had given him a philosophy of his own, remarked: "By the way, I'm not a fellow citizen of yours, Herr Udacher. You come from Pomerania or somewhere, and I'm a South Tirolean."

"Right! Bravo, Hoermann!" cried the thin teacher, Tschudaeth, his hair flying.

At this Herr Feigenputz, who had recovered his poise, said reprovingly: "Don't interrupt! Go on, Herr Udacher."

The Gauleiter's answer was immediate praise: "Thank you very much, Party Comrade Feigenputz."

"I didn't know you belonged to the Party," said the priest.

"Is that a reproach, Your Reverence?" asked the Nazi leader.

"A statement of fact," replied the cleric quietly.

Herr Udacher looked over his head as if he were not there. "Fellow Germans," he went on, his voice now at its most cutting, "the question of who does or does not belong to the Party is not under discussion here. The point that is under discussion here, on the other hand, is what German men——"

"German men!" repeated Tschudaeth, the teacher, savagely.

"Yes, German men, for that is what we are," repeated Udacher in turn. "Men who speak German and feel as Germans—what such German men are to do when they are offered the opportunity to become German again."

"Repatriation?" asked old Mumelter. "Is that it?"

"Quite right," agreed the speaker, not realizing how the question was meant. And when the old man translated the foreign word and what he thought of it: "Going back home to some place where we never lived and never shall feel at home!" he said scornfully: "You will realize, fellow Germans, that I cannot undertake to argue every childish remark," and he was about to go on.

But this was too much for old Mumelter's ninety-one years. He banged on the table with his flat hand, and said: "You. You may be a good Nazi. But if you're going to be impudent, I shall take you by the ears, which you are still wet behind. Do you hear?"

"Right!" "Bravo!" came a murmured chorus.

Herr Udacher was a skillful political speaker and equal to any heckling. He pretended to be listening exclusively to the wilder and wilder shouts in the square outside, and observed with a gesture toward the window: "The people who aren't dry behind the ears can get themselves a hearing even so!"

"Sieg, Heil!" came crashing from outside.

The priest had been whispering to his neighbor, Tschudaeth, the teacher. Now he asked: "To what do we owe the honor, Herr Udacher? As you see, we're in the midst of a session."

"Which is quite useless," said Udacher. "After all, a session can hardly mean anything unless there are several possible courses. Here, however, there is only one."

"Nonsense," said one of the two Paechl brothers, who so far had not opened his mouth. "You said yourself we could vote for Italy."

"In the first place," declared the Nazi leader, "it is unthinkable for a German man to do so; and in the second place you would only be getting something immeasurably worse in exchange. You would land in Abyssinia or the Pontic Marshes, or some other place that would be the last in the world you would choose. You can't stay here in any case. I know that officially."

The voice of a speaker was loud in the Waltherplatz. One heard it word for word, since none of the twenty-four was speaking: "Fellow Germans!" said the speaker outside, and the speaker in the room likewise said: "Fellow Germans! In the name of the Führer, whose special care you have been ever since he took power, and long, long before, I solemnly require you to enter your answers in the list which I present to you herewith."

He put on the table a sheet headed: "National Socialist German Workers' Party, District of Bozen, District Directorate," and containing the names of the twenty-four in alphabetical order. First name, last name, when and where born, religion, race, occupation, domicile; a vacant column after each name left space to answer the two questions provided: "Prepared for departure? When?"

The pastor picked up the sheet. After reading it carefully, which took some time, he said, "Men! This is a form issued by the Nazi party. Herr Udacher wishes——"

"Excuse me!" interrupted the latter. "It isn't I that wish it. The Führer wishes it!"

"Wishes," the pastor repeated, ignoring him, "to have you write on it whether you're prepared for departure and when. Naturally—as I hardly believe I need specially point out to you—none of you is under any obligation whatever to fill out this form. If anyone cares to, let him come forward."

No one moved.

"I suppose you realize that everything that happens here will reach the Führer's ears?" observed the Gauleiter, this time avoiding the term "Fellow Germans."

Thereupon Herr Tolloy inquired doubtfully: "May I see the paper a minute?"

Before the pastor could hand the sheet to the apothecary, Andreas stood up.

Something was happening inside him that he could not explain. He hated to listen to speeches and had never made one. The mistrust he felt toward people was even stronger toward words. If anyone had told him that he would now stand up and speak, nothing could have made him do it. Nevertheless, he had got up, and wanted to speak. He wanted to say just a few words, because no one had yet said them, and because, he thought, they must finally be said. He would not make a speech—he didn't want to and couldn't. He would only fill the yawning gap that, for some mysterious reason, the others had left.

"May I," he began, "inquire of our self-invited guest upon what he bases his statement that the Führer has made us his care and has our fate so very much at heart? So far as I know," he went on slowly, but without giving the other a chance to reply, "after the annexation of Austria he made a speech, I think it was in April of 1938, in Mussolini's presence at Rome—pardon me, it wasn't April, it was May—yes, May of 1938——"

He had lost the thread of his discourse, and a deep wrinkle appeared around his nostrils. "In that speech," he continued, "he solemnly promised Mussolini that he would respect the Brenner frontier for all time."

And although it was unspeakably repugnant to him to use any oratorical device, he turned to the assemblage and asked: "Do you remember, gentlemen, that on the day of the annexation of Austria —or wait a minute, it was the next day, the twelfth of March 1938 —the Führer telegraphed to Mussolini: 'Duce, I shall never forget this'? 'This' was Mussolini's broken promise to guarantee Austrian independence. Mussolini let Hitler annex Austria, so Hitler guaranteed the Brenner frontier for Mussolini."

When Andreas began, the group had listened to him intently. The longer he spoke, naming and correcting dates with pedantic exactitude, the less interesting they thought him.

Herr Udacher, indeed, seemed to feel otherwise. Taking note of every word, he said, "That is only one proof the more of our Führer's higher wisdom. He knew, you see, that the union could be accomplished in another way."

Andreas could feel that no one was listening. Nevertheless, he drove himself to say: "Apparently the Führer himself did not think his higher wisdom would be very popular with the South Tiroleans. Do you remember, gentlemen? The train that took him to Rome was ingeniously routed in such a way that the Führer passed through Bozen here at four in the morning instead of eleven-twenty in the forenoon, thus depriving the German South Tiroleans of the chance to put on before his own eyes a tremendous demonstration for their freedom."

They all were listening to him now. They all remembered, for the occurrence had created talk enough, though no one had put upon it the surprising and convincing interpretation that Andreas now offered: "Why did the Führer not want to see you, gentlemen? Because, thanks to the higher wisdom mentioned by Herr Udacher, he knew beforehand that he would betray South Tirol in Rome, and because he would therefore have found it extremely unwelcome if you, gentlemen, and thousands of South Tiroleans with you, had solemnly asked the contrary of him just before. Hence the journey in the dark of night."

Andreas' voice was not halting now. It carried. And speaking was no longer a torment: he found it almost a pleasure.

Udacher's lips were tight. "I protest against this travesty!" he cried.

"Why?" asked the old man, motioning to his grandson not to be put off. "Is there anything insulting about the dark of night?"

"Let's stick to facts and not become involved in hairsplitting!" said Herr Feigenputz, expecting from the Gauleiter a word of praise that he did not get.

"Much obliged that you didn't say 'Jewish hairsplitting'!" retorted Andreas, and in his excitement he spoke as he might never have done in cold blood. "For that matter, Herr Feigenputz, we *are* sticking to facts, and nothing else!" he emphasized. His voice grew hard and menacing. "Herr Udacher here has told us that we South Tiroleans were the special care of the Führer—not were, still are; and that the Third Reich is only waiting to clasp us in brotherly or fatherly arms. All right. But, gentlemen, have you seen so much as a single word about South Tirol in any Reich German paper? I lived there for three years, and I, at any rate, never saw a one. But there were innumerable words about Danzig. There seem to be German minorities of varying importance to the Reich, and Danzig is undoubtedly more important to it than we are. A fact, Herr Feigenputz! But whereas we—as you can prove for yourself at once in the Café Greif—are offered whole columns of news about Danzig every day, the subject of our present meeting is not given a single syllable in the Goebbels press. A fact, Herr Feigenputz. After all, you might suppose that a country so deeply concerned for us would shout with joy at the moment when it was relieved of this concern—and particularly a country like the Third Reich, so fond of boasting about its accomplishments. Wouldn't you suppose that a country like that would celebrate the glorious liberation of the South Tiroleans with trumpets and rejoicing? Nothing of the sort! Instead the agreement between the Axis powers has been kept absolutely quiet beyond the Brenner so far. Accordingly, it can't be either so glorious or so helpful—but more likely a dark-of-night affair better not mentioned by day. And if the Nazis themselves, who, God knows, are total strangers to the word embarrassment—a fact, Herr Tolloy—become officially embarrassed, we can pretty well imagine what they intend to do with us, and how we shall feel when clasped in their outspread arms!"

Here the Gauleiter could no longer contain himself. "I protest once more against these unheard-of distortions of the true facts!" he interrupted. "And I am not inclined to go on listening to them."

"Bravo!" cried someone ambiguously.

Andreas, thrusting forward his lower lip, looked about him. He no longer felt that people were withholding their attention. On the contrary, he saw the eyes of all twenty-four, Udacher included, on him, and his excitement grew.

"Fellow Germans!" The Nazi leader tried once more to assert his authority. "In the name of the Führer I demand a vote upon my motion!" This was obviously directed at his neighbors, Herren Tolloy and Feigenputz, and also at Herr von Hueber and his neighbors on the left, Herren von Fenner and Dorfner zu Steyerheimb. "You must decide!" he insisted, "between friend and foe!"

"Have I still got the floor?" inquired Andreas.

"Yes, Andre, you still have the floor," replied the pastor to the boy he had baptized. And he added quietly, "Furthermore, I might observe that Herr Udacher is not a member of the council and accordingly has no right to make motions."

"The council," objected the Gauleiter, "is an illegal body, created quite arbitrarily and not in conformity with the laws governing associations, neither registered with nor recognized by the prefecture, and therefore null and void."

"If that is so, then why do you want our decision?" asked one of the Paechl brothers, who spoke seldom, but logically.

"Because in a sense you are the mouthpiece of the former Austrians here, and because—whether rightfully or no I will not discuss—you enjoy their confidence," was the Nazi leader's equally logical answer.

Andreas, still on his feet, replied. He did not stop to consider; the words came to him and he used them. They poured into his mind; he had no hesitations now. "I have the floor, Herr Udacher," he said, "and you haven't. We here are former Austrians, and you aren't. We love South Tirol, and you don't. Wrong—we are devoted to it with all we have and all we are, and you aren't."

He stretched out an arm in the Gauleiter's direction. "You warn us to choose between friend and foe, Herr Udacher. We shall. That is what we are here for. But the bitter truth is"—and his arm dropped—"that, alas, we must choose not so much between friend and foe as—yes, between foe and foe. Our old enemy Italy has broken her word to us once again; the same Italy that solemnly promised us after the World War—through the mouth of General Pecori-Garibaldi, through the mouth of Prime Minister Tittoni, and finally through the mouth of the King—that Italy, the great and united nation, would assure us German-speaking South Tiroleans the preservation of our own schools, institutions, and associations; that Italy had no thought of oppressing us; she not only would tolerate, but wholeheartedly desired the unchanged national existence of South Tirol, and welcomed us as Italian fellow citizens on an equal footing; that this Italy, whose Prime Minister Salandra said five years afterward: 'Legally speaking, no minorities exist with us,' and whose Prime Minister Mussolini, one year after that, forbade not only every word of German, but even the name of South Tirol, so that we are obliged to write and print 'forbidden name' instead of that dearest of all names—that this same Italy should betray us again is not surprising. It *is* surprising that our father, our brother Germany has sold us out. For if what you, Herr Udacher, told His Reverence this morning is true, she has sold us out. In order to be quite sure, therefore, may I ask you here in the presence of us all, Herr Udacher: where will the German government send those who vote for Germany? Or, to be still more precise: where will those persons live in future who answer 'Yes' to the question 'Prepared for departure?' on that sheet there?"

Andreas paused, and the man he was speaking to considered his answer for a moment, so that a fragment of oratory outside became audible: ". . . with a magnanimity exceeded only by his wise statesmanship . . ."

Udacher was ready with his reply: "The German government will reach a decision on that point at a later date."

But Andreas would leave no room for evasions. "Does that mean that any one of us might possibly be settled outside North Tirol?" he asked.

"I have already answered, and do not wish to repeat myself," Udacher evaded the snare. "The German government will make that decision later."

"Just a moment," insisted Andreas with Tirolean persistency. "Might it happen, then, that one of us twenty-four here or one of the hundreds of thousands for whom we are taking counsel might be sent, let us say, to East Prussia or Silesia or Bohemia or the Hungarian frontier—I mean, might he be forcibly settled there? Take good care how you answer me. You see, we'll take you at your word, for once."

The Gauleiter made use of the opportunity that offered. Following the saying of his Führer that a great lie is more readily believed than a small one, he put his right hand where he supposed his heart to be, and said with all the sincerity he could muster: "I know from the highest quarters that the South Tiroleans will be given consideration above all other Germans." And he repeated significantly in a lower tone: "From the highest quarters."

Not only Andreas but the old man and some of the others had no doubt that he was lying. But the impression on the majority of his listeners was by no means unfavorable. Many eyes were trained on the sheet lying before the pastor.

Therefore Andreas, to forestall any precipitation, offered a motion: "Before we fill out this sheet, about which everyone may do as he thinks best, we must make sure of the Italian government's intention in regard to us. Herr Udacher has interpreted the plans of the German government in a way that each of us may, or may not, understand. But so far we do not know what the Italian government thinks. In order to find this out I move that the council appoint three of us to go to the prefect, and if this brings no results, then to Signor Mussolini himself, who, I suppose, will have to receive a deputation from more than 220,000 people. The three delegates are to ascertain definitely whether, if we vote for Italy, we may remain at home in our own houses and occupations, or whether we shall have to leave South Tirol, and where we would have to go in that case."

As this motion was about to be voted on, the Gauleiter played his trump card. "As I hinted before, fellow Germans, that is something I can tell you," he declared. "You can gather the attitude of the Italian government toward you, and what you may expect in that quarter, from this decree of the Ministry of the Interior, which reached the prefecture from Rome a couple of hours ago, and has, presumably, been published by now."

Following the old theatrical formula, he allowed the fixed attention of the assembly to grow for a while as he reached with studied leisureliness into his breast pocket, which contained, neatly folded and fresh off the press, the chief instrument of his persuasion, hitherto withheld. He pulled it out and passed it around the table. There was a smell of fresh printer's ink.

"Within forty-eight hours," said the three lines of Italian, "all aliens now in the Alto Adige are required to leave the country."

The orator's voice in the Waltherplatz was still lauding the superhuman virtues of the Führer as the paper passed from hand to hand.

That the three-line document could not refer to those present or to other former Austrians in South Tirol was quite clear. For it expressly said "aliens." Nevertheless, the Nazi propagandist gained the advantage he expected from the word (which, after all, was vague and subject to interpretation) and the conspicuously short time limit of the expulsion order. If you read it hastily, particularly when you were already deeply dismayed, you might even think the order meant you, and that you would have to pack up and go in the next forty-eight hours. With one or two exceptions, furthermore, these men were not lawyers and unfamiliar with Italian official language. Consternation was the result. At one blow it quite transformed the men, most of whom had so far confined themselves to listening, to a yes, a no, or an interpolation.

Even now their excitement was expressed less in words than in the deadly earnestness of their faces. Several stood up; others looked to the pastor, as if that could do any good, and a few surrounded Andreas.

". . . Not only abroad, in the overwhelming triumphs of his statesmanship that have amazed the whole world, but primarily and above all within the Reich. So what could possibly be closer to his heart than the German home and the healthy, happy, carefree . . ." came the harangue from outside.

Indoors, Herr Udacher was asserting with impeccable logic: "The sooner you sign, the more promptly the arrangements will be made for your arrival in the homeland. As you see, it is perfectly possible to be run across the frontier here within forty-eight hours."

"But not for us. This doesn't mean us!" said Andreas after he had read the notice over and over again and recovered from the shock that had stunned even him at first. "Don't be taken in, you fellows!" he cried. "That only means summer trippers, Englishmen, Frenchmen, Swiss, and that sort of thing. Not us. It says *aliens*. Not *Italians*. And by law we're Italians!"

"Right," said the old man thoughtfully, his face stony. "But even so, it's a bad sign."

"How so? What do you mean, Mumelter? Tell us!" The men crowded around, importuning him.

He looked at the printed sheet that now lay beside Udacher's form in the middle of the table.

"Well. They don't want any impartial witnesses here for a while—to the things that are going to happen," he said slowly. It sounded like a solemn verdict condemning the twenty-four and all those on whose behalf the twenty-four were here.

But the grandson did not give in. "That may be, but it needn't necessarily be so," he declared. And again, more surprisingly to him than to any of those present, who, after all, had more or less lost sight of him for the previous three years, he found that words were not his enemies; they obeyed him; there was nothing about them now to mistrust or be ashamed of. Indeed they convinced Andreas himself and carried away others. He showed how preposterous it would be to give up for lost a game that one had not even started to play.

"If we might ask Herr Udacher to leave us alone now?" he requested. "We'd like to be among ourselves—we South Tiroleans, I mean. And anyway I am sure Herr Udacher will find ways and means to keep himself well informed of our discussion and of our decisions." At "ways and means" he glanced toward Herren Feigenputz, Tolloy, Von Hueber, and Von Fenner.

"Does this mean, young man, that you are showing the representatives of the Third Reich the door?" asked the Gauleiter, frothing with rage.

"This means," replied the pastor quite unexpectedly, "that we wish to continue our deliberations, already long delayed, without outside influence, and that only members of the council are entitled to a seat and a vote."

Without a word or a salutation, leaving the papers behind him in his hurry or by design, the representative of the Third Reich left the private room.

Numerous cries of *"Heil* Hitler!" presumably in his honor, could be heard from the Waltherplatz, where the speech was still going on.

"Do you think that was wise?" asked Herr von Fenner. "After all, we shouldn't make enemies of them."

"You mean the Nazis, Herr von Fenner?" asked Andreas. "In that case, don't worry. They're our enemies anyhow. At least I don't know what else to call people who want to drive me away and make me utterly miserable." And he put before the council what he thought should be done. Since the formerly Austrian South Tiroleans were to vote for or against Italy—that is, as he said, to hold a sort of plebiscite —three things must be assured. He enumerated the three points on three fingers of his left hand. First, the world, deprived of all witnesses through the expulsion of foreigners, must learn what it needed to know, and be brought to think the case of South Tirol as important as that of Danzig, which was talked about everywhere, whereas—he emphasized angrily—not a soul so much as mentioned

South Tirol. Second, this option or plebiscite or whatever you chose to call it must take place without interference, "uninfluenced" as had been promised—that is, uninfluenced even by such people as Udacher or Dr. Luig, and certainly without any such ignominy as the plebiscite forced upon the Austrians after the Anschluss was completed. He told of seeing the ballot forms that the Austrians had to use on April 10, 1938: transparent white envelopes through which the printed "yes" and "no" could be read perfectly plainly. Third and last, there must be some assurance that the people who voted for Italy would be able to remain and pursue their occupations in South Tirol.

The priest put these three points to a vote.

They carried with one nay and Herr Tolloy abstaining—that is, by a majority of twenty-one. A committee to attend to them was chosen, consisting of Pastor Gemaassmer as chairman, Konrad, the elder of the Paechl brothers, and Andreas. By eighteen to five the council voted them complete authority to do as they thought best.

The session was then adjourned.

The demonstration in the Waltherplatz was already over, so that when the twenty-four left the airless room after three anxious hours, the accustomed nocturnal silence of Bozen reigned once more.

"Gruess Gott!"

"Auf Wiedersehen!"

"Gruess Gott!" said the men to one another, then they scattered in various directions.

Grandfather and grandson started home together.

"Have you any hope?" asked the old man with an entirely unaccustomed note of uncertainty, nay of respect for his junior.

"Oh, a very great deal!" replied Andreas truthfully.

At this the old man patted his shoulder, which did not reach to his own. "Bravo!" he said. And the first real smile of these last few evil days played upon his thin lips as he looked inquiringly for a hint of the next day's weather before they went on. "There! Look at that! Those are stars for you, eh?"

The heavens were spangled. Star after star sparkled against their deep, dark boundlessness. White light seemed to drip from them upon men, monuments, and stones.

"A lovely night," said the old man, taking a deep breath of the crisp air.

"Wonderful!" replied the grandson. And they went into the garden. For their house had a little garden between the Silbergasse and the back of the Laubengasse, through which they had come. Garden was too big a word for it. It was more of a spacious courtyard, in which trees flourished—one pear tree, the rest apples. They rose motionless into the silent night. The stars shone upon the apples along the branches, turning the fruit and leaves to silver.

"Looks like Christmas trees," said the old man, taking the big key to the front door off the key ring where he had carried it since his father's death, fifty-seven years before.

Thrusting it into the keyhole of the gate, which was always locked on this side of the house, whereas the Silbergasse entrance had remained unfastened at night for generations, he asked: "What do you think? Shall we still be here at Christmas?"

"Certainly," promised the grandson, surprised by the question and the tone in which it was asked.

"Good," said his grandfather. "You go ahead."

Motioning Andreas into the old house, he locked up and followed. It was as if, after a long reign, he were abdicating to the strength and confidence of youth, which alone might still save them.

Chapter 4

By direction of the committee Andreas went to Meran the following morning. Each of the three members had received his assignment: the priest was to mobilize papal Rome through the archbishop at Brixen; the taciturn Konrad Paechl was to raise the money needed for propaganda; and Andreas, who was organizing this propaganda, would secure the necessary world-wide echo for it by approaching the democratic press, some of whose Swiss and English representatives he had become acquainted with in Berlin.

The fact that a man like Mr. Joseph P. Hoffman happened just then to be staying within reach, namely at the health resort of Meran, was a particularly fortunate accident. For Hoffman, whom several members of the council had described to him as a man particularly influential in his native America, was connected with machine factories in Detroit, and, according to Andreas' informants, with an American newspaper organization as well. In addition he loathed the Nazis. He was, therefore, the very man to approach at the moment, and if Andreas proceeded with even a fair amount of address, this happy accident would bring great results.

He told himself this as he rode toward the meeting that he had arranged by telegram, and during the short train trip he considered all the arguments he would use to awaken the American's interest. He was feeling rather surprised, but in a way also really excited, that his fellow citizens had put such trust in him, who was by far their junior, and that he, who had never mixed in with politics before, was now discovering in himself qualities which suddenly pushed him that way. At the same time it fitted in admirably with the plans of the young mechanical engineer that Mr. Hoffman was a machine builder.

Once arrived in Meran, Andreas had not long to wait before seeing him face to face. They met at the Hotel Meranerhof on the Kurpromenade, where Mr. Hoffman was staying, and the first impression Andreas had of the American was that he looked typically American. The pink, smooth-shaven face, the thin hair turning white, the eyes looking through rimless spectacles, the broad shoulders, further emphasized by a loose-fitting suit, and the package of American cigarettes that he took from his pocket to offer to his visitor, all contributed to this impression.

Andreas was the more taken aback when Mr. Hoffman welcomed him in German with an inimitable Viennese accent in which only close attention could detect a foreign tinge and laughingly checked the English conversation that the Tirolean was prepared for: "Didn't you know I came from Vienna, or, to be exact, from Salzburg? Yes, I'm a native Salzburger, but I lived in Vienna till I was seventeen."

No, Andreas had not known this; none of his informants had told him. And it so reduced his expectations that he presented, with his protruding lower lip, a picture of complete disappointment. He did not even take the trouble to hide it.

This was a source of equally frank amusement to his host. "You came to see an American, then, not an Austrian?" he asked with a laugh, and insisted that his guest, disappointed or not, should sit down and have a cigarette. "Scotch?" he offered.

"Straight," replied Andreas in English, and neither of them could help laughing, because he had come so well prepared for this question.

"The purpose of my visit actually does have to do with the fact that I supposed you were American," he admitted formally. And, thinking he must offer some excuse, he added: "Judging by what I was told, and also by the spelling of your name, which I believe you write with one *n,* I was really justified in thinking so."

"If you've got to have an American according to his papers, I'm sorry," said Hoffman. "But if you can do with an American who has only kept his Austrian—beg pardon, German—citizenship because he stupidly kept forgetting to be naturalized, or, as we say over there, to take out his papers, then I'm completely at your disposal."

"Do you live in America, Mr. Hoffman?" asked Andreas with the woodenness that so often descended upon him when he was confronted with a new face.

"Yes, young man. For the last thirty years and more. You see, over there things are this way: when you immigrate you get your first papers, five years later your second papers, and then you're naturalized. But when I went over in 1909 because I couldn't stand this country of yours any more, I didn't like it so terribly over there either. So I didn't take out any papers. I thought to myself, once you've made a little money, you can go back. I was so busy with this idea of making money on the other side (which, by the way, isn't half so easy as you people think) that I forgot about everything else. Then the war broke out, and our Austrian consul sent for me and said, 'Why, a strong young fellow like you! Isn't it disgraceful for you to be here, running away from your military duty!' You don't know me, Herr Mumelter, so naturally you don't know that nobody can talk to me like that. 'Running away?' I said. 'When does the next boat sail?' To cut it short, I enjoyed four whole years of your filthy war, and then two years or so of your equally filthy inflation. With that I had more than a bellyful, and I did what I'd dreamed of when I was facing the Yankees in the trenches on the Somme—back again, boys! Well, and so I did, and when I got across for the second time I immigrated in proper form, with regular first papers. I can tell you, I thought I was practically in heaven when I saw the old Statue of Liberty (which, just between ourselves, is rather ugly).

Well, and then five years after that I should have got my second papers, but at that time I was in South America for the firm, and as bad luck would have it they sent me to China in 1933, and there was my naturalization gone to hell again. But if it will cheer you up any, my wife is an American, and so is my daughter, and when I get back this time I'll be only two months losing the dubious privilege of being a subject of Schicklgruber, the Braunau house painter. Why, you aren't drinking a thing!"

But Andreas took a good gulp of the excellent whisky before replying. "I'm glad to hear it." He meant both Mr. Hoffman's approaching naturalization and the remark about Hitler, which made his own task considerably easier.

"You see, Mr. Hoffman," he picked up this observation, "we don't want to be either. And that's what I'm here for." It was barely ten in the morning when Hoffman received him; it was after twelve when they left Hoffman's room together, both with shining eyes, Hoffman even pinker-faced than before, and Andreas with an entirely new look of hope.

It was out of the question for the young man from Bozen to go back by the one-o'clock train! Hoffman would introduce him to his ladies, then they would all take lunch together at leisure, and he, Hoffman, or his daughter Gwen, or both, would take Andreas over in the car. No arguments, please, this was definite.

This American who was none, and who, Andreas felt, was one every inch nevertheless, took his guest across the Passer Bridge, and then along the Gisela-, Stefanie- and Marie Valerie promenade (named after Austrian archduchesses) to the rendezvous with his ladies that he had every morning on the Tappeinerweg. As they went along the promenade, coolly shaded even against the noonday sun by the vivid green laurel trees and silvery poplars, Hoffman explained that they were here because of his daughter. The family had taken a boat from New York just nine weeks before in order to see Mr. Hoffman's mother in Salzburg. "Yes sir," he said, shaking his head, "that's how people are! I knew perfectly well how old my mother was, and that I should have hurried up my visit. But no, something always interfered. And anyway her letters and her handwriting were absolutely clear and amazing, let me tell you, in spite of her eighty-three years. And do you suppose I ever stopped to think how old she was, and that I had no time to lose if I wanted to see her again?"

He had not expected an answer; he was really talking to himself. Nevertheless, Andreas replied: "Yes indeed, I can well understand. I'm in that position myself, or rather I was." As he spoke he had the same uneasy feeling about his grandfather, for the second time in a very few days.

"Then you can sympathize with me all the more and imagine how I kicked myself when I got a cablegram from Salzburg that my mother was sick and wanted to see me," said Hoffman. "All right, I packed up and took my ladies, who hadn't ever been across—I mean here; I wanted to show them my Austria. I don't care what you say, it's a marvelous country. And there's a funny thing about it. If you haven't seen it for a long time, you forget everything that used to make you mad, and just remember how beautiful it is. Besides, I had no idea what the house painter had done to it, because of course I hadn't been back in such a long time. When we got here—— Well, I don't have to tell you about that, you know anyway. But I had to keep telling myself and my wife and daughter—I'd always raved to them about Vienna and Salzburg—but you simply couldn't recognize it under the Nazis. My God, what those thugs have made out of our lovely country! And of course I was doubly disappointed because of my mother's hopeless condition. I found her quite conscious, and in fact her mind was still so active that only a few hours before she died she made me promise her what I have just promised you so casually and, I repeat, so gladly—that I would do anything I could to make this gang of criminals harmless. 'Pepi,' she said to me—she always used to call me that—'be glad you don't have to live here. I'm so glad I shan't have to very long either. You know, they've made us strangers in our own country, and they don't know and don't care what we are or what we're like. And do you know why? They have no religion, and they've brought us to the point where we don't trust in the Lord ourselves any more, may He forgive me for saying so!'"

"Yes," agreed Andreas, who could understand this also only too well, and regarded it as providential that he had found this talkative man who thought as he did just at the moment of direst need. "Yes, that's just how it is!"

"Yes," repeated the other, whose volubility was almost that of a man trying to get rid of a burden that had weighed him down too long. "And that's how she died. In terror. She was afraid the Lord would hold her responsible—her, one of the most pious women I ever knew. She was afraid of God at her last moment!" Then, feeling that he had carried his confidences a little too far, he took out the paper package and said, "Cigarette?"

By now they had reached the beginning of the walk named after Dr. Tappeiner, the physician whose work established the fame of Meran as a place for the cure of tuberculosis. The promenade curved upward between espaliers of the celebrated Meran Calville apples, just beginning to ripen on their low, horizontal poles, on slopes rising one above another like terraces. The apples were large, oval, bright yellow, notched at the ends; as soon as they grew soft, with a sweet-scented flavor unequaled by any other apple in the world, you could break them into quarters by hand without a knife. Now in the sun they gave a hint of the magic perfume that was at once like wine and like flowers, incomparably fresh and sweet. As you climbed, the vineyards of the Kuechlberg spread luxuriantly before your eyes; here, too, the fruit was beginning to ripen, and the great, heavy green grapes were turning red. The walk went on among apples and vines until you were high enough up to see the southern part of the town with the shining statue of the Virgin and the Sandplatz, a square named after Andreas Hofer, whose inn had been at Sand in the Passeier valley, an hour from here. And you saw the so-called "Castle," where the Counts of Tirol had resided and ruled over the "Burggrafenamt" since the fifteenth century. As the walk curved, the hereditary castle of Tirol came in sight on the north slope of the Kuechlberg—a tremendous ruin that had been the cradle of these first Tirolean counts in the twelfth century, and that was nevertheless now called Castle Dante! The ancient castles of Schenna and Lebenberg, too, showed black walls that had defied a millennium. The vista, cradled in vineyards, overgrown with apple orchards, deeply shaded and green with mighty trees, opened step by step into a great past. There was no escaping the spell—neither the spell of the heroic testimony borne with such proud simplicity by these weather-beaten stones, monuments, and ruins, nor the blessed loveliness of this spot of ground, which was filled with glad harmony like music; it moved you deeply whether you would or not.

And indeed the American of Austrian birth cried out in delight,

"Isn't this one of the loveliest walks in the world?" Then, as they approached the round terrace next to the Powder Tower where his ladies awaited him, he hastened to end his story with the rather precipitate remark that his daughter Gwen's lungs, which had been ailing even on the other side, had grown worse during their stay in Salzburg, making necessary a cure for which a certain Dr. Paumgartner (a physician who had cared for his mother to her dying day) had recommended Meran. "So we've been here for five weeks now, and unless they're serious about expelling foreigners, we'll probably be here a while longer. Gwen feels much better here, and I'm firmly convinced that this'll completely cure her. You can't help being healthy in country like this!" Every time he mentioned his daughter's name an expression of infinite tenderness crossed his face.

He's a likable fellow, Andreas could not help thinking, and his mistrust of strangers faded away. It was all the more unwillingly that he found himself obliged to moderate his companion's optimism; he could not but point out how seriously the expulsion was meant. He told of learning in Bozen that very morning that a number of Englishmen, Frenchmen, Dutchmen, and numerous Swiss were having to leave the Province of Bozen by that evening. He even had a tale to tell of a Mrs. Dorothea Watts, an American, who, with her mother, had been routed out at six in the morning from a villa she had rented in Santa Cristina Gardena near Bozen, and forced by carabinièri to leave immediately.

"But why, for goodness' sake?" asked Mr. Hoffman, his confident optimism not in the least disturbed. "There must be some sense to it somewhere, surely, for instance these macaronis can't possibly know that Mr. Hoffman, of Boston and Detroit, promised Herr Mumelter of Bozen this morning to give the Fascisti and Nazis hell. To them all foreigners are simply tourists, and they want them badly because they pay in good money. Well, then, what does this mean?"

Andreas could only repeat what he had heard from the prefect, to whom he had spoken briefly before he left. The order of expulsion was issued by the Ovra, the Italian secret police; they thought it necessary to remove the foreigners—he quoted the prefect—"for reasons of a political and military nature."

"There you see the advantages of my not being officially a foreigner," Hoffman persisted unshakably. "If they bother me, I'll show them my German passport, which I'm sorry to say I've had since the Anschluss instead of my Austrian one. But it's good enough for things like that." Pointing to a bench in the rondeau near which they were, he said, "There they are!"

"Didn't you mention that the ladies were American?" the careful and unemotional Andreas felt obliged to warn him.

"Oh, the macaronis don't have to know that," Hoffman said scornfully. "I'll show 'em my passport, and that's that! To them women and children have the same nationality as the husband and father. Come on—let me introduce you."

Presentations were made. If Andreas had taken Mr. Hoffman for an absolutely typical American, the very opposite was true when he met the ladies. Mrs. Hoffman looked younger than she probably was—a slim, dainty little woman under a green parasol, which she waved eagerly at the newcomers. She was, if possible, in even higher good humor than her husband; her very first words expressed her delight in this heavenly day, and when Mr. Hoffman started to make excuses for being late she said, Oh, that was all right, she and Gwen had enjoyed sitting here more than they could say. Wouldn't the gentlemen sit down for a moment before they went to lunch? At least they ought to rest a little after the walk up. Besides, you grudged every moment you couldn't spend up here, she said, offering the guest a seat beside her. She spoke English, and ended almost every sentence with a question mark. The former was true also of her daughter Gwen when she was first introduced to the visitor.

Gwen spoke in a low voice, which Andreas laid to her weak lungs. But, as he soon discovered, it was actually due to her shyness. In any case, she differed almost completely from the type of traveling American girl whom he was used to seeing. She was rather taller than her mother and looked like her on careful comparison—the same questioning look; the same high forehead; the same line of dark brown, almost black, hair falling down her cheeks to the nape of her neck. Her eyes, under long lashes, were astonishingly beautiful, large, dark, deeply clear, and luminous. And her mouth was small, so that the eyes absolutely dominated the face. They were what you saw first when you saw Gwen, and it was not until afterward that you noticed there was a slim face below those magnificent eyes, rendered yet slimmer by the sweeping dark hair and the pallor. Until then Andreas had always thought his sister Riccarda had the most beautiful eyes he had ever seen.

"This is Gwen," said Papa Hoffman. "How do you like her?"

Goodness, thought the young man, *I suppose this is the moment for something flattering. I do like her, though; she's quite different from what I expected.* He was still frantically searching for an answer when Gwen said with a smile: "Don't listen to Daddy. You mustn't take him seriously."

That sounded more like an American girl, Andreas thought, and again he was struck by the beauty of her eyes. And of her hands, in which she held the kind of tiny green parasol that her mother used; but she scorned to put hers up.

Very soon—if he had looked at his watch he would have found it was hardly ten minutes—he felt as if he had known Gwen for a long time. She was perfectly natural, which prejudiced him at once in her favor. She had none, not a hint, of the forwardness that ordinarily made him so uncertain, impatient, and short-tempered in talking to girls from so-called rich families. Instead, oddly enough, she seemed to be the uncertain one. Yet at every word she said or that you said to her she looked you full in the face, although she obviously found it hard. Was she very young? Sometimes there was something positively childish about her, even in her tone of voice. Then, again, there would be something unexpectedly assured, as for instance when she said: "I hear from Daddy that you're an Austrian too? Or were?"

She tried to say this in German, which she managed without a mistake, but with an accent that was the first really American thing about her, the Tirolean thought.

"Yes," he said, and added in his usual matter-of-fact way, "that's why I took the liberty of calling on your father."

Her father, who seemed to have no secrets from anybody, took this as a signal to tell the ladies about his and Andreas' confidential conversation, and enjoyed himself royally in the process. He even got up and imitated, with gestures, the dismayed look of the young man upon learning that Hoffman was not a genuine Yankee. "I tell you, his mouth was like this!" he said, and Andreas was grateful to Gwen for glancing around at two men sitting on another bench, the only guests anywhere about.

"Never mind," Hoffman went on, with his back to the view, "Herr Mumelter is a nice young man anyhow, and we agree on a lot of points. Am I right, Herr Mumelter?"

"Certainly," agreed Andreas in embarrassment, and he was thankful to Gwen once more when she interrupted her father with a question intended simply to protect the visitor from the unpredictable effects of his loquacity.

"Is Mr.——," she stumbled over the name, which she could not pronounce, begged Andreas' pardon with an apologetic gesture, and went on without mentioning the name, "from Bozen?"

But Hoffman was not easily put off his stride, and he asked again: "Well, what do you think of our Gwen? Did you know that she types all my letters and handles all my correspondence? You'll have to make up to her if you want anything to come of our discussion!"

"Sorry to put her to any trouble," said Andreas stiffly.

"Oh, but you don't know what she's like," Hoffman declared. "She loves it. Am I right, Gwen? You see Herr Mumelter is one of the people that are supposed to be expelled by these macaronis here."

The two men, two elderly gentlemen who were highly amused and laughed continually without visible cause, got up and went down the steps toward Meran, leaving the little party alone.

"How do you mean expelled?" asked Mrs. Hoffman, all unsuspecting.

Andreas replied, uncomfortably but factually: "From Bozen. That is, from anywhere in South Tirol, wherever we happen to live."

Still she did not quite understand. "How so? Who's putting you out?"

"You know it's that decree against former Austrians, isn't it? They have to leave here," said Gwen, this time without looking at Andreas, and he was grateful to her again, for he could not possibly have discussed such things in ordinary conversation, giving an open-air performance, as it were.

"Good heavens," said the lady, "but that's awful?"

"Mhm," Andreas agreed flatly. And in order to avoid betraying too much emotion, which he despised, he asked in his turn: "I suppose you ladies know the region pretty well by this time?"

But Mrs. Hoffman persisted: "Away from here? And how long have you lived here, Mr. Mumelter?"

"Roughly thirteen hundred years," said that gentleman. To make up for his rudeness he laughed with an effort and changed the subject; he pointed down toward Meran: "Do you see the Rennweg down there, Miss Hoffman?"

Gwen nodded. This was the first time he had addressed her directly.

"And that gray house on the Rennweg?" he asked. She looked where he was pointing. "No. There, next to it. Look," he insisted. "First comes one with a wooden veranda—see? Then a white one. Then a big gray one. See it?"

"Yes," said Gwen in her soft voice, "now I do."

"That's number 28," he told her. "The house is called the Count of Meran. Take a look at it sometime if you feel like it. Andreas Hofer was locked up there overnight; that's where they tried him. And the next day they took him from here to Mantua—you know who Andreas Hofer was?"

"I think so," murmured Gwen.

But Papa Hoffman said indignantly: "What do you take us for? Why, even Mrs. Hoffman knows who Andreas Hofer was. Don't you, Evelyn—remember my telling you about it?"

Mrs. Hoffman, however, did not seem quite so sure, and was apparently rather prone to absent-mindedness in general. She said: "Why . . . of course. Isn't he the man who defied Hitler?"

Whereupon Gwen retorted with her unexpectedly assured tone: "In his way, Mother. But it was Napoleon he defied."

"Is that so?" her mother smiled. And said: "Well, quite a few years have passed since then, haven't there? But shan't we go and have lunch now?"

Gwen's face was red, which might perfectly well have been due to the sun and the fact that she obstinately spurned her parasol. But Andreas, whose head, goodness knows, was full enough of other things, took it for a blush, and told himself in his matter-of-fact way, *She has a tremendous amount of tact.*

This was the last observation of the sort that he made, and an hour later he had forgotten both of the ladies. He was sitting in the car with Mr. Hoffman, driving to Bozen, and they discussed point by point what was to be done. The moment facts were being discussed, the man at the wheel was like one transformed. His garrulity yielded to a definiteness that delighted Andreas because he, too, had this quality, and because it quieted the fears that had assailed him at lunch concerning Hoffman's dependability. The American, smoking an imported cigar, explained what he intended to do. Point one: a meeting with the American Consul General at Rome, who was fortunately staying with his family only three hours away, at Cortina d'Ampezzo; and, incidentally, another member of the American Embassy was also around the corner. Point two: that very evening he would put through a long-distance phone call to the Rome correspondent of the New York *Times,* whom he knew. Point three: here in Bozen, under the pretext of inquiring whether the expulsion of foreigners applied to him, he would have a talk with Mastromattei, the prefect of Bozen. Lastly: a night letter to a friend, a journalist, in Paris. After all that it would go hard if the neutral public were not up in arms by tomorrow night, or the day after at the latest. And certainly the macaronis—as he insisted on calling the Italian Fascists—would think twice before offending the democracies abroad, or, in other words, their best tourist customers.

He could not finish the sentence, for it did go hard, and when they had the chapel of St. Hippolyt behind them and the ruin of Mayenburg on their right, two carabinièri barred the road. They had signaled to the car from a distance; when Hoffman pulled up beside them, they asked to see the travelers' identification.

"Americani," observed the taller of them with satisfaction, noticing the foreign number plate of the Buick, while the other asked to see the passports.

Hoffman had his with him, Andreas had not.

With a look of sly satisfaction the American handed the gendarme the olive-green booklet whose cover bore the arms of the German Reich.

"No Americano? Tedesco?" asked the armed policeman suspiciously.

"See for yourself, signore," said Hoffman generously.

The carabinière began to leaf through the booklet, comparing the photographs with the image of good humor presented at the moment by the man he was examining.

There was nothing for the officer to do but to inquire: "But the car is American?"

"Si!" agreed Hoffman, using one of the few Italian words he knew, except for macaroni and spaghetti.

"And there's a foreign number plate on the car," the shorter gendarme prompted the embarrassed taller one. The latter brightened. "Yes! How do you explain that?"

The interrogation took place partly in Italian, partly in broken German when Hoffman refused to understand.

"How do I explain it?" he repeated in German. "By the fact that I came over with this car for a summer holiday. On the supposition, of course, that tourists would be made as comfortable as possible."

There was no objection to be made to this answer, either, particularly since the passport, recently issued, was in perfect order.

"Where do you live?" was the next question.

"Here or on the other side?"

"Here, of course!" said the inquirer impatiently.

"Here I live in Meran. Hotel Meranerhof. Quite a good hotel. A little old-fashioned, but good. Merano. Albergo Grande," said Father Hoffman, translating, to be particularly obliging.

"Where are you going now?" the gendarme asked.

"To Bozen, Bolzano, and right back to Meran. Merano. *Andare ritorno,"* said Hoffman, delighted with his linguistic prowess.

"You knew that you have to leave the province of Bozen not later than tomorrow evening?" inquired the shorter gendarme, who so far had scarcely taken part in the inquiry.

This question astonished even his armed colleague.

"No. I didn't know anything about that," Hoffman declared. *"Niente."*

Thereupon the gendarme took out of his pocket the proclamation of the Royal Prefect, dated yesterday, according to which all aliens in the Italian Tirol had to leave the country within forty-eight hours.

"It's nothing to do with me. That means *Inglese, Francese. No Tedeschi!"* said the American.

At this the gendarme inquired, quite logically: "Does it say so here? Read it."

As a matter of fact it did not say so.

"But that can't possibly mean German citizens!" objected Hoffman, a trifle less confidently.

"How do you know that?" asked the gendarme. "Hadn't you heard that the Italian and German governments had made an agreement by which all Germans from the Reich must leave the country?"

"But not in forty-eight hours!" put in Andreas, who had conducted the same unedifying argument only yesterday.

"Ecco! Vide!" Hoffman triumphantly drew upon his vocabulary.

To this the answer of the carabinière was: "Who are you?"

This was meant for Andreas. He answered in Italian: "My name is Andreas Mumelter. I live in Bolzano, Silbergasse *numero sette."* And he added, with a hint of the menace that he could sometimes give to his words: "That's our house. Has been for three hundred and thirty-six years."

Hoffman liked him better and better.

Although the opposite was true of the two gendarmes, the not-unfamiliar name seemed to carry enough weight with them so that they were cautious. A member of the Third Reich, and an old inhabitant, presumably an Irredentist—easy does it! So they contented themselves with taking down Andreas' name and address, and proclaiming oracularly that further developments would take place in due course.

They drove on, but the confident mood in which they had started was gone.

"You have to be prepared for anything," said Andreas. "My grandfather's right. They want to get all neutral witnesses out of the way as soon as possible."

"You actually think I'll have to leave?" asked the American.

"I'm afraid so, if you want to avoid unpleasantness," Andreas warned him. "Of course the decree doesn't include Germans, but like all Italian decrees it leaves room for chicanery and arbitrary interpretations."

"Out of the question! Gwen can't possibly leave! It's not to be thought of as long as she keeps on running a temperature!" said her father indignantly.

The two men were silent for the rest of the short drive. Hoffman stopped in front of the prefecture, and Andreas promised to wait for him in the car.

It was not long before he came back wearing his most beaming smile. The prefect himself, he reported, was not there, but in his place was an obliging gentleman, whose name he had taken down —Poschacher, it was. Poschacher had reassured him entirely. The decree about foreigners did not apply to Germans so long as they did not stay for more than three months. "And long before three months are up," he said happily, "we'll be back on the other side in our own better world, and Gwen will be better, and we shan't have to give a damn for the Prefect of Bozen!" He had hardly spoken before he realized he had been inconsiderate. "By that time," he declared, "your business will long since have been settled too. That's what I keep telling you—you mustn't take these macaronis seriously!"

Andreas said nothing but: "Poschacher?" And he remembered the baldhead whom his grandfather had treated so cavalierly in the garden of the Hotel Greif.

Hoffman's optimism was paramount, however. The statements of Mr. Poschacher and another gentleman who also spoke German, whose name he did not remember, showed that their bark was worse than their bite. What did Andreas want to bet that in a few days, possibly by Saturday, but in any case over the week end, he would be able to give Andreas encouraging news?

He declined the invitation to come in, saying meaningly that he must hurry back and look after his correspondence and his long-distance telephone calls. Andreas got the impression, however, that he was in much more of a hurry because of his daughter. She had to take her temperature three times daily, and in half an hour, about four, was the crucial time of day. For more than a week now she had had no fever at four in the afternoon. Another three weeks of lower temperatures—the anxious father had recorded them on a chart that he showed Andreas during the drive—and she could be considered cured.

It must be wonderful to have someone to care for you like that, thought Andreas, who had grown up an orphan. For a second or two the image of the pale, silent girl floated before him again. Then he thanked Mr. Hoffman and said good-by.

Three hours later, after supper, having reported to the members of the committee, he was sitting with the old man and Riccarda among the apple trees in the little garden, when Herr Antonio Udacher made his appearance. The conversation they now had would decide their fate.

Perhaps the old man was to be right when he said, months later, "We should have been wiser that evening in the garden!" For he was unshakably convinced that everything always depends on one's own efforts. Even at ninety-one it was possible to keep death at a respectful distance, and to teach a Herr Udacher or even a Herr Hitler to mind his manners, if only you wouldn't be fooled and wouldn't be bullied; of this he was absolutely certain.

Undeniably the second of these two was just what the Gauleiter of Bozen now attempted. Leading up to things was not his strong point, and he opened up directly with the question: "Back from your diplomatic expedition, Herr Mumelter junior?"

To do him justice, Herr Udacher was not in a very enviable position. Under orders from Berlin he had for years overtly and covertly resisted the Italianization of the province of Bozen, and impressed on anyone who would listen that "unless a Bozner is on the Fascists' black list, he's not a proper Tirolean." That Hitler would "deliver" South Tirol—that is, reunite it with North Tirol and make it into an independent German-speaking country—had been the whole substance of his publicity arsenal. And now, overnight, his Führer and master not only had carried out none of these high-flown plans, but had buried them forever and made common cause with the Italians against the South Tiroleans. It was not easy even for so adroit a propagandist as Herr Udacher, who had earned the praise of the Goebbels press, to turn the hawk into a handsaw, the glaring betrayal into German steadfastness. But here, too, he showed, as he had before the council of twenty-four on the previous day, that Berlin could depend on him. Furthermore, his position as against the twenty-four had improved since yesterday, because he had found out about Andreas' Meran expedition and certain other things that the three Mumelters did not dream of. The fourth, Sepp, was seeing Gigli's new picture, *L'Amore e morte,* at the Teatro Garibaldi.

Andreas said: "I've been to Meran. Yes. What business is it of yours?"

As none was offered, the visitor helped himself to one of his own cigarettes and said, this time quite frankly: "It's not for me to give you good advice. But I'm afraid the time will come when you'll regret having made an enemy of our Party. You're doing all you can to assure that, Herr Mumelter junior." He stressed the "junior," although he could scarcely have been much older than Andreas. He surveyed Riccarda with an enterprising look on his dashing, sophisticated, college-boy face. "Do try to reason with your brother, Fräulein," he said to her. "You've given so many proofs of your common sense in his absence that you ought to explain to him now what a big mistake he's making." And, being an apt pupil of his master, he followed up this flattery by showing his claws: "Quite aside from the fact that he's hurting himself tremendously, he's endangering all of you in the extreme."

"Not me," contradicted the old man. And, looking at his granddaughter: "Tell this gentleman that Andre isn't putting you in danger. Nor Sepp either, the donkey."

No one could have expected the girl to reply with such violence, such flashing of those eyes that her brother had considered, until today, the loveliest he had ever seen. "Yes! Whatever Andreas is doing must be right. We wouldn't think of interfering. And no matter what he does, I know one thing: There's no falsehood about it!"

Even the old man was struck by the passion of her answer. He kept a wary eye on his granddaughter.

The object of this reprimand shrugged his shoulders deprecatingly. "Too bad. Well, then, I'll just have to storm the fortress without an ally. What did the American promise you?" He made his thrust without further preliminary.

Andreas weighed every word he spoke. His mistrust was unbounded, and no one could have accused him of underestimating the danger. He replied slowly and with emphasis: "Gauleiter Udacher, I believe I have already made it plain to you that I shall give you no account of myself, because I owe you none."

"Whether you respect me or not——" the other started to reply, but Andreas was devilishly on his guard.

"Wait!" he interrupted. "I was talking not about respect, but about accountability. You heard me, Grandfather? And you, Riccarda?"

Riccarda was the first to say yes. The old man also agreed: "Yes."

"Good," Andreas went on. "Let's get our standpoints clear. We, my family and I, are going to stay here. Here in Bozen. And you, Gauleiter, with your Party comrades, are not going to stay here. It's quite simple, and everything else follows from that."

"Yes!" said Riccarda, again with a wild gleam of her dark eyes.

This led Udacher to renew his onslaught more fiercely. "And how, Herr Mumelter junior, do you know you are going to stay here?"

"I know I am," Andreas insisted.

"On the basis of your amateur diplomacy?" was the rejoinder.

"Never mind. We're staying here," he retorted.

"Very well, Herr Mumelter junior, that's what you think or hope, or whatever it may be," the other conceded. "But, nevertheless, suppose you can't stay here?"

"You mean in Bozen?" Andreas asked doubtfully.

"I mean in Italy," said Udacher, and Riccarda turned ghastly pale.

"What's the matter, lass?" interrupted the old man, who thought it improper to let oneself go in this fashion.

"Nothing, Grandfather," said his granddaughter, struggling for breath.

But Andreas seemed to take Udacher's words for a mere attempt at intimidation; he said curtly: "I shan't discuss that with you, because it is out of the question."

"It's too bad," the Gauleiter said to the girl, just as the crescent moon rose above the little garden, pouring its light over the old trees, "that a person can't talk sensibly to your brother. All I want is for him to see the facts. And the facts speak against your staying here. I mean all of you, Fräulein Mumelter. I believe there are four of you?"

What ails Riccarda? Andreas, too, could not help thinking, for his sister got up abruptly, took one wavering step, drew a deep breath, sat down again, and then replied in a voice as toneless as it was hostile: "Thank heavens it doesn't depend on you! Nor anyone of your sort! I'd like to see the man who could keep us from staying here if we vote for Italy. Will you stop me? Will you come and take me away? Will you pull my hands loose? I'll do like this—so—just try and see if you can get me away!"

With both hands she clutched the bench she was sitting on. Whether it was the moonlight or the agitation, her face turned chalk-white.

"Riccarda! What kind of a performance is this?" Her brother reproved this outburst of emotion, which he thought exaggerated, unnecessary, and quite unlike his reflective sister.

She nodded. With a vacant, shamefaced smile she released her grip, and took no further part in the conversation.

"Well, you know, in a way it's quite natural," said the Gauleiter, bridging the way to his next attack. "The Fräulein is simply one-sided in her partisanship, just as you all are."

"And you, sir?" asked the old man. "So you're two- or several-sided in your partisanship? I hadn't heard about that!"

But the nocturnal visitor now let fly at his target: "My time is limited. I'm not here to continue our absurd argument of yesterday, but to tell you two things, Herr Mumelter junior," he remarked cuttingly. "This very evening you will tell your American acquaintance —his number is Merano 212—to give up any attempt at sending news abroad. Second, you and the twenty-four or rather twenty-three other members of the so-called council will declare under oath to Prefect Mastromattei at nine o'clock tomorrow morning that none of you will take any step aimed against the Italian or"—he emphasized the *or*—"against the German government. In other words, you will swear neither to stir up nor to prejudice your fellow citizens against the Third Reich. From now on you will give up telling short stories about young Jewesses, for instance, who throw themselves out of windows. You understand me. You will now put in a long-distance call to Meran. Afterward you will make sure that the other twenty-three appear punctually at the prefect's."

All Andreas said was: "No."

"I should be very sorry for that," observed the Gauleiter, getting up. "Because there would be consequences." And he started for the garden gate.

Andreas did not move. Riccarda stared into space.

"What sort of consequences?" the old man asked.

Udacher turned. "You can answer that for yourself," he declared with cold venom. "By the way, Fräulein Mumelter, just to get that straight, too, it isn't I that will do the wrestling with you, but a couple of carabinièri. As you probably know, they're reasonable, useful lads to make less reasonable people see the light. Certainly they will be ready for use in cases where the Italian government has to expel South Tiroleans who issue lying reports to the foreign press through American accomplices. Good night!"

And the lover of theatrical effects marched out of the garden.

It was so still that for a time you could hear his steps dying away down the Laubengasse.

"Well," said the old man, getting up heavily, "come on to bed."

Andreas was about to follow him, but his sister said, "Stay a little while, will you, Andre? It's so hot inside. Don't you want to talk a little more, Grandfather?"

"There's been talk enough," said the old man, going toward the door. "It never comes to anything. Talking. And threatening. That's about the only thing they're good at." Then, putting his big key in the lock: "You lock up, Andre, when you go to bed. And put the bunch of keys outside my door. Isn't Sepp home yet? The young pup! Sleep well, lass. Sleep well, boy."

"Good night, Grandfather," the grandchildren replied.

And then his feet, too, were heard, step by step, mounting the stone stairs to the third floor.

The silence was unbroken again.

"What is it, Riccarda?" asked Andreas.

She shook her head. "Nothing."

They were silent; but their unspoken thoughts were loud.

"Riccarda?" said her brother again.

At this, her head drooping, she let both hands fall in a gesture of despair.

He sat down beside her and tried to lift her head, which she resisted. Her head rested stiffly on her chest like a piece of wood. She did not look up.

"As bad as that?" the eldest asked the younger, who had always gone her own way with such assurance.

She nodded.

"Going to tell me?" he asked softly.

"Yes," she replied as softly. "I'm going to have a child by Roberto. You know him. And his sister Elena."

Now she did look at him. Her waxen face was not ashamed; it was devastated.

The Mumelters had been brought up devout Catholics. The eldest son did not regard what his sister confided to him as a disgrace, but he did think it a sin. Her mentioning Elena confused him too.

"So that's it," he said, and took her hand. The hand was freezing cold. "Well," he said, as his grandfather had a moment before. "And when are you getting married?"

"When Roberto comes of age. His father is against the marriage." She forced out syllable by syllable.

"Why?" Andreas asked.

"He's supposed to marry an Italian," she told him.

The cold hand did not grow warmer in his; it lay like a piece of ice.

"And when does he come of age?" he pursued, asking what he needed to know.

"In October," she said woodenly.

"And," he asked, looking the other way, "what month will that be?"

"The fourth," she said in the same stricken tone.

"Is it as bad as all that?" He tried to console her; but he could hardly do it, because he knew what she was going to ask him next.

She withdrew her cold hand from his and asked it. "But suppose we aren't here by then, Andre? When Udacher was threatening us, I really got a clear idea of it for the first time."

The ripening apples were touched with silver in the moonlight as they had been not long before when Grandfather had asked whether they would still be here by Christmas. Christmas comes in December, and the wedding was to be in October.

Andreas had told Grandfather yes.

To his sister he said: "Oh, why not, Riccarda? Our sins aren't as great as all that!" He attempted a light tone, but it sounded as if he were in grim earnest. As if he were saying, "I don't believe we've committed any mortal sins, have we? And only mortal sins could be punished like this!"

"Are you giving it up for lost, Andre?" she asked hoarsely.

He grabbed her shoulder and shook her. "Don't talk nonsense, Riccarda!" By the time he let her go he had himself in hand again, and he promised her: "You'll have a pretty wedding. It's still lovely in October."

"It's still lovely in October . . ." she repeated.

"What's the matter, Riccarda? Surely you aren't going to go and lose your spunk, are you?" he asked.

She looked him in the eye. "No," she promised.

Whistling had been audible for some time. It was Sepp coming home from the movies, rendering the *canzone* from *L'Amore e morte*. Catching sight of his brother and sister in the garden across the low wall from the street, he called to them from outside: "You certainly were idiots not to have gone!" Coming in, he declared ecstatically: "It's the most marvelous thing you ever heard of! You simply must go see it! It's running until Friday." And, when there was still no answer: "Why, don't you believe me?"

"Of course," said his elders. "Come on to bed."

"You missed something!" persisted the youngest.

The day was over. The three young Mumelters would lie awake in the moonlit silence, thinking, dreaming, hoping, fearing, and forgetting.

Chapter 5

THE MOMENT Andreas heard Gwen's voice on the telephone saying in her painful, strongly accented, but correct German: "This is Gwen Hoffman, Mr. Mu-mel-ter. I was supposed to tell you that I'll be over in about two hours. You'll be expecting me, then?" he thought that the call had been a grave mistake. Nevertheless, he could not help feeling that the gentle voice was immensely charming. And although he had scarcely given her a moment's thought since their encounter of the day before, he looked forward eagerly to seeing her again. In talking to her over the phone, guarding vigilantly against saying or letting her say anything that any of the Herr Udachers could misinterpret, he almost forgot her face. He was dealing with nothing but a voice. And strangely enough this voice that spoke such disembodied words was the only thing he could imagine about Gwen. If you had asked him what she looked like, he would have said, "Very beautiful eyes." And still he would not have imagined her before him. But he could hear the voice even after she had hung up.

"It'll be nice to see you," he said. "I do hope the day won't be too hot. Please give them my regards at home."

"I will," she said. "Thank you. Well, I'll be leaving now."

Stupid of her father, he could not help thinking as he hung up after promising to meet her at the Talfer Bridge. He had been too long in the Third Reich to forget that wire tapping was among the methods now to be expected here as well.

Really, the stupidest thing a practical man like Hoffman could have done was to send the girl over here, he kept telling himself as he watched impatiently for the Buick that she would be driving. But this time his objectivity misled him. Mr. Hoffman's plan, far from being stupid, was very shrewdly thought out. He had concocted a scheme of his own, and Andreas' caution was not needed to keep Gwen from making unsuitable remarks over the telephone. Warned by her father, she would not have done so in any case.

"Listen to me, honey," he had said to her late the previous evening when they were talking it over. "As far as appearances are concerned, I'm going to drop out of the thing entirely. I'm not a big enough fool to stick my neck out, and yours along with it. We're here for you to get well, not so the macaronis or the Nazis can keep pestering us. That's that. On the other hand, we're here because I wanted to see your grandmother, and I made your grandmother a promise. I'm going to keep it. And so I've sent word of what I'm going to tell you now (being a bright girl, you're going to remember it instead of writing it down) by the diplomatic courier to our embassy at Rome, which will get in touch with the right man." He told her, and continued: "After that our consul general will look me up here, probably tomorrow or the day after, or else I'll see him; he's in Cortina. I've given up the idea of getting in touch with any other correspondent. These boys are a wily set of scoundrels, and they could pull a fast one on me easier than I could on them. And something else: after I talk to the consul I'll send a picture post card to young Mumelter (who seems to be a nice fellow, by the way). Or you can. Then he'll know he's supposed to meet you again, and where. You can fix up where. As I say, I'll fade out, and you'll take my place. Two young people—a little flirtation—who's going to see anything wrong in that?"

Mr. Hoffman could see well enough that he was not putting an unwelcome task upon Gwen, and this in itself was far from displeasing him. She had almost agreed with his remark that Andreas was a nice fellow, in so far as she was capable of agreeing with such a thing. And since he seldom did anything without considering the consequences, and always preferred to kill as many birds as possible with one stone, he was particularly pleased with the part he was assigning to Gwen. The thing that would do the girl the most good next to the cure at Meran, Dr. Paumgartner had recently written, was some psychological stimulus. In disorders of this kind, periods of depression—which he had been anxiously complaining of to the doctor—were an inevitable symptom. "Isn't there anything or anybody that she's interested in?" wrote the doctor who had cared for his mother in her last illness. Hoffman put down the letter with a sigh. Oh yes, the girl had plenty of interests, plenty and none at all. After graduating from Vassar she had started this and that, and never finished anything; he seemed to remember research for a study on John Stuart Mill, correspondence for a rescue committee, and even some kind of job in the election campaign. And what could be wrong with the child that she could be so preposterously shy of anything that even suggested flirtation? All right, the business with Bob O'Brien was a disappointment, and Bob hadn't behaved well, although Mr. Hoffman had to admit that Gwen's standards were much too strict. But even supposing he had behaved a lot more inexcusably than he had, that would still be no reason to draw any such conclusions from it. She had fallen ill just a month after that affair, and even though disappointment doesn't give you a lung condition, her father told himself, probably it slows up your recovery. The worst of it was that she took everything too seriously, and consequently was never satisfied with anything. Particularly not with herself. She expected too much of people; where had she got that from? Mr. Hoffman had reflected often enough that he was not of a demanding nature by any means, and anyone who was a decent fellow and not a chiseler trying to get away with something was O.K. with him. And what about her mother? No one, he thought, could accuse him of being unjust to Evelyn. She was the sweetest girl in the world, and the most absent-minded. But she didn't make things hard for herself or for others. Then where could it ever have come from? He racked his brain in vain.

He was the better pleased, then, in the rondeau on the Tappeinerweg and afterward at lunch, when Gwen had her first really interested conversation with a young man in a long time. His whole plan was built on this.

And so he sent Gwen to Bozen for a threefold reason. Primarily on her own account. Second, because he had promised his mother "to see to it"—and he had a great deal to reproach himself with on her account. Finally, because what the macaronis were doing to the former Austrians was really damned dirty. In a hidden corner of his heart Hoffman still cherished Austrian sentiments.

They met where the Talfer Bridge led into the Museumstrasse; for Andreas had happened to think meanwhile that it would be much more cautious of them to go inside the museum, where there would be scarcely anyone at that time of day, instead of out on the Talfermauerpromenade.

"Besides, it'll be cooler," he excused himself.

She was wearing a Lanz of Salzburg suit of unbleached hand-woven linen edged with red, with old silver buttons; although the Salzburg costume was quite different from the Tirolean, and no more natural to the place than the sign "Museo Municipale" on the "Städtisches Museum," Andreas felt more at home with the American girl than he had the day before, when she was dressed in city clothes, white or some light color—he couldn't remember. He was not apt to notice such things.

"Yes," she said, "let's go to the museum."

She did not offer her hand, which surprised and rather offended him. He did not know that the Americans do not shake hands on all occasions.

She left the car across the street, where parking was allowed, and the two of them went into the bare, sober stone building.

It was actually very much cooler the moment they went into the high entrance hall, and Gwen observed at once: "You're right, Mr. Mu-mel-ter. It's much pleasanter here." She spoke German.

Except for a sleepy attendant, who made sure that the gentleman had no cane and the lady no umbrella to check, nobody was around. It was quite a long time since Andreas had last been there, and a childhood memory of his first trip to see all the old things came back to him as they mounted the steps to the first floor. He could not remember whether it was the room with the national costumes or the one with the old furniture where he had slipped on the polished floor and fallen damnably hard on his bare knee. But he could still see as if it were today the smilingly severe look of his grandfather, as he told him: "Don't cry! When it really hurts a lot, that's just the time not to cry!" He had never forgotten that, nor ever cried since.

Neither of them spoke on the stairway; both were equally reserved, and he noticed Gwen looking around in every direction. So he postponed reproaching her for her lack of caution.

"Do you mind if I speak English?" she asked. "Don't you think people would find it a little harder to understand?"

"I am quite of that opinion," he answered, stiff and formal as ever. "I was of the opinion already," he added, and was about to continue, "that your telephone call was quite risky"; but, thinking better of it, he said instead: "We should have spoken English in Meran, too, don't you think?"

Yes, she agreed with him, and as they went into the room where national costumes were on display, and another sleepy attendant walked slowly and monotonously from end to end, she remarked: "I hope my news will be pleasant!"

"Have you good news?" he asked so quickly that a deaf person could have told how urgently he needed it.

And Gwen was keen of hearing.

She, too, had been thinking since her meeting with him yesterday. *What lies in store for this man,* she had thought, *is beyond imagining.* She had tried imagining someone's forbidding her to go back to Brookline, where she had lived since her childhood, when Daddy had moved away from Detroit. She had only started to imagine it, but had got no further than the thought that she would never see the white house under the locust trees again, never sit on the porch again with Pit and Pet, the poodles—*inconceivable,* she had felt. She had barely brushed the notion of someone's keeping her from seeing the States again, from ever hearing a Harvard accent for the rest of her life. *Impossible,* she had thought, and she had felt terribly sorry for the young man who had been talking to Daddy.

"I think I have good news," she answered him now, and as they stood before the faded wedding finery of a peasant woman from the Eisack valley, she repeated to him the message her father had charged her with. She forgot nothing.

She could see at once that he was disappointed. He tried to hide it with repeated "very good" and "that's fine," but she could see what he was thinking. "You don't think our consul general will succeed?" she asked.

He looked at her. She was wearing the childlike expression that made one so uncertain about her age; he decided to ask her later how old she was. "I don't know," he said. "Judging by what we heard over the radio this morning, your ambassador at Rome has already made representations at the Palazzo Chigi and been politely but firmly bowed out."

Gwen, who also knew this, tried to object: "But he wasn't making representations because of you!"

"No," said Andreas, laughing in spite of himself, "more because of you."

But Gwen did not care for his half-disappointed, half—she thought—disdainful laugh. She explained that she only meant to say that the ambassador had intervened not because of the South Tirolean question, but because of the Americans included in the expulsion of foreigners.

"Exactly," Andreas agreed, still laughing a little at Gwen's eagerness, which struck him as somehow funny; "that's just what I'm saying. He intervened less on our account than on yours."

At this she said, with the almost haughty superiority that upset all guesses at her age: "In other words, you're wrong, and I'm right. Representations haven't been made; they're only about to be made, as Daddy sent word to you."

He replied in his most careful English: "All right, Miss Hoffman. But from the fact that the American ambassador did not succeed even with his efforts on behalf of Americans it is easy to see what the answer will be if he makes representations on behalf of non-Americans."

"That's not quite logical," she declared, surprisingly, although he was convinced that nothing could be more logical. "It makes a difference whether you happen to be speaking for some tourists who might just as well spend their vacations somewhere else, or for hundreds of thousands who can't exist anywhere except where they are."

Again he looked at her. She sensed the amazement in his glance without replying to it; she went on to the next glass case, in which was another bridal costume, this time from the Passeier valley. Black satin bodice, black velvet skirt, gold-embroidered kerchief, shimmering, greenish silk apron with long ribbons, and a cap of gold lace.

"Well, I suppose that's true," he had to admit as he moved to her side before the glass case.

"Certainly," she said. "And there you were suspecting me."

"Of what?" he inquired.

"Being stupid," she replied with a candor that only surprised him the more.

"But, Miss Hoffman!" he protested in such confusion that her pale face brightened for the first time.

"Why?" she said, turning her great eyes upon him. "The Europeans do have a funny opinion of us!"

"But I haven't!" He unwarily admitted the accusation he was trying to deny. This amused her still more.

"Forgive me!" He collected himself at once.

"Mhm," she replied, not laughing now. She herself scarcely believed in the optimism she was trying to inculcate in him. Besides, she liked him. It was some time since she had taken a liking to a man. And she knew she would never let him know it—never. Every time she had grown fond of anyone, which had happened three times so far, she had never let the man know. That was her nature, and she couldn't help it. *It'll be that way this time, too,* she thought—no, she knew. *He'll never find out how much I like him.* But she forgot that her illness lay between the times she was thinking of and the present.

"Would it hurt you very terribly if you had to live anywhere else but here—I mean if things came to that point, which I don't believe they can?" The very next second she was upbraiding herself for the question, which she thought silly and unnecessary.

Andreas felt otherwise. No one had asked him this question since that Sunday broadcast on the Haselburg. And it was such an important question. *The* question. More than that, she had asked as though it meant something. *Flattery?* he wondered, and discarded the idea.

In the loveliest eyes he knew a book lay open to be read. Sympathy was plainly written there.

"Thank you," he said, which was quite wrong as an answer; but Gwen, whose hearing was as good as her eyesight, understood. She dug her nails into her palms as she fought back a sudden blushing and a rush of joy. His "thank you" was the finest, frankest, saddest, and most modest thing she had heard in a long time.

"I mean——" he tried to explain, but she interrupted.

"I know what you mean. And please do believe me when I say that I can imagine it, and perhaps even feel a little of it. But I'm quite sure everything will turn out all right."

He ran outspread fingers through his unruly hair—*like a small boy,* she could not help thinking, repressing an impulse to stroke it herself. She believed she knew more positively that this was and always would be out of the question, however, than that she was Gwen Hoffman, twenty-two years and four months old, once engaged to Bob O'Brien of Philadelphia and badly treated by him, in love with Jack Merton of Boston, who had never known it, and with Bill Armstrong of Boston, who had neither known nor wanted to know it, suffering from lung trouble in Meran during the past three months—not dangerously, but still enough to change her attitude toward people and things somewhat—slightly feverish at times, more often shivering with a chill.

"Well, you see," he said, scarcely realizing that he had led her into the second room, where besides the attendants there were a few people looking at the pictures, "last night I racked my brain wondering what to do. To be quite truthful, I wasn't counting on your father after our experience with the carabinièri yesterday—I don't know whether he told you about it. I said to myself, 'There are only two possibilities. Either we can make the same mistake that the Austrians and the Czechs made, by giving in and hoping for Hitler's generosity, or we can fight.' The first is out of the question. The second is possible. I want to tell you, Miss Hoffman, not only because you and your father are so kind to want to help us, but also because you have just asked about it so kindly—no one can take me away from here. My sister said the same—I hope you will meet her when you do us the honor to come to dinner; she's a fine girl—I mean—I was going to say, we'll fight. Even if we have nothing to expect from it, we'll still fight. I was quite downcast last night, I admit. Then I began to think it over. What do you mean? I thought. There are 220,000 of you here, of whom 150,000 at the least, at the very least, are able to bear arms, almost all of them with military training in the Italian army, a lot of them that were in the World War, and most of them owning their own weapons. You're an army, I thought, now you must march! Then I began to feel a little happier. I know eight people out of ten would say, 'This is nonsense, you can't hold out, and what are 150,000 against millions? Nothing! Besides, you can't mobilize and equip them all,' and so on and so forth. Granted. But if the Austrians had fired in March 1938 even a single shot, instead of yelling *Heil* Hitler! I guarantee you that the world would have pricked up its ears and stopped Hitler. And if the Czechs had fired in March of 1939, Hitler wouldn't have got to Prague, because France would have had to declare war. Do you know what? The things that have happened don't prove anything in favor of Hitler, but they prove everything against the people that are so terribly afraid of him. We won't make that mistake, you can be sure. So when your father talks to the consul general, please have him explain that quite clearly. Have him say we're going to shoot. We're going to fire so loud and so fiercely—we Tiroleans are wild devils, Miss Hoffman!—that the whole world shall hear us. Then maybe the world will think that this can't be allowed to go on. Because it can't go on. It simply cannot be that my grandfather—he's over ninety-one years old—will have to leave. It can't even be that I have to leave, or my sister, or my brother, or any of us who were born here and"—he was about to say "love the country so," but he thought this too emotional, and simply said—"and need the air here and the mountains here and in fact everything here in order to live."

Meanwhile, they had been pacing around the four walls, which were hung with landscapes, still lifes, and portraits. Neither Gwen nor he had given them a glance; they had not looked at the frighteningly realistic Astach Gorge with its wildly cleft and furrowed valleys, nor at the charming triptych of the first three German parishes, Vielgereut, Infraun, and Lusern; nor even at the portrait of Andreas Hofer by Altmutter, the only one painted from life, framed in gold and darkened with age, which was moving because of its simply speaking likeness. They had already walked past it twice, Andreas talking unseeingly, Gwen watching him, and so deeply stirred by his words that she scarcely felt the chill in the big, drafty gallery. The two of them, seeing none of the pictures and nothing but each other, or in Andreas' case not even that, attracted the notice of the few other visitors.

Gwen was the first to observe this, and she said: "Hadn't we better go down now? I've got to be back for lunch."

"Yes," he said, and once again, this time with anguish, she thought she heard disappointment in his tone.

"Then you don't give us the pleasure at lunch?" he observed stiffly.

She made her excuses, and mentioned what her father had said about the picture post card. His face brightened. He said: "Then I hope to see you again very soon. But only if it isn't too much for you to drive over in this heat."

"Oh, of course not," she said, suppressing the chills that her few tenths of a point of fever gave her punctually every noon. She felt like adding: "I'd love to come," but refrained. "Good luck," she said instead. "Next time I'm sure I will be bringing news that will satisfy you."

"Fine!" said Andreas.

Before she got into the car she held out her hand. She even waved for a second or two as she drove across the bridge and out along the Sigmundskroner Reichsstrasse.

Grand girl! he thought, somehow encouraged and comforted. On his way back he passed the building of the German newspaper, *Die Dolomiten,* and stopped to read the telegrams that covered the front window in three rows and were constantly supplemented by fresh ones.

"German Press reports today for the first time that an agreement has been reached between the German Reich and Italy for regulating the flow of migration back to Reich territory. Its terms have not yet been disclosed."

Next to this was pasted the following dispatch: "The first 200 persons covered by the German-Italian accord leave the Province of Bolzano tonight. Another 350 will go tomorrow, and 450 the following day. All of those being repatriated are German citizens who have been domiciled in the Province of Bolzano for less than four years. The destination of these groups is unknown."

Next came this: "According to Swiss advices Italy has leased the port of Trieste to Germany for a period of ten years."

Next: "Miss Barbara Rode of Chicago was affected today by the expulsion of foreigners from Bolzano province. She was touring in her car at San Vigilo di Marrede and was ordered by the police to leave."

In the second row: "Commenting on the Italian-German agreement today the *Giornale d'Italia* says editorially: It is a question of secondary importance, because it involves a ridiculously small number of German-speaking people compared with those Germans who were driven in a body from Alsace-Lorraine and Poland after the World War."

Next: "According to an unconfirmed report members of the Italian secret police, the Ovra, have searched a number of houses in Bolzano, Bressanone, Flers, and Aslago, and made a number of arrests. So far forty-five well-known inhabitants of the Alto Adige have been jailed."

Next: "According to a report in today's *Corriere della Sera* the Undersecretary for Domestic Affairs Buffarini stated to Giuseppe Stanza, deputy for Trento, that the inhabitants of Alto Adige who were subjects of the Austro-Hungarian monarchy before November 1918, and who have the right to cast their vote for Italy, are to be resettled in the provinces south of the Po."

Next: "The Duce as Minister of the Interior today presented to the Chamber of the Fascist Corporation a law ratifying the agreement between Italy and Germany in regard to the Alto Adige. Article 1 provides that persons affected must renounce their Italian citizenship before being transferred. Articles 2 and 3 provide that application must be made to the prefect, who will erase these persons' names from the register of Italian citizens. The fourth article states that citizenship may never be regained. Article 5 reads: The loss of citizenship extends to wives and children."

Below this, in the third row: "The magazine *Athesia Augusta* of Bozen declares in an article signed by the Prefect of Bozen himself: 'The South Tirolean agreement concluded at Berlin furnishes one more proof of the unanimity and effectiveness of the Axis. Contrary to certain malicious falsehoods that have been circulated, this is not an enforced evacuation, let alone a mass banishment of the entire population of the Ober Etsch (Alto Adige), but simply the return to the bosom of the Reich of the Germans and persons German in sentiment who live in Ober Etsch. The Fascist and Berlin governments have very properly assured complete safeguards of the economic, moral, and political interests of all those being repatriated; the agreement brilliantly embodies the spirit of honest solidarity and humane understanding that guides the governments of the two allied nations.' "

Just as Andreas was about to leave, the boy whose job it was pasted up a new dispatch: "Chancellor Hitler declares to Sir Nevile Henderson, the British ambassador at Berlin, that the fate of the German minority in Danzig is the fate of the entire German people. True to his policy of protecting and liberating the German minorities, he will under no circumstances continue to tolerate maltreatment of the Danzig minority by Poland."

"Who in thunder can make head or tail out of that? Can you?" asked a voice beside him, belonging to one of the twenty-four, Hoermann, the cemetery superintendent.

Andreas shrugged his shoulders. To tell the truth, he could straighten out the contradictory reports all too well. Pointing to the dispatch in the first row, he replied: "Did you read that, Herr Hoermann?"

It was the two-line report, almost hidden among the rest, concerning the leasing of the port of Trieste to Germany.

"Think so?" asked the cemetery superintendent thoughtfully.

Andreas nodded. "Certainly! That proves what they mean by it! Hitler relieves Mussolini of the troublesome Irredentists, and in return Mussolini hands over what he's refused for five long years to give up, the harbor of Trieste."

"Who knows whether it's true?" Hoermann objected. "They do think up an awful lot of lies!"

"I'd give something to have it a lie!" said Andreas, and walked on. The heat was growing more and more oppressive. *Keep your head clear!* he told himself.

But that was easier said than done. For these reports were not the end of it; one came hard on the heels of another that day and the days that followed. Not only the papers but the radio and, above all, the whisperers took care that almost every piece of news was followed by a contradictory or at least a misleading rumor. Berlin denied the agreement about Trieste. Rome confirmed the agreement about Trieste. It was not 1,000 persons who had left the province of Bozen, but 8,000. Those who cast their votes for Italy could stay here, Undersecretary Buffarini was reported as saying to foreign journalists, and His Excellency Prefect Mastromattei said verbatim in the great chamber of the Government Building, in the presence of all the zone inspectors of the Fascist Corporation: "The German-speaking inhabitants of South Tirol have the full and inalienable right, *il plento intangibile diritto,* to live in their birthplaces or residences in the Alto Adige, *di residere nel loro paese di nascita o di residenza nel Alto Adige.*" Heinrich Mann, the president of the Committee of Action for the German Opposition, issued an appeal to all the towns and villages of South Tirol: "Hitler has sold you out. He has not sold you for money. In return for the inhabitance of South Tirol he gets the free port at Trieste." Word came from the Vatican that the agreement was not approved by the Pope. Monsignore Sigmund Waitz, Archbishop of Salzburg, declared in a pastoral letter which Gemaassmer, the pastor, read at Sunday Mass, "Germany spoke to us as a mother does to her son. She has done the same to you, our brothers in South Tirol. But in Austria today National Socialist hatred has been unleashed against every Catholic, every Jew, every decent man, woman, and child. Austria has become an experimental area in which Nazism is trying to see how far Christianity can be destroyed. The same thing will befall you, brothers in South Tirol, if you let yourself be betrayed by Nazi promises. Rise and stand firm!" In a speech before the Party Council Mussolini declared: "Anyone who dares actively or passively to oppose the South Tirolean agreement will be court-martialed and shot."

Rumors buzzed, whispered, and hummed; no matter where you went they overwhelmed you. The hopes based on Mr. Hoffman were not fulfilled, and the picture post card that Andreas was looking for remained unwritten. The council met three times, and the Committee of Three went on day-and-night duty. There seemed to be no way out.

The result was an excitement swelling like a thundercloud from day to day, from night to morning, from hour to second. In the city of Bozen, which had been so proud of its quiet nights, people scarcely slept at all. They were not sleeping in Brixen or in Meran, in Klausen or in Brunneck. They were not sleeping anywhere in the country. They lay down exhausted from the bitter day, only to be startled up within a few seconds by the uncertainty of whether they would still be there tomorrow. Mortal doubt hung over them; to them the hot summer was stifling. Every day you heard of someone who had to go; some morning he was not there, and no one knew where he had gone. The authorities promised, reassured, threatened, disavowed.

When it was past bearing any longer, and the twenty-four could get no binding statement out of the prefecture, the Committee of Three asked to be received by the Duce.

The reply reached the prefecture very quickly, and was as follows: "Il Duce regrets that owing to the pressure of affairs of state he will be unable to receive the deputation of Bozen citizens headed by Pastor Gemaassmer. The deputation may be permitted to present its petition to His Excellency the Prefect of Bozen."

This was the last straw. The Duce didn't regard South Tirol as an affair of state, then? *We'll see about that!* thought the twenty-four savagely, or at least the seventeen of them with whom Andreas had shaken hands on the matter. They had succeeded in getting hold of the South Tirolean census, and found, to their triumph, that 267,907 souls were involved, and not, as was always asserted, 220,000—or, in other words, almost 50,000 more than they themselves had supposed. Of these, according to a very careful estimate made by Tschudaeth, the schoolteacher, at least 175,000, or twelve divisions, were able to bear arms. It was to them that a proclamation written jointly by Tschudaeth, the pastor, and Andreas was addressed.

Before this appeal reached the printer, Andreas was arrested.

Chapter 6

FROM HIS WINDOW Andreas could see a long way. Ostensibly because of overcrowding he was housed in the Palazzo Toggenburg instead of the court building in the Gilmstrasse, and so he could see the junction of the two rivers, the Talfer and the Eisack; across the Talfer he could see Bozen's pleasant sister town, Gries, and on the near side, to the right, the green villages of Im Dorf and Zwoelfmalgreien. The towering gray building above Santa Cuore church was the Casa di Risparmio, and the castle over there, untouched by time, was Castle Maretsch with the foaming cascade of Laurin's Fountain. And further northward the oddly twisting and rising white path was the Passeggiata Sant' Osvaldo. When he was a boy and it was still called the St. Oswald Promenade, he had run up and down it often and often, up to the Schloegl mill and down to the little church of St. Oswald.

He could see a long way, and he knew everything he saw. In the attic room where he was quartered, nothing interfered with his seeing, recognizing, and thinking. As soon as night fell he could recognize the church bells: first came the thin, clear, silvery bell of the

Sacred Heart, then the deep, brazen note of the parish church, then St. Johann and St. Oswald almost together, and then, with the minute's delay that had followed even in his childhood, came St. Augustin yonder in Gries. "Gries is always behindhand," his grandfather used to say, and not because of those sixty seconds alone.

When night fell, something else also fell on his listening ear. This it was that robbed him of sleep and left him counting the hours and comparing the bells.

He heard weeping. Night after night. It began about midnight, sometimes earlier, and ended one or two hours later with whistles and the sound of locomotives. At first he had not listened; he had had a great deal to think about those first few nights. But the longer he was there—and this was the twenty-seventh day and twenty-sixth night—the more intently he listened to what went on outside. It always began with the weeping and ended with rolling trains. At first he could not make out what it was. He had not even known what those distant sounds were that reached his ear now shrilly, now as a tremulous humming. He took them for vibrating telegraph wires, but discovered in daylight that there were none anywhere to be seen. On the other hand, if you leaned out of the attic window you could see the roadbed of the railway, whence the nocturnal sound seemed to come.

Once he found out that it was not telegraph wires but the people who were taken to the station in busses and there entrained, he never stirred from the window after dark. He could see the busses—the same green vehicles that had once taken the children from remote villages to the Bozen public schools, the boys' school in the Meinhardstrasse, the girls' school in the Runkelsteinstrasse, just below him. As a boy he had never ridden in one of these busses, because it was only a few minutes' walk from the Silbergasse to the Meinhardstrasse. But he always envied the boys who were so ceremoniously called for. Often they were tardy, and did not have to make up what they had missed, the lucky dogs! Now the green busses were gathering grown people. They began their night's work about midnight; sometimes he could tell the streets they drove to and the houses where they stopped. They never waited long; presumably the people whom they fetched were long since ready; and they went on and stopped and went on. When they came within range of one of the few street lights one could make out, from the spot where Andreas was straining his eyes, that the cars were green—still the same old school busses. As they moved away from the light they became shadowy; only the gleam of their headlights marked their trail as they went to the station.

A little while afterward the dreadful noise would begin.

It swelled and ebbed, ceased entirely and returned, was piercingly near, then distant again, and stopped. Locomotive whistles, hissing steam, and the thump of wheels drowned it. As soon as it stopped, the train left.

Now that Andreas knew the meaning of these trains leaving Bozen station about one o'clock at night, or sometimes just after midnight, he also knew what the weeping was.

From then on he could not sleep.

But so far as he himself was concerned, he had nothing to complain of. He had not been harshly treated; quite the contrary. He was even allowed to receive visitors; his grandfather came for ten minutes every Sunday, and his sister for the same length of time every Friday. Even Sepp had been there twice. He was allowed books and the *Popolo di Roma* newspaper, and Riccarda sent his favorite dishes by old Vroni. He had also been assigned a defense attorney in the person of the Fascist lawyer Ansaldo. They were treating him well.

He had been questioned repeatedly by the examining magistrate, and once by the sub-prefect. The crime they charged him with was attempted incitement to high treason. There was no question that he was bound to be held guilty, because not only the manuscript of the proclamation he had helped to write was on file, but also utterances of his, secured by some means or other, that were against Mussolini, or at least could be interpreted so. If he were very lucky he might get fifteen years, his lawyer said.

It was strange, on the other hand, that not another one of the twenty-four was under arrest. The public prosecutor had indeed tried to bring charges against all of them, partly for the same offense, partly for violation of the law regulating associations and for disturbing the peace; the latter, for instance, applied to old Mumelter and the pastor. But they were all at liberty, and pursuing their regular occupations.

"That's just it," said Ansaldo, the lawyer, during the new questioning—the eighth that Andreas had gone through so far, and the second one attended by the sub-prefect in person. "You accuse my client of attempting to incite high treason, quite forgetting that this alleged incitement was on his part nothing but a hypothesis, intended to take effect only under certain conditions. He does not deny that he had a share in writing the proclamation. But in doing so he presupposed that the Italian government would compel those former Austrians who voted for Italy to leave the country. Since that is not and never was the intention of our government, as you now inform us, Signor Sottoprefetto, he can only be charged with *dolus eventualis*. And according to our law *dolus eventualis* is not a punishable offense. I presume that is why our able state's attorney has prosecuted neither the other two co-authors nor the other sixteen co-signatories to the proclamation, but has left them at liberty."

This was a positive inspiration on the lawyer's part. It was so extraordinary that Andreas began to be in a good humor. The examining magistrate, an elderly gentleman suffering from dyspepsia and perpetually irritated, saw the force of the argument, and realized the blind alley into which they had been led by the statement of the sub-prefect, who embodied extreme Fascism with his black shirt and the black hair standing up over his low forehead.

But the man in the black shirt did not seem at all annoyed. Instead he gave a courteous *"Grazie tanto"* to the defense attorney, whose position was equally obscure. Did Dr. Ansaldo, the Fascist to whom the government had assigned the task of defending Andreas, have such a keen interest in acquitting his client, for whom he had prophesied a fifteen-year sentence from the outset? He smiled at the sub-prefect. The latter, smiling in turn and without the slightest trace of vexation, asked the question: "What have you been doing here, Signor Mumeltro, aside from the composition of treasonable manifestos? Did you come here in order to carry on Irredentist activities?"

Even this question was cruder than might have been expected, and if the almost bald-headed examining magistrate had had but a tenth of the bristling wealth of hair belonging to the sub-prefect, he would have torn out that tenth by the roots in exasperation. Why, he had recorded all this long before; everything was on file, and then this legal amateur had to come with incredible clumsiness and undo the neatly tied meshes of the law!

"We've got all that on file," he ventured to enlighten the smiling political functionary.

As if the question he was about to ask were less important by comparison with all that had gone before, the man with the rising helmet of hair said more or less conversationally, without even listening to the examining magistrate: "Didn't you bring with you some kind of plan or sketch or model of yours, Herr Mumelter?"

Andreas replied: "It isn't a model, it's a design."

"Va bene," conceded the sub-prefect, ready to agree with anything. "You published something about it, didn't you?"

Andreas almost laughed. You would hardly publish an invention while you were working on it! At most you might discuss it in order to find possible backers. This, as he explained to the uninformed sub-prefect, he had done in the *Zeitschrift für Maschinenbau.*

"Where is this magazine published?" inquired the other.

"In Berlin, sir," said Andreas.

"Then you propose to turn over your invention to the German Reich?" he was asked.

He said: "I was intending to turn it over to anyone who would finance it," and began to doubt whether the sub-prefect was quite so uninformed after all. The same thing was in the mind of the examining magistrate.

"At any rate, you published in a German magazine, not an Italian one," observed the smiling Fascist with perfect good nature. Then he asked casually: "What sort of invention is it, anyway, Signor Mumeltro? Isn't it something in the military line?"

The examining magistrate was all ears. Now this rogue whose South Tirolean obduracy had ruined four whole weeks for him seemed close to the gallows where he belonged!

Andreas replied cautiously: "I repeat, sir, it is not an invention to the extent that there is as yet no model of it. It contains proposals for changes, I might even say for important improvements, which would, in fact, amount to an invention if I could convince the proper quarters."

"Ecco!" nodded the man in the black shirt pleasantly. Once more he asked in a perfectly offhand tone: "With what field do these proposals deal? I don't believe you told us that."

"They involve the design of a new anti-aircraft gun," said Andreas with the bitterness of a man who had met with no encouragement in the very direction where he might have done his best work.

"Very interesting," agreed the sub-prefect. "But what was the reaction to your publication?"

"Practically nothing at all," he was told.

He had to put new lead in his pencil and accordingly had eyes for nothing else. Nevertheless, he inquired: "And have you communicated this invention, or—*scusi*—these improvements or suggested designs, or whatever you like to call them, to any military circles or industrial concern, or, shall we say, to a military attaché?" The lead, whose insertion required exactly as long as the question, was now ready to write with.

The examining magistrate rubbed his hands, which were always as cold as ice. Trapped! The rogue was trapped!

"No," said Andreas, shaking his head. "Professor Tomaschek, whom I was working under at the end, finally got the thing published and advised me simply to pick out the most promising of the inquiries I got. That seemed sensible to me. The *Zeitschrift für Maschinenbau* is very widely circulated, and if there had been any real interest in my project anywhere I should certainly have heard about it. But except for a trifling correspondence that led nowhere, nothing came of it. So apparently the experts don't think anything of my idea." He said this also in the manner of one who has managed to get over a keen disappointment, but does not like to be reminded of it.

Just then the sub-prefect was summoned away by a carabinière. He reappeared remarkably soon, accompanied by none other than Herr Udacher.

From this point on the scene changed so startlingly that the examining magistrate felt like tearing to pieces the file he had built up with such pains, guile, and ambition.

"I'm sorry to find you in this situation, Signor Mumelter," said Herr Udacher in Italian, nodding cordially to the defense attorney.

"I wouldn't say but what you'd had something to do with it," retorted Andreas in German. He was weary of the interrogations and maneuvers. What he felt like saying was: "Get it over with—sentence me, lock me up, or whatever it is you intend to do. None of this means anything anyhow!"

And while he was considering whether to say it now, Herr Udacher turned to him. "The sub-prefect has just been telling me about an invention you've made."

The "just" was conspicuous by its emphatic casualness. And the "has been telling" was conspicuous because there had been no time to tell anything. Nevertheless, the Italian official confirmed what the German official had just said: *"Si,* Signor Udacher." He pronounced it "Uddacce."

And when Andreas did not answer, the Gauleiter remarked: "It appears to be quite an interesting invention. And if the sub-prefect doesn't mind, I'd be glad to have a few minutes' talk with you about it."

No, the sub-prefect not only did not mind, but he even made the lawyer, now grown very silent, the examining magistrate, who did not know which way to look for sheer fury, and the police guard leave the room with him.

"We'll leave you alone with Signor Mumeltro," he proclaimed, pushing the three ahead of him. And he prophesied, too clumsily for even the Nazi's taste, "Possibly Signor Gauleiter may have proposals to make to you."

With this he, too, left the room, or rather was about to when Andreas stopped him with the question: "Do you hear the crying at night, Signor Sub-prefect?"

This time the diplomatic official was honestly puzzled. He looked at the other uncertainly.

"Do you hear the people crying at night, Herr Udacher?" Andreas turned to the latter. "Every night, punctually between midnight and one o'clock. When they're taken away. When they have to leave. Do you hear them?"

Herr Udacher had understood from the first. He said: "Now, Mumelter—not the same old refrain? I should have thought four weeks here would have given you better sense. Besides, one can't do anything about hysterical women and hysterical men—unfortunately some men are hysterical too. And that's all this is."

"Is it?" asked Andreas, turning pale. "What people are those who cry at night? I mean, I've asked everyone I could get hold of, and now I want an answer."

The sub-prefect interrupted; in this rejoinder at last his voice took on the cold, cutting quality that was perhaps usual to him when he was being less diplomatic: *"Basta! Basta!* You aren't here to ask questions, you're here to answer! *Capisce?"*

But Andreas persisted: "Signor Sottoprefetto, I want to know who the people are that are fetched night after night in the old school busses, taken to the station, and hauled away in two and sometimes three trains. You said before that the Italian government didn't want to drive us away from here. What people are those?"

"German subjects, of course." Herr Udacher came to his Italian colleague's assistance. "Germans returning to the Reich."

"And crying, Herr Gauleiter?" asked Andreas. "The Reich Germans going back home?"

"I told you before, there's no known cure for hysterical women!" Udacher retorted. "Incidentally, there's an abominable number of cats in the neighborhood. I tell you, Signor Sub-prefect, they have a tomcat in the next house to me—the love calls of that tireless creature drive me to despair every night of my life!"

The two officials shook hands, laughing, the sub-prefect said: *"A rivederla,"* the German replied: *"A rivederci,"* and Andreas was alone with him.

"See here," said Udacher, walking to and fro as he talked. "Let's not beat around the bush. That's not your way, still less mine. Let's lay our cards on the table. I know you don't trust me, but so far I've never misled you by so much as a single word."

"Of course, Herr Gauleiter," replied Andreas, standing with his back to the window. "The crying is the tomcat in your neighborhood."

"Nonsense!" retorted the other. "Never mind about incidentals now. You're done for, Mumelter, I don't need to tell you that. No one can save you from the penitentiary."

"Not even you, I take it," observed Andreas dryly.

"Me? Yes. That is, under certain conditions. Do you understand?" said the German.

"It's all the same to me," replied the Tirolean truthfully.

"It's all the same to you whether your family leaves here without you?" asked the other slowly. And, looking at a note that he had taken from his pocketbook: "Your family is due for it on August 29. There are three of them, aren't there? Laurenz Xaver Mumelter—he's your grandfather? Riccarda Mumelter—your sister? And Sepp Mumelter—your brother? This is the fifteenth of August. Two weeks from today, Mumelter."

Andreas sat down heavily on the window sill. "But you said only the Germans were being expelled," he said hoarsely, pressing both hands against the sill.

"And the undesirables, Mumelter," replied the German. "All the Germans. And also those among the former Austrians who are in disfavor with the Italian government. Your family is among the undesirables. Does that surprise you?"

"What? Say that again!" Andreas demanded, not yet able to control his voice.

"What is there about it you don't understand?" was the reply. "Look: the Reich and Italy have come to an understanding about South Tirol. There are people in South Tirol who want to sabotage the understanding. Obviously, naturally, these people are put out of harm's way; they're undesirable to the Italian government. Your family is among them. I saw for myself that your grandfather, in spite of his age, is unwilling to make any sort of compromise. Your sister and brother don't listen to anyone but you. And you're guilty of high treason. Is that clear?"

Clutching the sill with all his strength, Andreas asked: "Herr Gauleiter. Toward what cause am I guilty of high treason? Haven't you said, and hasn't your Führer said a thousand times over, that anyone who makes common cause with the Italians is a traitor? I didn't want to make common cause with the Italians. Am I guilty of high treason?"

"I don't say you are in my eyes or in our eyes, Mumelter," the German soothed him, watching the tremendous agitation that took hold of the Tirolean. "I will even go so far as to say—though of course I ought not to—that to a certain extent I can understand your fighting so stubbornly to stay here. But now you've got unequivocal proof of the thanks you get from the Italian government for your devotion to your native soil. I should hardly think in that case there was but one thing to do."

"Go to jail," said Andreas with bowed head, breathing heavily.

"Or else not to," said the other. "Instead you can be sensible and see to it that your life does some good. To yourself. To others. To your family, for example."

Andreas stood up. "Herr Gauleiter," he asked—the German had

difficulty in standing up to his eye, which seemed to be seeing an unbearable image—"how do you know that about my family?"

"There, now, Mumelter, that's the first sensible question you've asked," said Udacher. "I know it from Prefect Mastromattei himself. I always get—I mean we get the evacuation lists two weeks ahead of time. I got it today, and, as you see, I came here today."

"So it's you who sends the green busses?" asked Andreas; and although Herr Udacher was a stranger to personal fear, he decided to be on his guard against the menace of those all-too-resolute eyes.

"Ridiculous. That's the prefect's business," he observed. "But do try to stick to the subject!"

"I am sticking to the subject," Andreas contradicted, coming close to him.

The German weighed every word. "So much the better. In that case you can see your alternatives plainly. Either you will have the fantastic good fortune to be set at liberty—on certain conditions, naturally, be able to help your family get ready to leave, and go with them to a new but nevertheless old homeland; or else, Mumelter, you will have an unending prison sentence before you, during which your family will not only be lost to you forevermore, but (which is perhaps worse) will be thrown on their own resources in a strange country. Do you realize that?"

"I realize it," said Andreas, coming another step closer, and his fingers clenched and unclenched as if in a spasm. "I realize that the new homeland is an old one, and a strange country all the same. And I realize that I can enjoy a piece of fantastic good fortune. Fantastic good fortune was what you said, wasn't it?"

"And I'll stick to it," persisted Udacher, retreating not a step either in word or act. "They could have locked up your grandfather the same as they have you. They didn't. They could have sent you to Trento weeks ago, and held you in prison for investigation. They didn't. Why not, do you think?"

"It's all the same to me," Andreas repeated dully.

"They didn't do it," the German explained, unheeding, "because someone whose duty it was to examine your private papers—I wasn't the one, I might say—has called for opinions on your invention meanwhile. Mumelter, now listen to me, and be grateful: in spite of certain technical weaknesses that still stand in the way of your design, there is keen interest among the specialists in seeing it carried out. I'm not authorized to tell you more than that, but this much is certain: the German army wants to see you at work soon. Well, Mumelter, what do you think of that?"

"It's all the same to me," said Andreas for a third time, and the Gauleiter had trouble concealing his impatience.

"This obstinacy is just childish!" he objected. "It's all the same to you whether you are given a chance and the resources, under certain conditions, to work out an invention that may mean a great deal to you?"

Standing eye to eye with him, Andreas asked: "So all this is being done on my account?"

The Gauleiter congratulated himself on at least having broken down his adversary's obstinacy. "Suppose we stop the——" he began, but Andreas interrupted threateningly: "Hairsplitting?"

"Yes," Udacher admitted. "Don't forget that you've got into the most deadly hot water, Mumelter. And that you cannot only save yourself, but have an opportunity to lead a life that will bring you satisfaction, I might almost say an influential position, and that will of course make transplantation much pleasanter for your family too."

"Moving—where to?" asked Andreas. Now he was hardly a step from the other.

"That hasn't been decided yet," replied Udacher, prepared for the question.

"Not decided yet, when we're supposed to be leaving in two weeks?" the Tirolean insisted.

"Not decided yet, that's right," repeated Udacher. "In any case it will undoubtedly be a place where local arrangements will allow you to work on your invention as conveniently as you could possibly wish. That is, I'm simply assuming this. Once more, Mumelter: consider the great opportunities that are being put into your hands! If you'll give me your word of honor to engage in no political activity, here or anywhere else, the German government will request your immediate release from the Italians, and I have no doubt that it will be granted. You will then have two whole weeks to prepare for your family's and your departure. Well? There's hardly anything to think over, is there?"

"Herr Gauleiter," said Andreas haltingly, and one could see what was going on in his head, "does my—does my family know that they'll have to leave?"

Udacher thought the game was won now. "Not yet," he said. "That would be left to you too. You can imagine how hard a blow it would be to your family to hear the news from the mouth of a stranger. And what a consolation, not to say full compensation, it would be if they received your release and your company as the price of departure, so to speak!"

For a moment there was silence. Andreas turned toward the window. Then, with his back turned, he said: "No!"

"What?" asked the other with unaffected amazement.

"No!" repeated Andreas. His eyes were fixed on the Passeggiata Sant' Osvaldo.

"Let me tell you something," said the German behind him. "If you think anyone's going to take your part after we've dropped you, you're mistaken. The Hoffman family, for example—you know them—have booked passage for New York by the *Isle de France,* sailing from Le Havre on September 3. Incidentally, it may have escaped your notice lately that both Rome and the Wilhelmstrasse have given the cold shoulder to all diplomatic representations of any kind, no matter from what quarter. And so far as the reports to the American papers are concerned, the man who sent them will hardly be working much longer; that has been taken care of. By the way, I suppose along with the rest of the mail addressed to you you never got this picture post card? Someone who signs G. H. sends you regards from Meran. You were already arrested. Doesn't Miss Hoffman's first name begin with *G?"*

Andreas was scarcely listening. He saw the Passeggiata Sant' Osvaldo and the foaming cascades of Laurin's Fountain.

"No," he repeated. "No! No! No!"

"And one thing more," said the German. "If you shouldn't change your mind pretty soon, of course I would have no way of preventing the prefect's police from taking any measures they might find necessary for the evacuation of your family. Your grandfather, as you know, is not a patient man. If his truculent remarks should result in a rebuke, suppose we say a violent rebuke, from the Italian authorities, I wash my hands of it. You were telling us very movingly about the sounds of wailing that you say you hear at night. For my part I have no wish to contribute to their increase."

Andreas' boyhood stroll, the Passeggiata Sant' Osvaldo, swam before his eyes.

"What?" he asked, turning and standing rooted to the spot. "Do you mean that they might use force on the old man?"

"I don't mean anything at all," replied Udacher coldly. "Since you pay no attention to my opinions anyway, it doesn't matter. You will have to decide entirely for yourself whether you want to throw your family—that is, a man past ninety, a young and inexperienced girl, and a still younger lad—on their own resources at a decisive turning point in their lives. That's your business. Listen to me, Mumelter: this is my last word. It's two-forty now. I'll give you three hours. You are to make up your mind by five-forty. I'll hold up the notice of evacuation to your family that long. If you decide to await the verdict of the Italian court here, or wherever you may be sent, this is the last time you will see me. If, on the other hand, you decide to give me your word of honor, you will be at liberty by five forty-five, and at home with your family in as many minutes as it takes you to walk from here to the Silbergasse. I shall have an official from the Cancelleria come and get your answer at five-forty. He will be here from four o'clock on. You will answer either *'no'* or *'si.' Si* is your word of honor, and I know you won't break it. *Heil* Hitler, Herr Mumelter!"

With this the German left the Tirolean alone.

It was two forty-one when he left. At three-fifteen Andreas was still standing in the same spot. Then he began to walk up and down the room. It was a room of modest size, and he took eight steps to cover its length, six to cover its width.

The heavy sounds of his steps could be heard continually. He walked and walked, the length, the width. His eyes were fixed on the floor; they saw nothing; in his ears was a roaring, and all through his big frame a heaviness that kept him from thinking clearly. Again and again a new thought would intrude just as he was about to grasp an idea, or there would be an utter emptiness accompanied simply by this feeling of dull heaviness. "Away from here" were the three words with which everything began and ended. Away from here. He had thought them before, weeks before, that moment atop the Haselburg on Sunday, when the unspeakable news had come out of the little suitcase radio. But then, and each time since then, the three words had been followed by four more: perhaps not, after all? Each time the breathtaking blackness of the idea had been relieved and brightened by the thought that there were a hundred ways of averting it. At first there were a hundred. Then not so many. Fewer and fewer. But still there were some to be clung to. The plebiscite. Armed resistance. The sober second thought of a government that could not dispense with its best citizens. Best citizens! He laughed noiselessly now as this thought occurred to him again. The best citizens were being run out in the dark of night! Listen to them crying in the night! What if their families had been there for thirteen hundred years? Thirteen hundred years was less than nothing. Ha, ha! And if thirteen hundred years meant nothing, what did ninety-one mean? Why should anyone who had no respect for thirteen hundred years venerate ninety-one? He would be more likely to take pleasure in slapping them in the face or spitting at them. Why not?

He paced and paced. *I don't care a snap,* he thought, retorting to another idea that was running through his head. *That's all a fraud; he doesn't believe in my invention at all—preposterous!* First he said he had just learned of it from the sub-prefect, and a moment later he maintained people had been looking it over for goodness knows how long. The whole business was a lie.

For a second he stood still.

Well, then, why do they want to get me across the border?

The vacuum behind his forehead returned; he could not go on thinking, but only walking. Once again he measured the length and breadth of the narrow room.

Why do they want me away? he remembered having thought, and he found the answer.

Perhaps it was because of the invention, after all. If they simply wanted to get rid of him, all they needed to do was to lock him up with an endless sentence.

Riccarda! he thought. She was expecting a child. This sudden recollection crowded out the bare hint of encouragement he had just discovered.

I was always going to talk to Roberto, and something else was always more important! And I've always put it off, he admitted, *because of the girl, because of Elena—it seemed a painful situation!*

Ha, ha—painful! We undesirables can afford the luxury of thinking things painful!

Now the word "undesirable" came into his mind, and quickened his blood and his steps. *Just imagine,* he said to himself: *those who made the country—yes, under God we were the ones who made it. They're undesirable. And those that have nothing to do with it, to whom the Passeggiata Sant' Osvaldo is a promenade like any other—they're desirable!*

He was not walking now, but practically running, he was so excited.

Why not, he reflected, snatching at the scrap of thought that came to him, *why shouldn't I let myself be locked up? I've been locked up four weeks, and I'm alive and thinking; why shouldn't I be alive and thinking just the same after four months, four years, fifteen years? I'll survive it.*

At this something checked him. With a clarity that cut like a knife he saw the parish church cemetery before him. On the tablet of the Mumelter family vault, where the names of his parents, his grandmother, and his great-grandparents gleamed in letters of gold, his grandfather's name was lacking. *It won't be there when my fifteen years of prison are up, either,* thought the grandson. *Because meanwhile he'll have been buried somewhere where he didn't want to lie.*

He broke out in a sweat.

And Riccarda will have brought an illegitimate child into the world somewhere.

St. Oswald's church bell struck the quarter hour to five.

Andreas did not stop to think that time was flying, that he had only three quarters of an hour left in which to make up his mind. He was not trying to make up his mind; that was not what sent him racing around the room, pacing its length, pacing its breadth. The thoughts that were overwhelming him could neither be arranged nor reduced. They came down upon him like boulders, each one of them crushing. *They'll never see it again!* he thought confusedly, although he knew what he meant by "it." *And if I had a window like this one here, I'd be much better off than they through the whole fifteen years. I'd see it; they wouldn't!*

He went to his window. He concentrated into a single hungry, thirsty, longing look everything that offered itself to him—the mountains against the sky, the church against the mountains, the houses and the orchards against the mountains, their colors, blue, glacier white, purple, and green, their mixture of sweetness and magnificence. As he looked at them and embraced them with his eyes, they grew paler and more remote. The stroll of his childhood was more distant, more and more so, almost lost to view.

It struck five.

What was visible was the parish church and the cemetery next to it. Yonder on the north side.

What was visible was a landscape that had grown strange and hostile between quarter to five and five.

The mist parted before Andreas' eyes; the blood no longer pounded so loud in his ears; he took a deep breath, and knew what he must do.

Never mind the invention. That was not important, although but a moment ago it had seemed to him the very essence of momentousness.

And that Riccarda would bear, somewhere abroad, a child that might have no father—this was not decisive either, although it was a scarcely forgivable sin.

But that the ninety-one-year-old had no one to help him bear what no one could endure at twenty-five—that was what counted. It was as clear as the sharp, jagged edges of the gleaming Rosengarten yonder. Only a blind man could help seeing it. Only a madman could have taken so long to see it.

Andreas pounded on the door with such violent impatience that the police guard on duty opened in dismay.

"You are to take a message to Signor Udacher?" asked the prisoner.

"Si!" replied the soldier with military precision. "Through a gentleman from the Cancelleria. He's waiting downstairs."

"Va bene," said Andreas. "The answer is *si. Capisce?"*

"The answer is *si,"* repeated the police guard smartly, then closed and bolted the door behind him. He could be heard going down the stairs and coming up again at once.

Andreas sat down at the table to wait. On the table was a picture post card showing the Burggrafenamt of Meran. According to the postmark it had been mailed just four weeks before; the message read, in German: "Dear Mr. Mumelter, if it suits you I'll come at the same time day after tomorrow. Please be looking for me. Regards. G. H."

G. H. had meanwhile taken passage for New York. *And why not?*

The rats are leaving the sinking ship, thought Andreas, filled with unspeakable bitterness. The rats and the undesirables! He tore the piece of paper into a thousand tiny fragments, although he knew how silly of him it was. But he needed some outlet.

Before it struck quarter past five he was on his way home. The three hours of pacing the room had wearied him, the three hours' thinking had stupefied him. That was a good thing; he needed it now in order to tell his family what they did not yet know.

No one was expecting him home.

As always at that hour, Riccarda was busy getting supper in the kitchen.

And the old man, as always, was sitting bolt upright in his stiff armchair in the living room, smoking his pipe and reading the evening paper. The only change from former times was that seventy years ago, when he had first subscribed, the paper was the *Bozner Zeitung;* twenty years ago it had been the *Alpenzeitung,* and now it was *Die Dolomiten*. But the print and the words were German.

Sepp was somewhere at large, as always.

Andreas chose the entrance through the garden because he wanted to get into the house unseen and talk to his sister first. But Vroni, the servant, who had just taken Foxy the bitch outdoors, and was taking care by various "Come on, now, that's a good dog, Foxy!" that the old bitch should do what was expected of her, caught sight of him afar, and screamed piercingly toward the kitchen window, as if she had seen a ghost: "Jesus, Mary, and Joseph, Fräulein Riccarda! Quick! The young master's here, the young master!"

Whether the old man had heard her screaming was not certain, for the living room was at the front of the house. At all events, Riccarda rushed downstairs and into the arms of her brother, who stood on the threshold.

"What's the matter, Vroni?" said the enemy of emotional display to the old servant. "What are you bellowing like an ox for? Haven't you ever seen me before?"

"To think of your being back," said Riccarda blissfully.

And the elderly maid said apologetically, "It's so wonderful to have the young master back!" Going into the house with slightly wounded feelings, she called to the dog: "Come on, Foxy, we won't intrude any more."

"Won't you come in too?" asked Riccarda, still holding her brother's hand.

"In a minute," he said. Then, to make sure: "Grandfather home?"

"Yes. I'll tell him right away." Riccarda misunderstood.

But Andreas, still on the threshold, answered loud enough so that Vroni, who was in no hurry, could hear too: "No, never mind, Riccarda. I want to talk to you first."

The girl's sudden joy was gone. She could tell by the way he looked and talked how far from joyful he felt.

"Andre," she asked as they went over to the bench under the golden Reinette apples, "Are you free now, Andre?"

"Yes. Free," he said.

"For good?" she ventured.

"Yes. For good," he repeated.

They sat down, then he inquired: "See here, tell me—what about Roberto? Have you spoken to him meanwhile?"

"Yes indeed—why? Has something happened to Roberto?" she asked, her apprehensions now veering in another direction.

"Not so far as I know," he told her in a chilly tone that did not escape her. "So when are you going to get married?"

"You know we've got to wait till he's of age! That's only seven weeks away now. And for goodness' sake do tell me how you got out!"

"Not for seven weeks," he said, taking her hand again. "You see we shan't be here by then."

She looked at him. "What?" she asked.

"Mhm," he said, and squeezed her hand. "Now you've got to be a sensible, brave, unsentimental person, Riccarda—which, thank God, you are. That right, sis?"

She nodded and asked, with an effort: "What is it you know?"

"I know," he said, looking with all the force he could muster into her clear, beautiful eyes, which misted over now, "that we're on the list, Riccarda. We've got to go on the twenty-ninth."

She did not cry, and she did not scream. He was proud of her.

"One of the last things they said was," she declared, trying to defend herself, "that we Austrians could stay here! It was in the paper only yesterday, and this noon Grandfather heard it from His Reverence."

"Not the undesirables," replied her brother. "We're undesirable. We've got to go. And you two have got to get married first. Do you think Roberto will come with us?"

Her great eyes were filled with tears that did not flow. "I don't know," she said, swallowing the tears.

"Now, now, Riccarda! Surely you aren't going to cry!" he warned her, and as he did so he became aware of the stark lunacy he was talking. If there were such things as tears, when should they be shed if not at a moment like this? He remembered the sounds between midnight and two o'clock, and struggled desperately to maintain his composure.

"Oh no!" she assured him. "I'm not crying." And, in one last desperate effort: "Do you know it for sure, Andre? You aren't mistaken?"

"No—I'm sorry to say," he replied, putting a hand on her hair. He stroked it clumsily. This was the first caress he had ever given her in his life.

"All right," she said, making as if to stop him in her embarrassment. Then she asked: "Where to?"

"Unknown," he replied. "Somewhere."

Her eyes were moist again as she asked: "But how are we going to tell Grandfather?"

"Exactly," he said. "That's it. That's why you've got to pull yourself together, Riccarda. Even if it's hard enough for all of us, for him it'll be hardest of all!" His eyes turned to the apples, which had recently looked so silvery in the moonlight that Grandfather had been reminded of Christmas. Since then they had turned golden red, and grown almost ripe.

"That's true," she nodded. "It'll be dreadful for him."

At this a voice behind them said: "The same as for you. No more and no less."

It was the old man's voice; he had been standing for some time by the arborvitae bushes. For he had heard Vroni's screams, and had come down at once. When the servant tried to stop him, saying, "But the young master wants to talk to Fräulein Riccarda first, Herr Mumelter," he said gruffly: "Hold your tongue!" and went down the stairs to the garden, in order to find out for himself, as usual, what was going on in his house. In one hand he still held the paper he had been reading, which solemnly promised that the Austrians might remain and live here.

"Glad to see you back, Andre," he said to his grandson. "They couldn't prove anything against you, could they?"

The two had jumped up. But the old man's perfect composure led them to doubt whether he had heard or understood everything.

Accordingly Andreas replied: "No, Grandfather. Udacher has just been to see me and told me."

"Aha," said the old man, not stirring. "That business about the undesirables and having to leave—you got that from him too?"

"Yes, that too," said the grandson slowly, uneasily watching the old man.

"Aha," said the latter again. With a sudden fierceness that would have been natural to a far younger man, he crumpled and tore up the newspaper, just as Andreas had torn up the post card. He, too, had found his outlet.

"Grandfather," said Riccarda, going over to him, "oughtn't you to take a little rest before supper? You've been up and about since six this morning."

The old man's thin lips curled in a half-angry smile, and he inquired: "When did you ever see me lying down by day? I'm not going to start doing now what I've never done in all this time. Come on in. I should think Andre might want a cup of coffee or a glass of wine, eh?"

He knew perfectly well that Andreas wanted neither coffee nor wine. But whenever a guest had come to the house the old man had always offered him wine or coffee. And today Andreas was a guest.

Accordingly the grandson said: "Yes, thanks. A glass of wine."

And Riccarda said: "Well, I've got to look after my goulash now." As usual.

Now that the old man had come into the garden, the immobility of things past had been fully re-established.

Only when they were at supper—Sepp came late as usual—the old man ate and drank, but did not speak. Not a word.

And from the moment when Sepp, who knew nothing as yet, casually asked his brother: "I bet you're glad to be back home, huh?" the others were silent also.

Chapter 7

For two days the old man never spoke. He ate, he drank, he went to bed, he washed and dressed, he went out and came back, he smoked his pipe. But he did not speak. Vroni laid out the paper for him, and he threw it on the floor with such a violent gesture that no one dared give it to him again. So he did not read the death notice of Tschudaeth, the schoolteacher. "Sudden decease," the paper said.

After the two days of complete silence came a third, and that day the old man got up not at six, as usual, but at five, as he did on Sundays. It was quarter of six when he left the house.

He had on his black coat, his black trousers, and the narrow, factory-tied black silk bow tie with its ends tucked under his collar, as if he were going to Mass. Because of the thunderstorm that had been approaching for some hours he took along his cotton umbrella, his Loden cape, and his green Loden hat. But he was not going to Mass, he was going to confession.

Before entering the parish church he turned, as always, to the cemetery. Despite the early hour Jakob Hoermann, the cemetery superintendent, was already busy digging the grave for Tschudaeth, the schoolteacher.

It was windy, almost storming. Any moment might bring rain; the atmosphere, charged with electricity, let off flashes of lightning that blazed jaggedly over the Rosengarten and trailed long rolls of thunder after them.

Hoermann, the superintendent, was working three graves away from the Mumelter family vault, which the old man was coming to visit. Standing waist-deep in the earth, he called out: "We're going to catch it!"

"Mhm," the old man agreed.

"We can use it," said the superintendent. "Everything's dry enough. How are your golden Reinettes?"

"Fine," replied the old man. This was the first he had spoken in two days. "They'll be ready to pick in three weeks."

A flash of lightning split the slate-gray firmament.

"It certainly is a piece of luck, isn't it, about their leaving us here at the last moment after all?" observed Hoermann, spitting on his hands to go ahead with his work. "It just goes to show you how silly it is to be impatient. You might have thought he could wait for the good news! But no, Tschudaeth was always a hothead!"

The lightning was followed by the grumble of thunder, gradually dying away.

The old man, who had genuflected and was about to kneel at the graves of his wife, son, daughter-in-law, parents, grandparents, and great-grandparents, stood up again and asked: "Are you digging that for Tschudaeth, Jakob?"

"Yes," said he, once more busily at work. And he followed a tremendous shovelful with the query: "Don't you think it was the stupidest thing you ever heard for him to kill himself—God rest his soul?"

Thus the old man learned that Helmuth Anton Tschudaeth, the schoolteacher, had killed himself; and kneeling down to murmur a paternoster for his own dead, as he always did when he went to church, he could not help thinking: *Well, well. Tschudaeth. So he did what I'm here to see about.*

For he was here to confess, and also to pose a question. In the two days during which he had not spoken, and in the two nights during which he had scarcely slept, he had thought of nothing except what he now meant to ask his old friend and spiritual adviser.

"Don't you think so?" the superintendent persisted.

"Mhm," said the old man, crossed himself, stood up, dusted off his knees, went over to the open grave, looked for a moment into the black, dry hole in the ground, and then entered the church.

It was dark inside; fitful lightning sent a wan yellow gleam through the colored glass. Otherwise the twilight was broken only by the eternal light above the main altar and, for a few steps around, by a couple of candles burning quietly before the side altars of St. Jude and St. Anthony. Scattered individuals still kneeled in the pews at prayer, the Low Mass having just ended.

The pastor had celebrated it himself as he did every morning, and now he stepped into his confessional in order to hear confession, as he did every Tuesday. Laying his cheek against the narrow wooden grating, covered by a small curtain, which hid him from the penitent, and uttering his "Praise be to Jesus Christ!" he thought he recognized the voice that replied, "For ever and ever. Amen!"

But he obeyed the law, refrained from asking the name of the man kneeling before the grating and spoke the hallowed formula: "I hear you. Unburden yourself in holy confession. Speak!"

The voice outside the grating replied: "I confess before God that since my last holy confession I have committed the following sins: I was quick-tempered; I have taken the name of our Saviour in vain; I have cursed; I ate meat on Friday; I was unjust to our servant, Vroni; for the last two days I have not prayed."

It was the tone, not the substance, that terrified the father confessor. He had long since recognized the penitent, and, hearing him hesitate, he asked: "Have you anything else on your conscience?" He could not bring himself to say "my son," which he usually did.

No answer.

So he gave the penitent ten paternosters as penance, spoke the Latin words of absolution and a *Pax tibi,* and made the sign of the cross.

But the penitent did not go.

"Did you want to say something else?" he asked, trying to help.

"Yes," came the reply, and perhaps it was thus hard to catch because of the thunder that crashed outside as if lightning had struck somewhere. "I want to ask you something, Your Reverence."

"You may ask," the pastor encouraged him.

"If," the voice began, obviously struggling hard to find words, "a man has been decent to the best of his ability through a long, long life; if a man has been pious so far as in any of us lies, with our Saviour in his heart and not only on his lips, may a man like that —— Forgive me, Your Reverence, I know he mayn't! I asked the question wrong. I mean, is it just as much of a mortal sin for a man like that to take leave of this world as it is for a man who has slid through life more easily?"

The confessor was a full moment in getting out an audible answer: "Deliberately, you mean?"

"Yes," came the clear reply when the thunder had died away.

"Suicide, you mean?" the pastor repeated, lending to the word such an awful tone that the penitent could only beg: "Understand me, Your Reverence! Do you know who I am?"

"Speak, Mumelter," said Pastor Gemaassmer.

"You know," said the other, "we have to leave in twelve days."

"No! I didn't know!" replied the priest in the confessional, horrified.

"It's so," whispered the penitent. "Black on white. We're being fetched on August 29, at night. Everything has to be handed over, packed and ready, by the same morning. We have to apply for cancellation of our Italian citizenship. And we can take our clothes with us. No books, no written matter, no pictures, no furniture. We can't take our lire with us either; they give us German marks instead."

The whispering voice ceased.

"And where—where are you being sent?" asked the pastor, scarcely able to speak.

"Unknown," said the kneeling man. And in the new silence he implored: "Listen to me, Your Reverence! You've know me since you were a child. Would it be a mortal sin for me to leave here, but not the way they want me to? Think carefully, Your Reverence, take your time. I've been thinking about it for two days and nights. You have my fate in your hands. Because I shall do what you tell me—don't forget that. And if anything in my long life speaks in my favor—please, Your Reverence, remember it now. Tschudaeth couldn't stand it either, and he's got a grave in hallowed ground even so. Tschudaeth was a good Tirolean, God rest his immortal soul; but I'm at least as good a one. And now, Your Reverence, tell me the verdict."

A streak of lightning flashed outside, so glaringly that the high arches were as bright as day. Almost immediately after came rain, lashing the walls and windows with storm.

The confessor's mouth was sealed. There could be no doubt in his mind, not for a second, what he must say. But he dreaded the answer, and would have given anything between heaven and earth to avoid having to give it.

"Do you want to meddle with God's handiwork, Mumelter?" he asked at last instead of replying. "Would you pretend to play destiny? Haven't you always, and perfectly rightly, thought it the worst of mortal sins that the men under whom we are now suffering could put themselves in the Lord's place and toy with destinies? You propose to do that, Mumelter—you, who all your life have been among those to whom the Lord meant something, and who recognized His intentions? Must I ask you that, Mumelter?"

The listening man replied: "But it's *my* life, Your Reverence. I can do as I please with that."

"No! Did you give it to yourself? Then you can't take it away, either," he heard.

He asked: "What about Tschudaeth, Your Reverence?"

Almost angrily the priest replied: "Are you accusing me, blaming me for being weak enough to allow him a grave in hallowed ground and a church funeral—in spite of his mortal sin? Do you want me to be guilty of a second such weakness? I shan't, that I promise you. Once is no custom, and Tschudaeth was always a terribly sick man."

"And I'm going on ninety-two, Your Reverence, and don't know where they're sending me," said the old man, struggling for death.

"And, with the Lord's help, you'll live to come back from there ——" the pastor countered, but the penitent interrupted.

"Cut it short, Your Reverence. Don't try to tell me tales and don't try to convince me. If I must live, I shan't live to see anything but what I don't want. Must I? Answer me yes or no."

"Yes," said the son, brother, grandson, and great-grandson of the Gemaassmers, millers and bakers, who sat here in God's seat in the confessional.

"Thank you," said the penitent, and, kneeling, received the priest's blessing.

When he went outdoors, the cloudburst had almost washed away the fresh, half-dug grave.

Raising his cotton umbrella against the raging storm, lashed by the rain, the old man looked at the grave, and took it as a sign that the pastor had been right. Self-willed as he was, on this point he had no will of his own; the Lord had spoken to him through the pastor's lips. There could be only one thing to do—obey. And bury forever, or rather for the time yet remaining, the seductive dream of calling a halt after ninety-one years. Tomorrow morning he would take Holy Communion, and in eleven days he would leave. That matter was disposed of.

The eleven days that he still had to spend here he marked off on the calendar in his bedroom. Since time immemorial the Gemaassmers, the bakers, had sent their customers colored calendars at New Year's, and it was one of these on which the old man scratched off the days in ink. At the top was a picture of the Alpine sunset on the Rosengarten.

Eleven more days.

Ten more.

Nine.

Eight.

Seven.

A whole week still.

Only one more week.

As he was doing hundreds in the city were crossing off day after day on their calendars or in their heads. For like old Mumelter and his family, hundreds of others were among the "undesirables"—new ones every day, and daily some new time of departure was assigned to new people. Out of the twenty-four, only the pastor, his brother and sister, and, astonishingly, the elder Paechl had been spared so far. All had their dates of departure—on the twenty-ninth, thirtieth, thirty-first of August. Anton Tschudaeth, the schoolteacher, had got ahead of them.

Of those who occupied the hereditary seats in the parish church at six o'clock every Sunday, more than two thirds were on the list. Between today and August 29 only the Roell, Traxl, Malfertheiner, Praxmarer, von Sternbach, Tinzl, Psenner, Gemini families and the descendants of former Mayor Perathoner were leaving. But on the twenty-ninth the great exodus was to begin. The list posted on the bulletin board at the prefecture, open to public inspection, and surrounded daily and hourly by people come to see with their own horrified eyes whether they were included, listed three hundred and twenty-one for August 29, three hundred and sixty-four for August 30, and three hundred and eighteen for August 31.

The proclamation, in Italian, read as follows:

Pursuant to the decree of the Ministry of the Interior, regulating the settlement of the Alto Adige in accordance with a new treaty concluded with the German Reich, it is hereby ordered that:

For political and military reasons the following persons shall leave the Province of Bozen and settle abroad in the new domiciles to be assigned to them and announced later.

Then came Christian names, surnames, and occupations.

Of the above persons, the following will leave on——

Then came the date, the names, and addresses.

Such persons, provided they have applied for and been granted cancellation of their Italian nationality, are entitled to take with them all that part of their personal property consisting of clothing, and provisions for three days; furthermore, the equivalent of not more than 500 lire in reichsmarks.

All other real and personal property hitherto belonging to them shall be placed in my hands as trustee.

An appraisal commission appointed by the Ministry of the Interior will establish the value of this property at a convenient time, not later, however, than December 31, 1939, dispose of it, and transmit the proceeds to the former owners according to a conversion scale to be determined by the Royal Italian and German Finance administrations. The currency in which this payment will be made is the reichsmark.

There is no legal recourse against this decree, issued in concert by the Royal Italian and German Reich governments.

Persons opposing or attempting to evade it shall be punished by imprisonment up to twenty years and by confiscation of their entire property.

THE PREFECT OF THE PROVINCE OF BOZEN, MASTROMATTEI.

Bolzano, August 17, 1939.

A second notice dated the same day and signed by the sub-prefect read as follows:

AVISO!

The persons named in the accompanying proclamation are required to turn over their real estate, houses, dwellings, and business premises to a representative of the Royal Prefect forty-eight hours before the date of departure assigned to them, together with a complete inventory certified by a Royal Italian notary.

Any person attempting to make any changes in the status of his real or personal property with the purpose of concealing, diminishing, or removing the said property shall be punished by confiscation of the same.

Attention is called to the fact that the persons mentioned in the proclamation of the Royal Prefect must have their baggage, ready for shipment, prepared for inspection by the Royal Italian Customs Service at least six hours in advance on the day of departure. Customs inspection and bonding will take place from 7 to 12 A.M. of the day assigned at the dwellings of the persons departing. The removal of baggage and travelers will begin at 9:30 P.M. on the appointed days. From that hour forward the persons leaving shall be in readiness at their dwellings.

To cover the costs of dispatch and railway transportation including baggage (express train, third class), each traveler shall make a lump payment of 120 lire at the Finance Department of the Royal Prefecture not later than twenty-four hours before the appointed time of departure. The receipt for this sum shall be turned over to the official in charge before departure.

The word "undesirable" appeared neither in the proclamation nor in the Aviso, but it hung like an ax over the heads of 270,000 people, each one of whom henceforward might seek and find his name on some bulletin board at some South Tirolean town hall.

Yet this word, never officially mentioned any more than the name of South Tirol was, provided a key, found after long search, to lock a nation noiselessly out of its homeland while pretending that everything was done voluntarily, by desire of those concerned. Heavens above, surely these people had a right to decide for themselves whether they would go or stay. That this privilege could not apply to the "undesirables" who formed a "political or military" threat to the country, however, was as clear as day; and naturally the government decided who was undesirable.

So, at least, it was regarded by those who had stood before the bulletin boards without as yet finding their own names. And those who were listed felt the same. Their anger, their scorn, their anguish, their shame embittered the few days they had left.

Seven more.

Six.

Five.

On old Mumelter's gaudy calendar the thin, sharp strokes were accumulating with which he cut out of his life, as if with a dagger, what was no longer his.

In the next week more than a thousand would be leaving the city.

And since yesterday and the day before, the next seventeen hundred had been pinned to the bulletin board. They were to leave on the second, third, fourth, and sixth of September.

The great exodus was beginning.

When the old man went to bed after saying his paternoster (which he was accustomed to doing aloud, kneeling barefoot in his nightshirt before the iron bedstead) he would lay his head on the small, hard horsehair pillow that he still used despite his years, and think: *"Lord, don't take it amiss of me—but I can't see the sense! Nor the justice—I can't see that either!"*

He dared question the inscrutable ways of Providence no further, but stretched out, spread the thin blanket over his thin body, and thought with a too-wakeful brain: *I'll turn over the business to Paechl senior. He doesn't know a thing about it. Still I'd rather have him looking after it than one of those scoundrels!*

And if he happened to remember that the export shipment of carved crucifixes had to be made on September eleventh, or that the order for Baltimore, Maryland, must be ready to ship on September twenty-first, he brushed aside these worries with the reflection that he would no longer be here.

It was very hard to think this, and much harder still to believe it.

He tried to train himself to it—this old man who in all his life had never made way for anything, not for any pedestrian, carriage, bicycle, or even for one of the madly speeding autos that crossed his path, nor for any event either, whether birth, death, or war. Then why should he make way for banishment? He struggled to see the obstacle in his path now that he had been forbidden to choose what had seemed to him the suitable way out. He struggled with all his might to imagine it: *In five days more I shan't be here. Where shall I be then?* He did not know the answer. *What will it be like when I'm not here?* he asked himself. He did not know that answer either. It was monstrously hard to imagine, because it was unimaginable. But he struggled to imagine it, and, struggling, fell asleep.

During the nights that still remained, thousands upon thousands here in the city and here in the province were fighting the same futile fight. They could not imagine it.

But in the days that remained something incredible occurred. Bozen is not a big city, and though, with its 40,000 souls, it hates to be called a small town, still it has no small share of small-town ways —particularly its rigid, self-willed division of people into upper, middle, and lower classes. The families of the Counts of Sarntheim (now Sarentino), Welsberg (now Monguelfo), Thun (now Touno), Toggenburg, and Coloredo; the Barons of Uiberacker, Sternbach, Dipauli; the knights and vons, all associated with one another, but with the burgesses scarcely at all. Those burgesses, in turn, who were judges and civil servants, or otherwise in public life, formed a rigidly limited circle of their own; so did the schoolteachers, the industrialists, the landowners, the bankers, the artisans, and owners of vineyards and orchards; and so did the small country people. For hundreds of years the most scrupulous attention had been paid to the delimitation of classes, and even when people met at Mass or in some other place where distinctions do not exist, they still clung indefatigably to those distinctions. There was always a trace of condescension in the greeting bestowed by Von Hueber, the lawyer, on Tschudaeth, the schoolteacher; Countess Coloredo-Mannsfeld, on the other hand, gave Von Hueber, the lawyer, her coldest nod in return for his respectful obeisance, and Simmerl, the orchardist, considered for a long time whether he should allow his daughter to take coffee with Tieffenthaler the jeweler's daughter.

Pastor Gemaassmer had fulminated against this often enough in his sermons, and so had the priests before him on countless occasions. But, after all, Pastor Gemaassmer was himself only the son and brother of a baker, and his clerical predecessors almost without exception had been peasants' sons. How could they judge questions of rank, then? The Bozners, dating their consciousness of station back more than a thousand years, to the medieval times of the Counts of Tirol, and indeed even rather proud of it, had not heeded the pastors, not even the Italians who took possession of their city and country in 1918. In their judgments and prejudices, they had remained what they had always been. Not a few of them repeated with pride the words spoken half in earnest, half in jest to the old mayor of Bozen by Emperor Francis Joseph on the sixtieth anniversary of his coronation: "Dr. Perathoner, your Bozners are the most unteachable people I have ever seen in all my long reign!"

Thirteen hundred years had failed to teach them.

A single day did teach them now.

This was August 23, 1939. On that day, a Wednesday, the Bozen Wednesday market was held as always, and for those who were to leave on the twenty-ninth, thirtieth, and thirty-first it was the last market day. For one thousand and three people.

It was their last Wednesday here, and their last chance to supply themselves with things that could be got only at the Wednesday market, things that one felt like taking along a sufficient supply of to the place one was bound for, though without knowing where it was.

The mere fact that they wanted to take along a supply, and therefore were on their feet by early morning, patiently waiting their turn, made it plain enough how little they were capable of realizing what awaited them.

Provisions? How long were those supposed to last? How long could they last, even if these wares from the market had not, in the main, been things that spoiled easily? As they stood there in a long, unbroken queue starting at the Mercantile Building, waiting to buy Calville apples from the Burggrafenamt, sugared pears, plums, cherries, quinces, and nuts from Guntschen, Fagen, Zwoelfmalgreien, and St. Magdalena, herb cheese from Krummeck and Unterplatten, the country hams that are smoked so deliciously at Peterploner, Oberpayersberg, and Eschenbach, they gave the impression of people laying in supplies for a picnic.

Only their numbers, their patience, and their manner were not those of picnickers. The line pushed silently along, man by man, woman by woman, and child by child.

Some of them were buying only provisions, others also the trifles that had always been for sale in the fruit market at Bozen on Wednesdays ever since the first day the market was held, Wednesday, May 11, 704, when the Lombards bought and sold here, and the city already bore the name of Bauzanum, which later became Bozen. Even in those times there were the narrow rings supposed to bring good luck, only then they were made of iron and wood, whereas now they were of silver filigree. Today these were bought in great quantities, and immediately put on, although it had never been considered high style to wear such cheap trumpery oneself; such things were exported, and foreigners bought them as souvenirs or as presents for their housemaids and cooks. All proper Bozners and Meraners scorned them.

They scorned them no longer.

Some of the people, too, were buying religious goods for the first time in their lives, and it was they who showed most conspicuously the change that had taken place in the people of Bozen. The little pitchers and pewter medals of Sts. Jude, Anthony, and Christopher; the mother-of-pearl rosaries; the silver, nickel, and carved wooden crucifixes, even the carved madonnas and saints that the House of Mumelter had long been unable to sell here, but had had to export abroad—all these and also the bright-colored booklets of Tirolean proverbs and songs found purchasers. One of the songs was particularly in demand. It was the "Song of the Bozen Tirolean Volunteer Troops Defending the Country in the Year of Napoleon 1796," which begins:

The drumbeats roll; to do or die
Our mountain German hearts beat high
As forward now we march!
Our God, our law, our Emperor's name
To shield is every German's aim—
Brothers, onward march!

Who were buying these things, which ordinarily no one of the buyers would have taken as a gift?

The countesses were buying them, and the baronesses, and the knightly and noble dames, as well as the wives of civil servants and schoolteachers, of artisans, of countrymen; even the men were buying them. When they left here, one and the same sort of thing would be found in their oilcloth or plaited straw shopping bags, or simply wrapped in paper—fruit and cheese and ham and lucky rings and religious articles and songs. And just as they were all buying the same things, and waiting patiently and eagerly to get them, so on this twenty-third of August 1939, for the first time in their lives, they made no distinction among those whom they spoke to, talked with, and liked. For the first time Countess Sarntheim did not send her cook to market, but came herself. For the first time the Widow Aufreiter spoke to her mortal enemy, the widowed Frau Tolomei. For the first time not one of the hundreds who had been standing since dawn to get the few little things that they called their supplies nursed any grudge against another, or was even indifferent; they all felt for one another. A miracle had happened on this twenty-third day of August in the Bozen fruit market, by now almost cleaned out. The caste marks were gone from their eyes and foreheads, as if wiped away by an invisible hand touching all these people at the same moment. They could not yet fully imagine what awaited them, because they could not conceive of it. But there in that square at that hour they were already seeing with the same eyes and thinking with the same foreheads. There were no distinctions. And it was quite in the spirit of the miracle that not a soul found at all remarkable something that would under other circumstances have been a topic of conversation for days: old Countess Thun shook hands with the elderly peasant woman who was selling her smoked meat, and said in a quavering voice: "God keep you, dear Frau Mayr!" Not even the peasant woman was surprised; she simply said, "You, too, dear Countess!"

On this Wednesday that taught the unteachable people, Andreas had a conversation that so far he had kept postponing, and that could be put off no longer. This market day with its unspoken, universally felt impulse of fraternization, which he shared also (having bought three silver images of St. Genevieve, one for Riccarda, one for his grandfather, and one to send to someone who was about to take ship at Le Havre, and to whom he owed thanks for an unanswered picture post card), seemed to him the proper day for calling Roberto Maletti to account.

They had arranged to meet on the silent Passeggiata Sant' Osvaldo, Andreas' childhood walk.

Andreas said without preliminary: "You know we are leaving Monday. Are you coming?"

The young man from Trento, brought up in a city and a region where dissembling was part of living, put a vague smile upon his conspicuously handsome, distinguished countenance, and replied: "Herr Mumelter, you know I can't."

Andreas retorted: "I don't know that. Nor believe it either. What a person wants to do, he can do."

This made it easy for the other to reply: "If that were true, you wouldn't have to be leaving."

Nevertheless, he could have said nothing more ill-judged. In a fury Andreas inquired: "What are you going to do? It is astonishing enough that you wait for me to ask you. Don't you consider it your damned duty to do something?"

The queer smile had not yet faded from the smooth face. "I have offered to marry your sister the day I come of age," declared the boy from Trento.

"And you think that's doing something?" inquired the Tirolean.

"No, I think it's a matter of course," replied the other. "The point is that I am financially dependent on my father, and shan't have control of my inheritance from my mother until I am of age. If I married sooner, my father would get a guardian appointed for me."

"And why is your father so much against this marriage?" said Andreas. The whole time he kept wishing he could say: "Instead of talking about how lucky you are that a girl like Riccarda will have a fellow like you!"

"Because he doesn't want an Austrian for a daughter-in-law," replied Roberto, still smiling uncertainly.

"But he was an Austrian himself," observed Andreas bitterly. "And so were you."

"Perhaps that's just why," the victim of this snub ventured to say, thus exasperating the Tirolean the more.

"Much obliged for the explanation," he remarked. And, turning on him brusquely: "Well? What are you going to do? You know that Riccarda can't wait until you're of age, because she won't be here then."

The other conceded this with a nod, but said nothing.

"Are you going to marry my sister before she leaves?" her brother persisted.

"That's in five days?" said Roberto slowly.

"That's in five days," Andreas agreed.

"Impossible," said the handsome young man. Not loud, but very clearly.

"You're mistaken," Andreas contradicted. "I shall take care that you do not carry your cheap behavior to extremes!"

"You can't do any such thing, Herr Mumelter," said Roberto Maletti. And now the cause of his vague smile came out, for he said loftily: "You haven't the slightest cause to play the guardian of virtue around here! If my sister Elena is not in Riccarda's situation today, God knows she owes it to nothing but her own self-discipline!"

Andreas thought he must have heard wrong. "What?" he asked. "Say that again."

And the son of Dr. Maletti, the Irredentist, said it again. "Surely you ought to know, Herr Mumelter," he said. "If Elena hadn't resisted as she did, I'd be the one who was having to ask you today what *you* were going to do. And, just between men, fond as I am of your sister, and happy as I would consider myself to be married to her, still she's a grown woman, and I didn't force her!"

Now the smile vanished from his face, giving way to the look of one lurking in wait.

Too bad Riccarda couldn't see him now, Andreas thought. Then she would have seen his true face.

"For shame!" was all he said. He turned on his heel and left. *One can't marry a fellow like him,* Andreas decided almost with relief. For a moment he paused to wonder whether Elena had really been rotten enough to distort their meeting so abominably. He was almost inclined to believe it—judging by her brother. *For shame!* he repeated to himself, and began walking so fast that the other could not have overtaken him even if he had wanted to. But he wanted nothing of the sort.

As Andreas approached the prefecture he began to hear voices and shouts. They grew louder, and finally he could make out a German-speaking chorus: "We want to know where!"

"We want to know where!"

"Answer!"

"Answer!"

And immediately afterward, in Italian: *"Rispondete!"*

"Rispondete!"

Young lads were shouting this.

Sepp was among them. In fact, he was not only among them, he was actually leading them, as his elder brother now discovered.

"We want to know where!" he began, lifting both arms to beat time, as Andreas came around the corner of the Dr. Streitergasse.

"Shut up!" he shouted at his younger brother; but his shout was drowned in the uproar.

Meanwhile, adults had mingled with the young people; there were more and more of them. One of them said to Andreas: "Why do you tell him to shut up? Haven't we at least got a right to know where we're going? Mary and Joseph! Isn't it a shame and a dis grace for them to pack us up and ship us off like cattle without our having any idea of where, without our even being able to leave our new addresses for the ones that are lucky enough to stay? Let Sepp talk! He's right!"

She was the widow of Johanneser, the bookseller, and her three sons and two daughters were also among the demonstrants.

"No, Frau Johanneser," Andreas strove to make himself understood in the tumult, and to make himself understood by the woman at whose shop he had bought his copybooks and adventure stories as a schoolboy, his Schiller, Goethe, and Grillparzer as a young man, "Sepp is a silly boy, and he's not right. You see we have no such things as rights any more. I don't know why, but we haven't. Shame, yes. Disgrace, yes. Those we have. But no rights. We've got to pound that into our heads, Frau Johanneser! We've got to beat it into our skulls. Since August of 1939 we South Tiroleans have had shame and disgrace, but not any rights."

"But a person can't live like that!" persisted the bookseller's widow, who had to go on the thirtieth, leaving behind a shop over whose door it said, "Established 1809." And suddenly she was yelling with all the others, *"Rispondete! Rispondete!"*

"No," Andreas admitted. "Of course a person can't live like that."

No one heard his words; they were drowned in the tumult; a few moments later carabinièri, advancing at the double with fixed bayonets from three sides, had cleared the square. By order of the prefect no prisoners were taken from among the shouters, nor was any answer vouchsafed to their wild demand. In four days, the prefect knew, or in five, or in six, they would be well out of harm's way; so let them yell.

Four days before their departure, or five, or six, the thousands of undesirables knew only that, not where, they must go.

Chapter 8

THE SUN ROSE on the twenty-ninth day of August 1939 with a cloudless brilliance, a beaming splendor, a deep radiance such as only the late summer days in the Tirol can boast. It was five in the morning, and even thus early the outlines of the red Rosengarten were clear. When the old man arose from his iron bed, in which he had slept the last night quietly and dreamlessly, he looked at the sky, as always, and observed that it was going to be a glorious day; then he did what he had done every morning that he had spent in this room, which had been occupied by his father before him, that is, sixty-two years previously: he prayed, washed, and dressed. And today he also did what he had never done except on Sundays—awoke the sleeping house, and, after breakfast, went with its inmates to Mass.

All the three hundred and twenty-one who were to leave that night were in church. The prefect had allowed the German morning Mass, but neither organ nor sermon, and Pastor Gemaassmer, who was among those permitted to remain, recited the Latin prayers in a voice that failed him every other moment. There was in the church a silence that made every breath, every whisper, every sob clearly audible. There they sat in the hereditary seats of their forefathers, and in all their prayers was just one word: return, return, return. As they clasped their hands and bowed their heads, they kept asking themselves: *Won't the Lord whom we pray to and believe in perform a miracle now? Then we wouldn't have to leave.*

But today no miracle came to pass.

The Low Mass took its course. It went so terribly fast—now the Introitus, and now already the Holy Transubstantiation, and the celebrant was ringing his little bell. They touched their breasts and crossed themselves every time the bell tinkled. With all the clearness he was capable of, the pastor uttered his *"Dominus Vobiscum,"* made a great cross in the high, silent emptiness, and blessed the congregation that was leaving him.

Then they got up and went out of their pews to the altar, one after another. There they genuflected, and the pastor bent down to them, held out his hand to each of them, shook it, blessed each one, and said to him: *"Dominus cum tibi."*

And many of them raised their heads and looked up at him inquiringly, as if to say, "Isn't the Lord here, Your Reverence? Where is our Lord? Why does He not do anything?"

And the pastor, who would be standing here tomorrow and the day after tomorrow and the day after until all the undesirables had heard their last Mass in their native land, understood the mute, inquiring look all too well; he nodded. His nod meant: "Yes. He is here. And He is wherever you must go. He is with you."

Then even those who had looked up at him inquiringly nodded also and departed. Their heavy footsteps echoed on the flagging.

Old Mumelter went likewise, and Andreas and Riccarda and Sepp, and old Vroni. Old Vroni had gone to Mass, too, although she was not among the undesirables, but was staying in Bozen.

Outside, the old man dismissed his family. For that which he was about to do he wanted no witnesses; accordingly he waited until not only his grandchildren but most of the others had departed. It was not yet six, and the sun was barely touching the southern slope of the Rosengarten and the western ridge of the Schlern.

The ancient man took carefully from the right pocket of his black Sunday coat five flat, white, round candles; they were as high as a man's thumb, and sheltered from drafts and from burning too fast by a thin metal casing. From his left pocket he took five little bouquets. Each one consisted of edelweiss, gentian, and Alpine roses, tied to a small larch twig.

With these he went to the Mumelter vault, which was on the north wall of the cemetery between the hereditary resting places of the Perathoner and An der Lan families.

His actions were methodical. First he put everything on the tablet covering the vault. Then he distributed the candles: one, the first, for his wife. The second for his dead son. The third for his mother. The fourth for his father. The last for his daughter-in-law. He set them up and moved them until they were exactly in front of the names of the departed. Only then did he light them.

These are good candles that Figl the wax chandler sold me, he thought; *they light almost at once, and don't flicker.*

When they were burning evenly and quietly, he distributed the bouquets.

One to his wife.

One to his grandfather, one to his grandmother.

One to his mother.

The last to his son.

There were order and thanks in the way he proceeded.

Not the candles alone kindled the gold letters on the stone, but the sun as well, and in the double gleam the name of Mumelter shone from the white Carrara marble.

Only after his task was done did the husband, father, son, and grandson go down upon his knees and repeat the first of the seven paternosters that he meant to say, one for each.

The candles burned; the golden letters gleamed.

Having spoken the prayers with complete poise and devotion, the man of ninety-one said farewell to his dead and to the place that was rightfully his in death.

"Good-by, wife," he said in the windless stillness.

"Good-by, Mother."

"Good-by, Father."

"Son, good-by."

"Good-by, daughter-in-law."

"Grandfather and Grandmother, good-by."

"Good-by, all!"

He took leave of those whom he himself had known. Of his maternal grandparents, his great-grandparents and their forebears he did not take leave.

Getting up, he carefully brushed off the dust and soil, and, having made sure that no one was watching, stepped close to the cold stone. For a second he laid his haggard cheek against it, murmuring something, and then moved away.

He walked quickly, for somewhere behind him there were sobs, and this he could not bear to hear, because he was not going to break down himself for anything in the world. He had not cried since his son's death, and before that not since his wife's. He could feel that it would be child's play now to make him do this most impossible of all things. So he made off without delay.

But now, suddenly, there were people sobbing before him as well—and beside him. Everywhere. All over the churchyard they were crying. Had he not seen these people before, absorbed as he was in his prayers and his thoughts? Like him, they were taking leave of their dead. *But they ought not to be crying!* he thought, and halted beside the hereditary burial place of the Psenners, before which lay two women racked with sobs, the Widow Psenner and her daughter.

"You women," he said to them. "Stop reproaching the good Lord!"

Then, without looking back, he left the cemetery.

It was just after six, and he still had eighteen or nineteen hours. On his calendar he had crossed them off the previous evening before going to bed, and had then torn up the calendar. But it proved that in this he had been precipitate. For eighteen hours, well employed, are a great deal of time, and he used them wisely. First he went through the whole town. He was not tired; his feet carried him even to places where he had not been for a long, long time. For this farewell pilgrimage he knew he must use the time before the sun gained its full strength; otherwise it would be too hot. But to make this pilgrimage was for him the merest matter of course, and he made it with firm, steady steps, with occasional fierce anger when he found some new place ridiculously Italianized or some building or honest old name tortured into Italian. Like a stranger who had begun by asking himself what was the best and shortest way to see the town, he inspected the city once more by the shortest and most convenient road, enjoying as much of the shade as he could find under the arcades, along the walls of houses, and under trees. He began at the post office, went by way of the museum, the Sacred Heart Church, the Gerstburg, Maretsch Castle, and even the rather remote Lindenburg, turned down the Passeggiata Sant' Osvaldo, and went home through the St. Johann-Gasse. He looked at everything carefully and sharply, as one does when looking for the last time. It was a sort of inspection that he was making, or rather he seemed to be taking inventory. What part of his memories was still there, and what was not? To each thing he gave a long, steady look, impressing it firmly on his mind—the houses, the shops, the churches, the river, the bridges.

It was past nine o'clock when he entered the wood-carving shop on the ground floor in the house of his birth and old age, which had supported him and his forefathers. Having been on his feet for almost four hours now, he sat down in the brown wooden armchair at the brown wooden desk in the little room next to the shop, where he had always written his letters and invoices. He allowed himself the luxury of a pipe, took another look for safety's sake in the drawers of the desk, which he had long since cleared out and prepared for his successor, and told himself as he did so that it was a good thing the boys had not gone into the business after all. He meant his grandsons. The lathes next door were making the accustomed humming, grating noise, and the place smelled, as it always had, of wood, resin, and glue. There was nothing left on the top of the bare brown desk; it was painfully vacant. There were only a few letterheads, "United Tirolean Wood-Carving Shops, Christoph Mumelter's Heirs. Established 1752," in the box put there to accommodate them. The fact that the elder Paechl (with whom he had come to an agreement on all essential points a week before) was not going to change the firm name offered him some slight satisfaction.

He could see perfectly well through the glass door separating the little office from the workshop that the eyes of the men working there were fixed on him, and he could see just as plainly that his first and oldest workman, the lame Bernhard Tichtl, was taking off his apron and motioning to the other three; all four of them were standing together now, talking, evidently about to come in and solemnly wait on him.

At this he quickly wrote on one of the letterhead sheets in his thin, unwavering, old man's script, "Men! Take care of yourselves. God bless you and our Tirol land!" He signed it, "L. Mumelter," and added to the final *r* the long flourish with which he always concluded his name. Then he looked quickly at the brown-framed pictures of his father and grandfather, and went away from here, too, taking his third farewell on this beautiful August day.

It struck ten when he went upstairs.

The rooms upstairs were bare; they looked like rooms already abandoned. They looked like rooms that one would never come back to again, he felt as he went to his chamber on the third floor.

They did not look like such rooms to Andreas. He was destroying old letters from the drawers of the ink-stained desk in his boyhood room on the second floor. At this same desk he had started his studies. Sitting there now, he remembered when the larger stain and the three smaller stains were made. He could not help thinking that it was not the last time he saw them.

Next door Sepp was amusing himself by enlarging a tear in his wallpaper, stripping large pieces of the faded, flowered paper off the wall. He seemed to feel differently from his brother. To him the rooms looked exactly like rooms one would never see again, and he was young enough to find something adventurous in this, and to regard the whole departure as rather desirable than bitter. Of course he never said so. But as a matter of fact there ought to be a lot of fun in putting tedious old Bozen, which you almost never got away from, behind you, and seeing something new at last. Besides, the flag leader of the local Hitler Youth had been telling him simply fabulous things about the importance of all young people in the Reich. *Up and away!* he thought; *the sooner the better!*

So far as Veronika was concerned—she was just going into Andreas' room to hand him a special-delivery picture post card—she was so completely bewildered that she had to do almost every errand and operation twice. She couldn't get it through her head. For the young master to go away—that was all right; she was used to it. But the old gentleman? The old gentleman, who had never been away for a single day in the twenty-seven years she had served in the house? From the moment she had learned what the present day was to bring forth, she had been unable to look the old gentleman in the face. And when she stopped to imagine that tomorrow, no, this very night, she would be the only one sleeping here in the house——? The old gentleman had given her permission to stay on in the house. But this Vroni did not want to do. How could you live here without the children and the old gentleman?

"There's a special-delivery letter just come," she said, making a letter out of the post card in her confusion. And as this was the first opportunity she had had in a long time of speaking to Andreas alone, she screwed up her courage to ask him: "Young master, do you think the family'll be coming back?"

She had dreaded a no.

But Andreas looked at her and said: "Certainly, Vroni. Just be sure you keep everything in good order meanwhile!"

And, most amazing of all, Andreas had managed to make himself believe what he said. Since that morning he had believed it. A feeling stronger than his reason, which said no a hundred times over, was now saying yes a hundred times over. He would see these mountain silhouettes again. This room. This stained desk. And he would even sleep again in this bed, which, for the first time since Vroni had been in the house, was not yet made up by ten-thirty, but had the covers tossed around just as they had been during the night, when sleepless reason had uttered its hundredfold no.

"But that's——" said old Vroni, enchanted, and started to take the special-delivery post card away again for sheer confusion.

On this card Gwen Hoffman informed him that she was arriving here with her parents at 12:30 P.M.; they would go to the Hotel Laurin, and were expecting the whole Mumelter family to lunch at one o'clock. Lunch was crossed out, and *"Mittagessen"* was written above it. "We thought," Gwen wrote, "that you might rather enjoy talking to friends before you left." As, according to the postmark, the card had been mailed in Merano yesterday, Monday the twenty-eighth, at 11 A.M., and had been a full twenty-four hours in traveling a ridiculously short distance by express service, it had obviously had other readers besides Andreas.

It pleased him all the same. He thought it tactful in every way. *Mr. Hoffman or Gwen or all three of them*—he was rather inclined to think Gwen was the sole author—*are not only trying to tell me that they know about our leaving, but probably they want to let me know something else important,* he told himself. The rectangular piece of pasteboard with the view of the Tappeiner-Weg improved his humor. *No, it's not silly optimism,* he thought; *I absolutely have a feeling that it does mean something good.*

To convince the old man of this was hard work, though. And it was harder still to make him go and eat dinner at the Hotel Laurin. "I have never once," he began, but checked himself, realizing that this was scarcely the day to abide by former rules and habits. Besides, Andreas insisted that Mr. Hoffman could do a great deal for the Tirolean cause.

So far as Riccarda was concerned, she didn't care. She was just putting beef on the stove. It would do quite as well for supper, she declared—why not?

Sepp, on the other hand, was wholly enthusiastic. Just once in his life so far he had had the privilege of taking a cup of chocolate at the grand and sinfully expensive Hotel Laurin. *Swell,* he thought; *the adventures are beginning even before we leave!*

Thus it was that the whole Mumelter family greeted the Hoffman family in the lobby of the Hotel Laurin at one o'clock with a punctuality that was a matter of course to the old man and a source of satisfaction to Mr. Hoffman. Each of the seven, Sepp possibly excepted, was aware that someone in the big lobby had been assigned to watch what they did and said. In any case Hoffman left no doubt of it, for immediately after the greetings, and not even in an undertone, he said: "How many of us are there? Let's see. There are four of you and three of us, makes seven, and the man that's spying on us makes eight. If there are two spies, that makes nine. Well, my eight or nine friends, let's go in to dinner."

This they did; and from the moment when the Bozen family took their seats at their hosts' table in the imposing dining room of an imposing international hotel, they were strangers in their own city. It was five minutes after one, and Riccarda, accepting no pretenses from life, but taking things as they were, had a feeling that instead of being ready to leave in twelve hours, they had already gone. Strangers among strangers. She saw her grandfather stiffly and uneasily spooning his soup, and she saw her brother Andreas looking with strange eyes at the American girl; it was the first time she had ever been aware of such an expression in her brother, and it made her jealous, so far as she was capable of it in her apathy. Yet she did like the American girl. At first glance one saw the attractive quality she had. At the second—and Riccarda was not sparing of her glances—one saw that this attraction came not from the outside, but from within; and this was just what made Riccarda jealous. As for Mr. Hoffman, who first attended carefully to the choice of the dinner, and then to Riccarda herself, she decided he was a man who talked too much. His wife, on the other hand, smiling at everything and saying it was all charming, won Sepp's admiration. He ate, drank, and got on famously. This was the first time he had ever enjoyed the privilege of conducting a dinner conversation with a lady much older than himself, and though his English was not up to much, Mrs. Hoffman smiled and nodded at the German words in which he told her about the Davis Cup tournaments of that summer.

Soft, pleasing music by the red-coated hotel orchestra accompanied the meal. The Rosengarten, gleaming in the afternoon sun, looked in through the windows at them. The fact that the Bozen family now at dinner would not see it again in the afternoon, but only in the evening, and then never again at all, was like an icy hand upon all of them, aside from Sepp; it suddenly took away their breath as they spoke, fell silent, or ate. But it is a curse, or a blessing, of civilization that it covers up all ultimate moments with the duties and habits of convention: even a condemned man's last meal becomes mere eating and drinking, and a last conversation an everyday chat. There they sat, being played for and waited on like rich holiday-makers, talking about tennis and Greta Garbo, about the goodness of the Meran apples and the sweetness of the Bozen grapes, about the London trip of Henderson, the British ambassador to Berlin, which would probably end the Danzig crisis; they made tourist conversation that even spies could not have twisted into anything. Five of the seven realized that one had to be on guard. Mrs. Hoffman smiled and enjoyed the cold trout; Sepp laughed and enjoyed everything.

The condemned man's last meal, Riccarda told herself, and the old man had long anticipated her thought. Sitting stiffly with two corners of his napkin tucked into his collar, as was his habit, he ate things that were strange to him, and said things that sounded strange to people who remained strangers.

Andreas, however, had a question of Gwen's to answer.

The question was: "Is it worse than you expected?"

This was the first question that had touched upon real things. The band was playing "Ramona." Where was it that he had last heard "Ramona," he wondered. . . . "Yes and no," he said. "It's worse because it suddenly takes on such an irrevocable reality. And it's not as bad, because I absolutely do not believe in finality." Now he remembered where he had heard "Ramona." On top of the Haselburg, the Sunday after he got home. A girl had asked him something then too.

"That's wonderful!" she said.

He did not suspect this of being flattery, with "Ramona" rippling on. He could see it in her superb, shining eyes; they really were more beautiful than Riccarda's, he decided with a glance at his sister.

Riccarda saw, felt, and understood his look.

"You're going to New York?" she asked Gwen.

"Yes," Gwen replied. She, in turn, had caught the meaning of the question.

"When?" asked Riccarda in a curt, almost hostile tone.

"Today," said Gwen.

"Indeed?" said Andreas, who had not expected this.

"Yes," Gwen agreed.

"When does your train leave?" he asked.

"At eleven fifty-five tonight."

"Ramona" was finished.

"By the same train that we're——" Riccarda asked, and her words were so obviously unfriendly that she checked herself halfway.

Gwen answered: "By the same train that you're taking, I believe. You're going at eleven fifty-five, too, aren't you?"

To one at that table it was like music—not what the orchestra played to follow "Ramona," which was Grieg's "Solveig's Song," but what Gwen had just said.

Andreas thought: *That's wonderful of her!*

The old man cared nothing for any of it. He was wondering whether he could smoke his pipe here, and thinking it would be good sense to go home. Why, this American had not said a solitary word about the South Tirolean cause. You just wasted your time sitting here, and he still had things to do. It was almost two o'clock by his heavy silver watch.

The host offered around cigars and cigarettes to go with the black coffee.

"Well, you know," he said cheerfully, "we figured out that it might be nice to go with you a ways—that is, Gwen suggested it. We've got to be in Paris day after tomorrow, and at Le Havre the second of September; the *Isle de France* sails on the third of September."

"You were the one that suggested it, Daddy," Gwen corrected him, whereupon he said with a laugh:

"All right, then it was I. Don't you think Gwen looks much better, Herr Mumelter? We've got rid of the temperatures—definitely." His pink face beamed. Then, offering Andreas a light for his cigarette, he said almost inaudibly: "On the way I'll tell you various things that ought to please you."

With this everyone got up.

The old man, Riccarda, and Sepp went home. They declined with thanks the offer of a drive home, the few steps across the Waltherplatz, also said "thank you for all your kindness," and took their leave. Riccarda looked back twice at Andreas before she went. For Andreas stayed behind.

Mr. and Mrs. Hoffman likewise went to their room.

Before this Gwen had asked Andreas: "I'm sure you still have a lot to do?"

And he had replied: "No. Nothing at all. Have you?"

"Not a thing," she said.

So they stayed together.

First they sat for a while in the lobby, from which they were dislodged by an elderly lady who had also sat near them in the dining room. It was too hot to go for a walk. Should they take the car for a while? Then neither elderly ladies nor anyone else could eavesdrop on them.

As they got into the Buick, which bore on an oval plate the international number that had been assigned to it on debarkation at Le Havre, the elderly lady was standing in the roadway just behind the car, writing a post card.

"Are you getting in the shade of the Buick?" Andreas inquired testily.

"Yes," replied the lady. "Many thanks." She spoke in German, and went on writing.

When they started off, Gwen asked, "Was she taking our number?"

"Obviously," said Andreas. They drove out toward Sigmundskron.

"Are you feeling very sad?" Gwen asked.

He confessed it now: "Yes. Very." Although that wasn't the word; he was empty—utterly hollow.

"Did they treat you badly in prison?" she asked, only as a way of showing that she knew. She expected no answer, but told him how often her father had tried to do something, not only for him but for the whole South Tirolean matter. "You know," she said after a silence, "I think the worst of it is having to sit there with your hands tied and not be able to do anything about it. Don't you think so?"

They were passing Frau Fingeis' newsstand, where Andreas had bought three picture post cards weeks before; he had meant to tear them up then, but still had them. In giant type the Italian papers proclaimed: "Goebbels announces Hitler's conditions for solution of German minority problem in Danzig. Settlement favorable to interests of Danzig Germans virtually assured. Arthur Greiser's appointment as German governor of Danzig expected."

"You're right," said Andreas. "That's about the worst of it."

They drove along the highway in silence again for a while.

"Isn't the dust bad for you?" he asked.

"Oh no," she said. And then, slowly, "I'm very grateful to this country here. It's given me my health."

"Grand," he said. "Are you all recovered now?"

For a moment she smiled uncertainly. "I think so—yes, quite recovered," she said immediately.

Had he not understood what she meant?

Gwen was not accustomed to being direct. She did wish she could have said, "I meant something else before." But she did not say it.

She was unspeakably sorry for him. Since the last time she had seen him, she had been thinking about him a great deal. Hearing of his arrest, she had implored her father to do everything humanly possible; and when she learned in this way of his approaching departure, she had got him to come over today, and, by a special dispensation from the Italian Railway Ministry, requiring complicated official intervention, to get tickets for tonight's train. "Even if we can't help them any, Daddy, at least we ought to show them we know what it means to them," she had told her father. "You used to be an Austrian yourself!" And as he would never leave anything undone that Gwen wanted, he consented at once. He was far too happy over her cure, or what the Meran doctors called her cure. Besides, she was right—he had once been an Austrian himself, and he did cherish a fellow feeling for the South Tiroleans in general and Andreas in particular.

No, she did not take her hand off the wheel. Nor did she tell him that she admired the way he and his family were taking it. All she managed to force out was: "It's incredible how active your grandfather still is. Didn't you tell us he was almost ninety?"

"He's ninety-one," replied Andreas, matter of fact as always.

That's right, the Germans in Danzig! They're being protected! he thought savagely. *The world hears about them in great headlines! But how about us? Has there been a single word about us in the papers? Does it say that people of ninety-one are being hounded out?*

He was filled with such fury that he flung up both arms violently.

She looked at him, startled. Had she hurt him somehow?

"Let's go back!" he demanded, almost roughly. What was the use of going driving during these last hours with an American girl who would be on the high seas within five days, not giving a damn if a person's heart was breaking at having to go? By September 3 she would long since have forgotten that she had ever been here at all.

"Thank you for the lovely figure of the saint," she said softly. "I've carried it with me ever since. Excuse me for not thanking you before, but I thought I'd be seeing you today."

She took out of her handbag the silver figure of St. Genevieve that he had sent her on Wednesday.

"Oh, that doesn't make any difference," he said, meaning the belated thanks. "I hope it will bring you luck."

There was not much sincerity in his words, she felt.

"Perhaps we had better go back," she agreed, taking the next opportunity to turn around.

He never noticed at all.

His feelings today were shifting incessantly. If Vroni, the servant, had asked him now, he would have said, "No! We'll never be coming back, never!"

Despair gripped him as they drove toward the city in the hot sun—a feeling of utter forlornness, forsakenness, betrayal. No one in the whole wide world who would lift a finger for you!

Oh, of course they would invite you to dinner, or write letters, or do other things that cost a little money, practically no trouble, and no courage at all. The whole world was talking about the Germans in Danzig. About the Germans in Bozen, not a soul.

Hopeless, he felt, absolutely.

Gwen did not know what he was thinking; she could simply feel that the man beside her, his lower lip protruding beyond the upper lip, staring dismally into space, needed consolation—all the consolation in the world.

She felt it so overwhelmingly that she downed all her inhibitions. The blood raced away from her heart and back again as she put her hand on his and said tonelessly: "I'm here for you."

When she had caught her breath again, she added: "On the train Daddy'll give you some news I don't know about. All I know is that he was very optimistic when he heard." She wanted to add: "Daddy isn't usually an optimist." But this lie was more than she could manage. Her hand still touched his hand.

From the depth of his despair he looked at her absently. Not until afterward was he to realize what this strange girl had achieved in putting her hand on his.

"I don't believe there's much that can be done by now," he replied to her last words, not to the first. Then, seeing how her expression changed as she snatched her hand away, he replied to the first as well: "Anyway, I'm infinitely grateful to you."

"You don't believe what I just said?" she asked, and once more she did her absolute utmost for him by fighting down her restraint. Without looking at him she repeated: "I'm really here for you. Please believe me. And please believe that I can imagine very well what you're going through now."

She kept her eye on the heavily laden apple cart that she had to overtake.

"Thank you," he said. "That's wonderful of you!"

She could feel more sincerity in his words now, but she did not give so much as a glance to make sure.

She said: "I know I can't do much of anything for you. Nothing at all, really. But I wouldn't like you to feel deserted altogether." She had overtaken the apple cart.

What she's just been saying isn't flattery, nor empty chatter either, he admitted to himself. *It's what everyone in the world ought to be telling us, writing about us, and shouting to others. Even so, better one than none.*

He was not quite so angry any more. Nor quite so desperate.

"Yes. It is wonderful of you!" he said.

Only she alone knew what she was suffering now.

She was prepared for him to approach her, to touch her. She wished it with all the restrained fire of her thwarted body; at the same time, with the full horror of her conscious mind, she dreaded it.

But he did not touch her. Instead he said for the second time, and this time there was utter sincerity in his words: "I'm very, very grateful to you, Miss Gwen."

From that moment on she began to love him passionately, and the interest she had always taken in him, the deep pity she had felt for him, were flamingly transformed into something greater. She repeated also: "I'm here for you." Remembering that she would be on the high seas within five days, she went on: "No matter where I am. Do you believe me?"

"Yes," he replied.

She drove him to his house, which he showed her from outside; then they said good-by for the present.

It was four fifty-five.

As he went up the steps, Riccarda ran down them and past him without a word. Below she saw the American car driving away, and the driver turning to look back at the house. This, too, made the errand she was going on all the more bitter. She was going to meet the man whose child she was carrying; she had admonished him to be on time, which ordinarily he was not. For she had only half an hour to give to him, since by half past five at latest she must be home to get supper, which was eaten at seven sharp in the Mumelter household.

She knew she could expect nothing, and when she saw Roberto coming down the Helenenstrasse—late, even on this last day—her heart bounded with rage and love. She still loved him; even now she would give herself up to him at any moment, without reflection. And it redoubled her fury to think that she lost this power of reflection the moment he laid his eyes on her.

"Forgive me!" he said. Those were his first words at every meeting, and he said them even today.

"You aren't in any hurry?" she asked. She vowed to herself that today she would tell him nothing but the hard, unmitigated truth.

"Well, you see, I——" He began one of his hundred ready-made excuses, but she interrupted him.

"All right, Roberto. We'll say *addio* now. For today or for always—what do you say?" She was not going to make it easy for him, the beloved rogue, she thought; she would spare him none of the bitterness that filled her heart—this worthless, beguiling Roberto who had no more conscience than a schoolboy.

"Look, Riccarda," he said in his soft, sensual voice, trying to take her arm.

She resisted this and the voice and her love.

"You didn't answer my letter," she said. "That was why I wanted to talk to you. Just because of that. You aren't going with us?"

"Look, sweetheart," he began again, and again she interrupted him.

"No, of course you aren't going. Why should you sacrifice your comfort?"

"Riccarda, I'm ready to marry you the day I come of age, and I'll stick to it," he replied grandly.

"But I'm not, Roberto," she said, looking him straight in the eye, so as not to miss the gleam of relief there.

But she saw nothing of the sort, though she wished she might, because it would make everything much more bitter, and yet easier.

Instead he asked: "You're angry with me, then?" She gave him a long look that took him all in. This was how she would see him always. Half sly, half naïve. Half childlike, half cruel. And irresistibly attractive.

"No, I'm not angry with you," she said. "I simply see you as you are. You were the best thing I ever had in my life—which isn't saying much, for you or me either. I wasn't mistaken in you, Roberto. Perhaps I overrated you a little. But so did you me. I don't love you. We're quits."

He had come prepared for anything—anything but this. His face betrayed it.

"No," she retorted to the expression of astonished innocence that he could sometimes put on, and that she loved in him, "I'm not reproaching you. You didn't lead me astray—ridiculous; we aren't children. And our going suits you very nicely. Now please don't put on an act for me. The idea of having to marry me horrified you —all right, I'm not reproaching you; everyone is the way he is, and I might have seen long before this what you're like——"

"What am I like?" he flared up.

"Egotistical," she said. "A great egotist—but so are all of us, more or less, including me. There's no sense in arguing about it, and besides I only have fifteen minutes left."

As she said this, her bitterness gained the upper hand, and neither his look of innocence nor the appeal of his velvet eyes had any power over her.

"Listen to me," she said. "I'm not asking anything of you. Just one thing. When the child is born—because I'm going to have it—you're to adopt it. I don't want it to grow up anywhere but here. You're going to come and get it, you're going to take it, and you're going to see that it is well cared for. Will you promise me that?"

"Why, of course," he said casually, and now those velvet eyes showed the relief that she had expected before, which made matters easier for her.

"Oh no, Roberto," she contradicted. "I'm not going to make it as easy as that for you. You're going to give me a different kind of promise. We've still got twelve minutes. Come in here with me."

He followed, unresisting, into the Sacred Heart Church, which they had just reached.

She knelt down with him before the little altar to St. Anthony, which was lighted by a few candles. In the candlelight she could see his face clearly—what was hidden there, and what lay open.

"Promise," she said. "Say it after me."

This he did. He repeated after her a vow to care for his child that she was carrying. "So help me God!" she finished, and he repeated: "So help me God!"

Those were their nuptials.

"Thank you," she said as they went out. The church clock pointed to seven minutes before half past five.

She might have spent those seven minutes with him, but when she looked at him in the clear late-afternoon light, a little subdued by what had just happened, a little hurt at having been somehow taken by surprise, she dropped the idea.

"Well," she said. "Good-by. I've got to be going."

"Why such a hurry?" he asked.

"I've still got things to do," she said, holding out her hand.

"I'll come to the train," he offered.

"No, you won't," she declined. "You like to be in bed by one, and anyway this is no occasion to go with somebody to the train. Either one goes with them all the way, Roberto, or one stays where he is. Forgive me. I'll send you my address. You might kiss me, or are you ashamed in front of all the people?"

They kissed each other in the shadow of the church. For a moment she felt the wild, unbearable anguish of futility as she lay in his arms, trying to squeeze a lifetime into a kiss. Then she pulled free and left him. Five minutes too soon.

It was five twenty-five, and a few moments later old Mumelter came out of the house in the Silbergasse. He had been waiting for the moment when the sun reached the western slope of the Rosengarten, conjuring up the Alpine sunset that made the evenings here such fairy spectacles; at the same time it lost its burning intensity, which was what the old man had been waiting for. It was his second walk around town that day, but this evening journey did not take him so far as that of the morning. A person seeing the old man now, dressed for departure in his green Loden suit, would hardly have known what to think of the way he was walking. For old Mumelter was moving very, very close to the walls of the houses, which could hardly be on account of the sun, since it was setting. He also seemed to be touching the walls with his right hand as he passed them, feeling them or clutching them as if to press them or hold himself up. He was not doing either. This was the old man's farewell to certain houses. He was taking his leave, clasping hands with the stones along with which he had grown old.

First came the Silbergasse, where he was born. Here he brushed house after house with his right hand—number 1, where Platter, the veterinary, lived; number 3, which had belonged to the Winigers for twenty generations; number 5, where the Leiterpergers, related by marriage to the Mumelters, had dwelt since 1714; number 7 was his own; number 9 had been built by the Johanneser family in 1664; across the way, from number 2 to number 12, the Hohenprunn, Wollinger, Gemaassmer, Lechner, Campi, and Web families had lived as long or longer.

Then, still keeping close to the wall, and brushing or stroking it, he walked around the school building (which stood free of other structures), where he had learned to read and write; and he paused for a while before the shop of Stauff Brothers, Fruiterers, meanwhile three times renovated and imposingly enlarged, where he had met Anna, who became his wife and died at twenty, after the birth of his only son; she died in 1877, and he could remember as if it were today how he met her here for the first time. She was standing in there to the left, where the cashier's desk was now; she was nineteen, and he was twenty-seven. Her maiden name was Anna Wegleithner; she was the most beautiful girl he ever knew, and, during the year and a half that the Lord left her to him, the best wife in the world. Here he stood on the threshold, seeing and hearing himself say what he had said to her sixty-four years before, when old Stauff weighed out for her the nuts, pears, and candied quinces that she had bought: "But that's much too heavy for you, Fräulein!" This was how they had become acquainted. His right hand brushed the doorframe of the fruiterer's, and he hurried away on his evening journey of farewell to his memories. Here, in the chapel of the Franciscan Monastery, they were married; here, in the parish church, his son was baptized Thomas Paul Mathias; here, in the parish church, the last blessings had been said over Anna—the baptism one day, the burial the next. Now he brushed the wall of the Mercantile Building, where they elected him vice-president of the Board of Trade in 1888. And he touched the brown oak door of the former district command, which had since become the sub-prefecture, even going up the few steps to the door for the purpose. For here, in 1898, the district captain, Count Coloredo-Mannsfeld, had pinned to his breast the Imperial and Royal Silver Cross of Merit with the Crown, which he was taking with him into banishment.

Of people he took no leave. He was bidding good-by to the summits and the depths of his life. Now he had only to shake hands with Walther von der Vogelweide's monument, pass close by the Schgraffer, Mondschein, and Greif inns, lean over the bridge for a moment at the point where the Talfer and the Eisack met, watching and listening to the clear green water for a while, and then—it was striking quarter past six—to go back to the Silbergasse. Returning, he chose the opposite sides of the streets, saying his farewells there, too, with an occasional touch.

During his three quarters of an hour's walk he had spoken to no one; now, entering the old house from the front for the last time, as he well knew, he was dizzy for a moment, and had to cling to the copper knocker to keep his balance, but he soon recovered himself. He managed to walk erect through the gate and the entrance hall, and went directly out of the back door into the garden. Here Veronika, the servant, who was cleaning lettuce at the kitchen window upstairs, saw him doing strange things. He was going from tree to tree. Beginning with the one old pear that grew in the middle of the garden, and was heavy with fruit this year just as the apples were, he stopped by every trunk, reached high up with his right hand, then ran it slowly down the bark almost to the ground. At first the old servant thought he was picking fruit, which surprised her, because nothing was ripe yet. Then she thought he was looking for the beetles that infested the trees some summers, but not this summer; at length, completely baffled, she called Riccarda to show her these puzzling gestures.

They were no puzzle to Riccarda. She saw her grandfather touching and stroking the trunks that he himself or his father had planted, transforming the stone courtyard into a tiny green garden. She knew how he had loved those trees, how intimately he knew each one, how proud he was of their yield, what a delight the fruit was to him, what a worry the frost, and how much the seven trees had meant. From their turning green and blossoming early in April until the fall of the leaves late in October he had observed them long and carefully every day. It was perfectly obvious what he was doing now, and Riccarda had to turn away hastily to tell the maid: "Just let him be, Vroni. And now please give me the lettuce."

Down below, the old man was still going from tree to tree. The longer he went on, the harder it was for him to reach up so high. When he had stroked the last trunk, he sat down on the bench and looked around him. This also his granddaughter saw—saw him giving a long look at everything in the garden and hastily passing a hand over his eyes.

At this she called out: "Grandfather! We're going to eat in a minute!"

"Right!" he replied at once, got up, and came into the house from the garden side, this, too, for the last time. He hurried, for he had never been late to a meal.

They were soon sitting at supper in the dining room—the old man, Andreas, Riccarda, and Sepp (who was prompt today). Each took his accustomed place, the old man sitting where his father before him, his grandfather before him, and his great-grandfather before him had sat, the seat that he himself had occupied for more than sixty years. Before that he had sat for twenty-six years where Sepp was sitting now, for he was barely five when he was first allowed to eat with the grownups. The seat on his right was vacant; for a year and a half his wife had sat there, and after that no one, for her place in the household and in the old man's heart remained forever unfilled. On his left sat Riccarda, where his mother and later his daughter-in-law had sat. Next to her was Andreas, occupying his own father's place.

Veronika, the servant, served as she always had, and as always the meal began with grace by the old man. As always the parish church clock struck seven while he was saying it. Not even the silence prevailing during supper distinguished this from countless other meals at the same table. "Meals are for eating, not for talking," the old man used to say, and he had not changed his mind today. Whether he was hungry no one knew. But he ate as he had always eaten, two corners of his napkin tucked into his collar, slowly, carefully, some of everything. He helped himself to the soup, to the boiled beef and vegetables, and finally to the fresh apricot compote. He did not look at anyone as he ate. Once, in serving him the salad bowl, Veronika could not help sobbing. At this he spoke his only words: "Stupid goose!"

This time it was Andreas who thought of a condemned man's last meal. In his eyes this noon had been more bearable. The food stuck in his throat; the clocks ticked like hammers. *Isn't it preposterous,* he told himself, struggling for composure, *that we're sitting here eating and drinking as if nothing had happened or was going to happen! Isn't it insane for human beings to go on eating and drinking immediately before death? We're five hours from death.*

It's a good thing people have this, Riccarda thought. *It's a good thing they can fool themselves with cooking, setting the table, eating, and drinking. If they couldn't, they'd go mad.*

Black coffee appeared on the table, and sugar and cream, as always. And as always the old man lit the china pipe with the half-length pictures of Emperor Francis Joseph and Crown Prince Rudolph, and said, as he had said on getting up from that seat for more than sixty years, "*Gesegnete Mahlzeit!*"

From some corner to which old Vroni had crawled away came a stifled sobbing in reply.

With this the meal was over, and everyone went into the next room, where the old man's stiff, high armchair stood between the windows.

The rooms looked different from what they had. Not simply because the furniture was covered with gray slip covers, or because the curtains were gone from the windows, the pictures from the walls, and the china and the hundred knickknacks from the glass cabinets and the tables. Even if everything had been unchanged, the rooms would still have looked entirely different. Even their proportions had changed; they were lower, smaller, Riccarda thought. *They have parted from us—even these inanimate objects!* she thought, exasperated. *Even lifeless things are giving us notice!*

Everything was different, particularly the ticking of the clocks. They raced; they flew. A moment ago it had been seven, now it was half past, and in another second it was eight.

The Alpine sunset, incomparably perfect that evening, was long since over, and the sky had faded from deep blue to blue-gray. The crescent moon, a slender white sickle, appeared above the Schlern; the first stars followed, without brightness as yet.

The family sat in a bare room that grew less familiar with every flying moment, looking out at a landscape that grew progressively darker and retreated into the night—a landscape that had always been lovely. Now it became awful and threatening. They sat mutely, listening to time flash past, and saw their shadows grow, and they were totally strange in their own house. The baggage was inspected and locked; they were waiting for it to be fetched. Darkness fell outside; they sat and waited to be fetched themselves, and ventured to think, *If only the time would come!* This waiting and the implacably ticking and striking clocks were worse than dying.

It struck nine; half past; ten.

They sat and waited. They got up and saw to this and that which they believed they had forgotten, but had not. The familiar objects stared at them more and more strangely. Nothing belonged to you any more, nothing obeyed you. And gradually you were overpowered by a boundless weariness that asked only to sleep and know nothing, nothing at all.

Thus the Mumelter family waited for deportation.

But so, too, at this time of night on the twenty-ninth of August, three hundred and seventeen other Bozners were awaiting it. And they had spent the day in much the same way, with last meals and farewells and racing clocks.

And in the same way thousands of other South Tirolean families would endure their last days at home, tomorrow, and the day after, and who could say for how long?

Isn't it mad, Andreas thought, *what human nature can endure? Let's cross out the word unendurable from the dictionary once and for all. If a person can endure this, he can endure anything.*

A cloud of anguish shrouded Bozen now, and for all those who looked beseechingly heavenward the stars, now shining superbly, had lost their radiance. They were simply cold. And meaningless.

The monstrous meaninglessness of all this, barring every retreat, was almost the worst part.

None of those affected could see any meaning in what was being done to them; they all felt that there was none.

Time flew. Then suddenly it stopped.

The hour when the green school busses were to drive up and fetch the baggage and its owners lasted an eternity.

But old Mumelter never let himself go for a second; he saw by his silver watch that they would be called for at any moment now. Living with full consciousness through that which was taking place, he underwent the operation without the narcosis of fatigue or the anesthetic of false hope. He knew he would never come back here. And he knew he had been robbed of the fulfillment of his existence, robbed at the last moment by an act of madness. Now—for the time was at hand—he put on his Loden cape and green hat and said to the others: "Come, children. Better get ready."

And in fact one heard the clatter of the busses in the silent town, grown strange and hostile now.

Was there no one to help and save them at the last moment?

No one.

As time went on the busses stopped before many houses in Bozen. There were only five available, which had to keep going to the station and back to town. This delayed the process.

It was two minutes before eleven. The green bus stopped at the door of number 7, Silbergasse.

Without a backward look the aged man and his granddaughter got in. Andreas looked back. So did Sepp. Riccarda, never removing her eyes from the old man, had tried to take his arm and hold him up, as if casually, when they went out of the front door. But he said, "Never mind that!"

Veronika reached a hand thin with old age and icy with emotion into the bus, which already seated twelve other people. They neither offered any salutation nor seemed to have eyes for the newcomers; all had the same fixed, stony look.

"Have a good trip now!" she said, as was proper and fitting when the family was going on a journey and the servants were staying behind to keep the house.

"Good-by to you, Vroni," the old man replied. His voice was perfectly audible.

Whatever the grandchildren said was drowned by the noise of the self-starter. The school bus drove off.

Anyone who chose could look out of the window and see the Waltherplatz once more in the moonlight. But no one did. The sixteen passengers stared at the floor. There was not a sound—only the motor.

Now the sixteen of us in the school bus at least know why we went to school here! Andreas could not help thinking, and once again he was filled with a monstrous anger.

Riccarda, next to him, looked anxiously at the old man. He, however, was sitting erect beside his youngest grandchild, holding in his lap with both hands a worn black leather bag that he had taken to Innsbruck and Vienna in 1898; he had not been on a journey since.

Of the sixteen, nine had never been on a journey at all. These were the wine growers Landegger, Schwerth, and Zantner, with their wives and children. Like old Mumelter, each of them tensely clutched a bag or basket on his knees.

Where is the Saviour? thought Andreas. *Who's carrying Him ahead of us as they did on that colored post card that Frau Fingeis sold me outside the Virgl Station?*

Somebody should, he felt. The silvery outline of the moonlit Walther monument gleamed through the windows now. *Who will carry the Saviour before us?* Andreas thought.

Riccarda whispered to him.

"What?" he asked.

"Keep an eye on Grandfather!" she said softly. "He's so dreadfully pale!"

But the old man's hearing was infallible. "Don't talk nonsense," he corrected his granddaughter. "It's only the moonlight! Do you think I'd give them the satisfaction of looking different from what I ever do?"

This was his longest speech in days.

They stopped at the station. They got out.

No one except those who were leaving might enter the building.

All entrances were under double guard, and before each individual passed the main entrance he had to identify himself with the receipt for the fare he had paid. Directly beyond the main entrance a double line of carabinièri were drawn up the whole length of the station lobby and out on the platform; the travelers had to pass between the two uniformed and armed lines. Their baggage had been taken from them and loaded on hand trucks that reached the platform from the baggage room.

They went singly, one after another, down the armed lines.

The platform was scantily lit on purpose; a train stood waiting on Track 2, where Andreas had come in a month and a half before. It was what the authorities called a "sealed" train, one whose car doors are locked for the duration of the journey; unauthorized leaving or entering of the train is punishable with instant death.

It consisted of a locomotive, two baggage cars, and nine coaches. None of these coaches, eight third-class and one first-class, bore the customary sheet-metal tags announcing their destination. Instead there were the chalked words: "Via Brennero."

All the platforms, even those on the opposite, incoming side, were constantly patrolled by carabinièri with fixed bayonets.

An official from the prefecture was calling out a long list of those being entrained. They were expected to answer *"Ecco!"* and board the train at once.

"Landegger, Alois!"

"Ecco!"

"Landegger, Ludovica!"

"Ecco!"

"Schwerth, Andreas!"

"Ecco!"

"Schwerth, Maria!"

"Ecco!"

"Schwerth, Margareta!"

"Ecco!"

"Mumelter, Laurenz!"

"Hier!" said the aged man in German, and the official, reading and calling off mechanically, looked up from his list for an instant, wondering whether to insist on the Italian answer. Then he dropped the

idea, and the old man climbed the three steps, much too high, to the third-class coach that was indicated to him.

"Mumelter, Riccarda!"

"Ecco!" she replied hurriedly, for she was horrified to see the old man, clutching his black bag, make a misstep in the dim light and grab at space. In a flash she was after him, holding him up and getting aboard with him.

Some twenty or more people were already seated in the car, one of the so-called open type, in which the wooden benches are placed on both sides, with a single passageway down the middle. Two lights were burning. A carabinière made sure that each person should sit in the seat assigned to him.

The Mumelters had numbers 27, 28, 29, and 30, which occupied a whole bench facing forward. Opposite them sat the four members of the Tolloy family.

"I didn't know that Nazis were undesirable to the prefect too," said the old man to his granddaughter as he sat down, stiffly upright, on the hard bench, facing his former colleague in the council, and never letting go for a second of the black leather bag in which were his money and the photographs of his wife and his ancestors.

The rhythmic footsteps of the patrols echoed from outside.

No one might look out of the window; the curtains were drawn, and their removal was forbidden. "No windows are to be opened. Curtains must remain closed," a printed notice over every window warned in Italian and German.

Nor might anyone be accompanied by a person who was not leaving.

Nevertheless, someone was there who was not leaving.

How she had managed to get here was her secret, or rather that of the handsome young officer of *Bersaglieri* with whom she was now taking occasional rides on the cable railway and elsewhere. At any rate, Elena was here, with a bunch of edelweiss in her hand. She even managed to give it to Andreas as he started to get aboard.

"Have a good trip," she said breathlessly, pretending she belonged with the family.

"Thank you," he said.

At that instant she heard someone calling from the running board of the first-class coach: "Good evening, Mr. Mumelter!"

"Quiet!" a voice ordered.

In the dim light of the one arc lamp burning on Track 2 Elena saw a young lady she did not know.

And in spite of the inadequate lighting she could see also that Andreas' set face came to life.

Now she wished she could have asked for the bunch of edelweiss back, and plucked it apart one flower at a time.

But Andreas was already aboard, and the military voice shouting "Quiet!" had scared Gwen away.

The waiting train stood gray on the platform. The locomotive had not yet got up steam, since not everyone had yet been fetched and entrained. Whether from exhaustion or apathy, complete silence reigned in the gray train. Those already present were sitting rigidly in their seats, and those who came to join them were wooden and unseeing as they occupied their own.

Occasionally one heard an order, a curt greeting, a question—nothing more. And the names called out, and the answer *"Ecco!"* and the tread of the patrols. "It may last another hour. Or possibly two," someone said, and the word spread.

"Where's Sepp?" asked the old man. "Is he going to be late even today?" But Sepp was aboard long since. It was so dark in the car that you scarcely saw him.

Four minutes before midnight.

Suddenly, as if cut off with a knife, the shouted names and the echoing footsteps ceased; steam began to hiss from the locomotive, and a jerk ran through the gray, deathly still train.

The silence was past bearing. *One second more and they'll be crying,* thought Andreas, who had heard the crying at night so often.

At this he got up from the wooden bench between his sister and brother and began to sing.

What he sang was the old "Andreas Hofer-Lied," and the first two lines he sang alone; at the third his grandfather and a few others joined in, and when he started the second stanza everyone in the car was singing. By the third stanza the whole train was singing. It spread from car to car, swelled, grew into a single, mighty, roaring voice. They all got up from their seats and sang:

"At Mantua in shackles our faithful Hofer lay;
In Mantua the foeman's host led him to death that day.

His brother warriors' hearts they bled;
The Germans wept to see him dead,
So too our Tirol's land.

His hands bound fast behind his back, Andreas Hofer strode
With steady steps; he scorned the death that lay upon his road,
The death that he full oft had sped
From Iselberg, a champion dread
In Tirol's hallowed land.

But when from Mantua's dungeon he saw his faithful men
Reaching their shackled hands to him in one last greeting: then
He cried to them, 'The Lord God be
With you and fallen Germany!
Farewell, my Tirol land!' "

"Farewell, my Tirol land!" sang the whole gray train, which now began to move very slowly. They went out standing, for they were singing their own proud, sacred song. The windows were closed. It was almost dark. With heads held high, singing, they went out of their native city.

Gwen, in the first-class car, heard the song. She did not understand all the words, but she understood the meaning, and her father, repeating it word by word, explained it to her. He told her how a hundred and thirty years ago Andreas Hofer and his South Tirolean peasants, with scythes and sickles and flails as weapons, had freed the Tirol from Napoleon's Bavarian troops, for which Napoleon had him shot at Mantua. But the Tirol had remained free ever since.

"The Lord God be with you and fallen Germany! Farewell, my Tirol land!" sang the gray, rolling train.

On the platform that it had just left stood two people who had forced their way in, and who now followed with their eyes a cloud of smoke growing ever smaller and more distant. One was a girl of sixteen; she had given away a bunch of edelweiss and wished she could get it back. The other was Pastor Gemaassmer. It was only when the train started to move that his earnest entreaties had been granted, and he had been allowed to say good-by to those who were going. If they had been permitted to look out of the windows, they could have seen him making a great sign of the cross again and again with arm raised high, and sending it after them in benediction.

The singing did not stop. When the last stanza was finished, they began with the first.

Shutting her eyes and humming the melody that mingled so fiercely with the pounding of the wheels, Gwen could not help thinking: *They have no scythes or sickles. But they have a song. The song isn't a weapon—but neither were the scythes and sickles. And still they won!*

They were going through the first hour of banishment singing. The carabinièri on the train did not interfere.

It was not a weeping train. Andreas had won his first victory.

Chapter 9

BY THE TIME they stopped singing they had used up all their strength, and were so tired that they fell asleep almost at once. Heads sank on chests, fingers clutched the things that they counted most precious, and in their dreams they held fast what they had just left. The singing train had become a sleeping train where the sleep of exhaustion and despair was being slept, and even this was a kindly beginning for the sleepers: they dreamed themselves back into the life they were leaving. Occasionally one of them awoke and started up with frightened eyes, closed them again at once, and fled back into his dream. Those who could not manage to sleep again would sit there, trying to grasp it. But as long as it was night, the unendurable still had a bare hint of the endurable even for those who were awake. Everything seemed more unreal, remote, veiled. Their exhaustion and the gentle, steady shake of the rolling train were like a narcotic. Those who could sleep were dreaming of what had been; those who were awake did not take full account of what was to come.

But the nights were still short. The sigh that went through the train when dawn broke and the outlines of the landscape began to appear through the thin brownish curtains did not come, as one might have supposed, from the locomotive. It was so steady and rhythmic, beginning and recurring so regularly, that it might have been groaning wheels encountering some sudden obstacle. But actually it was groaning people, meeting the obstacles with dreadful suddenness the moment the fog of night and sleep cleared from their heads; the naked knife edge of reality cut deep into their consciousness. With almost all of the three hundred and twenty-one who now awoke or let go of their last self-deception the first automatic thought, "Where am I?" was followed by the more alarming one, "Where am I going?"

Odd though it seems, until the present moment this second question had not been uppermost in their minds. The question whether and the fact that they must leave had crowded out any other consideration. But now that this was finally decided, what had previously been pushed aside came imperiously to the fore. Where were they going?

The older people asked this question as something that would affect their destiny but little. The younger ones were expectant. If they were like Sepp, who was still asleep and would scarcely wake up until he was hungry for breakfast, they even had some hopes of advantage; if they were like Riccarda, they simply wanted to know; if they were like Andreas, the answer would settle their lives: if they were going to North Tirol, it might perhaps be bearable; if not, a struggle would and must begin, the like of which had never been seen.

Where were they now?

Those who had remained sleepless were aware that the train had not stopped yet, and all three hundred and twenty-one knew their own country. Even through the thin brownish curtains with the woven FI, the mark of the Italian Railways, by daylight you could see fairly well where you were. The station they had just left was Brixen, now called Bressanone, and the proud castle whose blurred outline appeared on the right was the palace of the Brixen prince bishops. And that yonder, towering above all else, must be the old Austrian fortress of Franzensfeste, which had been rechristened by the Italian name of Fortezza. They were still in South Tirol; for some mysterious reason the journey was taking an endless time. The sealed train was traveling almost more slowly than the freights, perhaps because it was itself a sort of freight with a load too heavy for man to bear.

Daybreak was greeted in car 5, where the Mumelters were, just as it was in all the other cars, whose doors were guarded by carabinièri; six of these accompanied each car, and against unarmed and exhausted people this was no small force. But the nearer daylight came, the more swiftly they shook off their exhaustion, and when they had said their paternosters, loudly or softly, their tongues were loosened.

"Good morning," they said to one another, and the miracle that had taken place the Wednesday before in the fruit market at Bozen still continued. Frau von Fennperg, a lady proud of her nobility, asked the former proprietress of the stationery store in the Jesuitengasse: "How did you sleep, Frau Entleuthner?" and three seats away from the Mumelters Hoermann, the cemetery superintendent, offered young Baroness Dipauli a drink of coffee from his thermos bottle, which the girl consumed with relish, and which, furthermore, gave her a hankering for some of the loaf she saw in Riccarda's hand, a so-called *Striezel,* baked of white flour and raisins, the old man's favorite breakfast. He took with a nod the thick slice that his granddaughter handed him, spread his handkerchief on his knees, and, raising the tin vessel of steaming milk coffee to his lips, started his first meal away from home.

But they were still in South Tirol, and the sense of being abroad scarcely asserted itself as yet. They reached Grasstein, and Sprechenstein would be coming into view on the left, Reifenstein on the right; old Mumelter, his grandchildren, and most of the others in car 5 had come here often for the Sterzing autumn fair, which by rights should begin in a fortnight. If they had wanted to fool themselves they could have imagined that they were on the usual expedition to Sterzing fair to buy good things, particularly the tools that were needed for growing apples and plums and grapes.

Haltingly, with long intervals and no real interest, the people in car 5 began a conversation. Everyone talked to everyone else; of the thirty-eight people in the car, thirty-eight wondered, "Where are we going?"

As yet there was no sign or indication; the carabinière whom Sepp finally screwed up courage to ask said, *"Non so."*

Hereupon Hoermann, the cemetery superintendent, who, like old Mumelter, was sitting in the midst of his family, said: "Do you think they'll leave us together?"

The question was directed at the old man, who was sitting three seats away, for which reason, in order to be heard above the noise of the train, Hoermann spoke quite loudly. Almost everyone heard him, and heard old Mumelter reply: "What are you bellowing for, Hoermann? Do you think I'm deaf?"

He said this simply to keep from admitting how deeply the unexpected question had struck home.

Yet the superintendent had meant only to ask whether the three hundred and twenty-one would stay together.

The old man, however, was asking himself whether the families would stay together, which was something that neither he nor anyone else had yet thought of.

Had the sun still not risen? Or was it clouds or only the curtains that made the light so dim?

Answers came from every corner of the car.

"Of course we'll stay together!"

"What gave you that idea, Hoermann?"

"Why shouldn't they leave us together? They want to settle us just the way we've always lived."

Andreas asked: "Who?"

The further the night retreated, the more clearly the travelers saw this second question.

Tolloy, the former apothecary, one of the twenty-four, who was sitting on the bench facing the Mumelter family, answered it: "The Reich, of course."

"Of course," Andreas agreed. "And because it is the Reich, there's probably no hope of special consideration."

"What do you mean by that, Herr Mumelter junior?" inquired the apothecary. It was noticeable how much more vigorous and decided his behavior was today; in the council he had, after all, spoken on behalf of Gauleiter Udacher in a far more modest and diffident tone.

"I mean we shouldn't have any illusions," replied Andreas, who did not want to quarrel. And he, too, saw the question that the old man was pondering loom ominously before him: Suppose they tore families apart?

They were drawing nearer and nearer to the frontier.

After Sterzing came Gossensass or Colle Isarco, then Giggelberg or Moncucco, where the Pfersch valley begins, and then, following the course of the Eisack, whose clear waters foamed along below the railway, they would reach the frontier station of Brenner, now called Brennero.

They had been nine full hours covering the comparatively short distance from Bozen to Sterzing, for it was after nine when they left Sterzing Station.

They were still in South Tirol.

That they would be there for only an hour more, slowly though they might move, everyone realized. Even Sepp, looking at his wrist watch, said: "We'll be in Brennero soon."

"In Brenner, you mean!" objected his grandfather, and Andreas could not help thinking: *As long as we still say Brennero, at least it isn't the Nazis!*

But he only thought this, he did not say it.

Gwen, on the contrary, in the sealed first-class car, could scarcely wait to get to the frontier, because—at least so the carabinière had told Mr. Hoffman—you could get out there, walk up and down the platform, and see the people in the other cars. Her expectation of being able to spend the whole journey as far as Innsbruck with the Mumelter family had proved mistaken, since no one was allowed to stir out of his own car.

"What's the idea of shutting everything off this way, anyhow?" Mr. Hoffman had asked the carabinière, ignoring beseeching looks from his wife, who was trying to restrain him from making ill-advised remarks. "Do they want to keep people from throwing themselves out of the doors and windows?"

The carabinière had given him the usual answer: *"Non so."*

Be that as it might, it was scarcely two hours from the frontier to Innsbruck, where the Hoffmans would change for the Paris express. This, Gwen reflected, meant that she had two, at most possibly three hours left in which to tell Andreas all she had to tell him, all she was going to tell him even if she died of it. During the sleepless night she had fought with herself to decide whether she should, and finally had made up her mind. After those two or three hours, she knew, there would be no more chance, not for a long, long time. For they were getting to Paris tomorrow afternoon, embarking on the *Isle de France* at Le Havre and three days later, not even a week later they would be in New York. It would be at least three fourths of a year before she saw him again—for see him again she would; that was what she meant to tell him, and what she had been inwardly fighting for. At best she could not induce Daddy to send her back to Meran before spring, if she could convince him at all that she absolutely required it. Possibly she would also tell Andreas something else, which as yet she could not clothe in words or in thoughts either. If only they were at the frontier!

If only they weren't at the frontier! the emigrants thought. They were still in South Tirol.

But now, although it was a cloudy day and there was no sun outside the brownish curtains, the station sign of "Brennero" moved toward the slow train; one could make it out from afar after passing the curve that directly follows the Brenner Tunnel. They rolled very slowly into the frontier station.

"No one is to get off!" came shouts in German and Italian.

The train was still moving as Storm Troopers and S.S. men swung on to the running boards and were admitted to the cars by the carabinièri.

Then the locomotive whistled piercingly, and the train went clear through the station and stopped outside, next to the coal bunkers.

One heard the carabinièri laughing and talking with their German successors, and a moment later they got off. The train was now in German hands.

This stop was endless. The German detail that had relieved the Italians, six Storm Troopers and three S.S. men in each car, kept silent. They greeted the emigrants with a curt "*Heil* Hitler! Welcome to the German homeland!" After that their answers to questions were monosyllabic, evasive, or non-existent. Passports and baggage were not inspected.

Only in the first-class car was there an inspection. It was for the Hoffman family.

It began as a passport and customs examination; no one would have suspected anything further.

After the three passports had been examined and the baggage thoroughly searched without revealing anything contraband, however, the S.S. officer who accompanied the passport and customs officials, and who so far had acted quite uninterested, asked: "You are a German citizen, Herr Hoffman?"

"Really I'm an American, and it's only technically——" the latter started to explain, but the officer interrupted him.

"I'm not asking what you really are, but what you actually are, Herr Hoffman. According to your passport you're a German."

"If you know, why do you ask?" retorted the former Austrian, and Mrs. Hoffman made warning signs.

"You'll have to let me decide how I do my duty," observed the black-uniformed officer, avoiding the slightest hint that he knew every detail of the Hoffman case.

"My wife and daughter are Americans," persisted the other.

"No one disputes that," the officer agreed. And then he said no more except: "Thank you," and sat down in one corner of the compartment.

"Our passports!" Hoffman said to him.

"I'll keep them for the time being."

"What? We're taking the boat in a few days."

"That will be decided at Innsbruck."

"How's that?" Hoffman flared up.

He was told: "I shall turn you over at Innsbruck to the Secret State Police, who will decide on all further steps."

"Man, are you crazy?" cried Hoffman, quite beside himself. "You can't treat American citizens the way you do people of your own sort!"

"Herr Hoffman," observed the other, "in the first place you forget that you are a German. And in the second place we treat American citizens who oppose the German Reich exactly as we treat our own. It is quite useless for you to argue with me about it. In not more than two hours at most you will have an opportunity to tell your story to the competent authority."

"My competent authority is the American consul! And you can depend on it, sir, that I shall tell him what liberties you have taken!"

"Of course you are at perfect liberty to do so," replied the S.S. officer, taking the *Voelkischer Beobachter* out of his overcoat pocket and starting to read. The three passports he put into his breast pocket.

Gwen had watched all this with divided feelings. At first, with her innate aversion to police manners, she had been outraged by the intervention of the Nazi. But then, suddenly, she could not help thinking: *Perhaps we shan't be leaving so soon after all.*

The longer she sat facing the intent reader in the corner, the more completely this question occupied her mind—and, to tell the truth, the more temptingly. With a sense of humor inherited from her father, she confessed to herself: *I'm probably the first non-Nazi in the world who was ever glad of horrid things the Nazis had done to him!*

Her father, on the other hand, made no effort to conceal his indignation. Not only did he treat the black-uniformed reader to his fiercest glares, but he told his wife in English, not caring whether the other understood or not, what he thought of the whole affair. The absent-minded Evelyn, less absent-minded than usual, tried to tone down with a "Well, but on the other hand," or an "I think you exaggerate a bit, don't you, Joe?" anything capable of being toned down.

The man who was reading, at all events, gave not the slightest sign of whether he understood, and for her part Gwen had no objection to Daddy's remarks; she felt they increased her chances of staying longer in Europe. She simply could not help it: this did decidedly improve her humor. The desperation that had taken hold of her as they came closer to the frontier gave way to an expectancy that was no longer fear, but the beginning of a dizzy hope. *Meaning?* she asked herself, staring fixedly at the man in the black uniform. *Meaning, then——?* And she answered herself, turning pale at her own logic: *Yes! That's what it means!*

The man behind the paper saw her turn pale, as he had seen and heard all that went before.

Interesting, he thought. *I know faces. There couldn't be a guiltier-looking face than that girl's!* He did not dream that the guilt of which Gwen had just become conscious was the only kind that the Nazis are not experts on—love.

That it was guilt, even Gwen admitted. It was her fault. Andreas had done nothing to make her love him. And since shame was what she had suffered most from in her life hitherto, and what she had been too weak or too strong to overcome, she turned pale and blushed at the thought which so far she had refused to enunciate consciously.

Interesting, thought the man, who was reading in the *Voelkischer Beobachter* that the Führer was expecting Arthur Greiser, the future governor of Danzig, from Berlin, and would receive the British ambassador, Sir Nevile Henderson, at a special audience this evening: *She has a perfectly wretched conscience!*

At this moment a man in mufti went along the corridor and looked into the compartment; Mr. Hoffman thought he recognized him from his call at the prefecture in Bozen. Shortly before this Andreas had discovered that it was Herr Udacher when the same man, accompanied by three others in civilian dress, had rapidly approached the train from the coal bunkers a moment before it moved out of the station.

The travelers could now look out of the car windows; the Nazi guards had removed the nails and strings that had held the curtains shut. "A sign of better treatment that speaks for itself," Herr Tolloy observed. Nevertheless, the windows still might not be opened, and there was no air.

Everyone in the eight third-class cars (which remained sealed) knew that it was only a few more minutes to Innsbruck, whose green Isel Mountain now appeared before them.

"The death that he full oft had sped from Iselberg, a champion dread," Sepp sang thoughtlessly, and was fiercely silenced by his sister—a rare occurrence.

"Shut up," she said. "Or else think before you open your mouth."

Sepp had no idea what he had done, but the agitation of everyone in the car was unmistakable and obviously growing. It was equally plain that they were all thinking just one thing—Innsbruck! Up to 1918 this had been their provincial capital, and since then it had been the capital of North Tirol. *If we're staying in North Tirol,* they thought, *then we shall be getting off now. Do you suppose they'll settle us in Innsbruck itself?* Probably, or in the immediate surroundings, where, although there were no vineyards or apple orchards, there was good land, not too thickly settled, where one might dwell, sow, and reap.

"Innsbruck!" was shouted in resounding tones.

The train stopped.

The shadow of the station made the feeble daylight feebler still. Artificial light was almost needed, even at noon in August. Everyone in the eight cars got up. They all left their seats, and, clutching the most important bag or most valuable package, turned toward the tightly closed car door. Frau von Fennperg, accustomed to other journeys, even called: "Porter!"

It was five minutes now—or was it longer?—since they had come in. And Andreas, who, like his grandfather, was standing by the window, saw something that confused and puzzled him despite the tension of the moment: the Hoffman family, accompanied by an S.S. officer and three S.S. men, were going through the gate. Their baggage was carried after them. Was Andreas mistaken in thinking he saw Gwen stop, look along the train, and be forced on at once? He was certainly not mistaken in thinking he saw her wave before she disappeared. She waved in a direction where there was nothing.

There was no time to think about it, for the train was already moving. Without a signal, without a blast of the whistle, it left the dim station, and the posters, "Visit Innsbruck, the pearl of North Tirol!" faded from view.

The right bank of the broad, clay-brown river Inn appeared, and on the left bank, for a second, one saw the Maria Theresiastrasse. The train went faster. Much faster than before.

The emigrants were still in line, holding bags and bundles tight, facing the door through which they had expected to go.

"Then this isn't it?" said somebody, and sat slowly down. It was old Mumelter. Nothing could have made the disappearance of any last remnant of human hope more irrevocable than this slow, heavy sitting down in a hated seat. Gradually others followed his example, sitting down and staring in silence as he did. But still there were a few who went on hoping. This was only Innsbruck, and North Tirol is a big province. Perhaps their destination was Schwaz or Hall or Woergl or St. Anton am Arlberg or Kitzbühel, or one of the other places they knew by experience or had heard of in school. They spread the word around—maybe Schwaz or Hall or somewhere here in North Tirol; and again a tiny spark of hope was kindled and gleamed on the dismal journey. It was long past noon. The women unpacked their provisions—smoked meat from the Wednesday market, ham and country bread and hard-boiled eggs. Old Mumelter, too, received his share, but handed it back to Riccarda untouched, which was the first time such a thing had happened since the girl had been looking after him. "Are you sick, Grandfather?" she asked. He had never been sick as long as she had known him.

"No," he said. "But I don't see how you can eat!"

He said it loud enough so that most of those in the car heard him, and the reproach in his words was so bitter that the food stuck in their throats, and the hands carrying it to their mouths were struck motionless.

Herr Tolloy, cracking a hard-boiled egg on the window sill, shelling it, and carefully salting it from a paper folder, said, "A man has to eat!"

At this the old man said: "No!"

White stubble that had grown overnight on a chin usually shaved with care every day made his face seem emaciated. For the first time, his granddaughter thought, he really looked ancient.

Obstinately he repeated: "No!" The thin hands folded over the black leather bag trembled. "Anyone that can think of eating now is a scoundrel!"

An embarrassed silence followed, to be cut by a sharp voice: "Who was talking that nonsense?"

The voice belonged to one of the S.S. men who were accompanying the train, and who, so far, had remained in the separate compartment by the door.

No answer.

"Hey! I asked a question!" the voice repeated. It was the voice of a very young person, scarcely more than twenty.

No answer.

The station they had just gone through without stopping was Hall.

"Are you all deaf?" roared the young fellow.

A second and a third S.S. man appeared behind him.

The thirty-eight in the car looked silently at the floor. Only Herr Tolloy answered: "Anyway, I certainly didn't."

"Scoundrel!" the old man repeated audibly.

"What?" asked the young fellow, standing at one bound before him. "What was that you said?"

The aged man slowly raised his eyes to the boy. "I said scoundrel!" he replied, his voice full of immense defiance.

"And what did you mean by it?"

"That it's scoundrelly to bear tales, and just as scoundrelly to yield with a hearty appetite to the much greater piece of scoundrelliness that you're inflicting on us. Do you understand that, young man?"

If only Hoermann had not been incautious enough to laugh his approval at that moment! But he was, and the young Nazi roared at the old man: "You swine! You will apologize at once for such talk!"

Now, attracted by the loud voices, Storm Troopers and S.S. men had also appeared from the compartment by the door at the other end, and something happened that none of the three hundred and twenty-one Bozners in the train would have thought possible: free men had suddenly become unfree. With every turn of the wheels as the train hurried on, the liberty in which they had spent their lives, and to which they were accustomed as to the fresh air of their mountains, retreated further into the unattainable distance, and unfreedom enmeshed them like a close, paralyzing net.

With one motion the old man put the black bag on the bench beside him. "Hold that!" he told his younger grandson.

Steadying himself by holding onto the baggage rack, he got up, stretched to his full height, and said, "I'm an old man. If a pup abuses an old man, and forty witnesses sit quietly by, the old man will have to see to things himself."

He raised his fist like a flash, took a swing, and would have struck if Andreas had not grabbed his arm from behind.

"The worthless pup!" the old man could be heard repeating, breathing heavily.

His assailant gave way for a moment without a word, as if abandoning the field of battle. Another second and he had changed his mind, and slapped the old man in the face with all his force.

The yell that followed came from Andreas' mouth. He flung himself upon the young fellow, but the other armed men had already intervened, pinioning him tight, although he hit about him wildly.

"Quiet!" they roared. "You rascals, be quiet this instant! The next person that budges gets shot! Damned rabble!" So saying, the nine of them cocked their revolvers.

"For the love of Christ!" cried Hoermann, the superintendent. "Andre! Use your head! Andre!"

The red fog before Andreas' eyes melted away; he saw the revolver muzzles pointing, ceased to move, and said tonelessly: "You're right, Herr Hoermann. For the love of Christ."

And he sat down.

But the old man still stood, clutching the baggage rack with one hand. His eyes saw nothing. His ears heard only a roaring.

"There's going to be an end to this kind of thing, once and for all!" said one of the nine, a short, fat man in Storm Trooper uniform.

"Hell's fire! The idea of such lack of discipline! And just remember, you people: never mind about Christ! What's done around here is not for the love of Him, but because the Führer gives orders. Understand?"

No one replied.

"I want an answer!" yelled the man, raising his revolver. "I asked a question, and if you're too stupid to answer, I'll tell you what the answer is. The answer is: What is done here is what our Führer orders. All together! Come on, now!"

Nine revolvers were aimed.

Nine hammers on nine revolvers clicked.

"What is done here," the interrogator began. "I shall count three. If I don't get an answer by three, you can lay the consequences to yourselves. Damned South Tirolean thickheads! I'll teach you!"

The station sign whizzing by proclaimed: Schwaz.

"One!" the man counted aloud.

"Two!"

"What is done here," a shrill woman's voice began in the rear of the car, and others went on, "is what our Führer orders."

Free men for a lifetime had become unfree within the space of fifteen minutes.

"Don't forget that!" the short, fat Storm Trooper warned, putting the safety catch on his revolver. It was obvious to him and the eight other armed men that neither the old man nor his grandson had joined in the chorus of replies. Very well, the reckoning should be presented at a more suitable time; for the moment, at least outwardly, they had accomplished what they wanted and saved face. The nine consulted for a moment, then withdrew to their previous post of observation.

But the old man was still standing upright.

He put off with an instinctive gesture anyone who came near in order to make him sit down.

With his hand still clutching the baggage rack, he stood there, hearing nothing and seeing nothing. His face was ashen; the red mark of the blow he had received was still on his left cheek.

They had slapped a free man's face with impunity—that was what he could not grasp, what burned hotter than the marks of the five rude fingers.

"Grandfather!" cried Riccarda, for he had staggered. "Please! Grandfather!"

"It's all right," he said, as if from a great distance. "You needn't be afraid. I'm sensible again."

And he sat down in his seat, saying to the youngest: "Let's have the bag."

The journey went on in silence. Station sign after station sign appeared and vanished in the dim daylight.

They were out of the Tirol.

The provincial boundary of Salzburg was far behind, and the names of the towns grew stranger and stranger; but still it was the province of Salzburg that they were traveling through, and here, too, there were glaciers and green mountains, and the rivers foamed like the Eisack and Etsch.

But there was no stop in the province of Salzburg either, and those who still had hopes now thought: Vienna!

Probably Vienna was where they were being taken. Of course it was Vienna!

Sepp, who was among those for whom this journey had no terrors, tried to find out from one of the nine Nazis: "We're going to Vienna, aren't we?"

The Nazi answered: "Shut up!"

They had now been traveling for seventeen hours.

Before the train entered Linz in Upper Austria the nine reappeared. They got those who were sitting in the middle of the car to make room for them; the lad who had slapped old Mumelter was the spokesman.

He said: "You will now receive from me some instructions, or rather some re-education, which will hold good for your entire future life. Pay close attention, and repeat after me the answers I shall say for you. First: What is the German greeting? Answer: 'The German greeting is *Heil* Hitler!' There is no good morning, no good day, no good evening, no *Gruess Gott*. All those are unmanly, outworn formulas that mean nothing to a German. Away with them! There is only one German greeting: *Heil* Hitler! Repeat it after me! All of you—anyone who doesn't repeat it knows beforehand what the consequence will be. Repeat!"

They all repeated: "The German greeting is *Heil* Hitler!"

Old Mumelter, too, moved his lips, as his castigator plainly saw. Whether he said anything, and if so what, it was impossible to tell.

The young man went on: "Point second in your re-education: What is the German's song? Answer: 'The German's song is the *"Horst Wessel"* song.' Repeat!"

They all repeated: "The German's song is the *'Horst Wessel'* song."

The Storm Trooper gave the third point of re-education: "In whose name does the German people live and work and fight and die? Answer: 'The German people lives and works and fights and dies in the name of its Führer, Adolf Hitler.' Repeat!"

This answer, too, was repeated by people who had been free until that noon.

The same re-education was taking place at the same moment in the seven other third-class cars of the train.

As they came into Linz, three hundred and twenty-one people had given the same answer in chorus to the same three questions.

"So now you know!" the man charged with the re-education concluded his instruction in each car.

Yes indeed. Now they knew.

In Linz the Mumelter family and three young people by the name of Pacher, Baumgartner, and Gergl were detrained, and led to a waiting train bearing tags: "Linz-Budweis." As soon as they had got into a third-class carriage, just as airless as the one they had left behind, the train began to move.

Linz-Budweis?

They had seen the destination plate.

Budweis is a city in Bohemia.

Were they going to Budweis?

The banks of the Danube were still in sight; the Poestlingberg above Linz was still a sign that there were mountains in the world.

Then you saw no more mountains and no more rivers.

The country around grew flat, and it was hard to breathe in the airtight car, which was filled with the tobacco smoke of the people coming back from the weekly market at Linz.

Since having to repeat questions and answers, the emigrants had been incapable of speech.

In the continuing dim light, the fields after the harvest looked almost black.

"Do they speak German in Budweis, Grandfather?" Sepp decided to inquire, now that he had had to give up the idea of going to Vienna.

"Czech," replied the old man.

After that even Sepp, who had had such high hopes of the journey, said nothing more.

They were riding through brown, almost black, flat country.

Riccarda could not bear to look at the old man: occasionally he passed his hand over the spot where he had been struck.

They had been on the way now for twenty-one hours, and it was growing dark.

Andreas, however, did look the old man in the face; he did not miss a single one of the motions he made, and every time he touched his cheek, which still bore red marks, the grandson said to himself: "I'll give that blow back! As God is my witness!"

A monstrous hatred blazed in his bosom; his breast was almost too narrow to house his hatred.

"Grandfather!" he said.

"Yes?" said the old man.

"We won't forget—will we?"

The old man's mouth in the darkness was a straight line. "No," he replied.

The journey went on, it was night outside, and there were Czech names on the station signs.

"Wouldn't you like to eat something, Grandfather?" Riccarda begged. "You'll be getting faint!"

"Right," said the old man. "Give me something." He ate a piece of smoked meat and a small piece of bread.

Having to watch him while he ate to please her tormented Riccarda yet more, and further inflamed Andreas' hatred.

They were not going to Budweis, they were going further.

To Netolitz. To Strakonitz. To Horaždowitz.

When they came to a station whose name on the sign was Plzeň, and, in parenthesis, Pilsen, their names were called out.

"Laurenz Mumelter!"

"Andreas Mumelter!"

"Riccarda Mumelter!"

"Sepp Mumelter!"

"Here!" replied those who were called.

"Get off," they were told.

They took their trunks and bags and packages and got off.

"Well," someone in uniform said to them, "now you're in your new home."

It was night; they stood with their trunks, bags, and packages on the ill-lighted platform. The train that had brought them had pulled out. The three young people, Pacher, Baumgartner, and Gergl, waved to them from the train, but they could not see them. The air was thick with smoke.

A voice in the dark said in a language they did not speak: *"Pojďte, paní! Pojďte, slečno!"* This meant, "Come, gentlemen, come, miss."

But they did not understand.

Another voice interpreted: "You go with the man. He will guide you."

They went with the man. When he came out into the light, they saw that he wore the uniform of a Czech infantryman and was shouldering his rifle. On the rifle was a fixed bayonet.

Another infantryman with shouldered rifle and fixed bayonet followed them.

They were in their new home.

PART TWO

There stay and die . . .

Chapter 10

Homesickness is an almost entirely neglected disease. This is owing to the fact that until a few years ago a comparatively small number of people suffered from it, so that it was probably not worth while to investigate the symptoms. But since the advent of Hitler matters have changed. He made homesickness epidemic, and as not hundreds or thousands but hundreds of thousands and millions now suffer from it, it has been recognized as a disease. But still no one has taken the trouble to study its phenomena. If this had been done, it would be realized that the disease rises and falls in curves like fever, is as infectious as an epidemic, and as fatal as any incurable malady.

This was the ailment that afflicted the Mumelter family when they were forced to move to a town that seemed to them the opposite of Bozen in every way. Pilsen in West Bohemia, to call it by its new name, in the western part of the Protectorate of Bohemia and Moravia, is a big factory town, black with soot and choking with smoke. It is hard for people from the Rosengarten to breathe, because the soot and smoke get into your lungs; and it smells perpetually of a piercing mixture of tanbark, decoction of hops, pressed yeast, kaolin, wine vinegar, and excelsior, which are turned out or used in the leather factories, breweries, distilleries, potteries, and explosives plants that belch smoke day and night. And the further you go toward the western end of town, which forms Okres 3, the third district of the city, the thicker and yellower grows the smoke, the more biting the smell, for you are getting near the Skoda Works.

It is a town, too, where people from the Rosengarten have difficulty in looking. Not only because of the smoke and soot, but because their eyes find so little to look at that they can enjoy, and so much that offends them. Factories, factory districts, streets that lead to factories, and streets that start from factories. The factories are everywhere—in the middle of town, outside in the three suburban sections, the Imperial Suburb, the Saxon Suburb, and the Prague Suburb, and also for twenty miles around, toward Doubravka in the northeast, Doudlevce in the south, Lobzy in the southeast, and Skvrňany in the west. And the streets and alleys that lead to and from all these factories are streets and alleys inhabited almost exclusively by people who belong to the factories. The streets and alleys are lined with yellowish or gray or brick-red buildings, mostly three stories high and facing one another at close quarters. Or else there are remnants of the circular fortifications built during the Hussite wars, transformed into promenades and making a mock of the factory atmosphere.

There are squares and avenues, buildings, monuments, and even parks and gardens of which those who are born here speak admiringly. They say the huge rectangular Republic Square with the tall-steepled Church of St. Bartholomew is beautiful; they speak highly of the Měšťanský Pivovar, the Municipal Brewery, with its rock cellars, and the Town Hall where Wallenstein's generals swore allegiance in the Thirty Years' War. And they are charmed by the region around the Mies and Radbuza rivers, for Pilsen, like Bozen, is at the confluence of two streams. But this, the Bozners thought, was the only thing it had in common with home.

When old Mumelter looked out of the window for the first time in the building on Karl Hermann Frankgasse near the Nerudová, where he had been living since September 2, something seemed to grip his throat. He still had that feeling, although he took care not to look out of the window, and this was already December.

Out of the window you saw this: a line of three-story buildings opposite, steering a middle course between workingmen's and fresh-air colony houses; built in the super-modern style that the new Czechoslovakia had preferred, they were all absolutely alike—square blocks of rough brick, with concrete and iron framework, square windows, four steps up to the front door, and tiny lawns around them, on which thin acacia trees were already sprouting here and there. They looked neat and dismally uniform. Here and there on the ground floor would be a shop sign saying *"Krejči,"* which means tailor, *"Pekař,"* which means baker, or something else that the old man did not understand. Before the buildings was an infinitely narrow margin of paved sidewalk. The street was no more than forty feet wide.

It was the sign *"Pekař"* that brought old Mumelter to the verge of tears when he found out what it meant. For in the Silbergasse at Bozen, too, he had had a baker's sign across from his windows—entwined pretzels, with the name of Gemaassmer underneath. But where mountains should have towered to gleaming heights above roofs and steeples, there were roofs and steeples and nothing more. Eyes accustomed for a lifetime to one kind of light and colors began to ache when both were suddenly snatched away; if, furthermore, they were accustomed to heights and broad expanses, the everlasting narrowness and flatness hurt them.

"So we don't look out of the window," the old man told himself. "You can't do that here." But neither could you talk to the people. For most of them understood nothing but Czech, and those who understood German had been unwilling, in protest, to speak it since the Nazi occupation. Where the Mumelters lived, in a quarter immediately surrounding the Skoda Works, you had to be careful about speaking even a word of German. For despite nine months' occupation the Nazis had not yet succeeded in Germanizing the factory sections of Pilsen; every German word was taken for that of a mortal enemy.

They had now been living here for three months and three weeks, at 47 Karl Hermann Frankgasse, second floor, door two. Three months and three weeks before, on the day of their arrival, the war had broken out, and since then the hatred of the Germans among the Czech population had only grown the fiercer. At the time of the occupation only 8 per cent of the inhabitants of Pilsen were German, and no matter what the Nazis had done meanwhile to inflate this tiny percentage by artificial means, Pilsen was still overwhelmingly Czech.

Andreas was employed in the designing office of the Skoda Works, with an engineer's pay, on which the Mumelters lived, and had nothing to complain of as regarded either salary or treatment. The incidents on the journey and what had happened in Bozen were not mentioned at all. From the managing director of the works, Herr Schultheiss, down to the humblest employee he was received courteously, with an almost emphatic respect; except for the Czech element, which predominated chiefly among the workers, he might have convinced himself that he was actually receiving preference. The Czechs, indeed, showed him the reserved, monosyllabic courtesy that they had adopted since the occupation toward everyone who spoke German; it was part of the passively expectant attitude ordered by something called *"Beseda,"* of which no one knew what or where it was. Since the outbreak of the war they had grown more sparing of words, and were yet more careful not to show their true colors and their fanatical hatred. How Andreas wished he might have said: "You Czechs mistake me. I hate as you do!" But he, too, had to be unendingly on guard, as he well knew, despite the honeyed bait that was offered him. Nor could he speak a word of Czech.

The place where he worked was in Plant 5. Until Herr Schultheiss had taken over the management, Plant 5 had been called the Waldstein-Werk, because it was the building that had constituted the Waldstein Machine Factory in 1859; starting from this in 1868, Emil Skoda, nephew of Josef Skoda the great Viennese clinician, had created the Skoda Works, enormously enlarged since that time. But Herr Schultheiss did not like the sound of the name Waldstein-Werk. Arriving six months before to "co-ordinate" the plant, or, in other words, to adjust its management to the policy of the Nazis, he had named it the Goering-Hof.

Here Andreas spent most of his time, and here he had been working at his model for the last few months. He was given a free hand. Any technical requirements he had were quickly fulfilled; he had three engineers as assistants; the head of the experimental department, Mr. Uliř, backed him up; and a permit signed by Herr Schultheiss himself admitted him to Plant 9, formerly the Masaryk Building, now the Robert Ley-Hof, an establishment closed to everyone, equipped with a shooting range where the automatic rapid-firing guns were tested. Everyone could see that he was feverishly busy; he stupefied himself with work, so to speak. This was the narcotic that helped him through the first few tormenting months of strangeness, forcing his thoughts in new directions. Occasionally reaching the point of satisfaction at the progress of his work, he would be unspeakably ashamed. But the state of crisis that he was going through both forbade and allowed him to think certain thoughts. He saw nothing of the external world, and wanted to see nothing. Deep within him he was hiding what the Czechs were hiding: he built passionate hopes on the war, and almost had a breakdown when Poland was annihilated, while the victorious intoxication of the Nazis knew no bounds. That was when his crisis had begun. But someday he would break the word of honor he had given to Herr Udacher, he knew; and he knew that he must drag out the perfecting of his invention until that day came. The invention would be used against, not by, the momentary victors: this was the word of honor that he had given himself on entering the Skoda Works and that he justified himself with whenever he felt any satisfaction at seeing his work grow. This, incidentally, figured in the card index of the Division of Design under the non-committal code sign FAG-X, anti-aircraft gun or *"Flugabwehrgeschuetz X."* Not even the "division" knew that Andreas' invention consisted not only of substituting for rapid, successive machine-gun fire a simultaneous volley from a large number of parallel barrels, but of substituting the conventional pellets of ordinary shrapnel by means of a large-caliber shrapnel projectile containing explosive bullets. The Division of Design and the managing director were of opinion that Andreas could considerably increase and improve the number of hits; they did not know that his new weapon aimed at much more. "Fired at a mass formation of bombers," said his sketch preparatory to the patent application, "a shrapnel of six-inch caliber (or even larger) is bound to create a cone of danger that will force the plane formation to disperse, even if it does not immediately destroy any of them." In other words, when his work was finished he would have created a weapon to make bomb attacks on a large scale infinitely more difficult.

Herr Schultheiss (who allowed him a sort of privileged position and admired his feverish industry, the motives behind which he did not suspect) in turn occupied a privileged position of the first rank. He came from Vienna, where he had held a minister's post in Chancellor Schuschnigg's cabinet, and had expressed his enthusiasm immediately upon Hitler's entry by savagely attacking his former superior Schuschnigg in radio addresses, newspaper articles, and speeches, denouncing him as a traitor to the nation, while presenting himself as a martyr who had been an Austrian minister solely in order to pave the way for Hitler. Those who remembered the assiduity and devotion to Chancellor Schuschnigg that he had displayed during the latter's rule had no choice but to take Herr Schultheiss for either a rogue or a highly skilled diplomat. The Nazis chose the latter. They promoted him to a position that assured him not only a dizzying income, but an influence equaled by few in the Bohemian-Moravian Protectorate. To give a picture of the man's capacities, it will suffice to observe that he was the one who, in January of 1939, concluded the negotiations that noiselessly shifted the Skoda Works from the possession of the French armament firm of Schneider-Creusot to that of the protectorate. The Anglo-Czechoslovak and Prague Credit Bank bought the monstrous concern from the Union Européenne Industrielle et Financière for $10,300,000, so the papers said, and that was the official explanation given to the world. But what the papers did not say was that a certain Rudolf Paul Schultheiss had had the useful idea of assigning character roles to two great banks, dressing them up as buyer and seller, so to speak, in order to conceal a piece of outright robbery. For although the buyer was a Czech bank, leading one to suppose that the Czechs would control this vital property, the control passed one day later to four German concerns: the Krupp Works, the Hermann Goering Ironworks, the Otto Wolf Steel Works, and the Rheinmetall-Borsig Works. Be that as it may, Herr Schultheiss' idea of a bank masquerade strengthened the armament and metal industry of Nazi Germany by more than 50 per cent—at a price, incidentally, that was "debited," or, in other words, never paid.

No wonder such an expert as this was forgiven his lack of experience with machinery and put at the head of the fire-breathing, pounding, hissing, roaring mammoth enterprise that he had so noiselessly slipped up the national sleeve.

Riccarda said of this superior, who bestowed his favor on Andreas, "He looks like a matrimonial racketeer." That was the bitterest term of opprobrium she knew.

In about four months she was going to bring into the world a child whose father had been heard from so far to the extent of one picture post card. It said that he was being called up for duty, and would be in the Brenner region. That was early October. Now Christmas was coming, and he had not written again. Riccarda, who had written to him three times, expected nothing further from him. She even doubted that he had been called up, and she watched with complete fatalism and apathy as the days came and went. It was a conversation with her grandfather that made her consider ideas which but a little while before would have seemed utterly unthinkable.

This was the conversation: "You shouldn't take me for stupider than I am," the old man had said to her. "Whose is the child you are having, and why have you never spoken of it?"

There was such disapproval in his hard eyes that his granddaughter asked angrily: "Could you by any chance have done anything for us, Grandfather?"

The old man countered, instead of answering: "The Mumelter family has come to a pretty pass, I must say!"

"I suppose I'm disgracing the family name!" returned the girl, who had scarcely done anything all these months except to make the old man's life in a strange land easier by every artifice and dodge she could command; her tone was immensely bitter.

"Yes," replied the incorruptible grandfather. "And that's the only thing we have left—our good name!"

"You're really angry with me, Grandfather?" she asked after a moment's thought.

"Yes. I've been wondering the whole time: is it true or isn't it? And when there was no more mistaking it, I thought to myself, 'She'll at least have enough respect for you to come and talk it over with you, and not only with her brother.' But no! Not even that! I suppose that must be the spirit of the New Order? Going around like that in public, and thinking nothing of it, and not being ashamed!"

She had not been ashamed until that moment. Now she was.

Right, she told herself. *This won't do.* From then on, after many sleepless nights, she began to hear the protestations of Jaroslav Uliř with new ears.

In almost every way he was Roberto's opposite, just as Pilsen was in almost every way the opposite of Bozen. But these are topsy-turvy times, she admitted, and began to think more kindly of Jaro, who hid shortsighted, wild, lovelorn eyes behind horn-rimmed spectacles, and had a clumsy head with short, bristly hair mounted on a broad, ungainly body. He had vowed to her a hundred times how desperately he loved her, and a hundred times she had told him: "Nonsense!"

Now the nonsense made sense. When she thought of how she had met him, in the little fruiterer's shop on the Jýhlova Ulice (despite all Germanization the Pilseners continued to call the streets by their

Czech names), she was tempted to tell herself scornfully that this at least would satisfy her grandfather! For according to a story that he had often told, he had met Grandmother in just this way—in a fruiterer's where someone suddenly said: "Won't that be too heavy for you?" The person who said this to Riccarda here spoke with a strong Czech peasant accent, and although the girl did not know what her grandmother had replied in a similar situation, she had said curtly: "No, thank you!" And in a moment she was outside with her package of nuts, plums, and pears.

But if the South Tiroleans are tenacious, so are the Czechs. And if old Mumelter was the very essence of the South Tirolean, so was young Uliř the essence of the Czech. He would not be put off, not then and not later; as he, too, lived in Karl Hermann Frankgasse, there was more than enough opportunity. To this very day Riccarda did not really know what his business was. He, like Andreas, worked at the Skoda plant; but he also had something to do with an association that went by the name of "National Unity" party; and it was plain to her that he hated the German intruders with a mute, piercing hatred that waited grimly for its day.

"That being so, you ought to hate me," she told him with deliberate illogicality.

And with his accent and his wild eyes he replied: *"Ale slečno!* But my dear girl! You aren't a German! You're much too good for a German!" After a long pause and a deep sigh he added: "And much too beautiful!" That was his way of paying her compliments and urging his suit. There was something touching about him sometimes, she could not help thinking as she listened during the sleepless nights to the voices that spoke on his behalf.

They spoke so weightily on his behalf that in the end she made up her mind. The child must have a father. And Jaro, whose eyes were remarkably good despite his shortsightedness, had no illusions about the reason that suddenly made a "no" into a "yes." But he was willing. He was even happy. His shortsighted eyes gleamed wildly.

"Dobře," he said. "You aren't marrying me because you're fond of me. You're marrying me because the child is coming. But you're marrying me. Jesus, Mary, and Joseph, you'll have me!" It was such an outburst of unrestrained joy that Riccarda asked herself: *Does not the man who takes such delight in me deserve something better?*

She was beginning to regard him less as a nuisance and more as someone with whom she had a bond. She would not be able to love him, he was just too ugly for that. But there was something disarming and at the same time threatening about his blind passion. Sometimes he seemed to her like a big dog that could be very devoted and very dangerous.

They had discussed everything. They would move into his apartment on the other side of the street, and Riccarda would go on keeping house for her grandfather and brother. This was her stipulation. He accepted it with a quick *"Anō! Anō!"* which signified "Yes! Yes!" and also typified his impatient way of agreeing to anything and everything she asked of him. If she had demanded his death, he would have said *"Anō! Anō!"* impatiently and quickly. All she had to do now was announce her decision to the family.

Sepp was not living at home. He had joined the ranks of the Hitler Youth of the city of Pilsen soon after their arrival, and this obligated him to sleep at the former Praemonstratenser High School in the Smetanagasse, which had served as Hitler Youth headquarters since the occupation. This, like much else, was beyond the old man's imagining. His grandson in the Hitler Youth, which one day would strike old people in the face! He had not yet grown used to the idea that he and his family, thanks to their German speech, had immediately become German citizens; or, in other words, subjects of Hitler—citizens of the first rank, in fact; whereas the Czech population, which had been living here for a thousand years, had sunk to citizens of the Protectorate; or, in other words, of the lowest rank. If the old man had been able to speak Czech, he would have told the citizens of the lowest rank the same thing that his grandson Andreas felt like saying to them: "A fig for my first-class citizenship! Although I speak their language and not yours, the people that have made me a citizen of theirs are a thousand times stranger and more impossible for me to understand than you!"

The strangeness increased and the incomprehensibility grew the longer they lived there, and here, too, it was the old man, being unoccupied, who felt it most and worst. What he saw and heard, what took place almost daily before his own eyes, he understood less and less the oftener he had to witness it. He had gone to Weider's shoe store in the Födermayerova to buy galoshes, and had seen them selling everything without any ration card to the customers who spoke German, but nothing at all to those who spoke Czech, card or no card; he had gone out on the street along with the peasant woman who had despairingly shown her clothing card, complaining that this was the ninth shoe store from which she had been sent away empty-handed—why, my dear sir, why? He could not talk to her, but he understood her; his new fellow citizens he did not understand. He had been in Schimetschek's barber shop in the Dominikanergasse when its proprietor loudly declared to an elderly man who was already seated in the barber chair: "We don't wait on Czechs in my shop." And he had heard the other patrons murmur approval, and seen the elderly man get up, abashed, and go out in silence—why, my dear sir, why? In *Die Neue Zeit,* the German paper published at Prague, he read articles written in German and with a temper so strange to him that he had to read them two or three times even to grasp the meaning of the words; in the pamphlet, *Why the Führer Established the Protectorate*—every German citizen of Pilsen received one by mail—he had discovered the sentences: "The will of the Führer is the German law"—a quotation from a speech by Field Marshal Goering; and, "Law in the Third Reich is whatever benefits the German nation; that is illegal which is detrimental to the German nation"—quoted from a speech of Dr. Hans Frank, the Minister of Justice. The same publication also contained a poem, just one, and he read it, for he was fond of poetry. It was called "Oh My Germany," the author was Heinrich Vierordt, and it ran as follows:

"Oh my Germany, you shall etch upon your soul a hatred deep and ineffaceable. Choke down all human frailty, and haste to the fray.

"Oh Germany, hate! Lay low the foe, and pile a monument of smoking corpses rising to the clouds.

"Oh Germany, now is the time for hatred! No prisoners! Your neighbor lands shall be a wilderness.

"Oh Germany, the time for hatred is at hand! Forward, you batteries, battalions, squadrons! Atop a ruined world you shall review them, forever cured of your ageless folly—no pity for the stranger!"

Underneath, in black type: "This is the poem that every German should know by heart."

He had read the poem that every German should know by heart

over and over again, and had understood it, and been absolutely unable to understand it.

He was ninety-one and a half, and had been struck in the face, he, a free man; he would never forget it.

He was ninety-one and a half, and all his life he had said, *"Gruess Gott!"* and *"Auf Wiedersehen!"* He could not conceive how so fine a greeting could be discarded and he compelled to say *"Heil* Hitler!" instead. And so he shunned all greetings.

And all his life he had gone to church, to Mass, to confession, to communion. But here in Pilsen he could not understand the German Mass. It began with the reading of a page from *Mein Kampf.* The first time he heard it he got up, horrified, and hastily left, supposing he must have gone by mistake to a church that was not Catholic; but it was Catholic, the Church of Sts. Cyril and Methodius; here and everywhere, even at St. Bartholomew's in the center of town, Mass began with a page from *Mein Kampf;* and after the Post-communion Prayer came a short prayer as follows:

"Our Father which art in Heaven, bless our leader Adolf Hitler, Thy heavenly son."

After that, during the first few weeks of his residence, he had stayed away from Mass; later, regarding it as the lesser sin, he decided to recite enough Ave Marias aloud so that he could not hear the words from the altar during the reading of the page, and to say the Profession of Faith loud enough to drown out the dreadful prayer. Finally, in his desperate need, he wrote to Pastor Gemaassmer of Bozen, the only letter he had yet sent from here:

Your Reverence! Dear Friend!

We have now been here almost three months, and I have neither heard from you nor have you from me. I am writing you today because I am in such distress, and do not know what to do or not to do. At Mass here they read a page of *Mein Kampf* instead of the Gospel, and before the *Ita missa est* they say a prayer that I will not even mention, in which our Lord and Saviour is replaced by someone else. Your Reverence! Dear Friend! I need your advice and opinion. May a good Catholic attend a Mass like that? If not, where is he to perform his devotions, as all the churches here are guilty of the same abuse? Please forgive the expression.

We have an apartment, Andreas has a job as an engineer, Sepp is a kind of soldier, Riccarda is keeping house. There are no mountains here.

Not even hills. I can't tell you more than that. When I shut my eyes, at night or even by day, I can see everything there. Every house and every tree, and the light and the shade and how beautiful it is.

Your devoted
L. MUMELTER

Two weeks later the following answer arrived:

DEAR FRIEND!

I am delighted that you are so well off there, and that I can say the same of us here. We often think of you, too, and talk a great deal about you—the more so, the fewer friends and acquaintances are left to us. The number dwindles day by day.

It is a very good thing that you took the old Bozen with you in your eyes and thoughts. Thus at least you keep it as homelike and unspoiled as it was when we loved it, lovable as it once was.

Don't worry about the other. The Saviour is everywhere, and no matter where you call upon Him, He will hear you. Whether it is a church or a room or out of doors does not make any difference. His blessing upon you all!

Your old friend
GEMAASSMER, PASTOR

This, too, had started the old man on a long train of thought, because he well understood what was not written between those few lines. But what was around him he did not understand. On one of his walks—he was accustomed to exercise—he had come upon the barred gate of the J. S. P. (Jewish Settlement Pilsen); this, according to a sign on the high barbed wire fence surrounding some four hundred low shacks between the Imperial Suburb and the Skoda Works, was the name of a concentration camp that avoided the title; it was on the left of the highway, exactly at the point where the side road turned off to Redčič by the 14.8 kilometer stone. The old man would scarcely have gone so far if cries had not led him thither. They came from the mouths of men walking one behind another, who were being flogged with whips as they walked; he saw it with his own eyes and heard it with his own ears, until someone shouted at him to be off.

All this had been stored up inside him, to pour out the moment he was alone and unobserved with his thoughts; then he pondered it, and found it beyond his grasp. *Am I too old to understand it?* he asked himself. It seemed as if each and every thing that had meant life to him had been completely transformed—as if the hand of the clock were turning backward—as if exact opposites held good everywhere: shame for honor, paganism for faith, injustice for justice—as if the calendar were no longer a fixed succession of days and nights, but an arbitrary mockery of dull light and dreadful shadow.

Nevertheless, Christmas was on the calendar and was going to be celebrated even in this year and in this city. And then with the scrupulous disregard of tradition that drove the old man to distraction—and of which one never knew whether it was mere scorn or systematic destruction of what had gone before—the Pilsen city authorities proclaimed that as of December 24, the day when people gave presents, neither provisions nor other "necessary requisites" might be freely sold; starting with Christmas Eve, said the proclamation, a permit from the town authorities would be necessary for the purchase of articles "required for nourishment, clothing, or the carrying on of a trade."

This made it harder for Riccarda to get such Christmas presents as she had intended for her family. However, the proclamation applied only from the twenty-fourth on, and when that day arrived she had almost everything she had planned for each one—the fur cap, gloves, and pipe tobacco for her grandfather, the books for Andreas, and the shirts and socks for Sepp. Even something for Jaro Ulíř. Furthermore, a letter had come by the morning mail from Bozen, and at sight of the postmark she was happily startled; but it was only Veronika writing to wish the family merry Christmas. She added that Foxy, the bitch, was well, and she said nothing about herself, the house, and the business in the Silbergasse—simply that "other people" were living there now whose name she would not or could not even mention; she was not living there any more either, but gave her new address in case the family had "nothing better to do" and wanted to write to her. The sadness of these awkwardly penned lines was indescribable, and Riccarda decided to withhold them from her grandfather. But she gave him Veronika's Christmas present, a tiny silver fir planted in earth from the back garden at the Silbergasse, in a carved oak container from the firm of Mumelter; the giver mentioned the source of the earth in an accompanying note.

Another letter also came by the morning mail, postmarked Innsbruck. It was addressed to Andreas, and even if Gwen Hoffman's name had not been on the return address, Riccarda would have recognized the handwriting as identical with that on the picture post card that Andreas had been carrying for months in his pocketbook along with three other colored post cards bearing no writing, for which she had several times made fun of him. Good, she thought, that at least is a Christmas present to please him.

It not only pleased him, it positively transformed him. When, because of Christmas Eve, he came home early from the plant, Riccarda heard him singing in his room—the first time any member of the Mumelter family had sung in this house. She did not ask any questions, because she knew he had read the letter that she had put on the table for him, and there must be something in it to make him sing; for this she almost liked Gwen, who was very seldom talked about. She knew from his rare remarks, too, that the Hoffman family had been stopping at Innsbruck since the outbreak of war, or rather had been stopped there. When the three had been fetched out of the sealed train, they had first had to submit to a long series of examinations regarding the South Tirolean plebiscite; two days later, after the outbreak of war, their departure had become a matter of utter impossibility; as a German citizen Hoffman was "hooked," as Gwen had said on the post card, or, in Andreas' translation, left to the tender mercies of the Nazis.

This Riccarda knew, and often it had been a sort of bitter consolation that Andreas got no more mail than she—just one wretched post card. If she had known that he and Gwen had been corresponding through general delivery since September and were working on a plan, she would probably have been less tolerant toward the American girl. It was Gwen who had thought of the plan, and Andreas who had carried it out.

"Since we have to stay in Germany," she had written to him one day, "why shouldn't it be where you are?" She had actually written "you and your family," and all told he had had four letters from her in the months of September, October, November, and December; today's was the fifth. He had fallen in love with the firm, beautiful handwriting and what it stood for, and a few days previously he had decided to admit this not only to himself but to the writer. The reply was this letter, sent not through general delivery but to his own address:

"I never knew that one could be perfectly happy. I *am* perfectly happy. Daddy is racking his brains about how to get away from Europe, and Mother sighs a good deal, because she misses Boston. And I'm perfectly happy, and racking my brains to figure out a way of staying here the rest of my life. Isn't that scandalous? Isn't it glorious?"

Then, in her tightly restrained way, the statement that had set Andreas singing: "So we shall be arriving in Pilsen on the twenty-fifth, and staying at a hotel for the time being. Daddy said he didn't care whether it was Pilsen or anywhere else, just so he got away, but if I enjoyed Pilsen, so would he. I'm very much afraid he won't. He's really in an awful fix. Imagine anyone's feeling so completely American as he does and having to behave as if he were a good German! And it's almost comical to see him trying to convince himself as well as Mother and me that the Nazis are better than he expected. Poor Daddy! He's a bad liar, and it's his best quality."

What if that letter had fallen into the wrong hands! Andreas thought, horrified, and stopped singing. He tried to see by the envelope whether this was the case or not, found no suspicious indications, and decided to go on singing. Not alone his joy at Gwen's expected arrival, but also a little pride and much hope made him so merry.

After long hesitation Managing Director Schultheiss had complied with his suggestion that Mr. Hoffman be employed at the Skoda Works. True, Hoffman was internationally known as a machinery expert, but he was or had been under investigation, and politically he was altogether undependable. Herr Schultheiss had these and other misgivings; nevertheless, he had finally agreed to employ him at a very substantial salary, and Mr. Hoffman had already accepted—not that he had much choice. For the Innsbruck Gestapo continued to keep a wary eye on his behavior; and not only were his foreign funds unavailable, but he must surely be glad to step from the position of a man more than half a prisoner into that of one with an occupation and an income: this was what Gwen had foreseen and suggested. But if it had not been easy for her to make the idea of the Skoda Works palatable to her father, it had been even less so for Andreas to gain Herr Schultheiss' ear. Gained it he had, however, the result was at hand, and promising new vistas were opened up. As he shaved Andreas sang Rodolfo's aria from *La Bohème:* "How chill this tiny hand! By your leave may I warm it?" Riccarda, listening to him in the kitchen, thought she saw a connection. But he did not even know he was singing; the song simply poured out of him, for the first time in almost six months.

With the scornfully scrupulous disrespect for anything venerable that had characterized the Nazi occupation of Bohemia from the very first, the black-out signal sounded on the dot of five in the afternoon of this twenty-fourth of December. The sirens screeched from the roofs of the Rasinův dům, the Narodopišne Museum, the German theater, and the observer post of the Skoda Works with such savage, earsplitting fury that the bustling city was dark and deserted within a few moments—just at the time, to a second, when the candles on the decorated Christmas tree in every house would be lighted for Christmas Eve. Riccarda, too, stopped in the act of lighting the candles on the tiny fir in the middle of the dining table and listened.

"Pull the curtains!" demanded her grandfather from the next room, putting down the book he was always reading, a history of the Tirol with a collection of Andreas Hofer's letters. "This sounds pretty much in earnest today," he said, and decided to open the dining-room door, but Riccarda called: "Don't come in!"

"Don't be childish!" he retorted. "Surely you aren't going to light the Christmas tree at a moment like this!"

Riccarda answered: "Why not? I've drawn the curtains, and the candles won't show outside. After all, Grandfather, one can't put off Christmas Eve!"

"Right," said the old man from the next room after a while. And again after a while: "Maybe it wouldn't be such a bad idea to leave a little light showing. Then at least they could see better where they wanted to chuck their bombs!"

Not a trace of fear in his voice.

Riccarda, however, was terrified. The sirens had not frightened her; what the old man said went to her very marrow. "On Christmas Eve?" she asked, putting out the one candle she had lighted.

At this he opened the door despite her admonition and stood on the threshold.

"And why not on Christmas Eve? Are you implying that it's against the order of our Saviour? Riccarda, so far I had supposed that you knew perfectly well what people here call the New Order. You've been a very good example of it yourself, haven't you? Must I come and explain to you that the order of our Saviour no longer prevails? They bomb on Christmas Eve, and justice is whatever Hitler wants, and honor is stealing and lying, and shame is what used to be honor, and decent girls have illegitimate children and think nothing of it—that's the New Order, yes or no?"

The question was asked in the dark, and in the dark the girl replied: "No, Grandfather. So far as I go, it's the Old Order. And it's going to go on being. With your permission I shall introduce to you this evening the man I'm going to marry."

The sirens had ceased to shrill; deathly silence reigned over the dark city.

"I see," said the old man slowly. "Did he come?"

"It's somebody else," was the reply.

"Who?" asked the old man.

"I'm expecting him after a while," said the girl.

Now the voice that had been cold and full of reproach for weeks grew warmer; he asked: "Are you fond of him?"

"No, Grandfather."

And he hesitated, and asked softly, knowing perfectly well what the answer would be: "Then why do you marry him?"

"Because I want the Old Order."

She had answered just as he had expected, and now she heard his steps in the dark and his voice asking: "Where are you?"

"Here," she said, reaching out her hand toward him.

Her hand found him, and he found her, held her hand and felt his way up toward her face. And found her face, and for the space of a heartbeat his lips brushed hers.

"That's a good girl," he said. "There's something I can respect!"

So after all she was the first in the family to get her Christmas present; she rejoiced profoundly, feeling that she received what anyone needs, something more necessary than food, more urgent than love, more irreplaceable than joy. One needs respect to live; otherwise one dies.

"Thank you, Grandfather," she replied. This was the first kiss she had had from him since her childhood.

The front door downstairs slammed, and then there was silence again.

A moment later, through the noiseless house, the voice of a radio announcer came with painful clarity from the first-floor apartment. He announced first in Czech and then in German: "This is the broadcasting station of the Czech patriots. Fellow Czechs! The air-raid alarm is nothing but a clumsy Nazi trick! Not an enemy plane is to be seen far and wide. For those whom the Nazis call our enemies are a thousand times more our friends than Hitler's and Himmler's bandits. They will not come to plague us on Christmas Eve. That is the Nazi fashion, but not the custom of civilized nations. Do not be afraid to light your Christmas trees. And remember: we Czech patriots are on guard! Have patience. Our time will come. Long live Masaryk's Czech republic! *Nazdar!* Merry Christmas!"

Static marred the German translation of this message.

A few minutes later, however, the lights blazed out again in the houses of Pilsen; though the streets remained dark and deserted, the fir trees from the beautiful forests of Karlsbad and Marienbad shone with a Christmaslike gleam.

"Do you believe what he's saying?" Riccarda asked the old man.

Instead of answering, he asked her in turn: "And you, girl? Do you believe it?"

She answered from the bottom of her heart: "Yes, Grandfather! I believe it surely!" There was such confidence in her voice that it impressed the old man.

"Grand," he said. "That's good to hear!"

And he docilely allowed himself to be sent back to the next room, to wait until the Mumelters' Christmas tree, too, was shining with white candles, lighting up the table covered with presents; it was more sparingly provided than it had been in Bozen, but still it was a table of presents, and a fir was lighted on it.

And those were good hours that the Mumelters spent there now, the best since they had arrived.

Even Sepp was on time. His Christmas was already behind him—doubly so, in fact: in the quarters of the Hitler Youth they had sung the "Horst Wessel" song, and after the line, "When Jewish blood spurts from the knife!" they had received the gift of the Party: a copy of *Mein Kampf* with the Führer's own autograph for each boy. And the one among the girls whom Sepp thought simply divine, Adelheid Walpurga Schimetschek, the seventeen-year-old daughter of a barber and hairdresser, had presented him with a perfume of which he smelled rather too strongly at the moment; furthermore, he had in his pocket a secret decree intended only for boys, which no one else was allowed to see, particularly not the girls—a marvelous decree, Sepp thought.

So far as Andreas was concerned, his humor was in no way inferior to his brother's; he, too, felt that he had every reason for rejoicing. Tomorrow Gwen was coming; he had just run over to the Hotel Waldeck to reserve rooms. Tomorrow evening he would meet her at the station, and then he would have someone who—— He hesitated, then thought: whom he could tell everything to, even what no one had yet suspected. Dear God, at last the burden of everlasting silence would fall from him, and there would be someone whom he could trust blindly, and who could help him, because this someone—— Well, who could help him. He had never needed help more desperately than now. He could not confide in Riccarda, very much in need of help herself in her condition; nor in the old man, whose days he did not want to make yet more awful with his hazardous plans; and otherwise there was no one far and wide who would not betray him instantly. How good it was to know that someone was on the way to go with him! Someone who—— Again he did not finish his thought. But in his soul, which he had thought utterly full and hopelessly scorched by all he was planning and suffering, there was suddenly room for love.

Nevertheless, it was obvious that the guest, Jaroslav Uliř, was the merriest of all. He was sitting at this family table for the first time, and his common face, with the short hair brushed even more stiffly upward today, was beaming not only in the light from the tree, but with the friendly reception that everyone here had given him, the mere son of a peasant and a peasant's wife; he found he was actually being honored here. With the innate humility of the Czech countryman toward the city and patrician surroundings into which he was being received as an equal, he took his place at the table of presents like one who had received rich gifts. The old man had said to him: "It is a great pleasure to meet you, Herr Ulir," to which he had involuntarily replied: *"Děkuji uctivě, pane* [Thank you very much, sir]!" omitting to make the correction that his patriotism almost invariably suggested whenever anyone pronounced his name Ulir instead of Ulirsh. And Andreas (who had long known him at the plant, and had heard—and approved—a week before of the tie that bound him to Riccarda) had actually shaken hands with him vigorously twice; and Sepp had immediately offered to call him by his first name; and Riccarda—well, she had only nodded to him, but she had smiled as she did so.

After he got there, the five of them sang "Silent Night, Holy Night," as always, and the old man's voice was very much in evidence. By their every action they were establishing the order that they had been born to and believed in. It was unconscious, yet sometimes conscious nevertheless; for instance, after the singing when the old man bowed his head before the shining tree and repeated according to the old Tirolean custom:

For all things pleasant
In past and present
Let us now be glad!
And He that gave us
These things shall save us;
Our prayers we'll add.

Lord Jesus Christ, all praise to Thee
Who diedst to make us sinners free.
We thank Thee here below
And when to Heaven we go
Thy children we shall be:
To Thee we go, to Thee!

When he came to the last line, his grandchildren repeated it, even Sepp, from childhood habit; and Jaro (who knew German but had difficulty in speaking it) nodded, emphasized "To Thee" like the others, and crossed himself.

When the presents were distributed Riccarda, too, had her surprise: at her place was a ring, and engraved in it were the German words: "I thank you for the loveliest Christmas gift of my life. JARO." The inscription served to announce Riccarda's betrothal as the ring passed from hand to hand, and she celebrated it by putting the ring on her finger under the shining tree and before her own people.

"Děkuji!" said the Czech again, only much more softly; his short-

sighted wild eyes grew moist, and the bliss that looked out from them was irresistible. Smiling, she gave him her hand, which he kissed. Certainty came now to a house of mortal uncertainty.

Sepp was deciding about his future brother-in-law: "He's old-fashioned!" but old Mumelter thought: "The man has kind eyes!"

They sat down to eat punctually at seven; Riccarda served the traditional Christmas dinner that they had always been accustomed to: boiled carp, and for each person a slice of the freshly baked Christmas *Striezel,* to make which Riccarda had been hoarding raisins and almonds, now almost unobtainable, for weeks. There was wine too—not Tirolean, it is true, but a good Mělnik from the Lobkowitz cellars; and before this they had drained foaming mugs of beer from the Pilsen Municipal Brewery. Cozy comfort reigned about the table with its white cloth, and this was the first meal here that all of them had enjoyed from first mouthful to last.

Jaro, the bridegroom-to-be, still a trifle abashed with happiness and the honor that was being shown him, and because he was having his troubles with the German tongue, looked at his watch, and found that the time had come for his second surprise. He took out of his pocket a little box not much bigger than his hand, put it on the table, fiddled with it, and a few seconds later they could hear Christmas carols from the British Broadcasting Corporation, and immediately afterward the voice of the former Czech president, Beneš, speaking from London to the Czechs of his homeland.

The Mumelters did not understand any of it, but they could see from the eyes of this young man whom they had received into their family that it must be good news. He translated it for them—a message bidding them wait until the time came, and then to strike and win. Afterward the Czech national anthem, "Kde domov můj," came from the astonishingly tiny box, and they all sang it—even the Tiroleans, without knowing the words. *"Kde domov můj* [Where is my home]?" they sang, for anyone who has a homeland can understand an anthem. And so they, who had had a homeland and lost it, sang the anthem of those who still possessed a homeland and had lost it nevertheless. And a third time sounds came from the box, of which Jaro was all the prouder because it had been made in his department, "One of the most sensitive existing instruments to receive short-wave broadcasts," as he explained in his harsh, stilted German; "with it, ladies and gentlemen, you can hear all the underground stations, if you please, in Czechoslovakia, in Austria, in Russia, and all the short-wave stations in the world!"

As if to justify him, the voice of the underground station in the protectorate now said: *"Pozor!* Attention! In a few moments bombs will fall! They are Nazi bombs, not Allied ones! They are terrorist bombs to make you think that the Allies are your mortal enemies. Take cover! And remember it is your true mortal enemies who are bombarding you, the very Nazis who said they were protecting you—so they called our country a protectorate. It is your protectors who are bombing you. *Pozor!"*

The voice had scarcely finished the German version of this warning before there was an explosion, without previous alarm or anti-aircraft fire, rather far away, in the direction of Lobzy. A second, equally far away. Roaring motors. No anti-aircraft. Then in rapid succession two very much louder and more violent explosions, shaking the walls. Then silence.

The five around the table, on which the Christmas candles were peacefully spreading the scent of glowing pine needles, did not stir. This was the first bombardment they had ever been through. They sat as they had been sitting, saying nothing.

Only the old man said in a voice that expressed all the contempt that he felt: "Bombs on the night when our Saviour was born!"

Soon afterward the guest took his leave. The night was still, hostile, black.

Before Sepp fell asleep he read the secret decree, the original of which was not allowed to be taken home: the standard leader had read it to them before the Christmas celebration, and every Hitler Youth had to affirm that he had heard and understood it by signing in a special book.

The copy that Sepp had managed to get said:

Decree of Reich Leader Heinrich Himmler to all members of the Gestapo, the S.S., the Storm Troops, and the male Hitler Youth.

Comrades!

Beyond the limits of perhaps necessary middle-class laws, customs, and opinions, it will now be a great task, even outside the marriage bond, for German women and girls of good blood, not in frivolity but with deep moral earnestness, to become mothers of the children of the soldiers going off to war, of whom Fate alone can tell whether they will return or fall for the Fatherland.

On the men and women whose place remains at home by order of the State, likewise, these times more than ever impose the sacred obligation of once more becoming fathers and mothers of children.

A personal representative will take over in the name of the Führer the guardianship of all legitimate and illegitimate children of good blood whose fathers are killed in battle, missing, or unknown.

The unavoidable death of the best men, regrettable though it may be, is not the worst. Far worse is the lack of children, not begotten by those living now who will be dead after the war.

Adelheid Walpurga Schimetschek, Sepp thought, was a girl of good blood. And he fell asleep with daring dreams while his grandfather was awakened from a brief nap by the voice of the tiny box, which he had taken into his room and forgotten to turn off:

"Germans in the Reich! Germans in the protected regions! Germans overseas!

"These are the combined German national stations and German short-wave stations for overseas.

"It is two minutes before midnight, Central European Time.

"We give you the German Christmas song."

Bells. Then singing women's voices, to the old tune:

"Silent night, holy night,
All is still,
All is bright.
Only the Führer stands guard in the night,
Watching our Germany's slumbering might,
Hitler, the blessed of God,
Hitler, the blessed of God."

Although the old man silenced the box, he could not get to sleep again.

Chapter 11

WHEN ANDREAS FACED GWEN in the hotel room where she was to live until they had got settled here, he began to doubt that love was what he felt for her. Whether it was because she looked at him so searchingly, so coolly, so composedly, as if she had quite forgotten who he was and what he looked like, or whether it was the consciousness that he had been mistaken yesterday in thinking he had room for anything but the one thought that he kept thinking night and day, hiding and shaping—no matter which it was, his first hour with her was full of uncertainty, indeed of such strangeness that he even began to doubt whether he could ever confide in her. *Perhaps we haven't seen each other for too long a time,* he thought; *perhaps we didn't know each other long enough before.*

But it was she, Gwen, who was creating this atmosphere. Ever since she had been dragged off the sealed train she had waited for this moment that she was going through now—waiting with a fierce, almost unbearable impatience; waiting with a vividness of imagination that borrowed fire and color from her illness as yet unextinguished. *When I see him again,* she had told herself, *we shall kiss each other as no two people ever did before. I shall let him know how I've longed for him—no, that's not the word—with what delight, with what dread of the deadly waiting.* And through all the hundreds of times that she had imagined, embellished, savored, and dreaded in advance these first moments of meeting, she had known what she would say and what he would reply. She would say: "I've been waiting all the time just for you." And he would reply: "And I for you." And they would fall into each other's arms, right in front of everyone. And it would be heaven on earth.

But when they had arrived an hour and a quarter before at the Pilsen Station, which had once been called the Wilson Station, and she found herself looking at the man who awaited her, just as she had dreamed of doing, there were Storm Troopers and S.S. men and a few Czech military police on the platform, and Mother had a headache, and Daddy said: "Well, it hasn't got any prettier here since they renamed it Pilsen instead of Plzeň! This makes Pittsburgh look like the Riviera!"

And it was rather hard work catching a porter, and she was fifteen minutes getting all their baggage together, and then, among a great many other people out in the lobby behind a rope held by Storm Troopers, there was a hatless gentleman in a short green sheepskin coat, and it was Andreas, a hundred times handsomer than she had remembered him. And she had trembled with joy when she saw him, but the people behind the rope stared at her, or at least she thought they did, and so all she could say was: "Good evening." And when he in turn said nothing but, "Did you have a good trip?" they had to hunt up the porter (who had stopped off goodness knew where for a smoke) and a taxi, whose driver discovered that the baggage was much too heavy when he heard them speaking German. A moment later he discovered it was as light as a feather, and loaded it on with his own hands, for Andreas whispered to him something that Gwen overheard: "They're Americans." Then the four of them had driven to the Hotel Smitka, No. 1 Smetanagasse, which had been called the Hotel Waldeck when Bohemia was still Austrian, and now bore that name again. And Mother said: "There's no air here; I can hardly breathe." And Daddy said with a shrug: "Well, dear, it's no health resort."

And now they were face to face, and she loved him unspeakably.

But that was just the problem. It was unspeakable. She could not get it past her lips, where it was held back obstinately by her inborn, insuperable, hostile restraint. She loved everything about him, his somehow disappointed, bashful way of standing there, his deep voice, his eyes, clear, firm, protective. But she could not say it.

He, in turn, took this for restraint and strangeness; his pride was sensitive, and he ended by doubting whether she liked him at all any more—good God, women are capricious, and particularly these American girls. Probably she'd changed her mind meanwhile; nothing to be done about it. For that matter he himself had no time or room for so inessential an idea as love.

And they were both mistaken.

He was the first to realize it. He found her more pleasing than ever; everything about her had a special touch that fascinated him. And he thought she looked healthier than she had in the summer, and told her so, forgetting the little bit of fever that colored her cheeks, while she, in turn, forgot to remind him of this inconsequential trifle.

For months there had been no room in his life for anything but hatred, dangerous work, and far more dangerous thoughts. They fell away from him almost instantly when she gave him a long, long look of the loveliest eyes he knew, and said very softly: "You have no idea how happy I am to be here."

He inquired: "Because your father got the contract?"
She answered: "On account of you."
Then he kissed her, forgetting that there were such things as anguish and homelessness and the mortal overthrow of everything that had been, and hourly peril of death; he could feel her lips like one perishing of thirst. And she felt his like one drowning.
But she was still Gwen, and she pulled herself free.
"Forgive me," he said.
"I'm afraid you'll have a great deal to forgive me," she replied.
So they celebrated their meeting.
The following day, December 26, St. Stephen's Day, Mr. Hoffman requested Gwen to ask the young man, "that young fellow," as he called him, to come for a business talk to the hotel first, and then, at eight, for dinner at the Municipal Brewery. She was only too delighted to do so, and telephoned him early in the morning. But the employees and workmen of the Skoda Works had a full shift on this second Christmas holiday, and it was almost eight before Andreas could leave the plant. There was no time left for the talk at the hotel, so he went straight in the direction of the Prague Suburb, where the brewery is located; but it was almost an hour before the tram took him across the Pecháckovy Sady Bridge to the other bank of the Radbusa. Here was the huge building of the brewery next to the Sokolova, the Czech gymnasts' hall; at this hour, with the brewery stopped at night and only the taprooms open, there was a constant stream of the hungry and thirsty. The burgesses of Pilsen were sitting in the three huge dining rooms as well as the numerous private rooms, striving to wash down the bitter taste of the day with their famous bitter beer.
Finding someone here was no joke; but Andreas managed to get hold of old Petrašek, the headwaiter, who had seen generations of beer-drinkers come and go, and asked him what room the "American family" was in. The presiding genius even nodded meaningly when the American family was mentioned, and inquired, astonishingly, "Are you from the police, sir?"
It was not until he went into the private room that the latecomer understood the strange question and saw that something must have happened of which only the epilogue and the excitement of those involved still continued.

Mr. Hoffman was not one to bewail what was bad as long as there was something less bad, or, above all, something good. On the very first day he took Mrs. Hoffman to the world-famous brewery, and urged her to keep trying the frothy golden-yellow beverage until she "acquired a taste for it." Mrs. Hoffman, who cared nothing for beer, but still worshiped him just as she had when she was young, did as she had always done: she gave in. And Gwen was doing well, considering, having emptied one of the glasses called *Seitels* while her father was already on his third *Krügel,* a glass with a handle, twice the size, whose luxuriant crown of snow-white foam sank lower with every gulp. Mrs. Hoffman, however, despite a most devoted resolution to think the yellow stuff marvelous, had ordered club soda after her first sip, and this was the only thing that disturbed her husband's high good humor at the moment. For he had also thoroughly enjoyed the roast goose, which both of the ladies thought too rich; and he was in the act of touching refilled glasses with his daughter, whom he had not seen so merry in a long time, when someone from the table opposite called out: *"Prosit!"*

The caller was a young and conspicuously good-looking fellow in the uniform of the Hitler Youth, who was sitting with three other young men in similar uniforms, and had—judging by the matchsticks lying at his plate (the method used to tally the number of glasses consumed)—done himself more than well.

Mr. Hoffman good-humoredly lifted his glass, said *"Prosit!"* and drank with him.

Gwen put hers down.

The young man, however, had meant not Mr. Hoffman but her, and if he had been noticed sooner, his *Prosit!* and the person to whom it was directed would have been no surprise; for almost half an hour he had been staring, and telling his three companions that that was a damn fine girl. Did he, by any chance, suppose she would see anything in him, he was asked derisively, and he retorted: "Why not? If I want her to she'll see something in me!" The three said skeptically, "Want to bet?" Accordingly the *Prosit!* was the product of an irritation that saw itself challenged to action, with a determination to assert itself at any cost.

When Gwen put down her glass without giving her admirer so

much as a glance, the three doubting Thomases burst out laughing.

The toaster sprang up, then sat down again.

But as he sat down he said loudly enough so that not only the Hoffmans but those sitting at the other tables could not help hearing: "I just drank to you, *mein Fräulein.*"

Even now Gwen did not look over or reply; her father whispered something to her, and Mrs. Hoffman, for her part, gazed in astonishment at the young fellow.

Gwen, the young fellow noticed, refused with a shake of the head to do what her father wanted. Her eyes, whose beauty did not escape even a man half drunk, took on an icy glitter.

"Fräulein!" he repeated, leaning across the table and pushing aside the beer glasses that stood in his way with a sweep of the arm. "I spoke to you. And I'm in the habit of being answered!"

If the one who spoke in this tone had not been in uniform, and accompanied by three others in uniform, all wearing holsters on their hips and daggers at their belts, people would simply have laughed at him, and that would have been that; after all, he was simply a boy overstepping the mark, and not even sober, into the bargain. But the townsfolk at the other tables, mostly German-speaking (for the Hoffmans had unknowingly sat in one of the rooms frequented by Germans), were so blindly accustomed to taking uniformed men with deadly seriousness, making no distinction between adults and children or between right and wrong, that there was only one laugh, and that was Mr. Hoffman's.

"Look here, young man," he said in German, although Mrs. Hoffman urged him in English not to get into an argument with the "tipsy fool," "I'm glad you enjoy this wonderful beer so much. But I think you ought to be satisfied with that pleasure."

The room, previously rather noisy, had grown quite still, and you could hear it when anyone put down a knife or fork.

The young man got up. "I have nothing to say to you," he replied in a strangely low voice. "I didn't ask for your advice, and I don't want it. But I did drink to the lady at your table, and I shall not tolerate her not returning the honor. A German girl whom a Hitler Youth drinks to is required to feel honored!"

"Bravo!" cried someone in the rear, thus remarkably encouraging the young fellow, who was not altogether sure of himself.

"Don't answer!" Mrs. Hoffman begged.

"What?" asked the boy in uniform. "What did that lady there say?"

At this Gwen replied in German, and her eyes were colder than ever: "I'm not a German girl."

This was so unexpected to the Hitler Youth that he hesitated for a moment. Then he took a step toward the Hoffmans and asked: "What are you, then, if I may ask? A Jewess?"

This was too much even for the good-natured Mr. Hoffman.

"My daughter is an American," he declared. And he added in a loud voice: "Stop this preposterous annoyance this minute! We don't owe you any account of ourselves, and have no notion of giving you any. I trust you understand!"

The difference in age between the two was so glaringly conspicuous that the three other boys in uniform grew uneasy. The word "American," too, made caution advisable. So far as the German beer-drinkers at the other tables were concerned, Hoffman's behavior had not been without its effect; they looked at him, some of them with obvious envy: "He's in luck—he can tell young whippersnappers like that what he thinks! But God knows we are condemned to hold our tongues!" their eyes said loudly; even now none of them dared venture a word.

The young fellow who had picked the quarrel quite gratuitously was now standing by the Americans' table. He touched the table with the two fingers that he leaned on; he was not sober enough and too much concerned with preserving his authority to stop and think.

"You there!" he said in a voice of almost unbelievable arrogance to a man at least thirty years his senior: "If you're an American then I can't imagine what business you have here. Be off with you; go on back to your Mr. Rosenfeld, and dance around the golden calf with him and the rest of the Jewish gangsters. But as long as you're here, you're to behave decently and show respect to the uniform of the Führer! Do you hear me? I must point out to you, and I would also point out to the young lady here, that I am in command of the local Hitler Youth! As commandant of the Pilsen Hitler Youth, Fräulein, I ask you to raise your glass and drink with me to the health of our Führer, Adolf Hitler!"

At the last moment the young fellow had had this inspiration; it was undeniably a cunning one, and it saved his reputation. For at that moment one of the silently listening townspeople, presumably one who wanted to silence his own eyes, which previously might have been too loud, brought him a full glass. He now held this up high in Gwen's direction. *"Heil* Hitler!" he said, looking her straight in the eye and carrying the glass to his lips. As if at a word of command everyone else in the room did the same; whether their glasses were full or empty, they carried them to their mouths, saying as they did so: *"Heil* Hitler!"

Mrs. Hoffman moistened her lips with club soda. Mr. Hoffman took a gulp of beer. Neither of them spoke. Gwen, however, neither spoke nor touched the glass before her.

His own glass still raised to drink, the young fellow stood before her, staring into her eyes.

Unstirring, icily she looked at him.

The people in the room grew restless; whispers were heard.

"Did you hear me!" the leader of the Hitler Youth roared at the girl.

At this she, too, got up. She said slowly, one word at a time, striving for extreme distinctness, as she always did when speaking German: "I hear that you're trying to insult a girl. But you're too insignificant for that."

The expression of her face, almost white, and her slow, decided manner of speaking had not escaped a single person in the room. No one knew quite what to think. She was very pretty, the German beer-drinkers thought. The German women thought her hair-do ridiculous.

Neither Mr. nor Mrs. Hoffman made any motion to interrupt their daughter, and astonishingly enough it was the timorous Mrs. Hoffman who nodded approval of Gwen's words.

Losing all control of himself, the young fellow grabbed Gwen's hand.

"Let go!" she cried.

"Not until you drink the Führer's health!" replied the Hitler Youth, trying to force the glass to her lips.

At this Mr. Hoffman grabbed the hand and squeezed it, hard; the hand dropped, and there was a cry of pain.

The young fellow fell back a step and reached for his holster with his uninjured hand. But Petrašek, the headwaiter, always on the spot whenever anything threatened to go wrong in the Municipal Brewery, and long since informed of what was going on, saved the situation by turning out the light, yelling "Short circuit!" and whispering in Czech to the waiters: "Leave them in the dark a while, the damned animals!" When the light came on again he and, for that matter, the other three lads in uniform had lined up before the intoxicated boy, and by the time Andreas came in just before nine o'clock outward calm had been restored. In fact, wise old Petrašek with his faked short circuit had almost succeeded in making the whole business a trifle ridiculous; a few of the German beer-drinkers departed, and the four Hitler Youth had gone away, threatening to come back and demand an accounting.

"They will too," said Andreas, after learning the details.

"So what!" said Mr. Hoffman, wondering why the fourth mug that he had ordered was not being brought. "They're simply ill-behaved children! They ought to have forty whacks. That's all the attention they ought to get."

But Andreas could not help thinking that one of these "children" had given a blow in the face to his grandfather, who had spoken in the same way. And it was this blow that still burned in his dreams at night and kept him working night and day to make sure that these "children" should never again be able to strike decency in the face. "I'm afraid you take the matter too lightly," he said, growing more and more somber. "They aren't ill-behaved children, they're children carefully trained to misbehave. By the way, did you say the young fellow introduced himself as the leader of the local Hitler Youth?"

"But not until much later," Gwen said.

"That doesn't change matters. If he really is the Hitler Youth leader, then it's Kuno Schultheiss."

"And?" said Mr. Hoffman, unimpressed.

"And," said Andreas, "he's the son of the managing director of the Skoda Works, your new boss."

"All the better," retorted the incorrigible optimist. "Then at least I can tell his dad what a lout of a son he has."

"Do," Gwen approved. And again the timorous Mrs. Hoffman, who could follow a German conversation only with some effort, and had had more than enough of it for tonight, joined the militant party: "Yes, dear. I think you should."

At this Andreas liked the three Hoffmans better than ever. Nevertheless, he urged them to leave undrunk the fourth glass, which would in any case never have been served, and to prefer the streets to a repetition of the previous incident.

Next morning, however, the following scene took place. The location was the office of the managing director of the Skoda Works, and the actors were the managing director and Mr. Hoffman.

"I asked you to step in," began Herr Schultheiss, and then interrupted himself: "Or would you prefer to speak English?"

"Not at all," Hoffman replied. "Why?"

"Oh, I was just wondering," said the other, taking from his gigantic desk a pile of cigar and cigarette boxes.

"Will you smoke?" he offered.

"Yes, thanks, a cigar," was the reply. Hoffman helped himself, cut off the tip of the imported Havana, took a light, and began to smoke, the very picture of enjoyment.

His interlocutor had lighted a cigarette. This took somewhat longer than it might have; through the three high windows of the office, prime-ministerial in its spaciousness and furnishings, came the pounding, drilling, hissing, and roaring of the plant, going full blast on the day shift. But despite the daylight the air outside was gray, thick enough to cut with a knife, partly from fog, partly from smoke, occasionally splashed with a rain of sparks that shot up high and red, then vanished. Otherwise nothing was to be seen. The lights in the director's room were on.

"Have a pleasant trip?" inquired Herr Schultheiss. He had a long face whose slender, pointed chin was its most conspicuous feature. Sparse, almost gray hair made the high forehead higher still. His eyes were colorless, scarcely present at all.

"Thanks. Very pleasant," replied the other, who was prepared for a variety of things, and resolved to give no openings to this lean gentleman.

"Glad to hear it," said his superior. Just then the telephone rang, and Mr. Hoffman heard him say: "Prague? Yes, put them on."

A pause.

"Good morning, Herr Reichsprotektor!"

Pause.

"No, the first I'd heard of it."

A longer pause.

"You don't say? Why, that *is* a surprise! A man with every appearance of being so cultivated too!"

A long pause, during which the voice at the other end was plainly audible.

"Why, this is an awful business!" Herr Schultheiss said.

Pause.

"No, I haven't laid eyes on him for days. The youngsters on duty are harder than hell at it just now."

Pause.

"I see. Direct from him. May I ask for the exact wording?"

Pause. The voice on the telephone dictated something, and Herr Schultheiss wrote something down.

"I'll be damned! How was that again? Wrenched? The police doctor said so? Might I have the exact medical opinion?"

Pause, dictation, notes.

"Dislocation of the right wrist. I'll be damned! Many thanks, Herr Reichsprotektor, much obliged for your call. I beg your pardon? Certainly. It'll be taken care of. *Heil* Hitler!"

Very effectively staged, thought Mr. Hoffman, who seemed to be enjoying his cigar more and more. He had had time to observe three things: a photograph of Hitler on the desk, with a dedication and signature; an oil painting of Goering in green hunting dress, the gold frame of which occupied the whole end of the office; and an often-repeated nervous twitch around the mouth of his interlocutor.

Although the telephone conversation was obviously about yesterday's incident at the brewery, Herr Schultheiss said not a word about it. Glancing from the note pad to a folder of papers lying on the left end of the desk, he moved them to the middle, opened them, and said: "You did good work on trucks on the other side. Or, as you usually say, 'a splendid job'?"

"Tolerable," replied Hoffman.

"Ford's you used to work at? I mean in Detroit?"

"Yes."

"Design?"

"And sales."

"I take it, or, as you say on the other side, I guess, you were making money there?"

"The Ford plant? Oh yes, I expect so. About like the Skoda Works. Maybe a little less."

The twitch around the interrogator's mouth grew more frequent. He gave Hoffman a quick sidelong glance, and said, skimming through the papers: "In any case, we're particularly happy to have an expert of your experience and connections in the plant. You still maintain relations with the Ford Company, don't you?"

Could he actually not know that?

"Not for years," replied Hoffman. "I retired from business, and am living in Boston."

"Oh, of course," Herr Schultheiss corrected himself with a smile. "You've chosen the better way. Boston! Lovely city. An aristocratic old tradition, just like London. The most English of the American cities, in fact. Just the thing I like. Do you know Hocking at Harvard? I mean William E. Hocking, the philosopher? Too bad. You really ought to meet him. Splendid man as a personality, and perhaps the deepest religious thinker alive today."

"Deeper than Alfred Rosenberg?" asked the American from Salzburg, looking with utter innocence at the Boston enthusiast.

At this Herr Schultheiss, the twitching of his mouth growing persistent, observed: "You have a sense of humor. Excellent. We shall complement each other as happily as we could possibly wish. You see I haven't any. I suppose you've heard that's one of the chief shortcomings we National Socialists are accused of—lack of humor?"

"Yes," said Hoffman, "I've heard of it. And judging by what I've seen so far, I'm afraid it's true." Again his utterly innocent gaze fell upon his partner in the conversation.

"It will be a pleasure to talk it over with you sometime," said the latter, and replied to the ring of the telephone: "No. I don't want to be disturbed now!" He immediately added, turning to his visitor: "When Herr Mumelter spoke to me of you—I take it I'm not mistaken in regarding him as your future son-in-law?—I very readily took the opportunity of bringing you to join us at Skoda. You are going to do very valuable work for us. By the time you've looked around a little and settled down to your work—just in passing, reports abroad about the arrangement of the plants and working methods are not allowed—I was going to say, I presume you'll take over the truck division?"

"That's what the agreement calls for."

"To be sure. And I am counting, I mean Skoda is counting on your manufacturing here the same excellent army trucks and lorries that you produced on the other side."

"How's that?" asked Hoffman.

"I mean, you'll improve anything here that you think needs improving."

"In so far as I can without infringing on any patents," declared the American, still smoking, still with that innocence of expression, in a very decided tone that brooked no contradiction.

"Naturally," the managing director agreed at once. But he added: "Naturally, patents mustn't be infringed. You simply apply for a new one."

"For that I'd have to make an invention."

"Oh well! An expert like you will very soon invent something. I'll send you Dr. Crusius from our patent department; he'll certainly know what to do. For my part, at any rate, I want to be as plain-spoken as possible, Herr Hoffman. We don't want anything from you except what you produced on the other side. Exactly the same. That's what we hired you for, and that's what we're paying you 2,000 reichsmarks a month and your quarters for. By the way, will you please take down the address of the villa, which is at your disposal starting today, and which I hope you will enjoy? Though of course you mustn't expect American perfection. We're old-fashioned Europeans. Villa Elfriede. Bendová Ulice 17."

"Just a minute," said Hoffman. "You want to speak plainly. So do I. I can't possibly do here what I did over there. That would be against our law."

"I beg your pardon? I suppose you mean against the laws of the United States?" Schultheiss asked sarcastically.

"Well, yes," replied Hoffman, abashed for the first time. His tongue had slipped and let out the "against our law."

"Exactly," observed the other courteously. "Please don't make any mistake about that. Our laws, which means your laws as well, are the laws of the German Reich. Is that clear?"

"Certainly," replied the other, annoyed at his slip.

"Because, I assume, your feelings are a hundred per cent undivided in favor of the German Reich? The same as Herr Mumelter's?" The managing director crushed out his cigarette in a bronze ash tray copied from the Lion of Lucerne.

"Certainly," replied Hoffman, slightly taken aback.

"Although," Schultheiss observed, leafing through the papers without reading them, "you and Herr Mumelter were not in sympathy with the Fascists, I mean with our Italian allies?"

"I don't quite know what you mean."

"Didn't you have some correspondence, long-distance telephone calls, and that sort of thing, aimed against the solution of the South Tirolean question? Or am I wrong?"

"A hundred per cent," was the answer, declining to give the other a second chance.

"So much the better. But you were questioned? I don't believe I'm mistaken there?"

"The questioning completely disproved the charges." Hoffman let his cigar go out.

"I suppose you know the words of our great German philosopher, Fichte?" asked Herr Schultheiss, toying with the wide ivory paper knife next to the folder on his desk.

"No, Director, I don't."

"I just happened to think of it because in Fichte's *Fourteen Addresses to the German Nation*—which, incidentally, I would urgently advise your reading, a veritable gold mine for anyone who has lived away from the Fatherland for some time—there's a passage that says: 'Anyone who is accused feels that his accusation is unfounded.' Very neatly put, don't you think?"

"Very," admitted the other with his most innocent smile. He said: "I take it I may be going along now?"

The more he smiled, the more nervously the other's mouth twitched. "You made a note of the address of the villa?" he detained him.

Hoffman, who knew perfectly well that the time for him to go had not yet come, held up an envelope on the back of which he had written, "Villa Elfriede, Bendová Ulice 17."

"This is your first trip to Pilsen?" asked Schultheiss, continuing the conversation, which was becoming more and more of a judicial examination.

"I've been here once before."

"Have you seen our plant yet?"

"No."

"But you have seen the second, or rather the first characteristic feature of our town, the Municipal Brewery?"

"Yesterday evening."

"Have a cigar, Herr Hoffman."

"Many thanks. Never two in succession."

"How did you like it there?"

"Marvelous beer, Director."

"And—I take it, as you say at home—you did some honor to our marvelous beer?"

"Just enough to make me comfortably ready for bed."

"Didn't you allow yourself the innocent pleasure of taking on something of a load, or, to use another of the excellent expressions that I learned to admire during my stay on the other side, weren't you a trifle 'high'?"

Hoffman saw what he was aiming at. More determined than ever not to play that game, he said with an expression of the most touching candor, "I've only been drunk twice in my life. The last time was when my daughter was born."

"In other words, you can remember everything that happened to you at the brewery yesterday?"

Hoffman, not setting foot on the golden bridge that was—for reasons he did not yet understand—being built for him, answered: "Everything."

"Then you probably recollect that the young lady, your daughter, behaved more than strangely yesterday evening. Or was she less moderate in her devotion to Gambrinus than you were?"

"Oh," said Hoffman, "I'm afraid you're mixing up the parts. It wasn't my daughter, but a young fellow who annoyed my daughter, that was rather high. Or at least so I assumed out of respect for the upbringing he may have had, though he showed no sign of it yesterday evening."

The interview was still just within the limits of social conversation.

"Are you alluding to my son?" asked Herr Schultheiss, the twitch scarcely stopped at all.

"I mean the young man who was so insolent. I should be sorry if he were your son. But as I said, I count as a mitigating circumstance the condition which neither my daughter nor myself was in."

"There's a mistake here," observed the managing director, balancing the ivory paper knife erect before him. "It isn't you that must find mitigating circumstances for the behavior of others, but, at best, we for your behavior."

Hoffman got up and came closer to the desk. "You mentioned that you were familiar with conditions on the other side," he said. "So you will realize that remarks of this sort are never permitted over there under any circumstances. I'm a man who thinks before he speaks. That's why you can take it as proved that your son's behavior last night was perfectly impossible. If he can't be excused on the grounds of drunkenness, he's inexcusable. Surely I may be running along now?"

He looked fixedly at the man before him; despite his good nature, Mr. Hoffman's gaze could sometimes be very disconcerting. Now he also saw the inscription on the photograph: "With gratitude for German deeds and German sentiments, ADOLF HITLER."

Schultheiss, who had kept his seat, returned the look. "Just a moment," was his civil reply. "I don't know whether you happened to notice my conversation on the telephone. I was talking to Reich Protector Baron von Neurath in Prague. The occurrence at the brewery was reported to him, and he considered it important enough to give orders that the guilty party should be held accountable."

"Just my opinion," Hoffman agreed. "It won't do the young man any harm to be taught a few manners."

"Herr Hoffman," said the other, "I admire your misapprehension of the facts. Your daughter refused yesterday evening to drink the Führer's health. You abetted her in it, forcibly, in fact. I still maintain you were not sober. But if you were, you must certainly realize what a monstrous error—to put it mildly—you and your daughter were guilty of. I will say nothing about its constituting a stupendous lack of respect for the head of the State; I will only emphasize that it is a slap in the face of the international courtesy you are so proud of on the other side."

"Listen to me, Herr Schultheiss," replied Hoffman, putting aside both the title of "Director" and his smile, "there is a limit to everything. Even to the twisting of facts. Possibly you can do that with people who will stand for it. I'm not one of them. Your son annoyed my daughter by staring and silly attempts to obtrude himself. When she didn't react, he tried to force her to drink his health; when that came to nothing, too, in order to avoid making himself completely ridiculous he substituted the Führer's health for his own; as he laid his hand on her, I snapped his behavior and his hand out of it. Those are the facts. And anyone who tells you anything else is a liar. If anyone has any complaint in the matter, it is my daughter and I. I would like to leave now."

Now Herr Schultheiss, too, got up. He stood facing Hoffman across the desk. "You are to apologize!" he demanded flatly. "You are to express, this moment, your daughter's and your own deep regret that under the influence of alcohol you were so little in command of your senses that you allowed a toast to the Führer's health to pass unheeded. I demand it of you as your present superior! Think before you answer."

"I shall not make such a statement," replied Hoffman without a moment's reflection.

"Then for my part I am sorry that I cannot be responsible for the consequences. Herr Hoffman! Don't be so perfectly unreasonable! You're risking your livelihood! Can't you see that?"

"I see all sorts of things. What explanation does your son offer?"

"You said yourself that you supposed he was drunk. Boys of that age often take a little more than is good for them. And I don't think your daughter would have lost any jewels from her crown if she had made an equally innocent return to a young man's innocent '*Prosit!*' Incidentally, *Prosit!* never means the health of the person who proposes it, but of the one to whom it is proposed. Do use your head, Herr Hoffman. Surely you aren't going to make an affair of state out of a matter that could be settled with a single word of apology, now are you? Well, then! May I take your word as said?"

"No." The good-natured face was greatly changed. It had grown cold and unyielding. "When someone has done me wrong, I won't let myself be put in the wrong. You won't get far with me that way."

"Your ideas of wrong are, I fear, rather antiquated," declared the other, and his expression, too, was stony, in spite of the twitch. "You will have to revise them." The managing director made a gesture that might have been interpreted either as regret or as farewell.

Hoffman took it as the latter. "We'll see about that," he said, leaving the room with its prime-ministerial furnishings.

Chapter 12

Mrs. Hoffman, working with Gwen to furnish the Villa Elfriede, also made strange discoveries. The first was the noise, going on day and night—a very different sort of noise from what she remembered in Detroit, where they had also lived close to the factory district. If she asked anyone here, she was told with a shrug that nothing else could be expected so near the Skoda Works, for the Villa Elfriede, a stone structure in the baroque style with green wooden verandas, was half an hour's walk from the plant. But Mrs. Hoffman felt as Andreas had a few months before in Bozen, when he thought he heard weeping night after night, and no one would admit hearing anything but cats; night after night, and sometimes by day as well, sounds reached her ear that she was willing to swear had nothing to do with the pounding machinery that drowned them out; she was even willing to take oath that they were human cries, shriller than any she had ever heard, and human groans, as if someone somewhere were suffering awful pain. Strange that neither Gwen nor her husband, whom she kept questioning about it, would admit to hearing anything. She had even taken occasion to consult Dr. Paumgartner about the possibility of its being due to illusions of the ear; and the Austrian doctor, with that cynical face of his, had replied oracularly that it was quite possible: this was an age of hallucinations, and one saw and heard a great many things nowadays that actually didn't exist.

But Mrs. Hoffman also made other discoveries that were, if anything, yet stranger. Above all, one had to consider every word one uttered as carefully as if one's life depended on it—and she was so accustomed to saying what she thought without much consideration.

When you went into a shop the thing you could not understand was not the language or the extreme difficulty of getting anything at all, but rather the fact that you had to refrain from all conversation with other customers or with the salesperson; at most you might say yes or no, and for heaven's sake not a word of opinion. When Mrs. Hoffman remembered what a pleasure it had been to go shopping in Boston, she could understand it still less; how many hundreds of pleasant conversations she had had with her grocer, from the praise of the weather to the elections. Or with the milliner and the hairdresser!

Here, on the other hand, you weren't allowed to open your mouth —ostensibly because of the American accent. But she soon saw that this was not true, for the others said almost nothing either as they stood in line for five or six hours, and what little they said was in a whisper.

This whispering! Was one gifted with speech so as not to use it? You might think that every single human being here had a secret that he would not betray for anything in the world. Wherever two people were standing together, they whispered. The Czechs, whom she did not understand, whispered in Czech, and those who spoke German, whom she understood quite well, whispered in German, unless they were people with swastika arm bands, and even they were sometimes seen to whisper. You whispered in the street, but you whispered at home too—that was what passed Mrs. Hoffman's understanding. All right, she had paid very little attention to the whole Nazi business so far, and had always thought the people who complained of it so bitterly were rather exaggerating. But what she saw now with her own eyes was far worse. You didn't even dare to say out loud within your own four walls what you had to say to your own husband and daughter—no, you whispered, and before you whispered you opened the door and shut it again to make sure no one was listening outside. And yet no one could possibly be listening except Božena, the stupid peasant girl that Mrs. Hoffman had finally got to help her after an endless search, a nineteen-year-old who hardly understood German, so that they had to communicate with her by signs. Yet every second sentence spoken at the Villa Elfriede was, "Not so loud! Božena might overhear!"

Mrs. Hoffman, with little inclination toward critical study of the world and her fellow men, could not seem to find her way. As far back as she could remember, trust had been the be-all and end-all of everything. Now it was distrust. There was a wall between people. A cloud hung over their faces. Dealing with them had always been so easy, so pleasant, such a matter of course—now it had grown dangerous and problematical. Mrs. Hoffman, avoiding problems wherever she could, felt she must be in some spectral dream from which she must awake at all costs.

Gwen, on the other hand, was fortunate enough to be living in a dream that she wanted to go on dreaming. Never to wake up—never to let her thoughts drag her to the point that would suddenly open her eyes; to shut them as best she could, opening them only when Andreas came in view; and to surrender, for the first time in her young conscious existence, to a love that was really worth loving. The oftener she saw Andreas, and the more closely she watched the man, his life and being, the stronger, deeper, and more inevitable grew their relationship.

"You're getting more European every day," her father would tell her. Quite possible. If that was European, then she had always been European.

Standing between her mother, who could not understand this life, and her father, who understood it all too well, she was the only one of the family who knew that it was hell, and to whom it was nevertheless heaven. She even knew whence the screams came that her mother heard and asked about so persistently—from the J. S. P. (Jewish Settlement Pilsen), whose fence she had repeatedly looked through from outside; it was twenty minutes to the west of the Villa Elfriede. There, she knew—and so did her father and Andreas and the Pilseners—people were flogged daily; the screams were from pain and fear. The moment this came into Gwen's mind was the moment to open her eyes suddenly and be abysmally ashamed that she was happy.

But when she could stand it no longer, and asked Andreas: "Can such things possibly be? Human beings being flogged twenty minutes' walk from here, roaring with pain and terror, and nothing done about it?" he gave her an answer that soothed her conscience. She could not tell anyone about it, not even her father, but still the consolation of his reply was unfailing. Whenever her eyes opened in horror now, this consolation allowed her to shut them again and return to the dream she was dreaming. "You *like* to worry," her mother had been in the habit of telling her; to her, life had not been much of a problem until lately. To Gwen, life had been a problem all her days. Not because she liked to worry, but because she did like to think.

But of the three Mr. Hoffman was the one to whom life here was the greatest trial. Spied upon as he was, every step he took watched, every word he spoke suspected and diverted through dark channels to people who interpreted and misinterpreted it, he had to behave like a defendant out on bail, expecting arrest with every passing second. For the moment his refusal to apologize had remained without immediate results; but someday it was bound to have consequences. Accordingly, he had only the one chance that Andreas, too, had discovered as a means to assure his comparative safety: to make himself so indispensable in the plant that interest in keeping an irreplaceable associate would outweigh the desire to remove him as an adversary. Without stopping to wonder what it was that actually threatened him, Mrs. Hoffman could feel the threat constantly, and his "Not so loud! Božena might hear!" did nothing to reassure her. Every time he was late for a meal she was panic-stricken. As the hand of the clock approached the hour when she expected her husband, her fingers grew stiff and the blood froze in her veins. Every time the telephone rang it lashed her to her feet. She would stand at the window of the living room, furnished in Biedermeier style, staring along the street, and never recovering her composure until Mr. Hoffman's car appeared. Even then her calm lasted only until he left the house again. But you simply couldn't live like this! "A person can't be afraid forever!" she had complained to Dr. Paumgartner, who occasionally stopped in on his way to or from the Skoda plant, where he was the factory doctor.

"Can't they? There are eighty-four millions living like that in our fortunate Third Reich!" he had told her, and with him one never quite knew how he meant it.

"Do be sensible!" Mr. Hoffman had begged her. "What are you afraid of, anyway? Are you afraid that someday I may just disappear off the face of the earth?"

Yes. Exactly and literally that was what she was afraid of.

However, everything would have gone its accustomed way at the Villa Elfriede, and after a while Mrs. Hoffman might have got over her terrified waiting and starting and listening for inexplicable sounds, or even with the miraculous adaptability of human nature, have grown accustomed to it, except for something quite unconnected with the Hoffman family, which nevertheless had a bearing on everything that came later—the murder of Madeleine Roux.

She was a twenty-one-year-old Alsatian girl who had been living in Pilsen for nine months, earning her living by giving private French lessons. The graceful little brunette had not turned her heart into a murderers' den, and she told anyone who cared to listen what she thought of the Nazis. This did not prevent her from giving lessons in a number of decidedly Nazi families, among others to the ten-year-old daughter of Managing Director Schultheiss, which she did with the same enthusiasm as in the Czech and German-speaking anti-Nazi families. Among the latter was the Hoffman family. Every Monday, Wednesday, and Friday, from three to four, she held French conversations with Gwen in the Villa Elfriede; and those afternoons she came from the J. S. P., where she taught the children from one to a quarter of three. The Nazis had at first made objections to her teaching at the Jewish Settlement, but the Alsatian girl had apparently convinced them in the end that it would be better to give the Jewish children some sensible occupation than to leave them to their own devices.

The murder took place on the third Friday in April. The most incredible thing about it was that Mademoiselle Roux, mortally wounded, managed to drag herself as far as the Villa Elfriede, where she collapsed on the stairway just inside the door. Gwen heard the dull sound of her fall, and found the dying girl lying on the stone floor. She said in French: *"Vite! Un médecin! Cunnaux m'a assassiné . . . Télégraphiez à mon frère . . ."* Then she lost consciousness. Dr. Paumgartner, to whom Gwen telephoned, appeared a few minutes later. At 3:30 P.M. he pronounced Mademoiselle Roux dead, giving the cause as stabbing with a knife or dagger. Before leaving the villa he reported to the state's attorney, who dispatched a homicide detail to the spot; they recorded the facts, but, to Mrs. Hoffman's horror, left the corpse behind, with strict orders not to touch it or change anything in the house. The women were also instructed not to leave the house, not to telephone, and in every way to follow the instructions of the two Gestapo officials whom the homicide detail left behind. When Mr. Hoffman came back from the plant as usual at six, he found his wife and daughter half mad with horror. An hour later the evening papers of the Protectorate, both the two German papers, *Die Neue Zeit* and the *Volksdeutsche Zeitung,* and the Czech papers, *Vlajka, Venkov,* and *Añ Zet,* reported in banner headlines:

RITUAL MURDER OF AN ARYAN

Jew boy stabs French teacher, and drains her blood for Easter rites.

Below, in identical wording, came a story from the D. N. B.:

Pilsen, April 23. A bestial crime was perpetrated in Pilsen today. The victim was Madeleine Roux, twenty-one, a French teacher from Mulhouse in Alsace. Miss Roux, who was compelled to leave her native country last summer because she had bravely spoken and written in favor of reincorporating Alsace-Lorraine in the German Reich, was earning a modest but adequate livelihood by giving lessons in Pilsen. Members of the best German circles were among her pupils, so Miss Roux scarcely needed to give lessons at the J. S. P.; however, she allowed herself to be induced by the bribery and ingratiation of the Jewish families housed there to give three French lessons a week to Jewish children. These lessons regularly took place in the barracks where the so-called bank director, more correctly the usurer, extortioner, gouger, war profiteer, and swindler, Leopold Israel Jellinek, is quartered. This eastern Jew, who immigrated after the World War from Galicia to Brünn, where he unscrupulously amassed a huge fortune as branch manager of the Živnostenská Banka, is, like all his eastern compatriots, an Orthodox Jew, clings to the ritual customs of his curled-haired forefathers, and recites his swindler's prayers every morning and evening in ritual costume, donning the so-called prayer shawl. As it is nearly time for the Jewish Easter celebration (Passover), he incited his almost feeble-minded nineteen-year-old son, Richard Israel Jellinek, to secure Christian blood, which is well known to play a most important part in all Orthodox Jewish Easter celebrations. The plan must have been prepared far in advance. For when Miss Roux arrived to give her lesson in the settlement at 1 P.M., she found herself alone with the feeble-minded youth. Only a few minutes after she had been seen arriving, four Storm Troop sentries heard piercing screams for help from the direction of the Jellinek barracks. Going to investigate, they found the French girl sitting at a table with young Jellinek standing before her in a menacing attitude. Being questioned as to what was going on, she replied: "Nothing. Richard was just joking." At 2:30 P.M. the same Storm Troop sentries saw the Frenchwoman leave the settlement and proceed as usual in the direction of the near-by Villa Elfriede, where she also gave lessons. As she passed the camp gate, the group leader on guard noticed her pallor, and asked whether anything was wrong. She replied in the negative. Fifteen minutes later she was found dead at the Villa Elfriede.

Prompt investigation by the state's attorney's office of Pilsen and the secret state police led to the sensational discovery of a water pitcher full of blood and a bloody bread knife in the Jellineks' shanty. Confronted with the overwhelming evidence, young Jellinek realized the futility of denial and confessed to having been incited by his father to stab Miss Roux with the bread knife and catch as much of her blood as possible in the water pitcher. Both the murderer and his father, who continued to protest in true Jewish fashion the innocence of his half-animal son and, of course, of himself, were held for trial at the Pilsen Provincial Court.

Students of Bohemian history will remember an analogous case that took place forty-three years ago, also at the Jewish Easter season, and at no great distance from Pilsen, stirring the entire civilized world to horror and indignation. In this case Leopold Hilsner, a Jewish distiller, butchered an Aryan maid by the name of Agnes Hružova in the little town of Polná, on the Bohemian-Moravian frontier, drained her blood, and buried her. The trial of the Jew, who denied his guilt, dragged on for years—striking testimony to the incapacity of the judiciary and the legal order of the time, which finally ended, with mistaken kindness, by sentencing Hilsner to thirty-three years' imprisonment.

This time, thanks to the New Order in our judicial system, the matter will be subject to no such delays, and the ghastly misdeed will be more promptly and radically atoned for. Such crimes as this cannot but open the eyes even of the blind, for they reveal with incomparable brilliancy the abysmal horror of the Jewish criminal soul, the unabashed and egotistical cruelty of its instincts, which is to say the menace to life and limb that it represents within any civilized national community.

Five hours before this appeared in print Gwen had informed the homicide detail at the villa that the dying girl had given the name of her murderer as "Cunnaux."

Accordingly she read the story with blank astonishment—read it over and over again. Looking for the murdered girl's last words, she found not a syllable. She read the contradictions, inconsistencies, and obvious distortions, which, however, when taken together, gave the impression of being facts, and she was utterly aghast.

She repeated one line of the story aloud: "Such crimes as these cannot but open the eyes even of the blind." Her eyes were open now. Now she saw.

How can this be? she asked herself, before she could ask Andreas. *A dead girl, here on our stairway, said to me, "Someone by the name of Cunnaux is my murderer." She was lying down there as she said it—I heard her. And I repeated it to the examining magistrate, or whoever he was. Verbatim. I even spelled it out for him, and he wrote it down. And the German News Agency never mentions it! It tells a story simply teeming with improbabilities and distortions. For example, I know that Mademoiselle Roux gave lessons at the J. S. P. free of charge out of pity; I also know, I, Gwen Hoffman, know (because our French conversation was almost entirely about the J. S. P.) that she gave her lessons not in one of the dormitory shanties, Jellinek the banker's or anyone else's, but in the so-called medical shanty, where the ones who had been flogged were bandaged so that they could be flogged again; therefore, the Storm Troop sentries cannot have heard her screaming in the Jellinek shanty. And I also know that she spoke of young Jellinek, whom she called Richard, as her best pupil, so that he can't have been feeble-minded. Besides, the Villa Elfriede isn't "near by," it's twenty minutes' walk from the colony, and it's unthinkable that a person who had lost a water pitcher full of blood could walk all this way when mortally wounded!*

The consequence of this reflection and of the thoughts that rushed in upon her was that Gwen told one of the two Gestapo officials she must telephone.

"To whom?" the man asked.

"To the state's attorney," she said.

"No," said the man.

"But I've got important information to give about the murder!" she persisted.

"No," repeated the man. "I have orders not to let you telephone."

"You got those orders at a time when you couldn't possibly know that I would have important information to give," she objected.

"Yes, I could. We foresaw that sooner or later you would want to give some sort of information. My orders apply to that case," he replied.

"But this is mad!" she almost screamed. "It says here in the paper a man by the name of Jellinek is the murderer! It isn't so! I know the murderer's name, and besides that I know other vital things that I've absolutely got to tell!"

"If I may give you a piece of advice, Fräulein," the man answered after looking at her fixedly for a moment, "I mean, if I were you, I should be extremely glad that any murderer has been found at all. I wouldn't let out another peep."

"How so?" she asked, puzzled.

"The dead woman is lying in your house, isn't she?"

"Yes."

"And you," the man went on, his gaze growing more penetrating, "discovered the murder. When she came in here she must have been alive, or she wouldn't have got in. She died here. In the house. At your place. There was no one with her but you. Do you understand?"

"No," she replied. She actually did not.

"Slow on the uptake!" jeered the man. "You just be glad and give thanks to your American guardian angel that you aren't being suspected yourself! Now do you understand?"

"Yes," she said harshly. Her dream was dreamed out at last.

Just then the focus of her dream, Andreas, appeared. He had the day's hard, dangerous work and his depressing supper behind him—supper with his grandfather, who could not get used to the new life; his sister, who meanwhile had become Frau Uliř, had given birth to a boy and was already keeping house again; his lovelorn brother-in-law; and his brother Sepp, who had already got used to things, and found less and less to object to about the Nazis as the days went by. Andreas was coming over as usual during his brief evening leisure, to make bearable an unbearable existence. Word of the murder had already reached him through Sepp, who reported it at dinner with the most fantastic embroidery. And old Mumelter, remembering the Hilsner case well and taking that as a starting-point, had admitted it was not altogether improbable that ritual murder in this region had somehow struck root. No one at table had quite escaped the impression made by the old man's words, for he told about the Hilsner case from the storehouse of his infallible memory, and thus invalidated the objection that such things were impossible. Old Mumelter had heard too much about the Hilsner case, which had filled the newspapers for years. He had considered Hilsner guilty at the time, and still did.

Countless others who could themselves remember the turn of the century thought as he did at this moment; many younger people had heard stories of the historic Bohemian ritual-murder case. And so there was an unprecedented situation—an utterly unlikely accusation losing its improbability in the shadow of a similar accusation, long since made, confirmed, buried, and forgotten.

Even Andreas had not quite freed his mind of the conversation at home when he entered the Villa Elfriede. He had not known that the body was here in the house, and he laid Gwen's unusual agitation to that fact. Going into the living room with her as usual, he greeted her parents (who regarded this regular evening caller not as a son-in-law or their daughter's suitor, but as someone without whom they could not have imagined life here), and asked the girl: "Where did you meet this Mademoiselle Roux, anyway, Gwen?"

His "this Mademoiselle Roux" seemed rough to her, for some reason which she could not explain; she also held it against him that he had not come at once, but gone home first. Of this, naturally, she said nothing. Instead she remarked, not answering his question: "The whole newspaper story is a lie. The poor girl was murdered by a man named Cunnaux. And they won't let me telephone!"

"Wait!" he said, looking at her. "Not so fast. How was that again?"

She repeated the name of Cunnaux.

At this Andreas, usually so self-contained, sprang up from his chair, demanding: "Again! What did she say? All of it!"

She repeated the dying girl's last words: *"Vite! Un médecin! Cunnaux m'a assassiné. Télégraphiez . . ."*

He did not let her finish.

"How do you spell that? I mean the name?"

She spelled it out: "C-u-n-n-a-u-x."

"No," he said very softly. "Not *C. K.* K-u-n-o."

For a moment there was silence around the family table, and the two Gestapo agents could be heard talking on the stairway below.

Then Mr. Hoffman asked slowly: "Isn't that the name of the——?" He did not finish.

"Yes," said Andreas quickly. "That's his name. You know him, Gwen. The civil young man whose name I had to tell you once before. At the brewery—remember?"

And as she looked at him wide-eyed, he said more to himself than to her: "So that's why Sepp knew so much about it!"

Only Mrs. Hoffman seemed unable to make anything of all this. She looked inquiringly from one to another, and finally requested of Andreas: "You explain it to me!"

But Andreas again said rather to himself: "That's just like Schultheiss, inventing this analogy with Hilsner to get his son out of a trap!"

This meant still less to Mrs. Hoffman, and with a shrug she abandoned the attempt.

At this Andreas, who so far had been looking at her, turned suddenly, with a visible start, to Gwen: "Tell me. You haven't told anyone else what you've just told me? To strangers, I mean?"

From the stair came a woman's scream, and then immediately the voice of a Gestapo man: "You ought to be ashamed! A grown-up young girl!"

But Božena, who had emitted the scream, scarcely understood German, and besides she did not care what the man might say. The sight of the dead woman lying at the foot of the stairs, her white face lighted up by the bronze darky bearing a torch in the stair niche, struck the maid as ghostly. Every time she had to go past, she put her hands over her eyes and roared.

"I told the homicide detail verbatim, and they wrote it down that way. I even spelled out the French words for them," said Gwen in reply to Andreas' question.

He said nothing, and began walking hurriedly up and down the room, whose windows looked out on the rather wide, ill-lit Bendová Ulice; the sidewalks were bordered with acacias that had not yet blossomed.

"Then you've done everything you possibly could do," he said tonelessly, stopping at one of the windows and looking out.

"How do you mean?" she asked.

"They can't ask anything more of you," he said, fixing his eyes on one of the acacias. They were late in blossoming this spring. In the Dorotheenstrasse in Berlin the sidewalks were bordered with acacias too.

She took him by the arm and forced him to turn toward her.

"They?" she asked. "Who? You don't mean you?"

"Yes," he said. "Even I."

"Please, what are you talking about?" asked the lady of the house, whose nerves were at the breaking point.

Her daughter replied: "About the fact, Mother, that I know who killed poor Mademoiselle Roux. And that neither Andreas nor Daddy wants me to tell."

"But," Mrs. Hoffman objected, "the murderer has been caught—didn't you read it to me in the newspaper?"

"No, Mother," Gwen explained. "The one that's caught isn't the murderer. I know who the murderer is. So I've got to tell. That's obvious!"

"Yes, I think so," said Mrs. Hoffman slowly. "I guess that's obvious."

"The thing is this, Evelyn," her husband spoke quickly, "Gwen made a statement of everything she had to say to the homicide detail that was here this afternoon. You remember that, don't you?"

"I think so," said Mrs. Hoffman helplessly. "There were so many people here. And they asked us so many questions. By now I can't remember what I said and what Gwen said."

"The thing is this," Andreas also now explained, and she was taken aback by the sudden unaccustomed attention that everyone was paying to her: "If Gwen says one word more in this trial than she has said already, or takes a single step that I don't approve of, I won't be responsible for anything. From that moment none of us can be sure of his life for a single second." He was standing by the table, speaking English, but so softly that Mrs. Hoffman had trouble in understanding him.

"Is that so?" she asked blankly.

"Literally," he said. "That's why I don't want Gwen to go on exposing herself in a matter——"

Now it was Gwen who interrupted him: "That's no concern of hers. That's what you were going to say, isn't it? That's what people say in a case like that, isn't it, Mother? Isn't it, Daddy? Didn't you tell me about a case, I mean you, Andreas, where a twelve-year-old girl jumped out of a window? You saw her dead on the sidewalk? A case that was no concern of yours. And still it's pursuing you. There's a dead girl lying downstairs, too, more than twelve years old, but I don't want to reproach myself the way you do—that's the difference!"

He had turned pale and was struggling for breath. Finally he said: "Gwen, listen to me!"

"Gwen," said her mother too. "You do what Andreas tells you. And your father. They know best!"

But no one had reckoned with the fact that Gwen's dream had been dreamed out on this evening and that her eyes now were opened wide. "No, Mother," she replied. "They don't know best. They let twelve-year-olds jump out of the window and don't stir. If I don't stir either, somebody will be convicted who's innocent."

"Listen to me," Andreas repeated, recognizing her complete transformation. "I can understand your excitement, Gwen. I can understand what's going on in your mind—if anyone in the world can understand it, it's I. You're a witness in the trial—someday everyone who lives in the Third Reich will be a witness in the trial. No matter whether it's this trial or that trial, it's the trial of the Third Reich. What counts is the question of what the person who realizes that he has become a witness does from that moment on——"

"Nothing," Gwen interrupted him again. "After all, it's a case that's no concern of his!"

"Let me explain it to you. It hit me just as hard as this—it does everyone, supposing they're like us. He says to himself: 'I was a witness of it, and now I must bear witness against it.' "

"And he's satisfied with that!" she interrupted for the third time.

"Gwen!" he said. "Was I satisfied? You know perfectly well it isn't so!"

"Forgive me," she said. "There's a dead woman lying downstairs. And you want them to take vengeance on an innocent man for it."

Andreas had been hot-tempered from childhood. "What I want is common sense," he said vehemently. "I want you to think. I'm assuming the quite unproved fact that the young fellow I mean is actually the murderer. We have no proof of it—now please don't interrupt me—except for the confused words of a dying woman, which you may have misunderstood into the bargain. But even assuming things are as we suspect, then, I still insist, you must do nothing more on your own initiative. You told the homicide detail what you know. If they don't pay any attention, or reach other conclusions, that's not your affair."

"Are you defending the homicide detail?" she asked, and her beautiful eyes grew more and more uncontrolled.

"I'm defending you! You're trying to save two lives that are lost anyway. Did you lift a finger for those two lives as long as they were being flogged daily just twenty minutes' walk from here? No, you didn't. You had qualms of conscience, true. And I reassured you. Is that true too?" His voice was harsh.

"Yes. You told me about your plan. But that's it! Now that you know you are a witness, as you call it, you've got your plan, and with it your road. I haven't. I've got to find mine. I don't know yet how a person behaves when he knows that he's a witness."

He saw that the girl was in a state of excitement not accessible to reason. But he felt a reproach that embittered him. "How about it?" he asked her. "Would you prefer to risk not only your own life but your parents' and mine, or, to put it more plainly, do you want us all murdered so that two prisoners in a concentration camp may endure their torments longer and lose the chance of quick escape from their inhuman existence?"

"Andreas," she said, looking at him so piercingly that he lowered his eyes, "why do you make simple things complicated? You're forgetting what I know, and that the dead woman told me so that I might tell. There's nothing to think over about that."

"Very good," he replied. "You're going to do what you think is right. And you'll take the responsibility. Won't you?"

"I think I shall," she said, with the superiority that sometimes gave her a look of being so much older. She added: "I'm surprised, Andreas. I'd been hoping so much for your help."

"And I for yours," he retorted fiercely. "You'll remember what we've talked over so often! And try to see which is more important!"

"I don't think I'll be putting you in danger," she replied, after a silence. "I shall try not to with all my might. But I made a promise to a dying woman. Surely I've got to keep it, haven't I? Andreas! Say something!"

At this, quite unexpectedly, Mrs. Hoffman said: "Yes, Gwen. You've got to."

Andreas, however, was at the end of his patience. "Don't fool yourself," he said. "What's happening to those two prisoners from the concentration camp isn't any worse than what has been happening to them and the hundred thousand like them and hundreds of thousands of others in the Third Reich for years, and what's going on every second. Every one of those hundreds of thousands is innocent. Have you found that so unbearable since 1933? When you were in Boston did you tell yourself: *Innocent people are being tortured at this moment in Dachau or Buchenwald or Oranienburg?* No, you didn't. You knew it, but you didn't think about it. All right. Boston is on another continent. But did you find unbearable the fact that hundreds of innocent people were being tortured twenty minutes' walk away from you, a hundred Jellineks, from the moment when I told you my plan? No. You put your hopes in the plan, and meanwhile you slept and ate and laughed here, twenty minutes away from there, you went to the movies and came back from the movies, twenty minutes from there. What's changed since yesterday?"

She replied with trembling lips: "You've just said it yourself: 'I've become a witness.' Maybe you have to be born somewhere else to be a proper witness."

"You forget that I come from somewhere where things are altogether different too. Or are you measuring capacity to open one's eyes by the number of miles you travel to do it?"

"By the number of days that you've been able to eat, drink, laugh, go to the movies, and sleep. You're perfectly right. And you have none of that to reproach yourself with. Because your eyes have been open ever since you saw. Mine weren't open until today!"

His mouth, too, was trembling as he spoke. "Aren't you afraid that what you intend to do will mean sacrificing not only yourself and us, but my plan along with us? I have to remind you at last! You seem to have forgotten!"

At this Mr. Hoffman, who did not know about the plan, but remembered his conversation with Schultheiss, broke his silence and put in: "It's just as she says."

"Yes," said she, knowing about the plan. "It's just as I say. I know it!"

Never had Andreas seen her like this. Was it the fever goading her on? What was it? He tried the last recourse: "I don't think I'm a coward. Are you trying to give me lessons in courage?"

But she persisted: "I am a coward. It isn't a matter of courage. Only of seeing."

Pale and wide-eyed, she spoke as steadily, as realistically as if she were insisting that one and one made two. Then after a brief silence she asked: "Don't you remember, Andreas?"

He could not bear her look. Yes, he remembered. *When the twelve-year-old girl was lying there with her eyes shut, her head smashed, it happened to me just as it has to her. I saw it like this. Just like this. It isn't fever. It's the truth.* His anger passed away. He implored her: "Gwen, promise me one thing. Wait before you do anything. Wait until I know more about the business. For my part I'll promise you not to waste any time. Will you?"

She promised.

Chapter 13

ON MAY 28, when the Belgians laid down their arms and the French defeat took on undreamed-of proportions, the hopes of the Czechs and anti-Nazis in the Protectorate collapsed like a house of cards. They had followed the German offensive with bated breath—with secret rejoicing when it finally began, relieving the uncertainty of the long, deadly winter; then with horror as the Nazis trumpeted their daily victories abroad, and with fervent prayers said before all the altars of Bohemia and Moravia for the success of France, which was still regarded as an ally despite the Munich disappointment. When the news finally extinguished the last spark of hope, a despair prevailed even overtopping the consternation of that early morning of March 15, 1939, never to be forgotten by any Czech, when the radio suddenly announced: "German troops have marched into Bohemia and Moravia to maintain order."

The streets were deserted in broad daylight now as they had been then, although no air-raid alarm had driven people indoors. The thing that drove them off the streets, what they simply could not endure, was the sight of the blood-red swastika flags, triumphantly hoisted everywhere, and the rasp of the loud-speakers, ceaselessly broadcasting reports of victory, introduced by trumpet blasts and followed by words that seemed to set the seal of eternity on the intolerable state of the country. So far even the downhearted and the skeptics had regarded the occupation as a passing stage that the present war would and must put an end to; not even they had doubted that the Nazis would be beaten, as the Germans had been in 1918. That the German domination in Bohemia, however, would not vanish like a nightmare after a few months, or at worst after a year or two, was something none of them had realized until today, and it cut them to the heart. In March of 1939 they had been able to tell themselves there was bound to be a war that would liberate them; in September of 1939 the war came; now, at the end of May 1940, the trumpets blared out that the war was lost for France, that is to say for the Czechs.

"It must be admitted that they did a marvelous job!" said Sepp, who had come home in the early morning to ask for money. He needed it to buy himself pigskin gloves for the victory parade that was taking place at one o'clock in the afternoon on the main square of Pilsen, the Náměstí Republiky, which was now to be rechristened the Adolf Hitler Platz.

"Who?" asked the old man. He had heard the boy speaking to Riccarda, who was washing the breakfast dishes in the next room.

"We, of course!" replied the lad, admiring his dress uniform in a small hand mirror.

"The Tiroleans, you mean?" countered the old man, with a resentment in his voice that did not escape his granddaughter; she drew her younger brother's attention to it by signs that he saw in the mirror but did not heed. He was tired of these ridiculous goings on. After all, they were Germans, and would be for the next thousand years, and that was that!

"No, I mean our German army," he replied, therefore, putting into his answer all the impatience he had long felt at the folly of mourning for what was gone—or, as the leader of the Hitler Youth, Comrade Kuno Schultheiss, had so dashingly and convincingly put it this morning at roll call: "Being too deaf or too idiotic, because of the senility of old age and the ossification of conservative brains, to hear the dynamic marching tread of the New Age!"

"Look here," said the old man, stepping into the open door. "What way is that to talk?" He, too, was venting the impatience and irritation stored up during the victorious howlings of the last few days.

"For whom to talk, Grandfather?" asked the boy, and the defiance that had always been his weakness blazed up openly, as it had when his elder brother had come home to Bozen, and his grandfather had treated him, the youngest, like a little boy in front of everyone.

"You, you pup!" said the old man.

"There's no reason for constantly reproaching me with being young," retorted Sepp. "I don't reproach you with being old." The senility of old age, he thought. And realizing that the old one wouldn't give him the money anyway, he used another verbal flourish of the Youth leader's: "Old age is no merit, and youth no drawback."

True, the old man had heard tell that lack of respect for elders was making incredible strides among the younger generation, and he had even heard of cases where schoolboys had reported their own parents to the Nazis, and, inconceivably, been upheld against their own parents. But his only personal experience of the sort had been on the dreadful journey, and then it was a fellow who had nothing to do with him, none of his own flesh and blood; but in his own family he did not mean to see such a thing, as God was his witness! So he said, with a hardness and determination that were his South Tirolean heritage, and not at all those of a man who would be ninety-two in just three weeks, "Hold your tongue! You're an impudent little boy that doesn't know anything! What you need is a couple of good boxes on the ear. And I'm the one to give them to you!"

Now Sepp did what he would never have dared do in Bozen, where the family's and city's respect for old Mumelter had been a matter of course; he retorted: "I won't stand for this any more from you!" and he even had the daring to add: "Do you hear me?"

Riccarda cried imploringly: "Grandfather! Sepp!"

But it was too late.

With unexampled fierceness the aged man flew at his grandson, who fell back before the unexpectedness as well as the violence of the outburst. Grabbing the boy by the chest, he demanded: "Apologize!"

"Do!" Riccarda motioned to her brother.

But the lad's new surroundings had taken their toll. He considered what his companions would think of him if he were to apologize. And so he said: "I haven't done anything!"

"Apologize!" repeated the old man, and his grip was as iron.

"No!" Sepp contradicted, trying to twist away.

"You hear me," said the old man strangely slowly, while his face turned red. "You'll——"

He did not finish. The iron hand relaxed; he took an unsteady step and had to sit down. The sudden red was followed by a deep pallor.

Riccarda had rushed out to fetch a glass of water. She held it to his thin lips, which he moistened. He was breathing quickly, and his mouth kept opening because his breath would not obey him.

"Oughtn't you to lie down, Grandfather?" she suggested.

He made a diagonal gesture that meant no. When had old Mumelter ever lain down by day? And he made a second diagonal gesture in the direction where Sepp was still standing, now rather dismayed. That meant *get out!*

The young fellow left the room.

The eyes of the old man, who was breathing heavily, followed him. His lips formed words, which Riccarda had difficulty in understanding. They were: "This is the New Order!"

His breathing did not improve, and after a while the old man was willing to lie down. But not to undress—that condition he insisted on. He lay down in his clothes and shoes on his bed in the next room, and said all kinds of things that Riccarda did not understand. He was not so pale any more.

When his condition turned to a sort of drowsiness, his granddaughter started to tiptoe out. But she had not reached the door when the old man motioned her back.

"Stay here!" he articulated.

She said: "Grandfather, mightn't it be a good thing to have a doctor take a look at you? Let me call Dr. Paumgartner. You know, the Salzburg doctor that the Hoffmans have. He's no Nazi, Grandfather."

"I—don't—want—anyone," was the halting but audible reply; the old man struggled for breath after each word. "I never—had—a doctor. And—I want—to—die—without one."

"Grandfather! What a way to talk! You're going to take a little rest, and then you'll be perfectly all right again."

At this the old man sat up slightly in his clothes (he was wearing the green Loden suit), and contradicted her: "No. I'm—going—to—die."

After a pause during which she went through agonies of terror, he added, less haltingly, "Thank God!"

The rattling and whistling sounds in his breathing gradually decreased. A few minutes later he was asleep, and his expression was almost as usual. His granddaughter listened for a while. Taking fresh hope, she went to look after the baby in her apartment across the street, and to telephone Andreas and ask him to come home just in case, bringing Dr. Paumgartner with him. But she could not reach him, although it was only nine in the morning.

At that hour the trial of Richard Israel Jellinek, nineteen years old, for the crime of murder, and of his father Leopold Israel Jellinek, forty-seven years old, for the crime of instigating the murder, was just beginning before a military commission at the courthouse.

The courthouse in Pilsen is between the Veleslavonova Ulice and the Ottokar Promenade, close to the Náměstí Republiky Square, which was to be rechristened the Adolf Hitler Platz today at one o'clock, and whence preparations for the solemnities were constantly heard.

Trials in the Protectorate were conducted according to German military criminal law. Only the presence of two Czech assessors indicated that the court was being held in Bohemia. The commission (a so-called special commission for capital crimes) was made up as follows: Presiding, Lieutenant General von Herrdegen; assessors: Colonel Kettner, Colonel Baron von Putlitz, Major von Dohna, Captain Fischer-Detmold, Captain Fischer-Gleiwitz, Captain Kageneck, Captain Stobral (of the Czech army), and Captain Zelený (of the Czech army); court stenographers: Lieutenants Rohnstedt and Bingen; prosecuting attorney: Judge Advocate Koetzschen; defense attorney: Dr. Schmidt.

On the witness bench, in the order of seating, were Gwen Hoffman, three Storm Troopers, Dr. Paumgartner, the physician, the murdered woman's landlady, Frau Smetana, the proprietor of a tobacco shop named Havermayer, Countess Hohenwart, and the murdered woman's brother, Monsieur Gaston Roux of Mulhouse in Alsace.

The journalists' bench was vacant except for one representative of the D. N. B. All others, including correspondents of the foreign press, had been refused admittance.

The Hall of Assizes (at the head of which a painting of Emperor Francis Joseph I in field marshal's uniform had hung until 1916; of Emperor Charles I until November of 1918; and of the civilian T. G. Masaryk until March of 1939; while a portrait of Hitler now occupied the place on the wall behind the judges' bench) was flooded with May sunshine. It glittered on the polished candlesticks beside the crucifix, and on the yet brighter buttons, medals, and gold of the uniforms. In this glaring light everything was visible—bodies, things, and the shadows they cast.

The two defendants before the judges' bench, guarded on both sides by Waffen S.S. men, presented a spectacle that wanted some getting used to. The elder of them was a little man who, to judge by the clothes that flapped around him, had once been portly. If the word pallor means conspicuously pale, then some new one was needed to describe the color of his face; it was gray. So was his hair. His lips moved constantly, even when he was not speaking. In contrast to the civilian dress that he had been allowed to retain, his son was wearing the gray garb of a convict. And by contrast with his father's immeasurable agitation, the son was not only calm, but positively sleepy. His eyes often closed, and unless all signs were misleading he seemed to nod off for minutes at a time. He was also small, with spectacles, a shaved head, and sharp, clever features. If he had been differently dressed, one might have taken him for a theological student.

The charging of the defendants, during which the witnesses had to leave the room, now began.

In the involved language of the German penal law, the charge asserted that Richard Israel Jellinek did proceed on April 21, 1940, in Pilsen, against Madeleine Roux with deliberate intent to kill by stabbing, in such wise that her death ensued; that the said Richard Israel Jellinek did thereby commit the crime of felonious and willful murder, as defined in Article 211 of the Penal Code; and that Leopold Israel Jellinek had procured him to do this act by direction and by furnishing the implements for said murder, and was according to Article 48 guilty of the same crime. The words "ritual murder" did not occur in the charge.

The presiding lieutenant general, who had been questioning the father, turned to the young man for the first time, inquiring: "Now tell us, what was your purpose in going at the Frenchwoman with the bread knife?" This was a leading question, intended as a trap, since the previous interrogation had produced nothing pointing in that direction. It was therefore illegal, and any lawyer knew that the correct question should have been, "Do you plead guilty?" But no one in the hall made any objection, neither the defendants (the elder of whom wore an expression of panic, while the younger stared dully into space) nor the judge advocate, and not even the defense attorney.

"Well," said the lieutenant general, a man with a strikingly handsome, open face, "kindly answer when you are spoken to!"

Apparently, however, Jellinek junior had not understood the question; he stared at the presiding judge, yawned, and said nothing.

Assessors Colonel von Putlitz and Major von Dohna whispered together; Captain Fischer-Gleiwitz made a note. Someone said: "Obviously an idiot!"

The father, hearing this, winced. "My dear sirs!" he cried, "I don't know what's happened to my son. He's completely changed! I've never seen him like this!"

But the presiding officer disposed of the interruption: "This constant Jewish outcry will not be permitted here! This isn't the stock exchange! Incidentally"—he turned to the court—"the second defendant's feeling interjection is without factual importance. We have here the opinion of the court medical expert, Dr. Wagner, stating that the first defendant displayed signs of pathological feeble-mindedness throughout the time he was being held for questioning. Item No. 7," he dictated to the stenographer, holding up the paper in question, and quoted from it: "Signs of dementia."

"But my son has always been healthy and in full possession of his faculties!" persisted the father desperately. "He was at the head of his class for eight full years at the First German High School at Brünn, where he graduated last year. For heaven's sake, it must be possible to ascertain that by simple inquiry at the Brünn High

School, since all our papers, even my son's school reports, have been taken away from us."

The lieutenant general repeated his warning: "Second Defendant Jellinek! If you take the floor again without being asked, I shall have you removed!" And, speaking to the commission: "The Brünn High School replied, Item No. 9, Lieutenant: 'The progress of Richard Jellinek, a pupil at this institution'—the gentry at the Brünn High School don't seem to know yet that all male Jews must be called Israel—'displayed mental and physical backwardness.'"

"This is unheard of!" cried the father. "They can't possibly have answered like that! He was always the best student, and graduated with honors in all subjects!"

Lieutenant General von Herrdegen seemed intent on proving to himself and the audience how long-suffering he could be: he let the shouting father finish speaking. Then he remarked: "You gentlemen can see from this extravagant lack of understanding and self-control that pathological tendencies prevail in the Jellinek family."

Nevertheless, one of the two Czech assessors, Captain Stobral, now asked in German: "Herr Jellinek senior, when did you first notice these signs of apathy which we observe in your son?"

The lieutenant general was annoyed not only at the "Herr" but by the question as such, and he displayed his annoyance by tapping the table with his pencil as the defendant replied: "Today is the first time, Captain."

"May I see the medical opinion?" the Czech member of the committee asked the presiding officer. He received it, read it carefully, and made a note of something on his pad. Then he handed it back to the lieutenant general with a bow.

The latter, meanwhile, had been striving to get coherent answers out of the defendant Jellinek junior. But the only thing the young fellow said was, "I don't know," and, "I can't remember."

Over the head of his neighbor, Captain Fischer-Detmold, Captain Stobral handed to the second Czech assessor, Captain Zelený, a note that said: "Van der Lubbe!" This was the name of the defendant in the Berlin Reichstag fire trial, who had behaved just as young Jellinek was doing in court; afterward a rumor got around that Van der Lubbe had been put into a state of total apathy by means of narcotics before each day of the trial.

"May I see that?" the presiding judge now asked in turn, meaning the note. Having read it, he passed it around the table with a smile, put it among the documents with a written notation when it came back to him, and closed the interrogation of the defendants preparatory to questioning the witnesses.

But Captain Zelený, the second Czech assessor, a man with a pockmarked face and huge hands, rose and said: "Pursuant to Article 218 of the Military Code of Criminal Procedure, I request a medical examination of the first defendant in the presence of the commission."

Whether the commission had been prepared for this motion, which had to be granted if even a single member offered it, was doubtful. In any case, the court decided through the mouth of its presiding officer: "The motion is sustained. Dr. Wagner, please."

But now Captain Stobral stood up, with neither medals nor gold glittering on his blue-black tunic, and said, "The statement of the court medical expert, Dr. Wagner, asserts that the signs of so-called dementia were observed in the defendant, Richard Jellinek——"

"Richard Israel, Captain!" the lieutenant general corrected.

"Richard Israel Jellinek on April 22. The first examination, however, as the testimony shows, did not take place until April 26. Accordingly the opinion—I refer to Article 219, a, of the Code of Criminal Procedure—is self-contradictory in essential points. Pursuant to Article 219, b, I move a new examination of the defendant Richard Israel Jellinek by a physician other than the court's physician, who has contradicted himself 'in essential points.'"

No objection could be brought against this either, provided it was correct.

The presiding justice leafed through the dossier; his handsome face, now marked with two deep wrinkles of annoyance, seemed to be saying: "How the devil did this Czech rogue get a chance to go poking around in the files so long?" However, having convinced himself of the discrepancy between the two dates, and wished the court doctor, who should have paid more attention, to hell, he said in a matter-of-fact tone: "I consider that a sheer waste of time. Because there can hardly be anyone who would impugn Dr. Wagner's authority! The divergence in the dates is obviously due to a typing error. But if you absolutely insist on it, Captain Stobral——"

"I repeat my motion, General, and request a ruling."

The presiding judge decided: "Chief Staff Dr. Heinecke, please."

Before the guards could carry out this order, the pockmarked Captain Zelený rose to offer a motion: "Dr. Heinecke is a staff doctor, but not a court doctor. As the examination has to be made by a court doctor, I move the examination of the first defendant by the court doctor and plant physician of the Skoda Works, Dr. Paumgartner. As he has been summoned as a witness, and is present, the loss of time that the presiding officer has objected to would be reduced to a minimum."

This, too, was indisputable. And Lieutenant General von Herrdegen, considering which would be wiser, to shut up the saucy Czech and refuse to be told his own duty, or to show the public—there were not more than twenty carefully selected people admitted—how faithful to the law these proceedings were, plumped for the latter. In any case, he chanced to remember that this fellow Paumgartner attended a number of perfectly dependable families.

So he ordered: "Dr. Paumgartner!", the S.S. guard opened the door, called out the name, and the man came in.

The person that entered was skilled at dealing with puzzles, and up to this moment had been one himself to his fellow men. It was not easy to read Dr. Karl Viktor Maria Paumgartner, and he made it as difficult as he could. Cynicism, along with an almost infallible gift of diagnosis and a passionate love of music, which he tried to express as an amateur composer, were the characteristic things about him. Tall, sloppily dressed, stooping, with drooping shoulders, his boisterous manner of speech indicating the former dueling university student and the tradition of the celebrated Viennese medical school, he was a typical Austrian in appearance, behavior, and thought. He criticized everything, himself above all, and made jokes about everything—jokes so deft and telling that people passed them around. A bachelor, he had spent his life without witnesses, and been brought here after a long practice in Mozart's city of Salzburg and Schubert's city of Vienna because Herr Schultheiss, a Vienna patient of his, was determined to have him near. For this and other reasons many people regarded him as a Nazi.

"Before I take your testimony, Doctor, you will please examine the defendant Richard Israel Jellinek," the presiding officer said to him.

Hereupon the not very manageable doctor made his first difficulty. "Examine him in what respect?" he asked, hands in trouser pockets.

"The opinion in the dossier," the lieutenant general explained, "diagnoses dementia. One of my colleagues questions this diagnosis. I would like to have your opinion."

Dr. Paumgartner looked up to the handsome man in the general's uniform.

"You mean a supplementary opinion, then, General? That would have to be a faculty opinion, for which the young man would have to be moved to the psychiatric clinic at Prague. Furthermore, my field is internal medicine, not psychiatry."

The lieutenant general, at the end of his patience with all these people who kept bringing up articles and stupid technicalities instead of carrying out the Führer's terse will, contradicted: "Any layman can see that the defendant is not in full possession of his mental faculties."

"In that case," replied the doctor, "an expert should hardly be necessary. May I humbly repeat that I am in no position to give an offhand opinion on his mental condition. And if I am to make a general examination of the defendant, I would request the assignment of a room for that purpose."

"What for?" asked the presiding officer. "There's more than enough room here. We aren't bashful, and besides, we're used to ugly sights!" This was meant as a joke, and was laughed or smiled at by all the members of the commission except the two Czechs.

"Well, let's get about it," said Paumgartner with a strong Viennese accent, and began, before the eyes of all, an examination that lasted some fifteen minutes, and was watched by the defendant with indifference, his father with profound agitation, and the members of the commission in complete immobility. Putting his stethoscope and instrument for testing reflexes back in their case, Dr. Paumgartner finally said: "The young man enjoys perfect organic health."

"That was not the question," admonished the irritated lieutenant general. "We want you to tell us to what you attribute the apathy of the defendant."

The doctor put his hands in his trouser pockets. "To bromine, General. A good deal of it."

"You mean the defendant was obliged to take sedatives to calm his excitement?" The presiding officer indicated the answer he wanted to hear.

But Dr. Paumgartner replied: "I have nothing to go on in saying that he needed bromine. That he got bromine, and in excessive doses on the other hand, is evident."

"How is it evident, please?" asked Captain Zelený.

"From the acne condition of his skin. A typical bromine rash, Captain."

"I think that will suffice," the presiding officer interrupted the exchange, which was growing more and more unwelcome.

"It quite suffices for me," retorted the pockmarked Czech officer.

And Captain Stobral agreed with the typically Czech phrase: "Ditto for me."

Gwen Hoffman was called as the next witness.

She made sure by a glance around the room that Andreas was not there. No one was present whom she knew except Dr. Paumgartner, whom she had occasionally consulted, and who had given her good advice. He nodded to her as she came to stand beside him before the bench, for he had not yet been dismissed; the presiding officer had decided it was better tactics not to have the unmanageable fellow's testimony follow immediately upon his expert opinion.

In response to questions Gwen Hoffman identified herself.

"You are an American?" the judge advocate inquired; this was the first question he had asked since the opening of the proceedings.

"Yes," said the witness.

"Then how does it happen that your father is not an American?"

"He didn't take out his papers in time."

"He's an accidental German, then?"

No answer.

Major von Dohna, one of the assessors, inquired: "What does that mean? The father German and the daughter American?"

Gwen explained the American law.

"It must be a fine state of affairs in America!" the major observed, to be immediately admonished by Lieutenant General von Herrdegen: "Major, please!"

Hereupon the major was silent, and the presiding officer opened the questioning by asking: "Is there any motion to put the witness under oath?"

No. They would dispense with the oath, which brought a smile from Dr. Paumgartner.

"On the day of the crime," the lieutenant general began, "the murdered woman came to you, Miss Hoffman. When was it—at what time, I mean?"

"Ten minutes after two."

"How do you happen to know the time so exactly?"

"Mademoiselle Roux always came punctually at two. This time she was late, and I looked at my watch."

"At what watch?"

"My wrist watch."

"Have you got it with you?"

"Yes."

"Will you please let us see it?"

"Certainly." She removed the little platinum watch from her wrist and handed it to the presiding officer.

He studied it and compared it with his own. "Your watch is six minutes fast," he observed, making a note of the fact. "Is that always the case?"

"It isn't so far as I know," replied Gwen.

"It is so. Do you wish to convince yourself?"

"No."

"Here is your watch back, Miss Hoffman. The murdered woman did not, then, as you said, appear at your house at ten minutes after two, but at four minutes after two. For certain reasons, that is of essential moment. Take care that there are no further discrepancies in your testimony. What did Mademoiselle Roux say when you met her? You testified before the examining magistrate that she spoke French to you. Is that correct?"

"Yes."

"How long have you been speaking French, Miss Hoffman?"

"Oh, quite a long time."

"What do you mean by 'quite'? May I ask you to be more exact?"

"Since I was a sophomore."

"Since you what?"

"Since my second year in college."

"And how long ago was that?"

"Three years."

"Do Americans in general speak French well?"

"I don't know."

"Well on the whole, or poorly on the whole?"

"Poorly on the whole, I think."

"And you yourself, Miss Hoffman? Well on the whole, or poorly on the whole?"

"Well on the whole."

"You have a high opinion of yourself, haven't you?"

"I say I speak French well on the whole."

"Then you are able to understand everything that is said in the French language?"

"Most of it."

"Accordingly you understood Mademoiselle Roux exactly? I suppose, like all native Frenchwomen, she spoke very fast and with an accent that a non-French person could scarcely acquire?"

"Mademoiselle Roux spoke with an Alsatian accent, or at least so she said, and never very fast, because she was used to conversing with her pupils. On the day she died she spoke particularly slowly, from exhaustion."

"You say from exhaustion. How do you profess to know that she was exhausted?"

Dr. Paumgartner coughed loudly.

"She was lying on the floor when I saw her," Gwen replied, "and could scarcely move. What she said to me was her last effort."

The lieutenant general paused briefly, and looked around. "Have any of you gentlemen anything to say?" he asked, and did not seem to be surprised that it was the judge advocate.

"It so happens that I don't speak French at all badly, General," declared Herr Koetzschen. "As I agree with your opinion that the extent to which the witness understands French is of vital importance, I would like to request that the witness be instructed to hold a brief French conversation with me."

Dr. Paumgartner coughed so hard that he was some time in recovering himself.

However, the judge advocate's astonishing proposal met with the complete approval of the presiding officer, who leaned back in his high chair, folded his arms, and declared, "Motion granted."

With a look that attracted Captain Stobral's attention, Gwen said: "I thought I was here as a witness."

"So you are," observed the presiding officer sharply.

"I didn't know I was supposed to pass a language examination."

"That probably isn't the only thing you don't know," retorted the lieutenant general, and instructed the judge advocate: "Please begin, sir."

Judge Advocate Koetzschen, a man of barely thirty, turned to Gwen: *"Comment allez-vous, mademoiselle?"*

"Merci. Très bien."

"Avez-vous commencé vos études de Français en Amérique?"

"Oui, monsieur."

"Êtiez-vous une bonne élève?"

"Comme ci, comme ça."

"N'avez-vous jamais fait des petites erreures dans vos compositions?"

"Certainement. Presque toujours."

"Vous aimez la France?"

"Profondement."

"Est-ce-que vous croyez que l'Amérique ressemble à la France?"

"Pas du tout."

"Vous connaissez sans doute la parole merde?"

"Pardon, monsieur?"

"Merde?"

"Non, monsieur."

"Ça ne fait rien. Mais vous avez entendu dire: 'Fîche-moi le camp'?"

"Comment, monsieur?"

The young judge advocate's face lighted up. "I wish to put on record," he said, bowing to the presiding officer, "that the witness speaks fairly fluent French with a strong American accent, but was unable to answer two out of eight questions. She is unfamiliar with expressions of daily use as well as of a more literary nature."

Just then the silence in the courtroom was broken by a loudspeaker: "Attention! You are about to hear the address delivered by the Reich Protector of Bohemia and Moravia, Baron Konstantin von Neurath, opening the ceremonies in celebration of the victory of German arms, in the Náměstí Republiky."

The presiding officer made a gesture of dismissal toward the court. He did not want to deprive himself or the commission either of the pleasure of hearing the Reich Protector's voice, which rang out forthwith: "Men and women of Pilsen! When in the course of the great migrations the German tribes began, for reasons to us inexplicable, to migrate from the territory which is today Bohemia and Moravia, a foreign Slav people made its way into this territory and established itself among the remaining Germans. Since that time the living space of this Slav people has been enclosed in horseshoe shape by Germans.

"The Czech nation is, in its origin, foreign to us. But in the thousand years during which the two peoples have lived side by side, a Czech culture has been formed, molded, and elevated in the main by German influence."

Someone shouted a Czech word that could be heard but not understood; the unctuous oratorical voice then continued. The two Czech captains on the judges' bench listened with tight lips, which seemed to please the presiding officer so much that he let the speech be, and picked up Herr Koetzschen's last remark: "Thank you, Judge Advocate, that was very instructive. Now I ask you, Miss Hoffman, pointing out to you at the same time that your American citizenship will not serve to protect you from the consequences of false or inaccurate testimony: do your depositions before the examining magistrate and the homicide detail contain the whole truth?"

"Yes. Of course."

"Before the examining magistrate and the homicide detail you testified to the following words, which you believed you heard: '*Vite! Un médecin! Cunnaux m'a assassiné! Télégraphiez à mon frère!*' This means: 'Quick! A doctor! Cunnaux has murdered me. Wire to my brother!' Is that right?"

"Yes," said Gwen.

"In your opinion a misunderstanding would be out of the question?"

"Utterly."

"How do you spell the name of the alleged murderer?"

Gwen spelled it.

"Do you know whether the murdered woman knew a person of that name?"

"Yes."

The presiding officer pricked up his ears. "Yes? Do you know that from personal observation? That is, did you yourself see the murdered woman with the person in question?"

"No."

"And do you yourself know a person of that name?"

Before the examining magistrate, two weeks previously, Gwen, complying with Andreas' urgent desire, had answered "No" to this question; accordingly the presiding officer expected the same "No" today.

But Gwen said: "Yes."

A stir went through the judges' bench and through the small audience. Even the two Czech captains turned their attention from the still-blaring speech.

"Who is it?" asked the lieutenant general. "Be very careful what you say, and do not venture upon any conjectures."

"Kuno Schultheiss," was the reply.

There was a pause. Glances were exchanged. Dr. Paumgartner, highly edified, regarded the tips of his shoes. The loud-speaker barked.

"Are you aware of the implications of your testimony?" Herr von Herrdegen asked.

"Perfectly."

"How does it happen that you have changed your testimony since your deposition before the examining magistrate?"

"Because I've succeeded in getting the proof since then."

"I beg your pardon?"

"I say, I've succeeded in getting the proof."

The presiding officer rose and announced: "For reasons of order and public safety the public is excluded."

During the following minutes, while the S.S. guards cleared the few listeners out of the hall, the voice of the Reich Protector resounded: "To those who overtly or covertly maintain that our marching into what was formerly Czechoslovakia has infringed on any rights, I say that the Führer, as he himself stated in his Reichstag speech on April 28, 1939, has taken no steps that violated the rights of others, but has only restored the justice that was violated twenty years ago. The Führer would have sinned against his call by divine Providence if he had failed in his endeavors to restore justice and the law of humanity to those who were deprived of them."

"When does your proof date from?" The lieutenant general continued the hearing in a hall now cleared of any audience.

Gwen could feel Father Jellinek's eyes resting upon her with such fervent gratitude that she turned away; the eyes of Dr. Paumgartner were equally intent upon her, but there was no telling what they meant.

"From yesterday," she said.

"And what sort of proof is it?"

"Ask Countess Hohenwart. She's outside."

"I'm not supposed to be told by you whom I should ask. I'm asking *you!*"

"It would be better if you asked the countess. You'll be more likely to believe her than me."

"No subterfuges, if you please! What has the countess to do with the matter?"

"Didn't you summon her here for that reason?"

"Your boldness is remarkable, Miss Hoffman. Countess Hohenwart was one of the murdered woman's pupils and is supposed to give information concerning her habits."

"She'll know more," Gwen retorted, taking courage from the father's eyes, which clung to her as if to a shrine, "about the habits of Kuno Schultheiss. He is in love with her."

The judge advocate, Herr Koetzschen, started to say something, thought better of it, and was silent.

"Where did you meet the countess, and what has she to do with the matter? I'm asking you for the second time," said the presiding officer.

"She invited me and my family to call on her at Castle Radno soon after we arrived."

"Did you know her before?"

"We were slightly acquainted in Salzburg."

"You say 'slightly.' To what do you owe the invitation in that case?"

"We're Americans."

"What do you mean by that?"

"So far as I have been able to observe, the European aristocrats regard us as somehow privileged, and like to associate with us."

"This verges on megalomania!" cried Major von Dohna furiously.

"Please, Major!" the presiding officer admonished.

"Begging your leave, General, this is going too far! This arrogance of people who are so conceited about dollars, with nothing else they can pride themselves on!"

"That's what I told Countess Hohenwart. But dollars fascinate her," replied Gwen, and now for the first time the veil was removed from Dr. Paumgartner's eyes; he beamed.

"I will say to the witness," cried the presiding officer, his voice quivering with annoyance, "that this is the last time I shall allow remarks not having directly to do with the case. You maintain you know Countess Hohenwart. Is your acquaintance intimate enough to give you the inside knowledge that you claim to have?"

"Yes."

"He has removed the ban of the Austrian nation, which prevented them from voting upon their own destiny, and carried out this fair, free, and honest plebiscite before the whole world . . ." the loudspeaker barked.

"When did you find out about this, Miss Hoffman?"

"Yesterday. Countess Hohenwart invited me to dinner. She knew I had to testify here today."

The lieutenant general raised his voice impatiently. "Witness. All you have told us so far is either hearsay or gossip. What, for instance, do you mean to imply by emphasizing that the countess knew of your appearance in court today? Do you intimate that she wanted you to denounce Schultheiss junior?"

"Quite the opposite, General."

"I beg your pardon?"

"The countess," said Gwen, looking into space, "wanted to find out how much I knew. To make me talk she tried to make me drink. But the attempt was a boomerang. She likes to drink herself."

Facing the witness squarely, the lieutenant general warned: "Listen to me, Miss Hoffman, for the last time. You're not here to tell us stories or exhibit your dislike of certain people or—institutions. You are here to testify to unalterable facts."

"That is exactly what I am doing, sir. Countess Hohenwart drank more than she may have intended to—in fact, so much that she lost control of herself. Her tongue slipped. This is what she told me:

'Don't blame the poor boy. Can you blame a young officer for strictly obeying his orders?' I quote her verbatim. That is an unalterable fact."

It was the lieutenant general's turn to cough. He did it briefly and softly. "Have you ever heard such inconsistency, gentlemen?" he addressed the court. Then, turning to the witness: "So the countess, who wanted to prevent you from accusing Schultheiss junior, forced you, so to speak, to do that very thing. And you ask us to believe that?"

Gwen's eyes grew hard. "I told you. The countess had lost her self-control."

"Extremely likely for anyone who wished to influence others. And what motive, pray, is young Schultheiss supposed to have had for killing an insignificant foreign girl who had never given any offense?"

"I do not know. The people whose orders Kuno Schultheiss obeyed will know. Ask them. Mademoiselle Roux maintained political relations with France." Again the witness looked into space.

"Is that all you know?"

"No. From another remark of the countess it became apparent to me that it was Kuno Schultheiss' father who invented and circulated the ritual-murder story because of its analogy to the Hilsner case. The remark I am referring to was——"

"Stop! Enough of this ridiculous hearsay orgy! That is not evidence, witness Hoffman. You may thank your lucky stars that I have had too much patience with you. But there are limits to everything. I won't tolerate any more of this. Does any one of you gentlemen wish to question the witness?"

Furious applause from the direction of Republic Square marked the end of the victory oration.

"Miss," said Captain Zelený, "I have a question. What interest had you in the investigation of the murder of Mademoiselle Roux? And why, furthermore, do you see fit to make a charge on what may after all be termed hearsay evidence? You're not a lawyer, I take it, and so may not know the difference."

Gwen looked up to him. "I think I do know the difference. From the mouth of the murdered woman I heard the name of her murderer with my own ears. Do you call that hearsay too? She wanted me to tell the authorities the name of the murderer. This I did. But nobody paid the slightest attention. Someone else was indicted. He is sitting in front of you. Do you still ask me why I was interested?"

"One more question," the Czech captain replied. "You must excuse me, miss, if I ask it. You see I do not believe in nobility. And, on the other hand, I think it would favor the credibility of your testimony if you were to tell us without reserve what caused your attitude. You are an alien, aren't you, and the whole thing is more or less nothing to you. What is it, then, that leads you to interfere here, so to speak?"

If Gwen had looked at Father Jellinek just then she might simply have said: "Look at that man." But she looked her interrogator in the face and said: "If it is nobility to try to prevent a ghastly injustice by a few words in court, I am willing to be called noble. Yes, I'm an alien. That's why it is inconceivable to me that you here—or somebody else—should quite ironically describe as nobility what would be a simple matter of course anywhere else in the world. The more I think about it the less I understand how this can be a question at all! Captain! If you were to see me being shot here, by His Honor the presiding justice, let us say—pardon the example—would you pay no further attention to the matter if your Czech colleague were to be accused? Would you be too much afraid of the general? Or not noble enough?"

"Miss Hoffman!" threatened the presiding judge. "Don't try to talk out of an open window. There is no representative of the American press on the journalists' bench. Your attempts at heroics are therefore quite futile."

"Captain," persisted the witness nevertheless, growing more and more passionate, "did you understand me?"

European judges are not accustomed to being asked questions in court. But the one addressed, although he said neither yes nor no, showed all over his pockmarked face how he wished he might have said yes. He wrote something down and handed it to his Czech colleague.

"Countess Hohenwart!" the presiding officer ordered in the midst of a tension that grew from moment to moment despite most of the commission members' obvious annoyance with Gwen.

A lady came forward and greeted the judges with a slight inclination of the head.

"Step up, please," requested the lieutenant general, while all eyes rested on the newcomer, whose motions were easy and graceful; her spring suit and tiny hat were as Parisian as possible.

"Your name is Klara Anna Marietta Countess Hohenwart?"

The lady nodded.

"What is your age?"

"Thirty-two," she said in a strikingly deep voice.

"Catholic, divorced, born at Castle Pardubice, maiden name Princess Erfft?"

"Yes."

"Related neither by blood nor by marriage to the two defendants?"

At this question, prescribed by law, Herr von Herrdegen laughed, and the lady, replying in the negative, laughed also. Her features were sharp; the enamel coating could not conceal the fact that they were dissipated.

"Your testimony is to be taken as a witness, Countess. In this capacity you must tell the whole truth. False testimony would constitute the crime of fraud. If you have reason to fear damage or disgrace to yourself in consequence of your statement, you have the right, according to Article 190, of the Military Code of Criminal Procedure, to refrain from testifying. Are you willing to testify?"

"Certainly."

"Is there a motion that the witness be put under oath?"

Before the members of the commission had reached an agreement, the witness had drawn the white kid glove from her right hand, preparing to take oath. It was a slender, long, remarkably beautiful hand. There was a motion for the oath, which drew another unobserved grimace from Dr. Paumgartner.

"How long have you known Mademoiselle Roux, Countess?" was the first question, the candles having been put out and the members of the commission, who had stood up for the oath, having resumed their seats.

"Since Christmas, I should say."

"How did you make her acquaintance?"

"She advertised French conversation lessons in the paper, and I asked her to take me on."

"How many lessons did you take?"

"Four a week."

"As many as that?"

"I originally wanted to take one every day, but Mademoiselle Roux hadn't the time."

"You paid by the hour?"

"Monthly in advance."

"What amount?"

"Thirty crowns per lesson."

"That's a large fee. Did Mademoiselle Roux ask as much as that?"

"I offered it to her. She was in straitened circumstances."

"Can you tell us anything about the character of the murdered woman?"

"She was an excellent teacher, and a charming, intelligent, and tactful person."

At this point the eyes of the witness wandered for the first time to Gwen, who had returned to the witness bench.

"I didn't mean it that way," the lieutenant general explained. "Do you know anything about any political activity on the part of the murdered woman? You said something of the sort before the examining magistrate."

"Only that she was corresponding with her brother in Alsace. She told me that. What the correspondence was about I have no idea."

"How was such correspondence possible? Her brother lived in an enemy country."

"I know nothing of that."

"Did you yourself ever attempt to arrange for this correspondence?"

"Never."

"You have acquaintances in France?"

"A good many."

"Was the murdered woman a French chauvinist? Or did she criticize her government and country?"

"Rather the latter. We hardly ever talked politics."

"How is that possible, in so many months of talking for a full hour almost every day?"

The witness smiled and shrugged her shoulders. "Women can always find a subject."

"You know Miss Gwen Hoffman?"

"Yes."

"How long have you known her?"

"For about a year."

"How did you make her acquaintance?"

"In Salzburg, at the festival."

"Have you remained in contact since?"

"No, our first meeting was very brief—in the lobby of the Hotel Europe, if I remember rightly. The Hoffmans had just had a death in the family and were not going out much. When they arrived here I invited them to visit me."

"They did so?"

"Yes."

"Did you receive all the members of the Hoffman family, or only Miss Hoffman?"

"All of them."

"Did you also see Miss Hoffman alone?"

"Repeatedly."

"Did you talk to her about the murder of Mademoiselle Roux?"

"Yes."

"Did you know Miss Hoffman suspected a certain person?"

"You mean Kuno? Of course I knew, and I told her how absurd it was."

Gwen rose, which Countess Hohenwart noticed. There was not the slightest change in her enameled face.

"If you please, Countess," said the presiding officer. "Each word now is of utmost importance. Please try to call everything clearly to mind. Did you ever, in the course of time, make any statement to Miss Hoffman that would lead one to conclude that any other person but the defendant Jellinek was guilty?"

"Never."

"Miss Hoffman, sit down! What took place yesterday, Countess?"

"What do you mean, yesterday?"

'Did you see Miss Hoffman yesterday?"

"Yes. Recently we have been seeing each other more often than usual. I believe she had an unpleasantness with someone close to her, and she came to see me more frequently than she had been. She had dinner with me yesterday."

"You alone?"

"Yes."

"What did you talk about?"

The witness smiled. "Yesterday was my saint's day, and we had a bottle of Pommery. Two, if I remember rightly. My brother Prince Erfft sent me some from Belgium, where he earned the Iron Cross, First Class, at Maubeuge."

The reference to her heroic princely relative went home. The colonels, majors, captains, and lieutenants made solemn faces. Dr. Paumgartner could not help coughing.

"Madam Countess is of opinion that you devoted yourselves a trifle too enthusiastically to the champagne?" asked the presiding officer with a smile, all understanding of the enjoyment to be had from a Pommery of such distinguished provenance.

"If you want to put it as diplomatically as that, General. I would say more crudely that I was a little drunk. Anyway, I have no idea what I said."

Gwen sat down. "Shame!" she said aloud.

The witness heard this, as did everyone else in the hall. "Goodness, what of it?" she turned to Gwen. "I didn't know you were so easily shocked. Yesterday, I must say, you seemed to enjoy the champagne very much indeed."

"I thought you couldn't remember anything about it?" was Gwen's quick counter-question, establishing her superiority.

But a moment later the countess repelled this surprise attack with the remark: "Naturally I don't remember every word we said. But I do remember two bottles. First they were full; then they were empty. That takes at least two people."

An amused and relieved smile crossed the lips of some of the assessors.

The presiding officer immediately pressed his advantage. "According to your recollection, then, you never discussed with Miss Hoffman—or hinted directly or indirectly—the possibility that anybody other than the first defendant was or could have been the murderer of Mademoiselle Roux?"

The expression with which the father of the alleged murderer now stared at Gwen was so agonizing that Gwen did not know where to look; the hope that had suddenly flamed up gave way to a baffled despair, and everyone who was not blind was bound to see by the man's every look and gesture that he had nothing to do with the whole charge. But none of the judges paid the slightest attention.

"Never," Countess Hohenwart replied to the presiding officer.

At this Gwen, her voice losing its hoarseness, and becoming clear, sharp, and resonant, said: "May I ask the countess a question?"

Permission was given her.

"Claire," she began, coming from the witness bench to the box where the other woman was standing, "I understand that you have reasons to conceal the truth, but I——"

"Miss Hoffman," interrupted the presiding officer, "I shall have to insist on your silence if you express opinions here, instead of questioning the witness about facts."

"I ask the witness," said Gwen, "whether she recalls the fact that she read two letters from Kuno Schultheiss aloud to me yesterday?"

"Must I answer that?" the witness asked the presiding officer.

"If replying might tend to damage or disgrace you, you are entitled to refuse to testify," the lieutenant general repeated his original instructions.

"There's no question of damage or disgrace!" cried the witness.

At that moment Managing Director Schultheiss came into the hall.

Half an hour before, over in the plant, he had summoned Andreas, and said to him: "Hitherto I have given you wholehearted support. I have also, for your sake—or at least for the sake of your work—tolerated the utterly preposterous attitude displayed by your future father-in-law. But under no circumstances will I allow your fiancée to behave still more preposterously. It had just been reported to me that at the trial of this Jew boy she had the perfectly fantastic boldness to drag in my name and that of my son. You are to stop this instantly. Do you hear me?"

Andreas had heard all too well. This was just what he had wanted to prevent, exactly this. Since their first discussion of the murder he had tried to keep Gwen from doing it, and she had taken it so much amiss that for the past few weeks she had been avoiding him. Either she was at the house of this countess, with whom she seemed to be striking up a remarkably quick friendship, or she sent word to the telephone that she was not there, or she found some excuse for not seeing him. She did not answer a letter he wrote to her.

"Miss Gwen Hoffman is not my fiancée," he told his superior.

"Herr Mumelter!" Schultheiss yelled at him, losing control of himself, "you will hardly suppose I am as naïve as that! I don't care whether the lady is your fiancée or not. At any rate, you have some influence over her, and I require you to use that influence. You will now go to court with me, call the lady out, and make it plain to her that she is to disavow her insane talk completely and without reservation. Otherwise, I shall bring suit against her for defamation, and I can promise you that Miss Gwen Hoffman will not leave the courthouse a free woman."

"I doubt whether I can do that, Director," Andreas replied slowly, pushing forward his lower lip, and seeing the full consequences that he had tried with such violence to forestall. "Miss Hoffman makes up her own mind."

"I would greatly regret that," was Herr Schultheiss' reply. "For the lady's sake and particularly for yours. Are you coming with me?"

This Andreas agreed to do.

When they arrived Herr Schultheiss showed his credentials to the Waffen S.S. guards outside the Hall of Assizes; the sentries saluted him, clicking their heels, and admitted him at once. Andreas waited in the anteroom.

The managing director went up to the judges' bench, in front of which stood a witness with whom he had talked the night before (in response to a telephone call from his son) just long enough to make her sober and induce her to give the testimony she had just given.

"I beg pardon for the interruption, General," he said to the presiding officer, just as Countess Hohenwart was repudiating damage and disgrace as something utterly foreign to her. "I have an important piece of information to give to the court in connection with this trial."

Captain Stobral, the Czech, looked triumphantly at his companion, Zelený. The eyes of the presiding officer, the judge advocate, and the German assessors, on the other hand, darkened. The defense attorney, who so far had confined himself to drawing little figures on the paper before him, put down his pencil.

"Director," replied the presiding officer, "after the deposition of the witness Hoffman I do not know whether I can take your testimony as a witness."

"General! Please!" the other flared up.

"Don't misunderstand me. The Code of Criminal Procedure requires me to point out to you that properly I should——"

"Question me as an accused party, you mean to say, don't you, General?" Schultheiss interrupted. "Well, I can help you out of your dilemma. I don't want to testify, I want to hand over something."

Here, too, a father was fighting for his son. And Father Jellinek, who had known a second moment of overwhelming hope when this other father came in and offered himself to the court, so to speak, realized quickly enough that it was hopeless, final. *That's the kind of father to be,* he thought with fierce envy, looking dismally at the self-assured gentleman before the judges' bench, and then at the young man staring into nothingness; *that's the kind of father,* he thought, *not one like me!*

Meanwhile, this other father had laid a letter and a book on the table. The presiding judge picked up and read the letter. His manner showed that it must be a remarkable document. "Thank you, Director," he said, and handed the letter to one of the two lieutenants with a look of infinite gratification and the order: "Please read it out."

Lieutenant Bingen shot up from his seat. He had in his hand a square white envelope containing a white letter. The envelope was stamped with a Czech ten-heller stamp, postmarked Pilsen, April 20, 1940, 11:45 P.M., and bore the address: "Mlle. Madeleine Roux, Pilsen, Radeckého Náměstí 9."

The letter in the envelope read:

MADEMOISELLE:

Please come at twelve-thirty tomorrow instead of one o'clock. I have something very interesting to tell you concerning your brother, which the others must not hear. Therefore, please do not come to the medical shack, but to ours. Please be punctual. A great deal depends on it for your brother. Your devoted pupil,

RICHARD JELLINEK.

As this letter was read out, the faces of the commission members brightened, and the judge advocate could scarcely wait to lay hands on the precious document. Having cast a glance at it, he exclaimed delightedly: "No doubt about it, it's his writing!" And he rose to move that the handwriting expert be summoned.

"Defendant Richard Israel Jellinek!" said the presiding officer. "Did you write this letter?"

"He never even had any letter paper! Any more than he had a

bread knife! Do you think they let us write letters or gave us knives in the camp?" cried the father.

"Be silent! Is that your handwriting, Jellinek junior?"

The young man on trial for his life stood swaying before the judges' bench, his shortsighted eyes on the white paper.

"I don't know," he answered almost inaudibly.

"For the love of God, Richard!" cried his father, jumping up, "you *must* remember! Pull yourself together! Richard!"

This time the presiding officer let the father go on; he almost wished he might have said more. But when the young fellow shrugged his shoulders with a completely expressionless look, the father sat down without a word, and said nothing.

Dr. Paumgartner observed, more to himself than to anyone else: "Nothing wrong with that letter, in style or logic either. No pathologically abnormal person wrote that."

"Doctor, we shall call on you for advice when we think proper," Herr von Herrdegen rebuked the interruption, and, turning to the young man, he added: "Your father is right. You must remember whether you wrote that or not!"

"I didn't write it," was the completely apathetic reply. And then immediately: "I don't remember."

"Then perhaps this forgetful young gentleman may remember this book," said the man who had provided the new evidence. "And not only he but the elder Herr Jellinek."

The book went the rounds of the judges, producing such a sensation that even the Czech officers stared at it in dismay. It was the publication of Supreme Court Justice Dr. Emil Hausmann concerning the Hilsner trial, published by the Wallishauser'sche Buchhandlung, Vienna, 1903, and passages were underlined in pencil on pages 111, 112, and 113. These pages contained the part of the charge that described in detail Hilsner's procedure in his alleged ritual murder. On page 2 of the book was a printed label representing the globe with an eagle flying above it; above this: *"Ex Libris,"* below it: "Leopold Jellinek."

"Defendant Leopold Israel Jellinek," said the presiding officer, "is this book your property?"

The man thus addressed took the book in his hand. His hand trembled; his voice trembled. His hand trembled so that he could scarcely hold the book, his voice so that the "no" was scarcely audible.

"Is that label your bookplate?"

"But I never saw the book! They didn't leave us a single book!"

"I ask you, was this your bookplate at the time when you were still cheating and stealing, and had a library like all the intellectual exploiters and parasites upon the national wealth?"

"That was my bookplate."

"How does your bookplate happen to be in this book?"

"I don't know. God is my witness! I don't know!"

At this someone said in piercingly clear tones: "But I know!"

And before the presiding judge could say anything, the person who had interrupted said to the man who had brought in the book as evidence: "This is the most infamous and cowardly thing I ever heard of! You know perfectly well, you and Countess Hohenwart, and I imagine even these judges here know that your son is the murderer, and that these two men here are perfectly innocent. Why didn't you bring the letters that your son wrote to Countess Hohenwart? Have you no shame—any of you?"

By the time she spoke these last words Gwen Hoffman was already between two S.S. men, who were removing her at an order from the presiding officer.

Andreas saw her for a moment outside as she was led along the corridor, and heard her crying out in utter desperation, with a voice whose completely unfamiliar sound went to his very marrow, "Shame! Shame! Shame! Shame!"

The cries died away; silence fell in the anteroom outside the Hall of Assizes, where the trial of the ritual murderers Richard Israel and Leopold Israel Jellinek now went tranquilly on. Someone else was also stirred to the depths by the woman's cries—a young man named Gaston Roux, a teacher at Mulhouse in Alsace, who had escaped from his native country six days before to attend the trial that would avenge the murder of his sister. On the day he left Mulhouse the Nazis were at Strassburg, and he had written on the blackboard in his classroom: *"Vive la France!"* Now he asked Andreas: "What did that lady call out?" Andreas translated.

The "Horst Wessel" song resounded from the loud-speaker, followed by the Reich Protector's voice: "And so I give to this beautiful square the name of the greatest German who ever lived, who has brought honor to Germany greater than any man before him. From this day forward and for all future time it shall be called the Adolf Hitler Platz!" Then the shrill Czech word was heard again, the one that had been impossible to catch before. Now it was plain enough: *"Hanba!" Hanba* means *shame*.

It was senseless to go on waiting in the anteroom. The two young men pacing to and fro there did not know what they were waiting for; they passed each other, met, parted, said nothing, waited.

Sepp, on the other hand, was marching in the triumphal parade that now goose-stepped the length of the Adolf Hitler Platz in their dress uniforms, with march music. Riccarda, running toward the courthouse, saw him marching stiff and proud directly behind the leader of the Hitler Youth, Comrade Kuno Schultheiss. For a moment she stopped to wonder whether she should call out to him that his grandfather was dying, but then she ran on breathlessly, around the edge of the square, past the Town Hall, down the Veleslavgasse, hurried up the steps of the courthouse, found the anteroom, and motioned to her brother: "Come!" Now Andreas knew what he had been waiting for.

Two death sentences were being prepared for in the hall inside.

In a convict's cell Gwen Hoffman kept saying: "Shame!"

On the Adolf Hitler Platz the Reich Protector was reviewing the triumphal parade.

In the house on Karl Hermann Frankgasse old Mumelter was making ready to die.

Chapter 14

DEATH DID NOT COME to old Mumelter out of ambush, like an enemy; it did not overtake him, did not surprise him. It announced itself like a visitor, whom one can expect and prepare for.

Having lain down in his clothes and shoes at this unaccustomed hour of the morning, he had gone to sleep, and his breathing had grown quieter; at least it seemed to Riccarda that he was sleeping. But it was not so much sleep as an exigent weariness that made him close his eyes. The dazzling flicker that had troubled him disappeared the moment his eyes were closed, and the senselessly quivering purple spots, stars, and circles joined kaleidoscopically into pictures that one could look at. He looked at these scenes as they appeared, vanished, were crowded out, and recurred with breathless rapidity; he saw them in his infinite weariness, which nevertheless left him perfectly conscious that he was lying in bed here in the Karl Hermann Frankgasse in Pilsen on a May Sunday morning because he had been so furious with his grandson. He even knew that he had wanted to say to his grandson something he had not said, which would have put the matter in the proper light, so that even a person completely blinded must have seen: *A world in which there was no fear of God, but only fear* —he could not find the conclusion of the sentence, although it was on the tip of his tongue, and he kept moving his lips as if to speak, which terrified Riccarda. It was not a terrifying sign, however, but simply meant that the old man was seeking and finding inner clarity. This was the moment when the flickering ended and the swift pictures began, carrying him far away from here, away from the Karl Hermann Frankgasse in Pilsen.

Old Mumelter had seldom gone to the moving pictures, although occasionally he had enjoyed sitting before the magic screen; now he made up for lost time: a long film in which he played a part was being run off before his closed eyes. Connections were often missing, time would shift about, and much that should have come first came afterward, but come it did, and the steadily breathing sleeper, who knew that he was neither asleep nor dreaming, had it all before his eyes. The bookkeeper of the firm of Christoph Mumelter's Heirs, in the little office on the Silbergasse, said in warning tones: "Sir, oughtn't we to give up these everlasting religious articles and crucifixes, which nobody wants anyway now, and go after those modern carved chessmen?" And he, the head of the house, returned: "Herr Höbel, that's nonsense. We'll go right on doing just what we've always done—Madonnas, crucifixes, and saints." Anna came in, who had been his wife for a year and a half, and he was delighted to see how beautiful and young and healthy she was, and that she was alive. "You aren't dead," he asked, "are you? I always knew we'd see each other again!" And she answered: "Can't you see that I'm alive?" There was snow on the apple trees in the garden; we don't get much snow in Bozen, but this February of 1896 we're getting any amount of it—it's a hard winter. A good thing I got that short fur-lined coat. He wondered for a moment where the fur coat might be. But there was the flag with the red Tirolean eagle fluttering upward above Castle Maretsch, and Pastor Gemaassmer was dedicating the monument to Walther von der Vogelweide. It gleamed in the moonlight; the Rosengarten towered silvery behind it. Why was Pastor Gemaassmer baptizing his grandson Andreas by moonlight? No. The old man saw that this was not a baptism but a burial—his son. "You know, Your Reverence," said the father walking behind the coffin, "children ought not die before their parents—it's against the laws of Nature!"

"In the name of the Father, the Son, and the Holy Ghost! Tell me the natural laws governing the fall," said Professor Baernhaupt to his pupil Mumelter, Laurenz, Class 4B, in the Bozen Realschule, and even now Mumelter, the schoolboy, still strove to answer the question that he had missed then. On his black coat was the decoration that His Majesty the Emperor had conferred on him—the thin, veined hand on the counterpane made an uneasy motion that frightened Riccarda again. But once more it was nothing frightening, for Grandfather was only looking for his Silver Cross of the Order of Merit with the Crown, and he found it in a moment, and his hand once more rested peacefully on the white coverlet. It was so pleasant to go for a stroll with the children when work was over—Sepp was not born yet, and Andreas was seven, and Riccarda was three, and both of them were lively children. Too bad that they had no parents. They stopped on the Talfer Bridge, for the boy wanted to know why the water underneath was so green, and whether they dyed it, because the tap water wasn't green at home. He kissed the boy, and replied with a laugh: "Silly lad! Everything's real around here, no matter where you look!" The laugh became a smile, curling his bloodless lips, which grew ever thinner and tighter; the way his lips moved soundlessly, remaining a little open, looked horrible, Riccarda thought. But she did not know that the old man was just laughing and smiling because little Andreas had asked such a childish question.

With closed eyes he watched the swift, changing, clear-cut pictures; they had no coherence and were not in order of time, and yet there was a larger coherence in them, Bozen, and there was an order of time about them—it was the long life coming slowly to an end on this day in May. Sometimes the old man's hand hastened across the white spread, seized something, trembled, rested, and hurried. The thin lips opened more often, murmuring silently, closing, and opening with a smile.

Why doesn't Andreas come? thought Riccarda. For the fourth time she tried to get hold of her brother by telephone at the Skoda plant, and for the fourth time she was told: "Herr Mumelter isn't here." Thereupon she ran down into the Bendová, where she knew a doctor had his sign out, and brought him back with her—Dr. Sramek, a Czech. But he understood enough German to see at first glance that a man was lying here on his deathbed; therefore he did not stop for examination, nor did he disturb the old man's dying, but simply felt his pulse, listened to his breathing for a while, asked how old the patient was, and then replied in the vestibule, half in Czech and half in German, to Riccarda's anxious inquiry about what he had found: "Just what was natural. You say the old gentleman is almost ninety-two? In that case you have to be prepared for it." And he took his leave hastily, for Riccarda had fetched him from the midst of his consultation hours.

But the amazing thing was that she had not been prepared for it. And was not. Not even now. From babyhood, Grandfather had been father, mother, family, and home. All of that. Now he was going to die. Once the doctor had gone, Riccarda felt as if her breath had been taken away in this city where it was so hard to breathe in any event. Standing once more beside the bed where the unexpected was going to happen, she thought: *And even if I had expected it, would that make it any easier? No! Even the expected is dreadful when it comes.*

If only the old man had been able to tell her what he felt now! In the pictures that capered about him, hurrying past him ever faster, more fragmentarily, more brightly and nimbly, an existence was sweeping past that had been filled with much that was good and much that was splendid; it had always been a full, strong life. The doctor who had gone away without examining him, even now, was the first doctor who had ever attended him in his life, and for his part he had not even consciously seen this first one. It was only now, when the triumphal parade was taking place in the Adolf Hitler Platz outside, and the dying man was reviewing the parade of his life, that he saw with overwhelming clarity what a blessed, healthy life his had been. Such radiance in the pictures—much more radiance than shadow; much strength and honor—far more honor than shame; such independence. Oh, it was lovely to see with those deeply weary, deeply penetrating eyes everything that one had possessed, and wanted to possess no longer, because one was far, far too weary, and ready to knock off work.

"Grandfather!" said Riccarda, for his hand on the coverlet now grew terribly restless. "Do you want something?" She spoke very loud intentionally.

At this he opened his eyes, and said with an unchanged but far softer voice: "Yes. Extreme unction."

She turned away quickly, and then back to him, and said: "But Grandfather! What are you thinking of? Surely you aren't going to die?"

And he said to her, as he said to her brother on the Talfer Bridge when she was three and Andreas was seven: "Silly girl! Of course I'm going to die." As he did so he tried to laugh just as he had laughed not long ago, nineteen years before, on the Talfer Bridge; he actually managed it quite well, yet it was unspeakably sad to see him twist his lips, which no longer quite obeyed him. He wanted to tell her what he had just been thinking: How fine it was to die when the time had come, and that it was nothing to be afraid of, and that he, Laurenz Mumelter, was departing with a light heart from a place where he could no longer stay. And he wanted to tell her too: "Silly girl, what are you so sad about? Can't you see how well off I am?" He had not the strength for all this, however, but only for a nod and the whispered words: "Bring me the priest."

She rushed away, tried again to get hold of Andreas, and finally found out where he was. But before she set out for the courthouse she fetched Father Felician, a Franciscan in the neighborhood, and left him alone with the dying man.

Father Felician was not Pastor Gemaassmer. But he had spent his canonry in Brixen, not far from Bozen, which fact had recommended him to the old man, who had confessed to him as long as he had been here, and had taken communion from him. The priest held the viaticum in his hand now, and he sat down by the bed to give it to a man who lay ready, even clothed and booted, to go on his last journey.

"Praise be to Jesus Christ!" he began. The old man, who recognized him perfectly, formed his lips into the reply: "Forever and ever. Amen."

Then the Franciscan repeated the first words of the paternoster, but the dying man made a gesture with his restless hand.

"Herr Mumelter," Father Felician interrupted himself, "is there something you want?"

A nod. The lips tried to speak, but they were too weak.

"Shall I ask, Herr Mumelter?"

Nod.

"Something to do with confession?"

The hand on the coverlet indicated "No."

"Is there some disposition you want to make?"

The same negative.

"Has it to do with your will?"

A nod, with one finger of the restless hand painfully lifted.

"You want to let me know where it is?"

Nod.

"Is it here in this room?"

Nod.

"I'll look for it, shall I?"

The same affirmative.

A while later the Franciscan was holding in his hand an envelope on which was written in the old man's thin, firm writing: "Last will of Laurenz Xaver Mumelter."

The finger motioned: "Give it to me."

Now the white envelope was on the coverlet, and the hand, growing more and more uneasy, could grasp it. He took and held it fast.

"Are you ready to pray now, Herr Mumelter?"

Putting things to rights and keeping order to the very last, the dying man nodded: "Yes." Now he was ready.

Then one might have heard in the room, filled with slanting arabesques by the afternoon sun, the praying of the priest and the repetitions of the dying man fulfilling the duties of his Church with complete concentration. He repeated the prayers that he had learned as a child just as he had said them as a youth, as a man, and as a graybeard—the immutable words, in the immutable order. After three paternosters came the Ave Maria: "Hail Mary, full of grace," and afterward the profession of faith: "I believe in one God, the Father almighty, Maker of heaven and earth." He moved his numbing lips to address God, the Father, whom he had believed in ever since he had been able to think—moved them, and renewed his faith.

Then he received his last meal on earth, the Host. He felt and swallowed the consecrated wafer that Father Felician put on his tongue, and felt the consecrated oil cool upon his brow and temples, where the officiating priest had made the sign of the cross.

And now he closed his eyes again in weariness, and, the work being finished and the time of rest here at last, waited for death. While the praying Franciscan guarded his sleep, his grandchildren came into the room.

He awoke, opened his eyes, saw his grandchildren, and had the strength to whisper: *"Grüss euch."*

At this Riccarda sobbed aloud so despairingly that he put matters in order one last time: "Come here!"

Leaning over, she heard him whisper: "What does this mean—girl? Can't you—understand? I've—got—to join—the regiment. My—class—has been—called—up . . ."

Then he made a sudden tiny movement with his left hand, his breath rattled, and he was silent.

Old Mumelter had joined the heavenly regiment.

There he lay, on a strange bed in a strange house in a strange city, with a smile growing deeper and deeper around his thin, open mouth, which seemed to say: "Dying is lovely." His cheeks were sunken; no need to close his eyes—he had taken care even of that in good time. In his hands (Father Felician having silently gone out, leaving her alone with her brother), Riccarda put a little cross; he had carved it beautifully for Anna, his wife, when she fell so ill. But she had died before he could finish it, and when he was through with it he had given it to Riccarda. Now she put it into his stiffening hands to take to his own Anna.

The two taciturn grandchildren said nothing. They had lighted candles at the head of the bed, and there was nothing else for them to do now but look at that face, whose expression seemed more and more assured and liberated the longer they looked and the further the candles burned down.

"Better for him," was the only thing Andreas finally managed to say.

Riccarda did not say, as she felt like doing: "And worse for us." She did not go home, but sent word to her husband what he was to do for the child, and that he should not come over; she would keep watch here. At that moment she felt keenly what a stranger her husband was—and her child.

Sepp did not come either. For the triumphal celebration went on into the night, and the Hitler Youth of the city of Pilsen, led by Kuno Schultheiss, held a torchlight procession. The gleam of it could be seen through the windows.

"He died of Sepp," said Riccarda when the first candles had burned down and she was lighting the second set.

"No," said Andreas. "He died of Hitler."

That he had died of old age never occurred to them for a moment.

Later that night, when they opened his will, they read:

This is my will and testament, written with my own hand, I being of sound and disposing mind and memory.

My property consists of the house and wood-carving business of Christoph Mumelter's Heirs, Silbergasse 7, Bozen; of securities and cash, deposited at the Banca Commerciale in Bozen; all appraised on December 2, 1939, by the Italian Appraisal Commission for the South Tirolean Emigrants at 87,000 lire. This appraisal is fraudulent. The true value is 258,764 lire.

This property and my other personal property I devise and bequeath equally to my grandson Andreas and my granddaughter Riccarda. My grandson Sepp is to be remembered proportionately by his older brother and sister upon attaining his majority.

I know that making my will at a moment like this is futile, because one of the most shameless crimes in history has been perpetrated upon us South Tiroleans, robbing us of our country and our possessions. But the day will come when this crime is atoned for. This you, Andreas and Riccarda, are to work toward with all your strength. And see to it that Sepp shall also be sensible and do his part.

Farewell to you all!

I beseech our Lord to punish Adolf Hitler and Benito Mussolini for the crimes they have committed.

The Lord, who has always been gracious to me, will fulfill this my last wish. That I know.

Long live the Tirol!

Pilsen, Christmas Day, 1939 LAURENZ XAVER MUMELTER.

Two days later they carried him to the grave. The funeral train was small, but it hardly included a single unmoved mourner. The dead man rested in an oak coffin in his green Loden suit, the Silver Cross of Merit with the Crown on his breast, and after him came Father Felician, Andreas, Riccarda, her embarrassed husband, Sepp, no less embarrassed, Mr. and Mrs. Hoffman, in mortal terror because of Gwen (who was still under arrest), Dr. Paumgartner, and three men whose names nobody knew, but who later identified themselves as South Tiroleans. They were a deputation of the new settlers on the Moravian-Slovakian frontier, and had learned of their fellow countryman's death from the German paper. So the South Tirol walked behind the old man's coffin, and when the coffin was blessed and lowered into the grave in the little Franciscan cemetery, two spadefuls of real South Tirolean earth fell upon it. They were the gift of Veronika, in which she had planted the little Christmas tree; the tree had died meanwhile, but the earth from the garden remained, and fell lightly upon old Mumelter.

"God give him everlasting rest," Father Felician prayed.

"God, let us carry out his last will!" prayed the two grandchildren, vowing to live for it alone.

Then the grave was closed, and two wreaths lay on it. The earthly career of old Mumelter was at an end.

That same evening another grave was closed at the same churchyard, the so-called Strangers' Cemetery. It belonged to Madeleine Roux, the French girl. The funeral train was yet smaller, for it consisted only of the murdered girl's brother and, again, Dr. Paumgartner.

Here, too, a vow was made by the open grave.

Chapter 15

THERE was such a rain of leaflets that the sky above Pilsen, never very clear, was darkened for moments at a time. At first it was taken to be an air raid, and the screaming sirens and the crashing and splintering of the anti-aircraft guns near the Skoda Works led people to fear the worst. Then the roar of planes and the firing ceased; but oddly enough, the sirens screamed on. Was a second attack expected, the first apparently having been beaten off?

With the inexplicable speed with which such things flew from mouth to mouth here, the word spread: "It isn't an air raid. They're dropping leaflets. Pick them up wherever you find them. Never mind the sirens. They're to make you stay at home or look for cover until the Nazis have picked up the leaflets themselves."

The result was that a few moments later thousands of backs would be seen stooping over pavements and plowed fields in Pilsen and the suburbs of Doubravka and Lobzy, picking up square, yellowish little slips of paper; wherever the wind whirled them into the air, they ran after them—boys, old folks, townspeople, workmen, peasants. The Military Police and the Gestapo, who had dispatched groups of their own to prevent this at all costs, found themselves faced with an impossibility. Hardly would they have scattered a few people and put them to flight before three times as many would have gathered in their place; besides which, a rather high wind kept blowing their booty back to them.

This picking up of leaflets on July 22, 1940—at least one third of the population was actively engaged in this—was the first sign of open disobedience in the Pilsen district. The leaflets, dropped from English Blenheims, were in Czech, and read as follows:

Czechs! Do not be blinded by the German reports of victory. France's misfortune does not alter the fact that the war will go on until the Nazis are defeated and you are set free. You know of nothing but German victories. What you do not know is that the English army has succeeded in reaching the British Isles from Dunkirk, making England an impregnable fortress. Protected by her battle-tried army, reinforced by the contingents from her colonies, England awaits the landing of Hitler. If he comes, we shall annihilate him and his Nazi bombs. If he does not come, then despite his European victories he cannot win the war, because England and her Empire are in his road. From today forward, therefore, you should think of nothing except whether he will come, when he will come, and what will happen to him if he does come. By that and nothing else you should measure the chances of your liberation. Whether he dares to invade the British Islands and whether he succeeds are the only questions that will decide the war. Listen to our broadcasts in the Czech language. Everything else is lying German propaganda. Hitler has not won yet. He will not win. Nazdar!

The rejoicing, the great, sighing relief that all these people felt from the moment when they hurriedly read and hid these leaflets, could not be concealed. On the evening after the rain of paper the cafés and beer halls of Pilsen and suburbs were overcrowded, and the Gestapo agents who were everywhere on hand could find nothing to complain of except shining eyes or the expression of unusual enjoyment with which the Pilsner beer, now growing much thinner and weaker in malt, was consumed, although this was not a week end but an ordinary Monday. People were celebrating nevertheless. Heretofore they had not dreamed that the evacuation of Dunkirk was so important as the leaflets had asserted. At one blow, with the willingness of despair, they saw everything in a new light. Someone thought of the quip that tens of thousands were repeating that very night, a scornful parody of Kaiser Wilhelm's statement, "Our future is on the water": "Hitler's future is in the water."

On the morning of July 23 these six words appeared as if written by magic hands upon every wall and corner. Wherever a wall left room for a chalk inscription, one was to be seen. They soon vanished as mysteriously as they had appeared; but by that afternoon the walls of the Městanska Beseda on the Kopecky Promenade were full of them again, as well as those along the Rasinův Dům in the Jagellonska and the Obchodní Academy on Dr. V. Petéka Square; in the afternoon, however, the writing was done not with chalk but with black paint, which was harder to remove.

The following news spread like lightning that Tuesday: the 2,700 employees of the tobacco factories in the Czechoslovakian city of Tábor, not far from Pilsen, had left their work and burned in the town square all the pictures of Hitler that they could lay hands on in their haste. The Janaček armament factories, near Prague, received a telephoned order from Berlin to get ready for shipment thirty thousand new rifles, which were to be fetched in German army trucks; the trucks appeared, the rifles were loaded on and carted away, when the Berlin order turned out to be fictitious; but by that time the thirty thousand rifles were already in safe hands. In the Masaryk-Realschule at Pilsen, which now served as barracks for German military police, disturbances whose cause and nature were described in various contradictory fashions broke out that same twenty-third of July. Some said a quarrel between a Czech and a German policeman was the cause, resulting in wild gunplay, with thirty-seven killed and more than a hundred wounded. Others asserted it was a dispute among the Germans themselves.

This raised the spirits of the town to fever pitch. But the unrest, growing hour by hour, was yet put in the shade by the excitement that spread abroad when the official broadcasting stations made the following announcement along with the rest of the news at seven in the evening: "Owing to the carelessness of a workman during the trial of a new casting process in the lead foundry of the Skoda Works, an accident took place in which the workman and several other persons lost their lives."

It was only a few moments until everyone who had a short-wave set heard identical accounts of the so-called accident broadcast from London and the Czech underground station. According to this story Karel Vaček, a fifty-four-year-old crane operator, had that morning at eleven tipped over his craneload of molten lead just as a commission of German officers inspecting the works was standing below. Fourteen were burned to death. At the same moment Karel Vaček, known in the plant as "Stary Vaček" (or Old Vaček), hurled himself from a height of sixty feet to the concrete floor, shouting "Long live Masaryk!" He was killed instantly. The head of the experimental department, questioned at once by the Gestapo, could only say that Stary Vaček had been one of his most dependable, skilled, and universally popular workmen, who had operated that same crane for twenty-three years. The name of the head of the experimental department was Jaroslav Uliř.

There was no justification at all for the wave of optimism that swept over the Czechs to a man. No one had time or skepticism enough to put under the magnifying glass what had happened since the day before. It was nothing, actually, except for a few English statements that might or might not be true, and a few open outbreaks of hostility that would be put down soon enough. But psychological moments do not depend on reason, and revolutions do depend on psychological moments. This was one of them. The strictly ordered and pursued policy of passive obedience planned by the Beseda and those who ran it had speeded the moment. People could no longer endure obedience to their hated masters, and still less could they endure the hopelessness brought by Nazi victories. This was what made Stary Vaček's act a valve through which poured out the now explosive impatience of a people fed up with silence.

A warning from the Reich Protector broadcast at midnight by all the German stations and the Prague Czech government station saw the situation exactly as it was, yet shortsightedly nevertheless: "Irresponsible elements in the Protectorate suppose the moment for disturbances has arrived. They may be assured that their action is sheer madness. Order has been completely restored at every point in Bohemia and Moravia where disturbances of the peace took place yesterday and today, and the culprits are awaiting sentence by court-martial. It cannot be too strongly emphasized that the unfortunate excesses of the last two days can have no consequence but redoubled and trebled severity. Let no one entertain the preposterous idea that the German government has not considered each and every possibility well in advance, and made its arrangements accordingly."

However, something seemed not to have been considered in advance: the execution of the two Jellineks, father and son, just at this point.

The two Jellineks were shot on the morning of Wednesday, July 24, 1940, in the courtyard of the St. Nicholas Monastery, which is some distance out of town on the bank of the Radbusa; the detonation of the twenty-four shots fired at the two men went unheard. It was too early in the morning, and the place of their death was too remote; neither the radio nor the papers carried a word of it. Nevertheless, no one could say how, the city knew the story when it rose from sleep. Here, too, something took place that had less to do with reason than with the people's immeasurable excitement. Under other circumstances the news would have left them quite cold; the alleged ritual murderer, Hilsner, was still darkly remembered—a proof of Herr Schultheiss' foresight—and people were none too fond of Jews. Now, however, the execution in the dark of night had a tremendous impact, reinforced by the fact that the authorities suppressed it, which led to the conclusion that they had a guilty conscience. That morning, therefore, in the official broadcast, the D. N. B. found itself compelled to break the silence. "Richard Israel Jellinek and Leopold Israel Jellinek, convicted of the ritual murder of the Frenchwoman, Madeleine Roux, were shot by court-martial this morning." No more. Not even that they were father and son. And again nc one knew the perpetrator, but on the dot of twelve noon, when the traffic was heaviest, there appeared on St. Bartholomew's Cathedral, on the newly named Adolf Hitler Platz, a gigantic poster asking in huge red letters:

Why?

Why was Kuno Schultheiss, the leader of the Pilsen Hitler Youth, not shot as the murderer of Madeleine Roux, the Frenchwoman?

Why is the American, Gwen Hoffman, who knows that Kuno Schultheiss, the leader of the Pilsen Hitler Youth, is the murderer of Madeleine Roux, the Frenchwoman, under arrest?

Why?

No one who set foot in Adolf Hitler Square could help seeing the fiery letters, for they covered the dial of the church clock at the precise moment when the Pilseners were in the habit of looking at the clock and hearing it strike the noon hour with a carillon and a mechanical procession of metal saints. The hour was struck, but the procession of saints, circling out of the clock tower and returning to it, failed to appear; the poster prevented them. It was so artfully put up that the German military police, using firemen's ladders, were a good half-hour in removing it; and in that half-hour innumerable people had seen it.

That afternoon the deputy Gestapo leader in Berlin reached Pilsen by plane, was received at the airport by the representative of the Reich Protector, Dr. K. H. Frank, and went to the Hotel Waldeck, where he took rooms. He held conferences with Dr. Frank; Managing Director Schultheiss; the commandant of the Pilsen garrison, General von dem Busch; the head of the Prague Gestapo, Stahlaecker; three German industrialists; a German lawyer; a German patent expert; and a Czech representative of the Orbis-Presse.

His arrival and the conferences were officially reported over the radio.

What was not officially reported was that the newcomer, Herr Reinhard Heydrich, was in a state of agitation concerning which the one Czech who had talked with him that evening made statements that spread quickly, confidential though they were. This Czech, Konopaček by name, belonged not to the National Unity party of the Czech president, Hácha, but to the Vlajka party, which included the Czech extremists, and whose support the Nazis were counting on. According to him Herr Heydrich had "bellowed like an ox," and taken the occurrences in Pilsen unexpectedly seriously. The man to whom Konopaček made his confidential statements was Jaroslav Ulíř.

"Take care, Jaro," he said, "they're on the trail of you and the Beseda! And just so that you'll know who this Heydrich fellow is—because I think you underestimate him!" From a filing cabinet in the office of the Orbis-Presse, where the conversation took place, he drew a mimeographed sheet, which said:

Reinhard Heydrich. Born in Halle. (Father, Director of the Academy of Music, Bruno Richard Heydrich. Real name, Süss.) Six feet tall. Slender. Well-groomed. Blond. Thirty-six years old. Thin nose. Thin lips. Nickname among the Gestapo: The Green Basilisk. Nickname among the Nazis: The Hangman. Nickname in Austria: Black Maria. Office in the Columbus Building, Berlin. Luxurious twelve-room apartment, 37 Kurfürstendamm, Berlin. Spends his yearly income of $150,000 on women and horses. In his dealings with callers, is courteous, attentive, affable. Never smiles.

Stands and keeps himself in the shadow of Himmler, along with General Kurt Daluege, who commands the uniformed police. More powerful than the latter, and perhaps than Himmler, absolute commander of the Gestapo, which obeys him blindly. Odious to the army because he convinced Hitler that Gestapo men must be assigned to every army unit from a battalion upward.

Career: at eighteen, member of the radical Youth group, the Stahlhelm. In 1920, cadet in the German navy, discharged for drunkenness and agitation against the Weimar Republic. In 1922, member of the National Socialist German Workers' party at Breslau; transferred to Königsberg as punishment for embezzlement of party funds. Learned that the Gauleiter of East Prussia, Koch, possessed correspondence with Hitler's schismatic representative, Gregor Strasser; initiated an affair with Frau Koch, and stole the letters. By threatening Koch with publication of the letters, extorted an introduction to Hitler, who recommended him to Himmler. Shot Gregor Strasser with his own hand in the blood purge of June 30, 1934. Has enjoyed Hitler's unlimited confidence since then.

According to his foreword to the book, *German Safety,* regards the following as the duty of the police: "Thoroughgoing understanding of the fundamental intellectual groundwork of the enemy; insinuation into his confidence on this basis; use of this confidence until the enemy unknowingly reveals his thoughts and actions, and thus becomes defenseless. Immediate annihilation at that moment by denunciation and arrangements for punishment."

"That's the man who's got his eye on you now, Jaro!" said Konopaček when Riccarda's husband handed back the sheet with a shrug.

"Hasn't he got his eye on you too?" he asked.

"Not so much. For the moment, at least, the Vlajka people are sacrosanct. But you National Unity and Beseda fellows will have to watch your step like hell!"

"Dobře," replied Jaro. "Good."

"Don't be so casual about it," the other warned. "There's too much at stake. If I were you I wouldn't lift a finger just now. Incidentally, I was the last one Heydrich talked to today. I gathered from his questions that he's had an alarming impression of the attitude of the local Nazis, whom he conferred with before he did with me. That would be glorious, Jaro! That's where it ought to come from!"

"Dobře," said the other again. Nothing more. The man who had given the warning had trouble in hiding his disappointment. Had he some mission that the man about whom he had so willingly given information knew of? Perhaps Riccarda's husband thought so. Or perhaps it was simply the caution rooted in the Czech national character that made him so monosyllabic.

He came home at the regular time; Riccarda, accustomed by her grandfather to punctuality, had supper ready and on the table, and the child, Laurenz by name, four months old, was asleep. Every evening the foster father began by standing at the crib, watching the child that was not his as it slept and flourished. It's like Riccarda, he thought in his infatuation. It's like its father to a hair, Riccarda thought. The oftener she thought this, the more seldom it occurred to her to remind the father of the vow she had made him give her almost a year ago, on August 28. She thought of him every day, and particularly every night, when the lovelorn man who had given her child an honest name begged for her love. Then she would shut her eyes and think of the other man. Jaro? She respected his passion; his devotion to his country was inspiring; the way he loved her was sometimes annoying, sometimes touching. She did not love him, and never could. She loved Roberto, who never sent a word, and whom she hated.

"Dobrý večer," said Jaro, coming in, for he was trying to accustom Riccarda to the Czech tongue. First he looked at the small sleeping

boy, as usual, and then they sat down to table and ate the Czech dish that Riccarda had learned to cook for him. She still could not get used to seeing him smack his lips, wipe his plate with bread, and talk with his mouth full; and, as always, so today there was a thin wall of aversion and submissiveness between them.

He said, *"Poslouchez,"* Riccarda," accenting her name on the first syllable.

"Speak German," she requested.

"Dobře," he agreed, with his favorite word. And went on in German: "Did you hear the radio today?"

She nodded.

"That business about Starý Vaček too?"

"Of course. Wasn't he in your department?"

"He was, *anō*. Yes. And I knew he'd do it."

They looked at each other. He spat out a cherry pit on the plate, making a loud noise.

"Good," she said. To please him, she even said, *"Dobře."*

It pleased him immensely. "You don't mind?" he asked.

"Naturally not," she said.

Now, having finished eating, he pushed aside the empty plate with the gesture that she disliked so. "The thing is this, Milačku," he explained, lighting a pipe—good God, how differently Grandfather had always lit his!—"that the balloon is going up now. And I'd like a talk with you first. All right?"

"Of course," she said.

He got up and unplugged the telephone. "Nothing like being sure," he said with the broad, good-natured smile that she liked about him, which had first spoken in his favor with her. They sat down face to face in the dining room, which at the same time was the living room and the place for entertaining guests, and which Riccarda had left (she often reproached herself for this) exactly as she had found it on moving into his apartment. The dreadful framed family photographs were still hanging on the green-papered wall, and so was the diploma, under glass and surrounded by a withered laurel wreath, certifying that Jaroslav Uliř, born in Plzeň, had graduated from the Technical Academy at Prague, and earned the title of engineer.

"I don't like annoying you with it," he began. "But Heydrich came today—you know who he is—and something may happen to me any day. Just in case, Milačku, I'd like you to know what's what."

"Yes?" she said.

"Yes," he said, rather embarrassed. "I think you'd better be prepared for it. Heydrich isn't like that idiot Frank. They may jug me at any moment. In that case, of course you know nothing at all, which is in fact true. I'm not in favor of pouring men's business into women's ears. I've never told you anything, and consequently"—he paused, then finished—"you have no idea of anything."

"But I'd like to know everything, Jaro."

The "Jaro," which she seldom, indeed almost never, called him, delighted him so that it was a moment before he could reply: *"Ne, ne, Milačku malý!"* In his delight he began in Czech, but immediately corrected himself: "No! That isn't necessary. It's quite enough for one of us to have his nose in it. And all I mean is, in case they do jug me—you'll just wait until I get out again. Will you?"

"Naturally," she said.

"I mean—please don't be angry—just in case—you wouldn't want to get a divorce? Or would you?"

"Don't talk nonsense!"

"Well, yes, but look. I do know I'm an annoyance to you. At least sometimes. I was thinking that in that case you might—— Well, the child's father is somewhere. And I know you love him. Forgive me—I understand that perfectly. Why, it's absolutely a matter of course."

This was the first time they had mentioned the subject.

She looked at the framed photographs and the diploma in the laurel wreath. And at the ugly face that was gazing up at her as if at a judge. She got up and kissed him. "Silly!" she said as she did so, "what do you think, anyway? Even if you don't tell me anything about it, I'm in favor of your doing what you are doing. Thank God there are men like you. I tell you. Everyone should be the way you are."

Fierce joy came over the ugly face; the whole man was one great expression of delight.

"But I'm so revolting," he said. "And you're so beautiful."

"Well," she admitted, "you aren't exactly an Adonis." That night he told her everything.

The following day, early in the morning, she insisted on having Andreas come over to see them. Thus began what Herr Heydrich's report was later to describe as the "Subversive action in the Protectorate."

Yet they neither betrayed their secret to Andreas, nor discovered his. And indeed this was not necessary. For every non-Nazi in the Skoda Works, whose uninterrupted and constantly growing production of arms and machinery was vital to the German war effort (just as vital as that of Krupp in Essen, and almost twice as vital as that of the Hermann Goering Works), knew that a definite moment was being awaited for a definite action, and that both moment and action must come, inevitably. The sense of the inevitability of this action was universal, although no one guessed or cared to guess more than the general outline. Everyone agreed that something would happen, many people without having any idea of what. This *what,* however, consisted of three independent plans: Andreas' plan, which no one but Gwen knew of; Jaro Uliř's plan, made in concert with the Beseda, a carefully guarded secret of Plant 9, which Riccarda had been told about that night; and a plan made in the cannon foundry, particularly favored by the Russians and Serbs who worked there, the vaguest of the three, and known to Jaro as "Project B." Riccarda knew what she was doing when she insisted on taking Andreas into their confidence; she respected Jaro's fanaticism, but she trusted her realistic brother's objectivity far more.

Without a moment's discussion of what it was to be, Andreas immediately said with all the emphasis of which he was capable: "Not now! Not under any circumstances! No matter what you do! Everything is premature now!"

"Is that so?" replied his brother-in-law, irritated. "And what do you say to Starý Vaček?"

"Magnificent. But insane."

"Don't say that! He has roused our entire nation from its lethargy!"

The Tirolean shook his head. "That's your mistake. Your nation is awake—too wide awake! It ought to be given sedatives instead of being roused. It's lunacy to start at the very moment when the Nazis have forced France to her knees. You have to begin at the moment of depression: that's so obvious that I can't see how any sensible person could imagine anything else. Any acts like the sheer madness that the Tábor tobacco workers were guilty of simply get the Gestapo after us; and we owe the fact that Heydrich is here to your friend Starý Vaček, whose personal courage I enormously admire. But courage isn't what counts! Haven't you discovered yet that the Nazis are the most utter cowards in the world, and never start anything until an overwhelmingly superior force and overwhelming preparations absolutely assure a success? Damn it, why can't you learn to fight your enemy with his own weapons? His weapons are the proper moment and proper preparations. We don't need courage—we need sober, mathematically exact intelligence."

His Czech brother-in-law felt wounded not only in his national honor but in his painfully won position with respect to Riccarda. With a furrow of anger between his eyes he contradicted: "Heydrich isn't here because of Vaček, or our people at Tábor either! He's here because of the legal murder of the two Jellineks, which has nothing to do with the Beseda. I'm astonished that you should forget that. Miss Hoffman didn't forget it, anyway! By the way, what have you done to get her released?"

Andreas, less sure of himself now, replied: "That's my worry. The question is, are we to sacrifice innocent human lives by premature actions due to impatience? Or are we to wait for the moment when they will at least not be sacrificed in vain?"

"Of course that's the question," agreed the Czech with utter positiveness. "But I tell you, brother, you'll have to sacrifice human lives at any time, and I'm afraid they'll always be innocent ones. After all, that's the reason why the Nazis have had their way everywhere in the world! Millions of people all over the world ask themselves: How has all this been possible? How could Hitler take Austria? And Czechoslovakia? And sell out your country? And pocket Holland and Norway and France? Because they were afraid, so much afraid that they were simply quaking, of sacrificing human lives—innocent ones! Because they feared that massacres would follow every assassination. But I tell you that and nothing else is lunacy! Innocent human lives? And what do they mean? What does Starý Vaček's life amount to by comparison with the fourteen that he disposed of? What does my life or yours count if we succeed in taking care of one of those who have long since forfeited all right to live? And what's the difference if a hundred or two hundred or two hundred thousand people besides us lose their lives for that purpose?

Nothing at all! You still reckon in human lives instead of ideas! Dear things cost a great deal. What if it does cost us dear?"

Here, Riccarda saw, a submissive man who sometimes looked as if he would not hurt a fly had been transformed into the kind of man who could say such things as this. *One should be as he is,* she again had to admit to herself.

Her brother, faced with a question that had kept him holding his breath month after month, said in the twilight: "I admire your confidence, brother. And your generosity. You toss around 200,000 people. But we South Tiroleans are scarcely more than 200,000 people. If they didn't exist there wouldn't be anyone to think of South Tirol. I've always thought that was important. And I've always thought one had some responsibility for human lives. You seem to deny it."

"Ale ne," the other objected, as if he took this wholly for granted and there was no problem at all. "All I say is, if one has the responsibility for a great many people, then because of this very responsibility one has to take great risks. How many Czechs are there here in Bohemia and Moravia? More than seven million. And if you or I or anyone can give back to these millions the existence that the Nazis have stolen from them, what, I ask you, do 70,000 or 700,000 of them amount to? And if we give it back to them, we shall also be giving it back to you South Tiroleans, and to the Poles and the Serbs and the Norwegians and the Austrians. Of course, it could have been done more cheaply—much more cheaply! One of us seven million could have taken it in his own hands: I mean our President, Hácha. And *Pan* Minister Chvalkovsky! On the night of March 15, 1939, they were entirely alone with Hitler in the Reich Chancellery. If those two had taken revolvers out of their pockets instead of the fountain pens they signed our disgrace with, and shot the greatest criminal of all time, there would have been two dead men and seven million happy on our side, *Dobře*. Two were cowards—the two who had the last right to be. But there can't be seven million cowards—is that what you want? We Czechs aren't cowards, and neither are you South Tiroleans. And the seven millions who aren't cowards will simply have to remake the fantastic opportunity that was missed. Maybe it won't be quite so good, because that kind of thing doesn't come twice. But at any rate an opportunity. And once it's made, we

must use it, without sentimental scruples. Jesus, Mary, and Joseph! We have the most unscrupulous opponent in history. And you have scruples!"

How convincing he sounded! And still he did not convince Andreas.

"Yes," Andreas said. "I have scruples. You're right about your president. He's an individual, and as an individual he can do as he pleases with his own life. But you can't do whatever you please with seven million individual lives. That's why you can't involve them in affairs that you can make but that you can't lead them back out of again. If you guarantee them death or the concentration camp, you must at least be able to guarantee the thing they die for or are tortured for. Can you do that? No. You'll have to wait until you can."

The Czech had leaned forward attentively. "And if I may ask, brother, when shall I be able to do that in your opinion?"

Andreas was silent, thrusting out his lower beyond his upper lip. Then he answered slowly, word by word: "I don't know. All I know is that someday you will be able to. We must prepare for that day. You must. I must. All of us must. Not haphazardly. Not impatiently. Not with bravado. Not amateurishly. Tenaciously, systematically, mathematically. It will always be an exercise in probabilities. But it mustn't be an exercise in impossibility. That's all I know. Thank you, in any case, for your confidence; it deserves mine in return. You have your plan, I have mine. And I suspect that aside from Project B there are countless others. Plans don't matter now—the best of them is bad if the time is bad. The time is bad. Listen to me, brother. Don't rush things. You ask him, too, Riccarda. Everything depends on his waiting. Not merely the success of my own plan—his does too. Everything!"

This was the first time that Riccarda had had to ask her husband for something. She said: "I believe Andreas is right. Will you wait?"

The Czech replied: "To do that I'd have to know and study his plan first."

"I'll promise you that," said Andreas. "When are you going to inform me about yours?"

Jaro hesitated. "Mine was worked out in concert with the Beseda. If I tell you about it, I shall be putting the Beseda at your mercy."

The Tirolean looked at him. His quick temper flared up. "Do you mistrust me? I've got a score to settle with Hitler too. At least as big a one as you."

"Then you want everything to go through your hands! Is that it? Yes or no?"

"Yes," Andreas admitted frankly. "My plan is a good one. That I know."

The Czech's patience, too, was at an end. "Excuse me, brother. You're a Tirolean. This is Czechoslovakia. And the Nazis are going to fall at Czech hands!"

Andreas shook his head violently. "The Nazis won't fall at Czech hands or South Tirolean hands either. Others will come after us. And all of us will do it together. But so that others can come after us, those who start must succeed a hundred per cent. And we're starting!"

"*Dobře*. And what gives you the right to impose your will on us? It's all fine for you to join us. But how can you insist on our putting ourselves under your orders?"

"I'm not imposing anything on you. Nothing, nothing, nothing! Only the time. When the time comes, act however you like. As idiotically as you like, I don't care. If I can't convince you by then, I'll carry out my plan all by myself. You may be sure of that."

"You'll do what we tell you to do, brother. I'm sorry to have to say it twice, but you're in Czechoslovakia!"

Andreas was more than hot-tempered; his sudden fury could make him foolhardy. At such rare, uncontrolled moments as these it was strikingly apparent how young he still was inside his shell of deliberation, precision, and restraint, which often made people forget that he was only twenty-six. "Yes," he said, "I am in Czechoslovakia—thanks for reminding me. And now may I remind you what your esteemed King Pržemysl Ottokar used to say: 'One Tirolean is as good as three Czechs'?" Before the words were out of his mouth he realized the mistake he had made, but he was too proud and far too stubborn to apologize. Besides, it was too late for apology.

"Brother, you will allow me to report to the Beseda," Jaro replied icily.

The three separated without reaching any conclusion. The two men had to go the same way to work, but did not walk together.

Nevertheless, an epoch in history dated from that six-o'clock-in-the-morning conversation between a Czech and a South Tirolean.

Chapter 16

Gwen was caught in the legal machinery of the Third Reich. For weeks she had daily interviews, sometimes two and three a day, with the perfectly courteous, English-speaking major in the judge advocate's department who was investigating her case.

"Miss Hoffman. Surely your extraordinary intelligence must tell you that what you are doing here is sheer quixotry!"

"Sometimes there has to be such a thing as quixotry."

"Why, Miss Hoffman? Please give me just one plausible reason for your utterly mysterious attitude! After all that has gone before, you cannot possibly believe that Kuno Schultheiss or his father has the slightest thing to do with the ritual murder. Why don't you retract your accusations, then, which the judge advocate characterizes as defamation?"

"Because two people are accused who have no more to do with the murder than we two, as I know and you know equally well."

She did not know that the two Jellineks had long since been shot; this had been kept from her.

"But Miss Hoffman! How often have I asked you to look at the case without prejudice! Do please get it through your head what you are basing your charges on: the words of a half-unconscious woman spoken in a foreign language, and sheer gossip from someone completely intoxicated. Can you not see that a state founded on justice cannot allow the validity of such proof?"

"It isn't a state founded on justice."

"If it will ease your mind any, I'm ready to assure you on my word of honor——"

"Major," she interrupted, with nothing now of that which had often made her seem so much younger than she was, "I don't want your word of honor. But I want you to tell me: did you see the two defendants during the trial?"

The major had seen them only at the execution, and therefore replied in the negative.

"Too bad," said Gwen. "Otherwise you wouldn't find my attitude hard to understand. There was a father there—I have one too. That father suffered as I have never seen a man suffer. No one paid any attention to him. I didn't either—I simply couldn't look at him. Nevertheless, he kept looking over at me as if I could help him. I never knew before that any man could be so utterly forsaken. And I actually can help him. That's what I'm doing—or at least trying to do—now. When I'm alone I can see his eyes. I have to look away, even though he isn't there."

"There we have it," said the major, finding his own opinion fully confirmed. "Nothing but feminine emotionalism. Because somebody gives you a sentimental look—the Jews are good at that!—you think he's innocent. But drawing conclusions from externals, instead of incontrovertible truth, is emotional justice. That's what they have in states not founded on justice, Miss Hoffman. In states founded on justice, on the other hand——"

"Major," she interrupted him again, "I take you for a very clever man. Why do you keep taking me for stupid? The word justice in connection with what I've seen is absurd."

"You're very much excited. We'd better stop."

"I'm calmness itself. If you don't want to say, 'For such and such reasons we are perpetrating a glaring, crying injustice,' then at least don't talk about a state founded on justice. I'm not naïve enough to believe it, and you have too much sense to expect me to."

"Shall I read you the article in the Code of Criminal Procedure dealing with evidence in criminal trials?"

"No, thanks."

"Then you are still so blind as to refuse to state that you have made a mistake and brought charges you cannot prove, and therefore regret?"

"I'm still so blind."

"Miss Hoffman. We have had infinite patience, and certainly far more consideration for you than they would have had in the states that you choose to say are founded on justice."

"Because I'm an American and you're afraid of complications!"

"I certainly don't think you are naïve, as you suggested before. But neither do I think you are an affair of state. Suppose we put an end to this exchange of irrelevant remarks and get back to the subject. I was simply trying once more to show you the senselessness—and, I would emphasize, the futility—of your attitude. Your parents are moving heaven and earth to secure your release. Your fiancé——"

"I'm not engaged."

"—Herr Andreas Mumelter on his part is doing all that is humanly possible to convince us that you acted in a state of extreme nervous excitement——"

"Is he? I'm sorry to hear it. And it's the only thing I'm sorry for. I would have expected him to realize at least what I'm here for."

"You are displaying a remarkable degree of illogicality. Your being here is doing no one any good—won't you see it? It isn't doing you any good, since it hardly improves your health, which is not robust, to say the least; it does your parents no good, since they are quite naturally tormented by knowing that you are here——"

"Are you always so considerate about what torments other people?"

"And it isn't doing the defendants any good. You knew that they were convicted?"

"I know. But as long as I'm here nothing can be done to them. The judge advocate himself told me so."

All the interviews so far had been very much on this order. The prisoner, Gwen Hoffman, would not give in. There were times during her imprisonment when she was ready to. But at such times she was simply afraid. More often, with her unceasing sense of watching herself, she felt she was ridiculous. *What am I doing, after all?* she told herself. *Playing a part in a melodrama? Attempting heroics, as the presiding judge said? I'm the very opposite of a heroine. I've never been interested in politics in my life. I'm afraid of mice; I fuss when they don't change the sheets often enough; I can't stand this hospital smell. And what's more, the major is right: my being here is doing no one any good.* But then somehow she could feel eyes upon her, and she would forget what she had been thinking. Everything would be plain, inevitable, and utterly simple again. She would not give in.

For that reason the major had now received orders to inform the prisoner, Gwen Hoffman, of the two Jellineks' execution, thus forcing her to realize the futility of her resistance. "The prisoner, Gwen Hoffman," said his instructions, "is to be informed of the execution of the two Jews." Signed: "Heydrich." Pursuant to orders the examining officer said: "Your being here isn't helping the defendants either.. That is, it was the case only so long as we still had to investigate your so-called evidence."

His tone terrified Gwen. "What does that mean?" she asked.

"That the sentence upon the two has been executed."

She had grown thinner during her arrest, paler than ever; she fell back a step. Her lovely eyes stared. She said hoarsely: "Is that true?" She believed, she hoped, that a trap was being laid for her.

"It took place within the period provided by law."

"You mean to say—the two are dead?"

"I did say so."

"And I ask you again. I care nothing for your impatience."

"What do you wish to know?"

"I wish to know whether it is true that the two are dead."

"Yes, certainly."

"Executed? I mean murdered—you—your state based on justice ——"

She got no further. The great eyes filled with tears. "I want to be removed!" she demanded.

"Miss Hoffman. I believe you can now see how senseless your behavior is. Pursuant to law, the two murderers——"

"I want to be removed!"

"I point out to you for the last time that there are limits to all forbearance and patience. The law of the Third Reich applies to you as it does to everyone here."

At this the prisoner, Gwen Hoffman, who heretofore had always talked to the major without a guard, flung open the door herself and shouted: "Guard! Take me away!" And back she was taken to her cell.

It was not a felon's cell, but one of the so-called "private" cells, reserved for special cases and assigned to privileged persons or those who were to be cut off from other prisoners. A whitewashed, fairly large room, with a large barred window, a white iron bedstead, and everything else that a not too pampered unwilling guest would need, even books; a combination of living room, hospital, and prison, it looked out on the Ottokar Promenade, which formed part of the fortifications that had been turned into footpaths. Gwen was thinking now with piercing, irrefutable clarity what she had always thought in this room without being absolutely sure of it: injustice was being done.

Strange that so commonplace an idea should amount to a discovery in her staring eyes. Nevertheless, such was the case. That which had been veiled before was naked now; that which might have been excused or argued or doubted was now inexcusable, indisputable, indubitable. There were no ifs and buts. No one could say, "On the other hand." Nothing but, "On the one hand."

And the one side that was glaringly obvious now to Gwen's open eyes was, *What is being done here is unjust. All of it.* The proof is given, the trial is ended. It ends with the triumph of injustice.

Gwen was not one of those people who had to have the absolute proof of things in order to notice and feel them. But because of her inhibitions she kept what she had noticed and felt at a distance until both came so close to her that there was no distance left. Looking down at the promenade that had been made out of the medieval fortifications, she could see with aching plainness that three things were going on here: laws were being used to commit lawless acts; no one did right, and no one received justice; everything that happened was unjust.

Injustice cried out. Who heard it? *Did I hear it until a few weeks or months ago?* the prisoner in the private cell asked herself.

No, she told herself.

But why didn't I hear it? she asked, examining herself more mercilessly than the major from the judge advocate's department had. *Why, since it jumps up and hits you in the face?*

Then she made a second discovery, almost more elementary than the first, and yet more alarming: You had to go through it yourself before you could believe and know it.

And the eye of the prisoner who was interrogating herself fell on a page of an American newspaper, which her father had sent in with magazines and books. "Keep us out of war!" it said in huge type. "We have no business in this!"

On the Ottokar Promenade across the way a child was sending

up a toy balloon. It was a blood-red balloon bearing a white swastika; it winged its way upward, and the child watched, fascinated, as it vanished in the smoky sky. By now it was no bigger than a cherry. "*Heil* Hitler!" the child shouted at the sky, nodding after the red cherry. Every day since Gwen had started looking out, children had been sending up toy balloons on the Ottokar Promenade and shouting "*Heil* Hitler!" after them; the fat woman who sold the balloons apparently taught them to. They were boys and girls, four, five, six years old.

You had to see it with your own eyes, Gwen thought. Otherwise you didn't believe it.

But, she told herself (having overcome her inhibition so that the distance shrank away to nothing), since it is as it is, we do have business in this. Everyone does—everyone who knows.

And then she made the third and last, utterly simple discovery. It had come to her upon hearing that people whom she might have helped had been murdered "pursuant to law": No one who knows can withdraw himself. If he does, then he partakes of the guilt. When Andreas had called it "becoming a witness," she had only felt it. Now she knew; it was proved; two people were dead.

She looked at the child as it stared raptly after the vanishing balloon. *Just suppose,* she thought, *that the child under the poplars should fall into the Radbuza, and I were to stand there without moving, letting it drown, although I can swim. Would anyone in the world excuse me? That is just our case,* she answered herself. *We're standing by, looking on, witnessing it, not moving, but waiting while children and men and old people perish. That child yonder is four or five, and will perish if it is not saved from staring fanatically after a toy balloon. Andreas' father was ninety-two, and perished because no one brought him back. The two Jelineks perished because I had scruples.*

The door was unlocked; Gwen automatically replied, "Come in," to a knock, and someone entered the private cell. Her thoughts filled her mind so completely and ached so fiercely that she did not turn. She was still looking at the child and the fat woman who sold the red balloons with the white swastikas.

The man who had come in said: "Miss Hoffman?"

She found herself confronted with a man she did not know. He was very tall, very thin, with a hook nose and thin lips; standing modestly by the door, he wore the black uniform of the S.S. Elite Troops. "My name is Heydrich," he said. "I'd like to talk to you, if I may."

"Please do," she replied, motioning to him to be seated in one of the two white chairs in the room. He went over to it, waited until she had sat down in the second, and then seated himself. Just like someone paying a call in a private house.

"Cigarette?" he asked, offering his case, and then, remembering: "I forgot. I take it you don't smoke? Do you mind if I do?"

"I do smoke," she said, helping herself; they both lighted their cigarettes. From where Gwen sat she could see the fat woman with the balloons. From where the visitor sat he could see a woman who seemed determined and ready for anything.

"I was sorry to hear that you've been suffering from a lack of fresh air," he began, and then, recollecting himself again, "I don't know whether you've heard my name."

"I have."

"Then you will know that I'm here officially. I wanted to ask you, isn't it about time to get you back into the fresh air that you've been missing? I am entirely at your disposal."

"I'm not missing anything."

The visitor knocked the ash off his cigarette, and, a little of it having fallen on the table, removed the mess with two fingers. "Let me tell you that I thoroughly respect your attitude. I've been meaning to call on you for a long time, but my time has been so taken up——"

"With murders? Or with protecting murderers?" she asked, starting to tremble.

The visitor heard the question and noticed the tremor. "Is it absolutely necessary to carry on the conversation in this fashion, Miss Hoffman? We shall hardly accomplish our purpose that way."

"I have no purpose." Her own voice sounded stranger to her than any voice ever had.

"That's a mistake, if you will allow me to differ. You've even got several purposes. Among others, the downfall of National Socialism. Am I wrong?"

She trembled so that she could hardly hold the cigarette. His frank, friendly eyes told him that it was not the trembling of fear.

"I don't care to talk to you," she said.

"I take the liberty of doubting that also. On the contrary, I have very much the impression that you would enjoy saying to me: 'Mr. Heydrich, does your conscience allow you to sleep?' You might put the question in rather more insulting words, but at any rate it is the question on the tip of your tongue. Agreed, Miss Hoffman. I am quite ready to reply. I'm even ready to reply to things that you have not asked, but that you ought to know before you despise and hate so obviously. Fair play, don't you think?" His voice was pleasant. He kept his cigarette in the corner of his mouth as he talked, which occasionally made his pronunciation careless.

She told herself that they were all alike. One looked just like another. And they all used the same methods. She said: "Since you can interpret feelings correctly, please don't trouble about anything further." She strove to speak clearly; but her voice refused to obey her.

"I've never gone through life the easy way. So I shall not take the easy way during these fifteen minutes either, Miss Hoffman. In your eyes, I'm a devil. We're all devils, defaming innocent, defenseless, estimable people, torturing them diabolically, brutally murdering them, and acting like angels of innocence as we do so. That is what you think of us now, isn't it?"

She did not answer.

"Suppose we change places for a little while. I'm the defendant. I realize that that's what I am in your eyes, and I'm ready to defend myself. Go ahead and accuse me."

"I don't care to talk to you."

He lighted another cigarette. "And you talk about intolerance! You're simply swathed in prejudices. Do you mind my telling you that they are the prejudices of your fatherland? America regards anyone as wrong from the start who exercises any power whatever. Sigmund Freud, whom I'm sorry to say a few overzealous Party members failed to keep among us—no new movement can be altogether free of hotheads, and they are the ones who compromise new movements—called it the anti-power complex. I'm afraid someday that will be the dangerous disease of your native country, which is so proud of itself for not servilely obeying anyone, although it has succumbed to an idolatry that no other country can match: it servilely worships liberty, and no dictator is deified as this scarecrow of a nebulous idea is.

"Since I am the accused, according to your principles you must allow me liberty to defend myself. I will defend myself with a question: What does your freedom consist of, Miss Hoffman? Doesn't it consist of an endless conveyor belt of material accomplishments, which everyone can buy for the same nickel, the purpose being to enjoy life and pursue happiness?

"I will defend myself with a second question: Does your liberty consist in the liberty of patriotism? In liberty to sacrifice for the Fatherland? In unlimited freedom to give your homeland everything you are and everything you possess?

"Miss Hoffman, you and your world think ill of us National Socialists, and you assume the right to condemn us. I will defend myself with a third question: What gives you, who talk so much about right, justice, and liberty, the right to do that? Have we imposed upon you our views concerning your fatherland? Have we ever asked you, the Miss Hoffmans all over the United States: what about your patriotism? When you sing 'The Star-Spangled Banner,' and the Stars and Stripes flutter in the breeze, your hearts beat higher, don't they? You love your fatherland. But you're so free that you neither must nor will lift a finger for it.

"Look here, Miss Hoffman, that's what we National Socialists want, the one thing *and* the other—to have your heart beat higher, *and* to have you lift a finger. We want to prevent a nation like ours —in spite of everything, it is one of the greatest in the world—from being humbled again. We want to make it proud for all time to come. And don't forget something else as you sit there full of venomous denial: that you yourself and the people who talk about our alleged injustice are committing an injustice that is positively monstrous. When we came into power, the injustice that your native country, Miss Hoffman, had imposed on us still prevailed. And we came to remove this world injustice from the world."

"With one a thousand times greater," replied Gwen. *They're all just alike,* she thought. *First that chest tone of honor and integrity; and when comes the grab for the dagger?*

"That has yet to be proved," replied the caller, crushing out his second cigarette and lighting a third. "But it does not require to be proved that a crying injustice has been done, and that it is being avenged exclusively upon those who committed it or allowed it to be committed. Among others, upon the criminals of Versailles; upon Messrs. Schuschnigg, Beneš, and their colleagues, who had not the courage to declare themselves for or against Bolshevism; upon the Church, which rolled its eyes and blessed those that bribed it; upon the intellectuals, who preached cosmopolitanism and destroyed love of home; upon the defenseless, innocent, estimable Jellineks. Miss Hoffman, in 1924 I personally asked Mr. Jellinek senior for 5,000 Czech crowns for a National Socialist worker whose right leg had been torn off in one of his steam mills; he gave me twenty. In the year 1929 the same Mr. Jellinek senior, by that time a bank director, invested four and a half million Czech crowns in the French armament factory of Schneider-Creusot; in 1931, three million Czech crowns in Sir Basil Zaharoff's English Vickers armament plant; in 1934 he established an annual subsidy for the *Pressburger Grenzbote,* the only German paper published there, in order to conduct propaganda against Germany. And in 1938, immediately after the fall of the Schuschnigg government, he was in Moscow to make a contract dealing ostensibly with arms shipments, but actually with anti-German espionage."

"Well, he knew who you were, that's all," Gwen defended the man who had sent her such imploring looks, and whom she had not assisted.

"Unluckily my fifteen minutes are up, Miss Hoffman. I didn't come to quarrel. I just wanted to tell you that you have no idea of the true background and aims of our movement." He tossed away his third cigarette half smoked. *Now comes the grab for the dagger,* she thought, and the hand in which she held her own unsmoked cigarette fought to keep from trembling.

"I, too, have a question to ask you," she said, looking at this eloquent man with his pleasant voice and friendly eyes, who never smiled for a moment. "May I ask it?"

"Please do," he replied like a guest at a tea party asking for a second lump.

"Did the two Jellineks murder Mademoiselle Roux? That's all I want to know."

There was no change in his friendly eyes. Not a shadow crossed them, nor was there any change in the resonance of his pleasant voice as he answered: "Of course. And just between ourselves, you know it too now, don't you, Miss Hoffman?"

"Yes," she said. "Thank you."

He hesitated for a second. He did not seem to have expected her to say yes. "Have I really convinced you? That would indeed be a pleasure!"

"Perfectly."

"Then you will make the statement that is expected of you?"

"And for which you came?"

"You have an odd way of putting things. Do you really mean what you say?"

"And you?"

"No matter how much you may doubt it, I do."

"So do I."

"We shall soon be seeing you released, then? I shan't be here much longer, and I would really be glad to have that pleasure before I left."

"Does my release depend on this statement?"

"There, now! At last you're being reasonable like most of your practical countrymen. I have a couple of lines here. If you signed them, everything could be taken care of in short order."

The dagger, she thought. And she read a letter headed: "Secret State Police, Pilsen Headquarters." "I declare of my own free will that I cannot sustain the charges brought against Herr Rudolf Paul Schultheiss, managing director of the Skoda Works, and Herr Kuno Schultheiss, leader of the Hitler Youth, both in Pilsen, during the trial for the murder of Madeleine Roux. I withdraw them as entirely unfounded, with an expression of profound regret toward the above-mentioned gentlemen." Even her name was neatly typed: "Gwen Hoffman," with adequate space above. She had only to sign.

She looked from the paper to the man who had handed it to her, who was now also offering her his fountain pen. It was a fat, expensive, green malachite pen. The friendly eyes did not urge her. There was neither impatience nor menace in them.

"You knew I wouldn't sign this," she said.

The green pen was capped again. The neatly typed sheet was

folded up. "You found my arguments inconsequential?" he asked quietly.

"On the contrary. I needed them to show me how dangerously genuine they could sound."

"Good day, Miss Hoffman. I was very much interested in talking to you. I believe you have a fiancé, or a good friend, who works at the Skoda plant?" The caller was already at the door.

"Why?" she asked, with more haste and interest than she had meant to show.

"Oh, for no reason at all. Good day again," and the caller left the private cell.

Nevertheless, Gwen was discharged the following day. Reasons of health, certified to in writing by Dr. Paumgartner before the major from the judge advocate's department, were the excuse, and a two-line item in the German and foreign papers reported and buried the story: "Gwen Hoffman, an American citizen, held on suspicion of libel and perjury by the judge advocate's office in Pilsen, was released under surety." Only the *Národní Noviny,* published in Brünn, headed this story: "Keeping on good terms with America." (For this the *Národní Noviny* was suppressed for three days.) The surety consisted in a promise by Mr. Hoffman to Herr Schultheiss that he would restrain his daughter from "further pieces of thoughtlessness."

Even so, when Andreas asked her if she would marry him, Mr. Hoffman could not keep her from answering: "No."

Chapter 17

THE SIGN, "Dr. Paumgartner, Internal Complaints, 2–4 P.M.," was at 38 Jagellonska Ulice. And the longer the doctor whose name it bore resided in Pilsen and gave consultations from two to four, the more patients came to ask his advice. Two classes of society chiefly preferred him—Nazis and aristocrats. The latter in particular, the princely and baronial proprietors of the old castles in the neighborhood, who had enthusiastically received Viscount Runciman, the harbinger of Munich, two summers before, now made a habit of consulting the new doctor. Snobs that many of them were, they chose and changed doctors according to fashion, and for some nine months past their choice had fallen upon the excellent man from Vienna—not so much, malicious tongues declared, for his medical as for his musical skill, because in his rare free moments Dr. Paumgartner was an amateur composer and a brilliant pianist. His most popular composition, it must be admitted, had grown rather untimely—the song, "Austria Will Stand Forever," which could have been heard sung or played in any Vienna night club and by every *Heuriger* band up to Hitler's arrival. Judging by that song, the composer must have been a passionately patriotic Austrian. But the people who molded public opinion here, and not the malicious tongues alone, nevertheless believed they could be sure of his Nazi sympathies.

Be that as it might, he treated Nazis, Czechs, and aristocrats with equal skill, in addition devoting at least a third of the day to his duties as a plant physician for the Skoda Works. There was an eighth reserved for music, however; and as he had, in addition to other passions that were laid to his charge, a passion for chamber music, it was quite natural that he should have evenings of chamber music at his apartment next to the consulting and waiting room.

They took place regularly every fifth Friday evening for a few specially favored listeners. In Pilsen and at the neighboring castles it was now very much the thing to receive a prettily printed card that said: "Dr. Paumgartner has the honor to invite —— to an hour of chamber music on Friday the ——, punctually at half past eight."

This hour on certain Fridays was prepared for on other weekdays, and even on Sundays, by the members of the quartet—for quartet it was; the rehearsals often lasted far into the night, and the neighbors along the Jagellonska Ulice had to get used to them willy-nilly; sometimes the same constantly repeated passage would penetrate their very sleep, much to their annoyance.

But such splendid performances as Dr. Paumgartner presented every fifth Friday cannot be accomplished without rehearsals, as even the least musical neighbors recognized. But when they learned that personages like Princess Zorotin, the families of the Counts of Kinsky, Dubsky, and Czernin, the city commandant, Herr and Frau Schultheiss, and even (although this was not vouched for) Dr. K. H. Frank, were among the guests, they dared raise no further objection. Only a Czech lawyer who lived in the same house heartily wished the music makers in hell every evening.

Dr. Paumgartner himself called it a stroke of luck that he had managed to assemble a chamber-music quartet made up entirely of outstanding amateurs who, like him, cared for music above all things. The instruments were as follows: piano, the host; violin, Monsieur Roux, the murdered teacher's brother, who had not left after his sister's funeral, but had become her gentle and popular successor in the families where she had taught. His playing was greatly esteemed by the music critic of *Die Neue Zeit,* who was sometimes among the Friday guests, and Countess Kinsky, who played the violin a little herself, even went so far as to compare him to Kubelik. Viola: another newcomer to Pilsen, and, like the cellist, an acquaintance whom Dr. Paumgartner owed to the Skoda Works. Olaf Herdal, the violinist, was a mining engineer from Narvik in Norway, which he had been obliged to leave because he publicly called his fellow countryman Quisling "a second Seyss-Inquart," thus likening him to the man who had betrayed Austria to the Nazis. Quisling, not the Nazis, insisted on his expulsion. Because of his reputation as an iron-mining expert, however, the Nazis willingly complied, sending this useful man to Skoda at Pilsen. So far as the cellist was concerned, he was Jaroslav Uliř. Riccarda was somewhat surprised to hear about this previously hidden talent of her husband's; he apologized to her for possessing it with the humble explanation: "Well, you know, we Czechs are all fiddlers to some extent."

Six performances had taken place so far, very much to the delight of the guests. If there was any complaint at all, it was that the music chosen, at first the very soul of intelligibility and melody—largely Mozart, Haydn, and Schubert—grew more and more difficult from performance to performance. Beethoven, even Gustav Mahler, Scriabine and Stravinsky appeared on the program, and the story was current at Castle Mlin that Dr. Paumgartner had been requested to eliminate at least Mahler, the Jew. But supposedly he had refused all advice, and this very thing had probably impressed the authorities.

The more difficult the works to be performed, the more necessary and time-consuming the rehearsals. This was willingly admitted by the members of the group, three of whom were bachelors; and even the wife of the only married member, Riccarda, began to realize it as soon as she understood what was involved.

And what was involved was a chance for meetings that no one, not even Heydrich's Gestapo, could call in the least suspicious. For at these meetings of an Austrian, a Frenchman, a Norwegian, and a Czech, who formed a superbly harmonious quartet in the opinion of musical Pilsen, the matters under discussion must not leak out if one hoped to see the light of the following day, and above all of that day for whose sake the quartet was playing.

Dr. Paumgartner was a systematic man; his cynicism reveled in the idea of combating the enemy with his own poisons, or, as he put it, "following homeopathic methods," not in medicine alone but also in politics. Accordingly he worked out a most minute order of business for the quartet rehearsals, which had to be equally scrupulously observed.

They met at eight o'clock. They ate, talking at random, for half an hour. Sitting with their instruments, they began their discussions at eight-thirty, never forgetting for a moment to keep playing, accompanying and covering with music whatever they said. There were no curtains at the windows, which stood wide open; anyone who cared to look in might see four gentlemen utterly immersed in the music on their stands. That they were really immersed in bringing the downfall of the Nazis, the four musicians alone could hear; Riccarda knew, and Andreas suspected. It was he, incidentally, who had brought about the sudden growth in seriousness of the programs, and the extensive rehearsals.

For after that morning's talk with Andreas, Jaro had picked up a conversation held with Dr. Paumgartner some time before on the eating of green plums, dysentery, and typhus; that sort of thing spread with tremendous speed, particularly in the none-too-hygienic army camps. Dr. Paumgartner had decided to put Beethoven on the program, and not even a piece of chamber music at that. Instead he took the first movement of the Fifth Symphony, an arrangement by Paderewski for two pianos, violin, and viola. He lacked the second piano. But, performing a minor operation, he gave the second part to the cello. In that way his quartet was able to attempt the music, making every effort and rehearsing far into the night.

Except for the cynical pianist, the members found it a torment to go through with the comedy. But they agreed with him that it was the safest way for the moment. Herr Heydrich had returned to Berlin with a statement that was published everywhere: "I am leaving the industrial center of the Protectorate with a sense of great satisfaction. Not only the Skoda Works but all the war industries are working at capacity. The disturbances that originally rendered my presence necessary have been cut off at the roots, and their recurrence has become permanently impossible. My presence, therefore, is no longer necessary. I have, however, appointed a deputy to maintain continual contact with His Excellency the Reich Protector and myself." The deputy, unidentified in the official communiqué, was named by the underground radio station. He was a Hans Otto Krueger; even the underground station knew no more than this. Yet the four members of the quartet knew what everyone else knew also, that in spite or rather because of Heydrich's departure the Gestapo was growing daily more suspicious.

They had distributed their parts among themselves with the exactness that the pianist demanded of them and of chamber music.

Monsieur Roux, violin: five of the houses where he gave lessons were closely connected not only with the Czech government but with the Protector, Baron Neurath; he was to spread rumors there, test their effect through his pupils (the oldest of whom was twelve), to follow them up with other rumors, and to collect news in return; his pretended ignorance of German, which as an Alsatian he spoke fluently, stood him in good stead; the other three profited by his permanent contact with the French Socialists.

Olaf Herdal, viola: in September Skoda was to send him to Essen (Krupp) and Steyr (Hermann Goering Works) on business regarding iron ore, and there he would spread the Beseda movement, which had made great strides among the Czech workingmen, in the factory cells of the forced Russian, Jugoslav, Slovak, and Polish workers. He had also undertaken, by means of a cipher correspondence with his fiancée, to include the Norwegian workingmen in the timetable that the Beseda was establishing for active and passive acts of sabotage.

Jaroslav Uliř, cello: his part was to put out of commission the Skoda Works and their nine branches. The preliminary stages were the replacement of the inadequate underground transmitter with a more powerful one; increase of the secret production (carried on in

Plant 4) of short-wave receiving sets to a million, and free distribution of the instruments among the members of the Beseda; sabotage of railroads and rolling stock. The local jurisdiction assigned to him by the Beseda included the Northern Railway line—Vienna, Lundenburg, Brünn, Prague, Prerau; the Prague-Buštiehrad Line; and the former Francis Joseph Line, Vienna, Gmuend, Prague, Pilsen, Eger, Karlsbad.

The host, piano: to continue the influence that he had been systematically exercising, since the annexation of Austria, upon conservative elements in the German army, with which he maintained touch owing to his treatment and cure of the third son of the German Crown Prince, stationed in Vienna; to destroy systematically the grain harvest in the Protectorate, which supplied 34.7 per cent of the Reich's entire consumption, by means of a fertilizer (Fecundas) manufactured at Linz, Austria, and already approved by the Chemical Experiment Station at Prague; systematically to induce dysentery epidemics in the garrisons of the Protectorate by supplying antiseptically cleaned plums (the cleaning fluid, an I. G. Farben product, had also recently been tested and approved by the Chemical Experiment Station); systematically to encourage Austrian resistance by smuggling news.

"Gentlemen," said the pianist when at last the first few bars of the Fifth Symphony were played to something approaching his satisfaction and each member had made his regular evening report, "I must refer to a conversation held by one of our members with a man who is pursuing the same aims that we are. This man has misgivings about our plan, or rather its timing, and as he is an expert, I wish to emphasize once more that our plan is only a preliminary step.

"Permit me a comparison drawn from medicine. This preliminary step will remove the paralysis of the will power that has heretofore affected the people of the conquered countries like some mass hypnosis. And it will also cure the blindness—as a diagnostician I have some experience of it—which has made them regard any resistance as hopeless from the start, so that they have not even tried it." Directing the andante from his seat at the piano, he continued: "Besides, any doctor can tell you that a major operation upon a gravely weakened organism requires all-important preparations; it is these necessary conditions that we want to fulfill—no less, no more. We must inject into weak patients who have been bled white enough of the blood of confidence so that they can undergo the operation and take part in it. The operation, as you know, is the revolution. That this operation will come—in it, of course, those whom we operate on will be the operating physicians—is a certainty. Whether we shall take part in the operation I doubt, because I do not question for a moment that the preparations will cost us our lives. G, Herr Uliř, not G sharp! Or do you think differently?"

Jaro obediently fingered G. While the three others accompanied him with violin, viola, and piano, he said: "I haven't the slightest intention of dying."

"Interesting," cried Paumgartner, playing the bass accompaniment twice as loud as necessary. "Do you think life is as pleasant as all that?"

"Yes," replied Uliř, reddening and bending hastily over his cello. But neither Monsieur Roux nor the blue-eyed Olaf Herdal found life pleasant. They rubbed out that possibility with their bows. As for Dr. Paumgartner, despite the one lover of life in his quartet, he had made a perfect choice. And while the second piece to be rehearsed, Mozart's "Kleine Nachtmusik," was sounding sweetly through the open windows, reconciling even the embittered lawyer on the ground floor, he could not help thinking that these were the only sort of people to prepare for the "operation": non-Germans whose eyes were not dazzled, and who therefore would not succumb to mass hypnosis; good haters; exiles who—the lover of life included—found a Hitlerized life on strange soil worse than death.

So far, so good.

The doctor, whom nothing except stupidity could possibly have annoyed more than a mistaken diagnosis, made no doubt that he had diagnosed the case correctly. He did not insist on people's noticing that he was a fanatic, a fanatical Austrian who could not endure seeing the country robbed of everything, even the name that had given music to the world (in his opinion music consisted of Mozart, Beethoven, Schubert, Brahms, Bruckner, Hugo Wolf, and Johann Strauss). That was his private affair, and he, burdened from morning till night with other people's private affairs, did not wish to bother others with his. No one would have believed it, not even Dr. Paumgartner, who hated to be reminded of himself, if anybody had said that this cynic whom Pilsen regarded as a Nazi had meant to commit suicide the night after Hitler's march into Vienna, and had had the hypodermic needle ready on his bedside table; that he had not done it for fear of the sin—he, the freethinker, the non-churchgoer; that he had cried without restraint that night and the nights that followed over the loss of Vienna; and that he, the man who was in the habit of admonishing patients: "Don't be hysterical! Pull yourself together—it's a scandal the way you're letting yourself go!" had driven through the streets of Vienna with his eyes closed for weeks because he could not bear to look at the posters with the picture of the Führer, the red swastika flags, and the beaming faces of the mob. A hardened bachelor, he had remained unmarried because he said cynically, "There is only one person who can stand me, and I'm it."

When the three others had left, and the music racks were put away for the night, he did what he had been doing night after night now for months: he paced the rooms, reconstructing in his mind every detail of the plan, its risks, its prospects. And he told himself, as he had told himself a hundred times before, that this was the first large-scale plan, the first that could be taken seriously; consequently, it was bound to succeed. But if this plan, which the world had been awaiting for years, was the product of ridiculous amateurishness and a sortsightedness that would leave a few or a few hundred dead behind it without bringing about the slightest change or improvement, then it must be dropped; if you could not stand waiting any longer, you could just give yourself a shot of strychnine.

And the diagnostician thought he observed this in his own case: an inability or unwillingness to wait any longer—in a word, impatience. *Why the hell,* he asked himself, putting away the arrangement of the Fifth Symphony and the music for the "Kleine Nachtmusik" on the shelves, *am I so proud about meeting the enemy with his own weapons? What Uliř told me about his talk with this fellow Mumelter is right: Hitler's most powerful weapon is his sense of timing. He times things superbly. Have I timed it right? Is it right to strike the blow when Herdal gets back? Herdal isn't impatient, that's true. He's a fanatic like me. Roux isn't impatient. He's a fanatic like me too. But Uliř is impatient. He's a fanatic, but he's in love. Women in matters like this are disastrous. They distort the proportions. If Schuschnigg hadn't had a passion for a woman, I'd still be living at number 2 Opernring, looking out of my window at the Vienna Staatsoper. Am I, too, impatient?* he continued the investigation of the patient Paumgartner's case. *Maybe. I can scarcely endure any more going on from morning to night, from night to morning, winning the confidence of these people whose dirty little motives I can peer into, and wearing twelve different faces instead of the one I want to die with.*

Two of us are impatient.

He observed this as he would have observed something in examining a heart case: tachycardia, second beat of the aorta not accented.

And, having observed this, he telephoned to Jaroslav Uliř.

Riccarda's voice answered; they had a strange conversation.

"This is Dr. Paumgartner. May I speak to your husband?"

"He isn't home yet. Wasn't he at your place?"

"Yes—he'll probably be there any minute."

"Do you want him to call you, Doctor?"

"Yes. That is, do you mind talking to me for a moment more? Or is it too late at night?"

"I'll be glad to, Doctor."

"I haven't talked to you for a long time. Not really since your grandfather died. Have you got over the blow? Silly question. I mean, over the shock of the blow?"

"We miss him."

"Natural enough when you've lived with a person so long. But it's undoubtedly better for him, although one always says that. In this case it's true."

"Probably."

"And how is your brother?"

"Which one?"

"That's right, you've got two. The elder."

"He's very busy."

"I take it he's to be congratulated on his engagement?"

"How so? No."

"Are you always so shy of talking, Frau Uliř?"

"I'm afraid so. At least so people say."

"Then I won't keep you any longer. Do please excuse me for bothering you so late."

"It was no bother at all. Oh, I hear my husband. If you'll wait a second, I'll call him. Good night, Doctor."

"Good night, Frau Uliř."

A moment later Jaro's hard accent: "What's wrong, Doctor? Did I run off with your music?"

"No, not that. But I wanted to tell you that you'll have to take the rondo in 'Kleine Nachtmusik' more slowly. Much more slowly. I'm afraid the way we did it today is much too fast."

A second's pause. Then: "You don't say, Doctor! I thought it couldn't possibly go too fast."

"That's a mistake that we'll have to talk over. I've just been thinking about it. I just wanted to have you correct the mistake in practicing at home. *Dolce,* and slowly. Good night!"

It was not a good night for the diagnostician. He kept forever thinking tensely along the same lines, and he was not even in bed before he began all over again with the conversation that Uliř had told him about, which had occupied his mind all evening. This Mumelter fellow wasn't engaged, then, and wasn't going to become engaged? Was that why he was less impatient than his brother-in-law? Accustomed, as he was, to tracing everything back to personal causes, he tried it in this case. He failed. Why was Andreas Mumelter so passionately in favor of waiting? The man gave the impression of being a good hater. Besides, he was young. Should the young be less impatient than the old? Nonsense! Quite the opposite!

He had not a moment's peace. He called another number. No, Andreas wasn't in bed yet. "Would it be too late if I came over now? I wanted to before, but unfortunately I simply couldn't get time. Feeling any better?"

Andreas realized that the doctor wanted to pretend a professional visit for the benefit of uninvited telephone listeners, and so he played up to him: "Rather, Doctor. I've still got a little pain, though."

The man's thinking is dangerously quick, the diagnostician told himself. Aloud he announced that he would be over in a few minutes.

In the infinitely lonely apartment on the Karl Hermann Frankgasse two bachelors met—one of them reported to be engaged, the other generally considered a roué and seducer. Even the doctor, accustomed to silent rooms and the stillness of death, could not escape the impression created by the apartment, whose furniture, books, and pictures did not prevent it from seeming absolutely deserted, as if the old man's coffin had just been carried out. For anyone to eat, sleep, or enjoy himself here seemed out of the question.

The inmate of the apartment was somewhat changed in his looks—lean, almost peaked. "See here," the doctor observed, "you look rotten. Maybe it's a good thing I came. Shall I have a look at you?"

Andreas declined with thanks. There was nothing wrong with him. A touch of overwork, maybe, and the irregular meals now that family dinner had been given up.

Every object here was bound up with the one who was no longer present. Never had the doctor seen such absolute dominion by a dead man. His books and pen still lay on the little table where he had been accustomed to read and write the few letters that he had written in exile, and his glasses were in the last book he had been reading—the letters of Andreas Hofer. His pipe with the double portrait of Francis Joseph and Crown Prince Rudolph was within reach, but it had not been cleaned, and was exactly as it had been when he smoked it for the last time. His green Loden hat hung on the hatrack. The cuckoo clock that had ticked out ninety-two years of his life was still ticking.

"I don't want to butt in here," the doctor said. "But what you're doing isn't wise. You're preserving memories. That's bad. For the memories and for oneself."

"Maybe," said the South Tirolean. "I never was wise anyway. It's very lonesome here."

This had such a dismal sound, coming from the mouth of a big, muscular man, that the belated visitor almost forgot what he had come for. He had come to make something clear.

It must be made clear that whatever was done would be done by him alone. No one was to intermeddle. Not even this big, muscular man, who had intermeddled already. He, Karl Viktor Maria Paumgartner, was by no means going to let the thing be taken out of his hands, particularly not by a fellow so much his junior. Not because he was vain, but because he knew more about it. Incomparably more. Never mind about impatience, it was maturity that mattered. Or perhaps it was because he was vain after all, he admitted to himself as he lit his long, thin, black Virginia cigar with the straw in it, and went on to the questions that he needed for his diagnosis. He had never been able to endure having any superior, which was why he had never become a professor. Perhaps he would come down to posterity as the man who overthrew Hitler. That was better than being a professor, anyway. And gave more assurance that there would be some posterity.

His long cigar was aglow, and so was his cynicism. The cuckoo clock ticked in the lonely, inhospitable room.

"What can I do for you?" Andreas inquired very formally.

"You can tell me the truth," answered his self-invited guest. "You have a plan directed against the present regime. And you think the moment for carrying it out is inopportune. Is that right? Don't be afraid that I'm a Gestapo agent. I wouldn't be so clumsy about asking questions if I were."

"Did my brother-in-law tell you about our conversation?"

"Yes. Truth for truth. I also have a plan, of which your brother-in-law's is part. You knew that, didn't you?"

"I suspected it."

"On the basis of information from your brother-in-law?"

"No."

"Then it actually was on the basis of information from your brother-in-law?"

"Might I make a request? Please take it for granted that I'm not lying."

"I can't take things for granted unless I see some reason for them. Why should you tell me the truth? Do you trust me?"

"No."

"Then there's no reason for you to confide in me, young man."

"I'm not confiding in you. You are in me, sir."

The clock ticked on its quick, hostile, dismal way.

"The question was wrong, so the answer was wrong too," the doctor began afresh, recognizing that this nocturnal conversation would be more trying than he had expected. "Suppose we begin by deciding what we have in common—I see that you dislike fine words as much as I do. My old teacher of anatomy, Professor Tandler, used to say, 'Skeleton conversation, please.' Suppose we talk that way. Our common point is the destruction of the Third Reich. Right?"

For a moment the Tirolean hesitated, looking searchingly into the face of this man who was the subject of so many conflicting rumors. Then he felt ashamed of his caution, and said: "Right."

"Good. I shan't abuse your confidence. Various roads lead to our common goal. Right?"

"Yes and no."

"Explain yourself."

"It isn't easy, because it sounds like megalomania."

"You mean your plan is the only one that's any use. I'm no clairvoyant, but I know that's what I think about my own too. Am I correct in my supposition?"

"More or less."

"Another point in common. Each of us has a plan that he finds convincing. What's the result?"

"That each of us will do what he thinks is right."

"That would be criminal!"

"Why?"

"Didn't you implore your brother-in-law to postpone his own scheme?"

"Yes."

"And wasn't your idea to prevent your brother-in-law from going into action before you did?"

"Yes."

"You know what your brother-in-law's plan is?"

"No."

"But to know that yours is better, you ought to know what his is, shouldn't you?"

"He wasn't willing to inform me. Everything depends on the execution."

"Is it your idea that all plans, considered as action, are equally good?"

"Equally bad. For that reason it doesn't make so much difference what is done as who does it. That's what I meant when I said I preferred my plan."

"You regard yourself as capable of carrying it out?"

"Yes."

"Another point in common, young man. So do I—myself."

"Then——" said Andreas, with a gesture almost of dismissal. The doctor's tone embittered him.

"Sorry. You won't get rid of me so easily, even though you do show your—shall we say refusal?—pretty plainly. Let's not be touchy, shall we?"

"No."

"Suppose I carry out my plan in the immediate future. Since you are of opinion that each of us should do as he pleases, you wouldn't care if I did?"

"Yes, I would!"

"That's inconsistent."

"I didn't think you'd be as unreasonable as my brother-in-law, and consider the present moment suitable."

"Does my plan interest you?"

"Yes. It does interest me."

Two things were plain to the diagnostician by now: that this was a man to be trusted, and that he was a man not to be underestimated. His eye traveled toward the telephone.

"I unplugged it before you came," Andreas said.

"Good. I hope—no, I don't hope anything. You make up your mind first." And he began, despite the telephone's being disconnected, to set forth his plan—the parts and the whole—in a voice that not even an eavesdropper in the same room could have overheard.

Andreas listened. Every muscle in his face was tense. If one of the two was a diagnostician, the other was a mechanical engineer. As he listened he was testing the materials in the construction, their solidity, their suppleness. When Paumgartner was finished, he said nothing for a moment. Then, after a while: "That's quite a plan."

He was always sparing of his praise; nothing was more repugnant to him than the exaggerated way in which the Nazis puffed up every trifle. This, he saw, was not a trifle. And yet there was no greatness in it, as he could see also, though he could not have told why.

The other was a diagnostician. He saw at once that he had not made the impression he wanted to make, and this gave him pause, not simply because he was vain. "Tell me in a word—you are disappointed?" he inquired.

The South Tirolean considered carefully. "That isn't the word," he said honestly. "The plan has possibilities."

"But," said the doctor, "because I take it the *but* is coming now?"

"Yes, there is one. Only I can't put it into words at the moment. The plan isn't—perhaps I should say it isn't convincing."

"You're not a flatterer, young man."

"Never was, Doctor. I thought we weren't going to be touchy."

"Good memory you've got. Haven't you?"

"Pretty good."

The Tirolean's gaze, his calm, his strength made a deeper and deeper impression on the doctor. Dropping his tone of superiority, he asked: "Even now, after you've heard what we intend to do, you still think it would be a mistake to strike the blow soon?"

"Absolutely."

"You don't want to tell me why?"

"I'm slow, Doctor. I've got to turn it over in my mind first. Then I shall be able to tell you what I miss in your plan, and what would have to be added to make it effective in my opinion."

"You mean your own plan?"

"Perhaps. There are a lot of good things about your plan." He counted up on his fingers what was good. "The men are good," he said, as if talking to himself. "Yes. The harvest business is good. The broadcasting station is good. The communications with Austria are good, and with Norway. Working on the cells in Germany is good."

"The rest is bad?"

"Not thought through—excuse me—and rather haphazard, I should say. It's more of a plan for propaganda than for action. Yes, that's it—that's what's wrong with it. But we need both. Propaganda to carry abroad what is done here, as well as what you might call assuredly effective local action. By local action I mean my own plan."

"Do you imply by that that you would put it at my disposal?"

"Under certain conditions, yes."

"Does that mean if you have command of the whole thing?"

"Not at all! Why, that doesn't make the slightest difference now!"

The cuckoo clock called the hour: one. The diagnostician looked up and felt ashamed. With this spontaneous "That doesn't make the slightest difference now," Andreas had accomplished something that Dr. Paumgartner would never have thought possible; it was a long, long time since he had been ashamed. "I respect your attitude very deeply," he said aloud, and to himself he said: *"Isn't it revolting that such a young fellow should impress me like this!"*

"Oh, it's got nothing to do with attitudes." Andreas brushed away the "flattery." "The more I think it over, the more clearly I see one thing. You mustn't do anything now, or it will all be for nothing. Look here. I'm going to tell you what I'm planning myself. You didn't ask for my word of honor, and I shan't ask for yours. The thing is this."

Without further ado he explained the matter as he saw it; he sketched or wrote it down where necessary. The further he went, the more excited his visitor became.

"Mumelter! This is magnificent!" he cried.

Andreas looked at him, delighted. "Thank you! Your reaction is the first I have had, with one exception. And to be quite honest, I was afraid you would feel the same about me now as I did about you before."

The diagnostician passed over the implied criticism of his own plan. "Really magnificent!" he repeated softly, telling himself again: *"Never mind age. He hasn't got my age. But twice as much brains. And something else besides."*

"There's nothing special about it," said Andreas, trying to weaken this praise. "What you call *the operation* can only proceed from an army, or rather with an army. I purposely don't say from *the* army, but from an army. The one that we can form and arm, as I have just shown you. Of course the whole thing is possible only because the nucleus of this army will be delivered to my door, so to speak—the South Tiroleans, most of whom"—he pointed with his pencil to certain spots on the map he had drawn of Bohemia and Moravia—"are to be settled here and here, on the Slovakian and Moravian frontier. In other words, it's the same army we wanted to muster at home, only they hate the Nazis worse than ever now. They're Tiroleans!" he said, a trifle too emphatically for the fanatically Austrian Paumgartner. "A hundred and seventy thousand men who can be absolutely depended on." He wrote down the figure. "Then come"—the pencil point indicated another item—"the equally dependable Czech students. You left them out of account in your plan. Bohemia and Moravia have at the moment 291,480 students between the ages of eighteen and twenty-four capable of bearing arms." He wrote the second figure under the first.

"And Austria has at least that many!" Paumgartner interrupted.

"Austria has about 224,000," replied the careful engineer. "But I can't get at them—with perfect certainty, I mean. It would be possible to arm them from Steyr, and that will certainly be done someday, but, as I say, I'm only using what I regard as a hundred per cent certain and practicable. The 291,480 Czech students are certain. Then another equally certain element is the soldiers of the regular Czech army: even with the disarmament carried out by the Nazis, they still amount to 218,000 men." He wrote the third figure under the second. "Finally, the last factor, which your plan also makes too little of: the workingmen. As you have seen by my figures, the industry of the Protectorate includes a total of 561,761 workmen; of these figures 109,618 are Germans and therefore omitted. That leaves 452,143. Of these roughly another 100,000 are omitted because of age or undependability. That leaves 352,143." He wrote the fourth figure under the third, drew a line, added up the total, and wrote it down: 1,031,623. Pointing to his notes, he said: "That, as I have written it down for you approximately, comes to about a million. That makes an army of eighty-five divisions, at least sixty of them with military training. And it will be *our* army the moment it is armed. But until that is the case, Skoda must go untouched. For Skoda is the one absolutely certain source of arms for us. And we cannot move until we have an army." He had given the proof he meant to give.

"When do you think it will be ready?" asked the other.

"Not inside a year. The emigration from the South Tirol won't be finished before that."

"A *year?*"

"What does that amount to, Doctor? What's a year, or even three, if the results justify it?"

"But, Mumelter, what are you talking about? In a year Hitler may have conquered Europe, if things go on as they have been!"

"Not England."

"Suppose he bombs her into submission?"

"Look here, Dr. Paumgartner. I made my plan when my countrymen began to arrive ten at a time in the Protectorate; that was in

October; by the time I had got together the figures and gone over them, it was the middle of November; when I reached an agreement with our rifle, machine-gun, cannon, and tank departments, I mean with the workmen, it was December. We couldn't begin what we call *plus production,* which is intended for ourselves, until January, and when Dunkirk came, we weren't even a third finished. But Hitler didn't take England even after Dunkirk. Therefore we have time."

There was a pause.

The two men in the inhospitable room, dominated by the life of one who was gone, had nothing mysterious about them, nothing of the conspirator. No movie melodrama flickered here.

"And your brother-in-law? Does he know about the *plus production?"* the Austrian asked.

"Except for the workmen, nobody but you knows about it. And one other person," the Tirolean answered.

Nothing divided the two now, not age, not suspicion, not vanity. Between strokes of the cuckoo clock they had come to trust each other.

"You're sure of the workmen?"

"Absolutely. They're Czechs and Russians."

"You couldn't do without the South Tiroleans?"

"I couldn't. And I wouldn't."

"You aren't impatient yourself, Mumelter?"

"Me? Why?"

"I mean, can you stand this life?"

"We shall die."

"That's no answer!"

"It's the only one to the question. All of us that are in it will die. We have about a year to live. Do you realize that?"

"Absolutely."

"In fact, we've got to want to die. Don't you think so?"

"The whole damn business came about because for such a long time we didn't want to die. Right?"

"Right."

A new silence.

"I'm afraid you've convinced me," said the doctor.

"You're afraid?"

"I'm impatient."

"To die?"

"To see Hitler die. If you insist on heroics (although in my case it's nothing but disgust), I have no objection to dying myself."

"Nor I!"

His tone was so peculiar that the diagnostician let his eyes rest upon the other for some time. Then he asked: "Didn't someone tell me that you were engaged?"

"I'm not engaged."

"Of course you haven't got to answer me. But it seems that future associates ought to know each other. From now on I'm your associate, please remember that, and consider yourself in charge of me and my orchestra, the first violin in which I hereby offer you. I was going to say, weren't you intending to marry?"

The grandson looked at the open book with the dead man's spectacles in it. "Yes. I was intending to. Then I acted wrong. I mean if I had gone on intending to, I would have acted wrong, and would have been in the wrong as well. But then I changed my plans. The girl I was going to marry saw what all my plans were, and said no when I asked her."

"And why did you change your plans?"

"A person can't become engaged to a dead man, do you think?"

Another silence, the last before the caller departed. "You're a man, Mumelter," he said. "Good night."

"So are you. Good night."

Chapter 18

A PROCLAMATION in a red border, headed by the German eagle and the swastika, was posted up at every street corner in the early hours of the morning:

> Without special permission no one is to remain in the streets after nine o'clock at night; physicians and railway workers are excepted.
>
> All places of public entertainment are to close at 8 P.M.
>
> All public meetings are prohibited.
>
> Arms, ammunition, and radio sets are to be turned in at the nearest police headquarters without delay.

Weekly withdrawals of more than 500 Czech crowns (or their equivalent in reichsmarks) from banks, savings banks, or other financial institutions are prohibited; possessors of a balance in excess of a million Czech crowns (or their equivalent in reichsmarks) may not withdraw more than 5 per cent of their balances.

Signed: VON NEURATH, REICH PROTECTOR.

Immediately afterward, and likewise by poster, a proclamation was issued by the Czech government (which consisted of the Prime Minister, General Alois Eliáš, the Minister of the Interior, Police General Josef Ježek, and the Vice-Premier and Minister of Transport, Georg Havelka); it was the first government publication in two languages, Czech and German, and read as follows:

The people are hereby informed that:

I. Effective today, the German language is a state language, on an equal footing with the Czech language.

The German language, however, takes precedence over the Czech language, and is to be used exclusively in negotiations between the Czech government and foreign states, and to express the following terms: Führer, Reich Protector, Protectorate of Bohemia and Moravia, National Socialism, National Socialist German Workers' Party, Storm Troop, S.S., Gauleiter, District Leiter, Party comrade, fellow member of the people, people's community, people's law, populist, living space, major-area economy, German Reich, Third Reich.

The inscriptions on coins, paper currency, stamps, street, railroad, and tram signs, as well as on public buildings, are to be in both languages, the German appearing first, the Czech following as a translation.

II. The Czechoslovakian army is dissolved. In its place there will be a new Czech army, consisting of 7,000 men and 280 officers.

III. The Czech Legion is dissolved. Continued membership in it is high treason, punishable by death.

IV. The Czech police is under the jurisdiction of the German Reich Police.

V. Decisions of Czech courts require the approval of the Reich Protector.

VI. Czech citizens of the Protectorate having one parent or grandparent of German nationality shall register as Germans at their local police headquarters within two weeks.

VII. Compulsory labor is to take the place of compulsory military service. The place where this compulsory labor is to be performed may be beyond the frontiers of the Protectorate.

VIII. The Czechoslovak National Defense Act of 1936 is valid not only for the Protectorate, but also for the German Reich.

IX. The Protectorate is to have a new national flag, consisting of three horizontal stripes of equal width, the top one white, the middle one red, and the bottom one blue. Display of the former flag is forbidden on pain of death.

These two proclamations utterly destroyed the optimism that had survived since the rain of leaflets; its effect was paralyzing. Everyone who read them knew that they were the death warrant of a nation; there was no Czech state any more, not even the puppet state that had been tolerated since March 15, 1939. The thirteen articles that Hitler had issued in his decree of occupation, "filled with an earnest desire to serve the true interests of the people within this living space and safeguard the national and individual characteristics of the Czech people," were a scrap of paper. This was incomparably worse than the occupation. The Czech language, whose preservation had been struggled for passionately for more than a thousand years, was a language not good enough, as of today, to occupy first place in its own country; it was only a translation. The Czech Legion, more than a hundred thousand patriots who had fought along with the Allies in the First World War for an independent Czechoslovakia, was outlawed. There was no army now, no flag, no justice, no police. And there was no such thing as property any more; the Protector could, if he chose, declare a state of emergency on the basis of the Defense Act of 1936—that is, Czech industry and Czech private property would all pass under his control.

The two proclamations were the murder of a state.

People stopped, read, understood. Those who did not or would not understand at once inquired of others. Then they understood too. Men and women who had been present on March 15, 1939, when Hitler marched in through a fierce snowstorm and in icy silence, and who had done their share to make that silence icy, today wept openly, unashamed. Making toughened and full-grown people burst into tears on the street was, then, the first success of the two proclamations. Those who did not weep clenched their fists and spat.

When the proclamations had been up for a few hours, loud-speakers bellowed into their ears. They heard the first bars of "Kde domov můj," and the trembling voice of Hácha, the president: "Recognizing the true situation of our beloved country today as I did on that historic midnight hour of March 15, 1939, once again I have not hesitated with full confidence to entrust the fate of the Protectorate to the magnanimity of the Führer."

Those whom this was intended for had grown accustomed to much that was grotesque, absurd, inconceivable; they were used to the fact that the black headlines in the papers and the hoarse voices from the loud-speakers hardly ever told the truth. But what the president of the state had dared do today surpassed anything their minds had ever imagined.

Had it remained for Pan Hácha to discover Hitler's magnanimity? To those who heard the trembling voice it was precisely the complete lack of magnanimity that seemed a typical sign of the New Order's pettiness. Every one of its promises was broken, every hope that it awakened was throttled. Had not Hitler screamed, likewise through the loud-speaker, "We shall display the magnanimity of the victor to Herr Schuschnigg!" and locked him up the following day and tortured him for years? Just a year afterward, had he not solemnly promised the Czech people, through the loud-speaker voice of his foreign minister, Ribbentrop, "Independence, protection, and prosperity"? Today he had taken it all back, word by word, and the pose of a guardian spirit had become the truth of a robber's purpose. Hitler's magnanimity was Pan Hácha's own discovery.

They spat, and if there were still tears in their mouths, they spat them out along with their contempt.

At noon the loud-speakers announced the new food rations. Every Czech was entitled to four ounces of sugar, five ounces of butter, and one pound of meat weekly. A quarter pound of household soap had to last a month, and toilet soap could be obtained only on a doctor's prescription.

"Wrong!" someone in the Födermayerová yelled into the lying maw of the loud-speaker. "The Storm Troops and S.S. and the German police can buy all they please! Just go at six in the evening to the same shops that close their doors to us at nine in the morning! They're open then! Just for Germans! And they send ten-pound packages home every week to their families in the Reich!"

The shouter, as the same loud-speaker was to report six hours later, was Maria Jindřich, a Czech, twenty-seven years old, born in Krch, wife of Václav Jindřich, a locomotive engineer; she was court-martialed and shot within five hours of her arrest.

Thus ended the day that shattered the hopes of a whole nation, and the night was the most unbearable that the Czechs could ever remember. Many of them were on their knees praying. And there were some who wished planes would come again, no matter from where, to level with the ground this city and country that had lost its language and its rights, and along with it themselves, who had not defended themselves fiercely enough and so did not want to outlive the day.

The following morning brought rumors of suicides, which tiny items (in the new state language) in *Die Neue Zeit* and the *Volksdeutsche Zeitung* called "sudden deaths."

Národní Listy, the official organ of the National Unity party, however, called them in Czech what they were, suicides, reported that the ambulance service had been active without pause all night throughout the country in seven hundred and sixty-seven cases, and listed the names of the better-known suicides. For mentioning these names *Národní Listy* was suspended for a week.

The Czech newspaper, *Aň Zet,* reappearing after a three-day suspension (it had printed a photograph of Hitler "deliberately distorting the Führer's lock of hair"), reported the death of twelve-year-old Věra Nemčová at Velvary, twenty-four miles from Prague. The child was picking raspberries in the field in front of her home when a piece of concrete from a Czech fortification that German engineers were blowing up struck and killed her. Andreas cut out this story. It was the second unavenged death of a twelve-year-old girl to take place in his time. The first was named Agnes, was poor at mathematics, and had awakened his conscience; this one was named Věra, was killed by the fortifications of her own country, and brought his awakened conscience to a decision.

Other papers also contained alarming news. *Venkov,* former Prime Minister Rudolf Beran's paper, was suppressed three hours after publication for printing the story that the following Czechs had escaped: Mgr. Jan Šrámek, former cabinet minister and Catholic leader, with his secretary Mr. Hala, to Poland; General Leo Prchala, former commander of the Czech Legion, to France; Jaromír Nečas, former minister of social welfare, and his associate Ladislav Feierabend, to France; General Neumann, former chief of the Czech General Staff, to France.

But although the street sale was stopped immediately on its arrival, the morning edition of another Czech paper, the *České Slovo,* passed from hand to hand with the list of those arrested during the previous day and night, a long one, over a hundred, in fact, including fifty-four unidentified Czechs, for having thrown acid in the streets of Pilsen.

This last had taken place before the very eyes of those Pilseners who lived near enough to the Skoda Works; they had seen it before the nine-o'clock curfew the preceding night. They did not know it was acid, but they saw the workmen being moved on by the German police, splashing out of blowpipes something that they supposed was water. Discovering now that it had been acid, they said to themselves and one another: *"Dobře."*

But it made no change in the paralyzing apathy to which they, like most of the Czechs, had fallen victims after the shock of the previous day.

The name of the journalist Josef Čapek, included in the list, however, awakened memories of something to counteract this lethargy. It was a prayer which Karel Čapek, his late brother, had published during the desperate days after Munich, hundreds of thousands of copies of which had been distributed as a leaflet by the government. Those who still possessed copies read it again:

A prayer for tonight.

O Lord, Creator of this beautiful land, Thou seest our suffering and our despair; to Thee we need not describe what misfortune has befallen us or how our heads are bowed. Not bowed in shame; we have no cause for shame, though fate smites us with an iron hand. We have not been crushed; we have not been wanting in courage. Our nation has not lost its honor; it has only lost part of its body. We are like a man caught in the spokes of a wheel, who feels from the very first and with excruciating pain that he is alive. Our nation lives, and, in this overpowering pain, feels how potently, how vitally it still lives.

We must take a solemn vow: to work for our nation. Our fate is a universal drama that will be carried through with great and glorious effort.

O Lord, we do not pray that we may be avenged. But we do pray that Thou wilt inspire each of us with the spirit of faith and hope; that Thou wilt let none of us yield to despair. We have no need of those who despair. We need faith. We need strength. We need an effectual love that shall increase our strength tenfold.

Never can a nation be called small whose faith is great enough to build a better future.

Those simple words rang out like bells. The man who had written them in the hour of dire need was killed. But these words of a martyr brought new life to the ruins of shattered faith in self. The music of their humanity welled up in many a Czech home.

The music of Beethoven's Fifth Symphony welled up. The four music lovers were rehearsing it again, and today they were joined by a fifth member, holding his violin and bow as his neighbor did. He carefully copied his neighbor's motions, for he was no violinist; neither was Beethoven's Fifth written for a quartet, but nevertheless its proud, triumphal beginning came through the open windows of Paumgartner's apartment, where Andreas the non-violinist was sitting at a rack for the first time, sharing in a discussion made imperative by the rush of events. He had only to meet the violinist from Norway; the others he knew. With one of them, quite long ago, he had stood outside a court of law, senselessly awaiting justice; with the second he had talked at dusk; with the third at night. Time had passed since that morning and that night. If anyone had asked Andreas, How long? he would not have known whether it had been days, months, or years. He knew only this, that of all the periods in his life it had been longest in loneliness and shortest in hope.

Gwen had almost entirely withdrawn from him; he scarcely saw her, nor did he try to. It suited his plans, and cut him to the heart. Since the old man's death Riccarda had grown bitter as she had never been before, Sepp incorrigible as he had threatened to be. His brother-in-law bore him a grudge because Andreas had repudiated him before Riccarda and Paumgartner. And the old man was dead. *It is simply this,* Andreas had told himself in the longest loneliness and deepest defiance of his life: *They want to make it easy for me.* The plural *they* was not quite right. The singular would have been truer. But he had said "they," kept saying it every day and every night, and he knew what he meant: when the time was ripe, it would be easier for him. But events seemed to be cutting the time short, which was why he sat here, holding a bow that he did not know how to use.

Solemnity was not the cynical Dr. Paumgartner's way. Nevertheless, he said almost solemnly, as solemn music covered up his words: "Herr Mumelter, who is doing us the honor today for the first time, will be a member from now on. I would ask you to bestow on him the complete confidence that he deserves. The five of us here all have similar destinies. We have lost our homelands. The five of us want to regain them, if not for ourselves, then at least for the Czechs, Tiroleans, French, Norwegians, and Austrians who will come after us. To that extent Herr Mumelter is in the same situation as we are. But in one point he differs from us—*je vous en prie,* Monsieur Roux, don't let it look as if you were listening to me! He has a plan of his own making, differing from ours, which, however, combined with ours, gives some assurance of complete success. After a series of long and detailed conferences we have agreed that he should make common cause with us, and we with him. There is just one difference between us: the question of timing our action. As I know your views upon the question, gentlemen, I thought it was best to have our new member present his own viewpoint here. If you please, Herr Mumelter!"

Andreas remembered the time in the Bozen council when he had got up to talk against Gauleiter Udacher. The South Tirol had been lost since then, and so was the country where he lived now. Talking was not much good, he thought, even if you did not have to stand up, but could sit there with a fiddle bow, behaving in a way ridiculous and unworthy of a man.

"Gentlemen," he said, "I am ready, as the doctor has just said, to work with you. I know almost all of you, know what you think, and am sure that our task could hardly be in better hands." (More sober than ever, and more averse to exaggeration, he said "almost" and "hardly.") "But I also know what your plan is, and have been discussing a number of additions and changes with the doctor."

"You definitely should have told us that!" said Uliř, meaning their host. The tension between the brothers-in-law had grown more acute since the Czech had learned that Andreas was making secret agreements with "our" workmen.

"You are being told now," retorted the doctor.

"But we don't like being faced with a *fait accompli!*" the Czech objected, growing more violent. "By your leave, this isn't a chess game with kibitzers. We're all playing!"

"Not so loud!" Dr. Paumgartner warned, and could not refrain from adding: "Unfortunately you aren't all playing! What about that G minor chord, Herr Uliř? Herr Mumelter, you have the floor."

"I could have wished," declared the Tirolean, unmoved, "that we might all advance on an even footing, none sooner, none later. I have always held to the view—you remember, Jaro—that we must give ourselves plenty of time."

"I don't remember anything at all!" the Czech contradicted angrily.

"Correct," agreed his brother-in-law dryly. "You were going to discuss with the Beseda whether I should be informed of your plan. You did forget about that."

"Well, Dr. Paumgartner was generous enough to inform you of my private concerns," said the object of the rebuke reproachfully.

But Andreas cut off the dispute. "My conviction that we must wait has only been strengthened by recent events. Dr. Paumgartner thinks differently. In his opinion the depression now prevalent among the people must be broken, and a spirit of resistance must at least be reawakened by active opposition. I don't share that view. Although I'm not a Czech, I've seen enough of the Czechs to know that they are every bit as much patriots as we are. Patriotism on that level does not need to be awakened; it exists. For that reason I was decidedly against the acid outrage. What was the result? Fifty workmen have been shot, and 2,200 transported to Poland. More than 300 of them were engaged in our *plus production*—the doctor knows what I mean; we are losing them."

"And of Skoda's roughly 44,000 workmen," retorted his brother-in-law, whose absolute disagreement could be read in every muscle of his flaming face, "roughly 41,750 are more resolved than ever, since the shooting of their fifty companions and the deportation of 2,200 others, to be shot themselves in order to atone for such vileness!"

"Not so loud!" the doctor warned again, vigorously repeating the G minor motif.

"I'm not forgetting that," declared Andreas. "I hope you will all believe, though you may know me slightly or not at all, that none of us desires the downfall of Hitler"—he hesitated. He wanted to say "more passionately," but decided the word was too emotional, and said instead—"more urgently than I. I repeat, the Czech nation needs no awakening. No patriotic nation needs it."

"Yes, they do," said the pianist, interrupting the bass movement for a moment. "There are some that do need it. You're a Tirolean, Mumelter, and you fellows have always been scrappers. Not all nations are. Maybe Monsieur Roux can speak for the French. I'm speaking for the Austrians. The Austrians, I mean the Viennese, the Salzburgers, the Linzers, the Steyrers, the Kärntners, aren't a nation of scrappers. Or, rather, they aren't until you shake them awake. Don't forget that the Nazis are absolutely right about one point: old, sloppy, easygoing nations are defeated; young ones win."

"And when is a nation young?" asked the Norwegian, his bright face shining. "When it wants to die! I don't know if that's the word, Herr Mumelter—I don't speak German correctly."

At this the brother of the murdered Madeleine Roux bent tenderly over his violin; coaxing from it tones of perfect purity and sweetness, he said in his Alsatian German: *"Parfaitement.* That's so true, so true! We French are very much the way *Monsieur le Docteur* says the Austrians are. Easygoing. Slop*py*." (He accented the word on the second syllable.) "We believe, *permettez la phrase,* that to live is to live well—*c'est à dire* to live well with the body. *Mais non!* To live is to live with your forehead; or with a principle, or with your will, or whatever you want to call it—only not with the intellect, of course. Because the intellect is misleading; it led us astray. The Na*zi*" (he also accented "Nazi" on the second syllable) "revolution is a revolution against high living. That was why we French were bound to be defeated. *Mais!* We French, who need thirty kinds of cheese and twenty kinds of hors d'oeuvres and many varieties of wine, and innumerable pleasures of the eye and body, to be quite ourselves—this is, to be Molière and Clemenceau—we have but one single honor nevertheless. And with that, *je vous assure, messieurs,* with that French specialty, which is perfectly identical among forty million people, whether they are free or unfree, in the occupied or unoccupied territories—with that we shall free France. We are a people that lives by its eyes! We need an example. We need a banner carried ahead of us, and—*oui, c'est ça!*—we need the fine and heroic pose with which it is carried. That is what intoxicates us—with that we march! That was why Jeanne d'Arc could only have been born among us, and could perform her miracle only upon us. But when this war began there was no banner. And no fine pose. And nothing to intoxicate us—only the sobering recollection of 1914. *Croyez-moi!* It wasn't the dive bombers that beat us. It was our totally un-French sobriety that beat us. We need enthusiasm; *Monsieur le Docteur* is right, we have to be shaken and waked up. We have to know *why* we are singing, *'Allons, enfants de la patrie!'* over and over. Then we can march as no one ever did. Then we can win as no one ever did! We are a great nation—*excusez-moi!*"

The young French teacher with the gentle voice, his eyes consumed with passionate shame and vengefulness, had spoken while he played, following the music and bringing out of it all the melody that was there.

All of them had now voiced their opinions.

How strange, Andreas thought, *that there is still disagreement at the moment that decides our certain death.* He did not propose to go on with the ridiculous farce of pretending to play the violin; putting down the bow, he called everything to mind: Twelve-year-old Agnes lying dead on the pavement of the Dorotheenstrasse; the radio voice on the Haselburg that told him he had lost his country; the hour when they arrested him; the moment when the school bus took him away; the blow in his grandfather's face; the arrival here in smoke and soot; Grandfather's dying; Gwen's Christmas letter and Gwen's *no;* twelve-year-old Věra torn limb from limb while she was picking raspberries.

Remembering each thing that had marked an epoch in his life, he replied: "Out of the question! We mustn't stir now. At least not as long as the Czech government is against us. Don't forget that! I haven't told you about the details of my plan, because the most important thing now is that the Czech cabinet, which was for us until recently, is taking the Nazis' part. The men whom the Beseda was in contact with, and whom we could have turned to, are not there now. Johanis has hanged himself, Nečas has escaped, Prchala has escaped, Soukup, Truhlař, and Preininger are in the concentration camp at Miskovice. And the Prime Minister, General Eliáš, has been at the Palace Sanatorium in Karlsbad since yesterday. Ježek, who admires Himmler, and Havelka, who congratulates Hitler on his birthday, are in charge of affairs."

"How can you say such things!" Jaro flared up, and he, too, turned from his cello, so that the burden of playing fell upon the shoulders of the host, the violinist, and the violist: "The old Beran government wasn't worth a damn! And the present Eliáš government tacked back and forth like cowards from first to last! What do you know about Czech politics and the Beseda? Not *that!* If the Eliáš government had been for us, this damned business of Hácha would never have happened—never in the world. Gentlemen, you mustn't think for a moment that the present government has changed its attitude. They were pro-Nazi from the first moment. Think it over—what did our President Hácha do? In a word, he tore up the Czech constitution. It provides that territorial changes must be approved by a three-fifths vote of the National Assembly. The president of the Republic is not empowered by the constitution to cede any part of Czechoslovakia. The agreement with Hitler that Hácha signed on his own responsibility in Berlin on March 15, 1939, is, therefore, null and void. And what did the Beran government do? Exactly the same thing that General Eliáš did, our alleged protector—not a damned thing! They swallowed it, and never lifted a finger!"

"Herr Ulíř," Dr. Paumgartner warned, still playing, but losing patience, which had happened to him often lately, "this isn't a political meeting. Besides, we only have twelve minutes left. By that time we've got to decide on the date. That's what we're here for."

"The Day," said the Norwegian fanatically, hitting a wrong note.

"Exactly. What our enemies call *Der Tag*. That's what we've got to decide now; all further discussion is unnecessary, and will only prolong our meeting, which I'm not sure hasn't been too long already. Herr Mumelter, what date are you for?"

Andreas ran his hand through his refractory hair. "Excuse me, Doctor, but I consider it not only impossible but absolutely childish to fix on a day now. What we need is not propaganda but a scheme of action, a timetable that isn't simply on paper, but that will be carried out. Everything else aside, that will be impossible, practically speaking, until the Tirolean settlement is finished and our *plus production* is adequate. You know that, Doctor, I've explained it to you often enough. And to you, gentlemen, I can only say again that a nation like the Czechs needs no stimulation."

He did not know that the nation was justifying him at the very moment he spoke. For at that instant, summoned by goodness knows whom, tens of thousands were standing bareheaded before the monument to the national saint, Jan Hus, in Prague, Prerau, Budweis, and here in Pilsen. Here in Pilsen, on the Klatovská, next to Svate Jan Nepomuk Church, they had laid innumerable little bouquets on the lawn before the monument steps so that the roses, carnations, pansies, and forget-me-nots formed the words: *"Pravda vítězí* [Truth prevails]." And going on from there they would bestow their flowers on the monument to President Wilson, and no one could prevent them, for they had done nothing but honor a saint and the late president of a neutral power.

"Put it to a vote!" cried the Frenchman. As he said this his gentle voice grew hard, for the first and last time that evening.

His motion was carried.

"Those in favor of immediate action say yes, those who share Herr Mumelter's view, no," the host requested, and called off the names.

"Herr Herdal?"

"Yes!"

"Monsieur Roux?"

"Yes."

"Herr Uliř?"

"Anō! Yes!"

"I myself," said Paumgartner, taking his fingers from the keys for a moment with an apologetic shrug in Andreas' direction, "say yes. With the express explanation that I think it irresponsible to let the Nazis have the psychological advantage they have unquestionably gained by their latest *coup d'état.* From that to the complete incorporation of Czechoslovakia into German Reich territory is only a step, which they will take.

"But then it will be definitely too late for us. The same thing will happen here then that happened in South Tirol—I'm surprised that you've overlooked it, Mumelter! They'll resettle the Czechs in Poland,

Silesia, Pomerania, some damn place. And when that happens we're done for. I admit without argument that the people here are nationalistic and patriotic in their feelings, but aren't we Austrians that too? And still the long period of timid inactivity rendered my countrymen incapable of action. At all costs we mustn't repeat that fatal mistake here. If the new decrees hadn't been issued—and of course they are the result of Heydrich's visit, for the purpose of forestalling any attempt like ours—I would have been in favor of waiting too. But as it is, I'm for action a hundred per cent.

"The more thoroughly and quickly we act, the more completely we can overcome the phobia, or suppose we say the crisis of pessimism, that the Czechs are going through at the moment, in spite of what Herr Mumelter says. It's a perfectly natural depression that has taken hold of them, and depressions mustn't be allowed to go on, or they turn into true melancholia. That kills people—I'm speaking as a doctor. The problem we have to solve here is not so much practical as physical: the nation is sick. We mustn't wait until the remedy is perfected, but useless owing to the patient's weakness. In a case like that it's a thousand times better to take imperfect remedies at once. I just wanted to make my standpoint quite clear." Another gesture of apology toward Andreas.

"It's quite clear to me," said the latter. "Just for the record, I vote no. Are any minutes being kept?"

"Here," said the doctor, tapping his forehead. "Gentlemen, the day is our next Friday concert. All details at tomorrow's rehearsal."

Then, motioning to everyone to join in, he played the leitmotiv through again. G G G E Minor, F F F D, the notes sounded triumphantly through the open windows, and the rehearsal was over in good time, fifteen minutes before curfew.

After curfew, however, there appeared on the walls of the town, written by hands that not even the constantly patrolling military police could discover, two Czech inscriptions:

"Mluvte Česky [Speak Czech]!"

"Nedáme se [We won't surrender]!"

Chapter 19

ANDREAS AND GWEN were walking along the riverbank. Everything in life comes back, and here they were walking along one river that flowed into another under a bridge. When the bridge was called the Talfer Bridge, and the rivers the Eisack and Talfer, life had been before them. Now that the bridge was called the Bethlehem Bridge, and the rivers the Radbuza and Mies, life had grown short. Fearfully short—the more fearfully since they had had so little of it.

It was perfectly obvious to Andreas that he was not going to disappoint the other four. The other four, at least so he felt, were, like him, representatives of the nations that had lost their homelands. Therefore, they were deputies in a parliament that did not exist; and in parliaments the majority decides. He would obey the majority. Not for its sake, not for his sake, but because he could not stop it next Friday. And there were just four days until next Friday.

This was the first conversation Andreas and Gwen had had together since she had refused him. When she had seemed at the limit of her endurance, after her arrest, he had asked if she would marry him, even though "one can't become engaged to a dead man." He had felt that here there could be no consideration of tomorrow, but only of today.

And she had said "no" without a second's reflection, with a decisiveness that made the word an irrevocable condemnation. He could hear it still; it still hurt and shamed him.

Why had she said no? Because she had thought he disapproved of her behavior in the ritual-murder case, wanting to retain Herr Schultheiss' confidence. But she knew what his plan was, before anyone else did! Well, she, too, had thought that there could be no consideration of tomorrow, but only of today. The plan was for tomorrow or God knows when, and the legal murder was today. That was why she had condemned him; it was perfectly simple. This was how he had thought it out through countless night vigils.

She, too, had an infinity behind her. Since her release she had scarcely gone out of the Villa Elfriede, where the cries of men being flogged could be heard on windy days punctually from five to five-thirty and at eleven in the morning and at six at night. Her health had not improved. Dr. Paumgartner prescribed this and that, which Papa Hoffman brought from the apothecary, and which the patient took or failed to take with an indifference that drove her mother to despair. Except for her parents she saw almost no one; once she had put roses on old Mumelter's grave, another time she called on Countess Hohenwart, who had been a witness at the trial, came back from this call more distracted than ever, and after that shut herself up entirely.

Mrs. Hoffman kept urging her to make up with Andreas; again and again the subject was introduced, and each time Gwen said: "You can only make up with someone you're angry at, not with someone you're on good terms with," which Mrs. Hoffman did not understand.

Mr. Hoffman, in turn, discussed the matter directly with Andreas, and implored him "to settle things with the crazy girl." Andreas, however, said the girl was not crazy, but knew exactly what she wanted and whom she didn't want, and that would have to be that.

Dr. Paumgartner, called upon for help by both parents, and having a technical name for everything, termed this an "apperceptive crisis," by which he meant to convey the condition of a "hypersensitive person who finds himself faced overnight with facts whose implications he fully realizes, without feeling equal to confronting them." Some time after their evening's conversation the diagnostician had even explained to Andreas himself: "Well, you see, it's a typical case. Apperceptive crises go hand in hand with confidential crises. A person who finds himself unequal to confronting a thing, at least wants someone else whom he has confidence in to do it; if this doesn't take place, he feels disappointed, and holds it against the other person."

With an irony that was ordinarily not his but the doctor's way, Andreas had observed: "The disappointed person should have given the other a little more time. The time was too short. Certain things, National Socialism, for example, can't be put out of existence overnight."

The time now had grown shorter still, only four days; and that was what he wanted to explain or at least hint to her today. His first surprise was when she came at once to the telephone, and told him she had tried twice already to call him; she also acceded forthwith to his request that she see him before curfew, and suggested the path by the river.

When he actually saw her he felt a start of joy and anxiety. But for the first time it struck him that she looked sick. She offered him her hand as if they had shaken hands not long ago but only yesterday, and said: "I'm glad you're here." There was no sign of hostility or disappointment. She was wearing a dress that he had once said he liked particularly. He did not remember, but she did.

"Are you sick?" he asked. She was well.

He avoided the streets where the decrees of the Protector and the government were still posted, and from whose walls the Czech inscriptions had not been erased so completely but what a fierce word or refractory letter here and there disturbed the artificial quiet.

The person who, like him, had just four days of life ahead must make a clean sweep, giving an explanation to those who were or had been something to him. He had only two such people, for Sepp no longer counted: his sister and this girl here. The order was wrong. This girl here; and also his sister. She was walking beside him, and something suddenly clutched at his throat as he thought that this would be his last stroll with her. Had he actually believed, at his loneliest, that the girl by his side no longer belonged to him? Had he proved to himself with a hundred arguments that this was so and could not be otherwise? She walked beside him and belonged to him. Where were the arguments now? Nowhere.

It was she, not he, who spoke first.

He had been determined to put the matter of the four days into words; but those words had to be carefully chosen and weighed in order to be bearable, and so he hesitated. At this she said: "Andreas, we haven't talked for a long time. So I guess I can begin by making a request. Mayn't I?"

It was the same voice that had spoken to him in front of a glass case with the bridal finery in the Bozen Museum; and when they were driving along behind the apple cart on the Sigmundskron highway; and here in the Hotel Waldeck at Christmas. It was not often that she had spoken in this voice. Three times altogether. Today she had again.

"What is it?" he asked.

"But you won't say no?"

"I'll have to know what it is, first," he said doubtfully, looking at her. Not say no? And she had said no, condemning him without hesitation! Her eyes were bigger than ever now that her cheeks had grown so thin.

"Just a minute," she promised. "First I've got to tell you something else. I know why you asked me to take this walk. Dr. Paumgartner considers himself an infallible psychologist, and even so—or perhaps for that very reason—he let me know what I've been trying to find out from him for so long."

"You asked him about your health?"

"I know about my health. I asked him about you."

"What?"

"Don't be so slow on the uptake. About the five of you, if you prefer. Do I make myself plain?"

He admitted that she did.

"So you don't need to tell me anything. Not even that you think differently from Paumgartner. I don't know whether he's such a marvelous doctor as he thinks, because I've seen some of his patients die—my grandmother, for instance, Mademoiselle Roux, the two Jellineks; I mean I wouldn't swear by him as a doctor. But he's right about Friday. And I think it's magnificent!"

"I see," said Andreas slowly. And he could not help thinking: *So I've wasted my time worrying about how to make her swallow the thing! She thinks it magnificent. She can hardly wait. That's right. It's easy to be generous with other people's lives.*

If he had looked at her just then he would not have gone on thinking so. Her eyes rested upon him with an imploring, overflowing, protective look such as only those eyes have that see nothing, nothing but two other eyes. But he was looking away. People are that way. They mistrust each other even at the moment when they are ready to die for each other.

"Yes," she repeated. "It's a deliverance!"

"For whom?" he asked, still looking away.

"For everyone. For me," she replied. "Now that I know it, I can live again."

Because others are dying, he thought bitterly.

"And now comes my request," she went on. "No. Go on like that —I'd rather you didn't look at me." She wanted him to go on looking bitterly aside. People are like that. At the vital moment they know nothing of each other.

"I'm listening," he said.

"I want us to get married."

She said that. All six words. Audibly. The business of talking past each other and not seeing each other was at an end. He looked at her.

Coming from her mouth, what she called a "request" was the most tremendous decision she would be capable of in all her life. Was this she, Gwen Hoffman, who had vowed to herself never to show a man that she loved him—who would rather have died than offer herself? It was she; she had traveled a long road. The red on her thin cheeks grew no redder. But the gaze of her protective eyes grew more protective.

He looked at her, and saw it. He was happy as he had never been in his life and could never be again, not if he lived to be older than his grandfather. He could feel what was in the question, could feel that it contained more resolution and action than any death in four days; that this was what you could live and die for. What the Nazis had stolen, making existence empty, tiny, gray, and meaningless, was there in plenty, in an abundance that gave back more than the robbers had been able to take away.

He had so much to tell her; and so much to ask. Why, for instance, had she said no, conjuring up an endless, unspeakable loneliness and shame? But he answered: "Yes, Gwen. I want it too." No answer could have been more matter of fact. But behind the matter-of-factness lay the jubilation of a man in bliss. I am perfectly happy, she had written to him once. Now he was the one. The ring of loneliness was burst, his shame scattered to the winds.

"There isn't much time, Andreas, I know. I mean, you'll be needing every moment during these days. For that reason"—she summoned all her strength to keep from collapsing or turning pale—"I got things ready to have it at six."

They were standing on the Bethlehem Bridge, with the clay-brown Radbuza foaming into its sister stream; on the other side the clock struck half past five from the Bethlehem Chapel.

He remembered that she was the one who had wanted to walk upstream. "Why, you're a conspirator," said he in the blissfulness that he made no effort to hide.

"So are you," said she in the boundless sadness that she hid so well.

"But—all unprepared——" he said, and the words eluded him at first. "Isn't this—I mean, it isn't your way, Gwen. Didn't you expect your wedding—— I mean, oughtn't it to be more elaborate? You have them very elaborate on the other side, don't you?"

She clutched the railing of the bridge. "Don't talk nonsense," she said, finally conquering herself as she had been struggling to do. "It'll be very grand and solemn. Isn't it solemn that you're marrying me?" *And I you?* she tried to say, but the three words died on her lips.

"But I—I've only got this suit on—and no flowers for you," he said in his immeasurable happiness. People are like that. Even at the minute of supreme bliss they cannot get away from everyday things.

She almost had to laugh at that, which made it easier. "Haven't you noticed that a few things have been changing in this world recently, Andreas?" she asked, seeing once more what had first enchanted her in him, his boyishness and straightforwardness, so dependable, so lacking in guile. He did not even know why she had said no! It was because, the longer she reflected upon Dr. Paumgartner's evasions, the more firmly she had formed her own opinion of her disease: she would be a wife for a year or two, and after that a burden and a disaster. "Among other things," she said—for since then her calculation of time had changed, growing far, far shorter, and now it was only a matter of being a wife for four days—"people don't get married in bridal gowns any more, with bridesmaids, or in fact even with a bridal bouquet. The bridegroom is enough." She succeeded in maintaining her lofty tone.

"But we aren't even engaged yet!" he objected with his incorrigible matter-of-factness.

Now she really did laugh. "Let us take care of that essential at once. Herr Andreas Mumelter, allow me to ask you whether you regard yourself as my fiancé."

"Yes," he said.

What she had imagined in her Innsbruck dreams of meeting him again took place at last here and now: she kissed him in front of everyone. That is, in front of the three children and dachshund that were also on the bridge; so far as the children were concerned, they did not even notice—they saw so many soldiers with their girls kissing each other on the bridge and then going over to the park along the bank. The dachshund barked a little.

"Anyway," said Gwen when he had released her, "I didn't forget the wedding rings. And your sister will be waiting over there now. My parents too. Please don't take any notice when Mother cries. She always cries at weddings, even strangers'. And say something nice to Daddy. He's behaved marvelously, as always. Come on."

They went away from the bridge, under which objects that might once have belonged to some household swam hurriedly and senselessly past—a charred bookshelf, a smashed armchair. The river, swollen by the rains of the last few days, lashed them brownly past.

Over in the vestry of the chapel they found four people waiting for them. Mrs. Hoffman, with tears in her eyes already, said: "At least you're on time. I was beginning to be afraid you'd be late. Gwen, your dress is hiking up behind," to which the daughter replied: "No, Mother. I'm afraid it's me!" which amused the second of the party, her father. Or at least he laughed. (He had a carnation in his buttonhole, and was wearing a cutaway.)

The third was Riccarda. Strangely enough, or rather perfectly naturally for anyone who knew her as Andreas did, next to the bridal couple she was the one most excited. Anyone looking in her handbag, from which she took a present for the bride and one for her brother, would have found she had also brought along a photograph: it showed a tall man in a Loden hat, with close-clipped side whiskers and a scrupulously clean-shaven chin, not showing his age, although he was eighty-five when the photograph was taken. He, too, was with them here now; as she looked along the empty, unlit nave of the chapel, his granddaughter seemed in spite of herself to see him there in the flesh, in the third row, just as he used to stand before his hereditary seat—God give him everlasting rest and let him approve of this moment when he was losing his grandson to a stranger, and she, the sister, was losing a brother.

The fourth member of the party was the chapel deacon. He was already in his surplice, and rather in a hurry, because he had just been called to administer extreme unction, and had promised to come over immediately after the marriage. The Host was all ready in the vestry. The deacon spoke no German at all, and so it happened that the American girl who held the Catholic faith of her father, the South

Tirolean who clung to the faith of his grandfather and of generations in the hereditary seats at the Bozen parish church, were joined in matrimony by a Czech who, though a trifle hurried, was more than willing to evade the strict regulations of the Reich Protector, asking for neither papers nor formalities, but only for the "I will" of the bridal couple.

It was too bad that the bride and groom and the others who served as witnesses before the beautiful little altar with its six tall candles and its red eternal light could not understand a word of what he said. For what he said was: "I don't know you. I hear that you have both come from far away. And you have met in the wide world, and do not want to go on without each other. That is a sign that you belong together. For nothing happens in our Saviour's wide world without some meaning. I always say to my congregation: Strike out the word chance from your dictionary. There is no such thing. Whatever happens, great or small, is the will of the Lord."

It was a good thing, too, that the deacon did not know or had forgotten in his enthusiasm or his haste that no one here understood him; for that would have put him off. And so he asked the bridal couple, who were kneeling at both sides, regarding each other during his brief speech with eyes that embraced the love of the whole wide world he was speaking of: "If thou, the bridegroom, Andreas Mumelter, wilt take this woman, Gwen Hoffman, to be thy wedded wife, to be her husband all the days of thy life, then answer yes so that all may hear. *Povíde jano!*"

The bridegroom, Andreas Mumelter, answered: "Yes!"

"If thou, Gwen Hoffman, wilt take this man, Andreas Mumelter, to be thy wedded husband, to be his faithful wife all the days of thy life, then answer yes so that all may hear. *Povíde jano!*"

And Gwen answered: "Yes!" It was such a surprisingly loud yes that one might have thought she had understood what "all the days of thy life" meant, and was replying to the threat in it.

Then they exchanged rings, in which their names and the date were engraved, and Andreas thought, *Next will come the organ;* but this was a war wedding. The deacon blessed the two of them, hustled away, and said in German with a great effort as he was picking up the Host for the next priestly function, "Good luck!"

It was a few minutes after six, almost three hours until curfew.

But the newlyweds were misers of their time. Three hours were part of eternity. And so they took leave of the people who had been their witnesses, and went home from their walk.

Home was an apartment that Mr. Hoffman had taken for them at the Hotel Waldeck, the same one where Gwen had lived with her parents a year and a half before, and where Andreas had kissed her for the first and also the last time. They walked into the same room, and found it decorated with roses; it was not a strange room, for roses and memories made it friendly.

Too bad that they had not understood what the hurried deacon said of their meeting and of chance. They had met like two stars in their orbits, had been bound to, and now the combined light blazed and gave off warmth. No smoke blackened, no regrets extinguished it.

How short are three hours of bliss!

Curfew was past. But still the night was before them, and until tomorrow morning all time was theirs. Well for them that they did not understand that it belonged to them all the days of their lives. Only until tomorrow morning. Then another night. How many more? Three? Four? Perhaps there might be more—they prayed that there might to the God who, according to the deacon, left nothing to chance. And God heard them. For time was nothing to the fulfillment that he granted them. In this city of misery, this land of misery, this continent of misery, there were two souls blissfully happy. Tell them not that their happiness is dearly bought because disaster will come with the tick of the clock. Leave them to their bliss, which is infinite because they can feel that they are free again, above all dictation. What befell them now was a miracle. Roses smelled sweetly in a city of smoke; restraint, the everlasting mortal enemy, gave ground. Had there ever been such a thing as restraint? Only when there was still dictation, and its time was past. Stars shone in the nightly darkness so strictly enjoined by the Nazis. The two could see the stars from where they were.

When day had dawned, the stars did not give way. The roses still smelled sweet.

"Are you sad?" he asked.

She answered: "I didn't know that anyone could ever be so joyful."

Chapter 20

"The day" dawned. A perfectly ordinary Friday like any other, on which people wake up, take breakfast, go to work, eat lunch, go back to work, eat supper, and rest after work. Not until then would "The Day" begin.

The guests and performers gathered in Dr. Paumgartner's apartment at six-thirty, for since the new decrees the quartet had begun two hours earlier. Today, as usual, neatly printed programs lay on the chairs in the living room where the quartet played: "Seventh evening of chamber music. Performers: Olaf Herdal, violin; Gaston Roux, viola; Jaroslav Uliř, cello; Dr. Karl V. Paumgartner, piano." A list of music to be played followed: "Mozart, 'Kleine Nachtmusik'; Beethoven, First Movement of the Fifth Symphony (quartet arrangement by Ignace Jan Paderewski); Viennese Waltz Paraphrase (arranged by Dr. Paumgartner)." Andreas' name was not mentioned, but he was sitting among the guests with his wife, who here made her first public appearance.

The guests had arrived punctually: it was known that the host, otherwise charming, might grow furious if anyone came late, arriving in the middle of a long and painfully rehearsed andante; and today's program had required far more preparation than any of the others. Usually there were no more than twelve guests, but this time, including the newly married couple, there were twenty-three; and although people were accustomed to seeing the flower of Pilsen society at these musical evenings, tonight all previous efforts were surpassed. Not only the owners of the feudal castles in the neighborhood, patronized by the mistress of Castle Mlin, Princess Zdenka Zorotin (a corpulent, red-cheeked lady who wanted to look younger than she was), were on hand, but in addition practically all the personages enjoying authority or repute. No one would have been surprised if the Reich Protector in person had decided to brave the short journey from Prague; however, he was replaced by Dr. K. H. Frank, and the former bookseller (who only three years ago had been accustomed to sell the *Prager Tagblatt* with his own hands to Princess Zorotin in his shop on the Old Meadow at Karlsbad) enjoyed the whirligig of time that had made him the second man in Bohemia.

Herr Konrad Henlein, too, had not scorned the invitation; his cold schoolteacher's face strove to shield behind a tense smile the fact that he, who had fought through the Eight-Point struggle and then Munich, was now a waning star. Managing director Schultheiss and his wife, a tall, well-dressed elderly woman, the commandant of the Nazi Garrison, General von dem Busch, the local directors of the S.S. and Storm Troops, von Maltzahn and Ross, and Lieutenant Colonel and Frau Hammerschmied of the German military police had also appeared; and that Herr Hans Otto Krueger, whom Herr Heydrich had accredited before leaving as his personal deputy at Pilsen, had also come was almost a matter of course, because Herr Krueger, a widower with two grown daughters, was fond of society. As an exemplary father he had brought along his daughters. The thing that struck even the aristocrats with Nazi leanings, however, was the fact that tonight's guests (aside from the Czech vice-mayor and Frau Hruby, and Countess Hohenwart, who had given people little cause to suspect her of anti-Nazi feelings) belonged exclusively to Nazi circles. *Has our mysterious host lifted the veil once and for all?* several of the guests thought, and felt it was all the more surprising, not to say tactless, to have invited the Tirolean engineer and his American wife; she had played a peculiar part in that trial —what was it again? Countesses Haugwitz and Huyn, both of whom were infatuated with Paumgartner, were particularly annoyed about Gwen. Excepting for her ridiculous pallor she looked simply dazzling, drew all eyes, and the gown she was wearing stirred the envy of not only the countesses, but all the women present. And she seemed to be in radiant spirits, which sensationally attracted the interest of the younger Krueger daughter, and drew from Frau Hammerschmied the observation: "American women certainly haven't a scrap of self-control! I really think the least she could do is not to flaunt her honeymoon like that. After all, there are young girls present!"

The newlywed husband, too, presented a picture of unblemished happiness, and some of the ladies from the castles regretted noticing too late how attractive he was. The serenely happy, attractive-looking young husband was thinking: *If all goes as it should, the first news ought to be here at seven.* His lower lip was thrust forward—the countesses took this for a fascinating way of smiling; his palms were cold. When Gwen's eyes fell upon him, they said: *Never fear. It's all right the way it is.* More and more frequently he looked for the eyes that held him up. *How madly in love they are,* the younger Krueger girl decided, feeling a shiver of delight.

What Andreas feared was not death or the arrest ending in certain death that he foresaw not more than an hour hence, but that the effort would be irrevocably squandered, and the great opportunity clumsily wasted forever. This made him furious. He crushed the neatly printed program, surer than ever that the four at the other end of the room who were now starting to play Mozart had picked the worst possible moment. Pathologically impatient madmen! Their lack of patience was robbing the world of its decisive opportunity. He hated them as he watched them play, and yet, he reluctantly admitted, there was something impressive about seeing those men handle their instruments and attend to every note as if they were not playing the overture to inferno, but merely Mozart's dainty "Kleine Nachtmusik." The guests' peering and whispering had stopped; they were listening, and some of them, knowing Mozart, smiled. *Good!* said Gwen's protective glance, which never left him. He felt as if he had never been without her, and yet it was only four days.

A gesture from the host warned him. Dr. Paumgartner's eyes were everywhere—on the violinists and the cellist, for now came the rondo, which had to be played *dolce;* on the guests; and even on Andreas, who looked far too often at his wrist watch, provoking the diagnostician's displeasure. Not a muscle in his face betrayed the diagnosis that he had made of himself and the others. The Norwegian's blue eyes gleamed. The Frenchman wore his tenderest expression, as if with his violin he were embracing revenge. The Czech at the cello rocked his head as if worshiping Mozart.

The rondo came, *dolce,* just as it ought to have been; a moment later the piece was finished, and the listeners applauded. Secretary of State Frank said very loudly to the princess: "I have seldom heard anything more excellent. Have you, Durchlaucht?"

Her Serene Highness, who had once bought the *Prager Tagblatt* from him on the morning walk that she took for her figure, replied, deeply honored: "Splendid, Your Excellency. I do adore these evenings."

After a one-minute pause the host again looked expectantly at the three other musicians, and the opening notes of the Fifth rang out, G G G E minor, F F F D. Five minutes more, Andreas found. Gwen, previously separated from him by Herr Krueger's daughters, was now sitting beside him; thus she was able to hold his hand, and could feel the cold sweat on it. *This lack of restraint is positively criminal,* thought Frau Hammerschmied, drawing her husband's attention to the newlyweds with a nudge in the ribs. Gwen was putting everything she could give into her touch and her eyes. *Don't forget,* the eyes were saying. *Nothing can happen to us two,* said her touch. *We are beyond all that. Don't forget that.* The fact that Herr Schultheiss was sitting in front and to the left, and directly behind him Countess Hohenwart, two witnesses and finders of evidence in the trial, gave her the strength she would otherwise have lost; she was no giant, and the last few days had used her up. The diagnostician looked sharply at her. *She mustn't collapse on me,* he thought. Then he thought: *I'm glad they all came.* The introductory motif was repeated—three short notes, a long one. Like a trumpet blast.

At that moment a detonation was heard from some distance off. It was not at all an alarming noise, and only Herr Krueger pricked up his ears. The others went on listening to the music; the quartet did not stop for a second. On the contrary, they went on with a dash as the motif grew louder and more expressive. Then the noise was repeated, equally distant, quite inconsiderable.

"Excuse me!" said Herr Krueger, jumping up. "Where's the telephone?"

"Why, Father, right in the best part!" objected his younger daughter, who could scarcely take her eyes off the newlyweds. It was so exciting to see him constantly exchanging glances with her, and literally hanging on her every look!

"To the left, in the bedroom," the host indicated from the piano. The music went on. The voice of the man telephoning in the next room was heard: "This is Krueger. No. What? No. They're here. I'll see to it at once. Be over this minute!"

Monsieur Roux squeezed his cheek against his violin as if the two belonged together. The host struck the bass with gigantic force.

"Awfully sorry," said the sociable widower, returning to the music room, "but something seems to be going on over at your place, Herr

Schultheiss! Five explosions, so far. There! That's the sixth! Hell's fire! Did you hear that? Can't you keep those accursed Czechs in order—forgive me, Herr Vice-Mayor!"

The blasts followed one after another, still far remote. The music had stopped. Several guests got up.

For a moment the leading officials gathered around Herr Heydrich's favorite; then they made their excuses, gave thanks for an enjoyable evening, and left in a body. When they opened the front door the explosions were more loudly audible, in rapid-fire succession.

Frau Schultheiss, Frau Hruby, Frau Hammerschmied, the Krueger girls, and the aristocrats remained. The leaving gentlemen had told them to stay.

"Dirty rabble!" said Frau Schultheiss. Strangely enough she turned a face positively distorted with hatred upon Gwen as she spoke.

"I say, Herr Uliř, you're at the Skoda Works, too, aren't you—and you, too, Herr Mumelter?" the host interrupted her. "Suppose you find out what's going on out there. I imagine Her Serene Highness will be interested. It won't be serious, I hope."

Accordingly the cellist stood his cello against the wall. A moment later he was to be heard speaking Czech in the next room, and when he returned, he said, with a ceremonious bow to the mistress of Castle Mlin: "Your Serene Highness, I'm sorry to say there's a tremendous explosion out there. I think I'd better get over right away."

"You should. I hate the idea to interrupt our little entertainment," Paumgartner said, "but shouldn't we all go? The men at least. We could be of some help, maybe?"

"Do you think that's very sensible of you?" observed the princess, regarding him most ungraciously through her lorgnette. "The best that could happen is that you could get killed yourself. Have there been any fatalities?" she asked the Czech.

"They don't know yet for sure, Durchlaucht," was the respectful answer.

"We'll know it right away," declared Countess Huyn, who was smitten with Paumgartner, turning on the radio. There seemed to be a good deal of static, but after a while she got Berlin, and Berlin was broadcasting a speech by Reich Labor Leader Ley. "There! Nothing doing!" said the countess, turning off. "Listen! All quiet again. Go on, Doctor, please do go on playing! The Strauss waltzes are next. I've been looking forward to them for weeks!"

"So have I!" said Countess Haugwitz.

The wife of the vice-mayor of Pilsen, however, had gone on spinning the dial, turning the volume down to keep from disturbing the others, who wanted the concert to continue. What she heard seemed to astonish her. She made a violent gesture, and said to the rest of the party in her harsh Czech German: "I'm sure it will interest you, ladies and gentlemen—they've blown up the Fiat Works in Wiener Neustadt!"

"What?" asked the princess, still more ungraciously. "Are the swine starting things in Vienna now too? Where'd you get that, Frau Hruby?"

"Please listen for yourself," replied the latter. It was the news from Prague, in Czech. Those who could speak Czech—and the aristocrats could, Jaroslav Ulíř could, Paumgartner could—listened to it. The two gentlemen last mentioned, however, were more concerned with preparations for the finale of the program, since the detonations had ceased and the countesses were so eager for waltzes; they were putting out the music, tuning up, and so could hear only fragments of the news.

Two freight trains on the Salzburg-Munich line destroyed, the radio reported. Four freight trains on the Linz-Budweis line. Steinhaeusl, head of the Vienna police, murdered. All the foodstuffs destroyed in the St. Marx Cattle Market and the Naschmarkt in Vienna. The Salzburg arsenal was on fire. Mutiny had broken out at the Floridsdorf barracks near Vienna. A munitions dump was on fire at Graz, the capital of Styria. At Klagenfurt, the capital of Carinthia, the Gestapo barracks were afire.

"This is all happening in that Austria of yours!" said the elder Krueger girl reproachfully to the host, the essential points having been translated for her.

"Yes, they're perfectly terrible fellows!" said he; the words might well have been taken for censure. Then he called the Norwegian's attention to what was just coming through in Czech: "Herdal, there's something for you!"

The radio reported: "Over a hundred German transports and supply ships were blown up by Norwegian rebels today. The underground organization must have been extremely well organized to plant explosives simultaneously in more than a hundred ships at the six Norwegian ports of Oslo, Stavanger, Bergen, Trondheim, Aandalsnes, and Tromsö. Most of the vessels were sunk or badly damaged, and the terrific explosions wrecked the port facilities as well. There were eight hundred and seventy-seven German sailors and soldiers killed or wounded."

The blue-eyed man had caught the names of his native ports. "Oh!" he said, tightening the G string on his viola with a strange rough note.

"But now for our Johann Strauss, and then a little wine! I think we've truly earned it after such horrible news, don't you, Countess May?" asked the host.

She was quite of his opinion, and, she assured him, really felt like dancing to the Strauss waltzes. So did the second countess.

The wife of the vice-mayor, however, in utter nervousness, had tuned in Berlin again, which said in German: "A conspiracy of terrorists, whose identity and center of operations will be uncovered during the night at latest, chose this evening for obviously organized acts of sabotage in the Protectorate. Aside from locally restricted explosions in the Skoda Works of Pilsen, which were immediately brought under control without material damage and with the loss of but a few lives, only the cutting of German army cables in Staměřice near Kroměříž by Oscar Stratil, a laborer, who has already been arrested, insignificant material damage to the oil refinery at Králupy, and an explosion in the Sellier & Bellot powder factory at Vlašin are authentic. All other reports of terrorist acts, particularly the alleged destruction of the main pylon of the Poldi Foundries at Kladno, of the electrical works at Třeběnice, and a bomb outrage in the Skoda branch at Mladá Boleslav, are complete fabrications, misleading propaganda unworthy of credence."

"Well, that's all there is to it!" Paumgartner said, while detonations from the region of the Imperial Suburb were heard again. "I'm awfully glad. Aren't you?" he asked the Czech lady, and gave the signal to begin the waltzes.

"Yes," the wife of the vice-mayor answered tonelessly.

All the rejoicing of the Vienna that no longer existed, all the immense rejoicing of the host, who saw that Vienna resurrected before his eyes, indeed almost regained, was in the notes of the dance and the playing of the quartet. It was so compelling that in their enthusiasm the two infatuated countesses could not keep their seats. But the elder of the Krueger girls, caring nothing for music but a good deal for the significance of news, and getting much less comfort out of the surprisingly clumsy reassurances issued by Berlin than the all-too-credulous host, said to her sister: "Let's go. This is really the worst possible occasion for bacchanalia!" She actually said "bacchanalia," because she used the vocabulary of her father, who in turn employed the favorite expressions of Himmler and Heydrich; but her younger sister, who was interested in nothing but the young couple (thanks to which interest she would be able to give her father more useful information than her elder sister), was extremely eager to stay. "Oh no!" she said. "It's really too cute the way they play!"

So far as the newlyweds were concerned, their eyes said what their lips did not. *I'm alive,* thought Andreas; *none of us has been arrested. Our plans are being carried out, and they're working. Even the order to cut the army cable has been literally carried out. And if that's true about Třeběnice, Prague will be without electric lights. And if they've done a good job at Kladno, Bohemia won't have any oil. And the explosion at Vlasin will deprive the army of occupation of its powder supplies.*

Slowly the expression in the other four men's eyes spread to his. He was not an optimist; he was a realist. He was not "credulous" either. He was slow and reluctant to believe things, good or bad. But when he did believe them, he was as capable of rejoicing as anyone. He rejoiced now, profoundly. If old Mumelter had been there Andreas could have told him: "Grandfather, the slap in the face has been washed away. Get ready, we're going back—perhaps not today, and not tomorrow. But soon. Did you hear all that? Good news. Splendid. It's on the way." Then he looked at the girl who had become his wife four days before, and in her eyes, too, the loveliest he had ever seen, the gleam in his own was reflected. She nodded; she needed to do nothing more, for their thoughts were the same.

"Danube, so blue, so blue, so blue," the quartet played, and the character of the four was expressed in the fire, the tenderness, the strength, the irony that they put into this waltz, which affirms life a thousandfold, deifies joy, and calls death a fable that is not true.

"Danube, so blue, so blue, so blue . . ." For generations that waltz has succeeded in turning the gray Danube blue, and now it succeeded in tinging panic with rejoicing.

The four musicians sang, and some of the guests as well. For that reason the guests could not hear the words that the host—whom the elder Miss Krueger thought too credulous—was singing; fitting the rhythm perfectly, these words differed from the familiar text of the "Blue Danube":

"Villain, your day is drawing near
You who rejoice by humanity's bier.
The hour's at hand: it bids you die.
Fade! In unhallowed earth you'll lie!
In the unending march of time
Not Judas himself could match your crime.
Hitler begone!
It is done!
'Tis we who will bury you in slime!"

It quite suited the host's ironical turn of mind that this new verse fitted a waltz, and it suited his diagnostic eye that the old waltz was so popular, since it would help him make the new verse popular overnight. They played and sang with utter rapture. Suddenly the host noticed that they were conspicuous, so he began intoning the waltz from "Die Fledermaus." It, too, was jubilant, but it extinguished the fire of eyes that were burning too brightly.

Afterward Mělník red wine and dried zwieback (the greatest delicacy to be had now) were served; the host himself, allowing no servants in his apartment, had prepared it, and he brought it out with his own hands, permitting one of the countesses to help him, which drove the other to despair.

People enjoyed the refreshments while the sky reddened in the direction of the Skoda Works. "Look here, Herr Mumelter," said Countess Hohenwart, who was smoking a cigar, to Andreas: "I hear you're a clever person; I'd enjoy having a longer talk with you sometime. Are you satisfied with tonight's results?"

"It was a very successful concert," answered Andreas, looking at the lady, who knocked off cigar ashes with one hand while she took a glass of wine with the other.

The sky grew redder.

"I don't mean the concert," she explained, drank, and put the glass on the table. "I mean the explosions, the arson, the sabotage, et cetera. If you insist on my giving a name to it, the revolution. After all, it is a revolution, or don't you think so?"

"I don't understand."

"Oh, you understand me. But naturally you aren't going to say so. For that matter, it wouldn't be the worst thing you could do if you did say so. Even though in your wife's eyes—just see how frantically she's staring away!—I'm a monster of wickedness. Still, people aren't as simple as that. The good ones aren't so good, and the bad ones aren't so bad. I mean, sometimes I could give you a hint that would be worth hearing. For instance, that it's nonsense for you to stay here so long. After all, you work at the Skoda plant, and logically you ought to be interested in whether your laboratory is still standing. Even if it was part of the plan not to destroy it. After all, you're making that wonderful invention—what was it, an anti-aircraft gun? Don't look like that—I won't eat you. I'll leave that to your wife, who's looking charming, by the way. Perhaps you'll both give me the pleasure, or you alone. If the English had any sense they'd bomb us now. Good-by!"

The sky had grown so red that one could see somewhat despite the black-out. As the guests were leaving, the air-raid siren went. A few minutes later the Saxon and Imperial suburbs were briefly bombed. A shrapnel splinter hit young Monsieur Roux, the teacher, as he went homeward singing, taking no cover. He was killed instantly.

Chapter 21

THE SKODA WORKS, or, as they are called in Czech, Škodovy Závody, are more than a factory and less than a city. Although with their 44,500 workmen and their staff of engineers and officials, also running into the thousands, they exceeded the population of Bozen, they were laid out with such economy of space that they occupied less than a sixth of Bozen's area. This was owing to the fact that they had been constantly enlarged from small beginnings, and had had to adapt themselves to local conditions, so that they could not be spread out at will.

What struck you first as you came from the Tylová or from the Hálková Ulice was less the vast dimensions of the works than their vast monotony; a more extended uniformity could scarcely be imagined. A private railway station, which had had to surrender the Czech word of "Závody" in favor of "Pilsen, Skodabahnhof," with twenty-eight miles of track, made it possible to unload raw materials and finished goods on the spot. Directly behind the station the bays of the factory spread out, flat concrete buildings with gray corrugated-iron roofs; each group of three forming a block, or plant. All told there were thirty-nine blocks and thirteen plants. Before the war not only arms and ammunition had been produced here, but also complete equipment for all sorts of power stations. From here electric traveling cranes had been shipped to Chile, cast-steel moving parts to Egypt, oil-refinery tanks to the Argentine, and tub mills for crushing gold ores to South Africa; Skoda built the bridges across the Chirrond and Kazimroud rivers in Persia, the Chapli Electrical and Water Works in Shanghai, the Casablanca sugar refinery in Morocco, the Hong Kong brewery. If you traveled on Chinese or Lithuanian railways, you were drawn by Skoda locomotives. Now Skoda and its nine great branches were making guns of all bores, rifles, machine guns, light field, aircraft, anti-aircraft, and coast defense guns, howitzers, mortars for battleships, shells and bombs of all calibers, marine and river mines, tanks, and armored trains.

The further one went toward the center (which was prohibited to non-employees on pain of being shot forthwith by the continuous military police patrols), the more smokestacks jabbed at the air like thin, black, giant fingers from the low factory buildings; for at the center were situated the cannon foundry, the tank factory, steel works, forges, and the airplane factory, added but two years ago. Even from afar these closely crowded smokestacks, two hundred and eighty-nine in number, constantly belching forth thick yellowish-brown, reddish, or deep-black, pungent smoke, indicated the center of the whole establishment. To the left, four miles along the railway in the direction of Mies, were the gun-proving grounds (part of Plant 9, called the Robert-Ley-Hof); to the south, with a direct entrance to the station, were the dining halls, swimming pools, shower baths, and athletic fields for the workmen; they, like everything else, were allowed only the barely essential space. The dwelling houses for those who almost never left the plant grounds—officials of the management, supervisors, electricians, the gas and water staffs (the Skoda Works had their own electric current, gas and water lines, just as they had their own coal, iron, and lignite mines)—were all distressingly close together; no such thing as open space existed here. The acacias and linden trees that someone had attempted to plant were withered, and the small patches of grass before the dwelling houses were gray.

It took about four hours to walk the whole area at a moderate pace; and no newcomer but would be stupefied by the monotony, rendered hoarse by the smoke, choked by the evil smell, and deafened by the noise after those four hours. Those who were accustomed to it hardly saw, noticed, smelled, or heard any of it at all. "The hellish place," the Czechs called it.

When Andreas entered his laboratory in Block 17 (Plant 5) the following morning, he had taken a walk and seen a spectacle that would not have disappointed even the vengefulness of the gentle Monsieur Roux, who had now silently followed his sister, and that made his brother-in-law's wild eyes wilder yet. To say that the works were "washed up," which Jaro kept asserting in his excitement, as did the underground station (which had begun yesterday to call itself the Nazdar Station instead of the Czech Patriots' Station), was a gross exaggeration. Andreas, a man who loved facts, recognized it as such; and, being anxious to preserve the source of the *"plus production,"* he did not mind. Nevertheless, the damage was terrific. The electric plant was completely destroyed to its very foundations; Block 4, the welding department, was still burning, despite all attempts to put it out; the machinery in the steel works was out of commission; of the cannon foundry, Block 31, three gigantic shops next to Plant 9, was simply wiped off the face of the earth, and deep craters marked the spot where it had stood; the whole railroad line from the Skoda Station to the junction with the Prague main line had been blown up, and the devastation was the more glaring with so much standing untouched directly beside the destruction. Smoke was going up from fires everywhere; walls were constantly heard crashing. The fire department and two battalions of the sapper regiment from Prague had been helpless for a night and a day. But Skoda was working. Its smokestacks, diminished by sixteen, were belching forth thick, acrid smoke.

All things considered, the man who loved facts was forced to admit that the course of events justified not him but rather the musicians, now reduced to a trio. Not only had that which took place the evening before and would go on taking place, according to the Nazdar Station, lashed the temper of the Czech population to new heights as Paumgartner had foreseen, but the thing the diagnostician had prophesied in addition to the "emotional effect" began to be evident: the "go-slow campaign" was taking form.

Overnight the decrees of the Protector and the government were torn from the walls, and on these same walls in the early morning the astonished Pilseners saw an unfamiliar symbol. A thousand times over, painted and drawn with pitch, red paint, or red chalk, they saw the outlines of a turtle. An oval loop made the body; two pairs of short slanting lines made the legs; in front a triangle with a dot made the head; and in the oval was a *P*. But this strange symbol, which Jaroslav Uliř was so proud of because he had designed it, could be seen that morning not only in Pilsen but everywhere in Bohemia and Moravia. And not on the walls alone. The turtle outline was stuck inside the saucepan that the German housewife would buy this morning in some Czech shop; it was on the bag of potatoes that the Czech peasant had brought to early market; it was stuck to the menu that the lunch patron at a Czech inn would pick up; it was everywhere. And as the Nazdar Station reported (here, too, Jaro had done a thorough job, for as of yesterday a fifth of the population of the Protectorate was equipped to hear these broadcasts with the three-wave-length boxes), the new symbol meant: "Go slow." The tortoise was the sign of slowness, and the *P* expressly stood for the Czech word *pomalu*—slowly. "It is," the radio voice said triumphantly, "an imperious command and a proud statement. The statement: our production is systematically receding; the command: slow down every kind of production to hamper Nazi efficiency." Only Riccarda knew that it was Jaro's voice.

"What can the best Gestapo man learn from a machine that wears out surprisingly soon, thus holding up the output of a whole factory for two or three weeks?" the voice asked scornfully. "How, I ask you, can the subtlest German spy outwit a hunger strike at the moment when the fire in the furnaces should be stoked? And what can the Gestapo man possibly say to a newly installed engine sent back for repairs on its second day of work?

"Listen to me, you Czech workers in Bohemia and Moravia! There are other ways of slowing down production. For instance, I know of an order for twenty million rounds of ammunition that had to be returned to the armament plants at Jinonice, Loděnice, and Hradec Králové. Why? Because it had not been properly assorted, and would have been dangerous to the Nazi retouch workers. How long do you think the re-assorting took? Four whole weeks. Let me tell you of another fine example. Take the Letov factory, where important casts for urgent work were found in the warehouse only after a fortnight's search. An even more remarkable record is held by a once-outstanding Czech factory—I think you'll all know the one I mean—which delivered one hundred and ninety-nine faulty out of two hundred airplane-motor castings. Yes, comrades, at the moment Czech industrial production is showing a decline of at least 40 per cent. The Kolben factory, which you all know of, has decreased its output even more—by some 30 to 40 per cent a month. Think of it! This means that one factory will produce in a year only about half the amount needed to equip a German Panzer division, which requires an average of eight hundred tanks.

"Let me tell you of still more drastic methods. In the Waldes factory at Prague the Nazis built a special section equipped with expensive and complicated automatic machinery to manufacture machine-gun ammunition belts. The whole section went up in flames after the first three or four belts were produced. This is what happened: complying with the Gestapo's desire for speed, our good Czech workers ran the machines so fast that the whole factory caught fire. Not bad, not bad! Only last night similar fires destroyed vital parts of the Vlašin ammunition factory, depriving the Huns of further powder production in this country. Not bad again. And the Baťa factory at Zlín, where the charcoal for gas-mask filters is ground, burned to the foundations. Last night, too, the Sochor factory at Králův Dvůr, which specializes in underwear for the Nazi armies in the field, by sheer accident grew so warm that it unfortunately burned down, with the result that Hitler's headquarters in Russia will be left chilly.

"That, you see, is what the turtle with the *P* stands for. I'm sure you'll like it. Such a pretty little sign! And I'm sure you'll use it from now on, for it can be very useful. And one thing more before we conclude this broadcast. From now on, starting today, listen to the Nazdar Station every hour. And read our newspaper, *V Boj,* every day. Keep going, Czechs. We are gaining. The Beseda movement has only started. It must and will grow more efficient by the hour. Help the Beseda! Go slow under the sign of the turtle. And never forget that owing to the perfection of Czech industry the Nazi war machine depends more than 40 per cent on the smooth running of our plants. Slow them down. Make them stop. Nazdar!"

Andreas, listening to fragments of the Czech speech, which he could not understand, from one of the tiny boxes that had been smuggled in everywhere, had before his eyes the fragments of the destruction that had begun yesterday, punctual to the minute. He was ready to believe he had made a mistake. He had not yet heard of Monsieur Roux's death; he had spoken to Jaro a few moments before, and to Paumgartner in the morning. None of them had been arrested. His and Jaro's block had been spared according to plan. The model, which was approaching completion, stood untouched in his laboratory; none of his papers had been interfered with; none of his cases broken open. He was just about to telephone to Gwen the "all right" that they had agreed upon in case of such unexpected good fortune when he was summoned to the managing director's office.

Herr Schultheiss was in a state of excitement that he could scarcely conceal at all. As the head of the Skoda Works he feared the grave damage to his prestige that might be done by the blow so unexpectedly struck, and, as it proved, so inadequately parried; for the moment, assisted by Heydrich's favorite, Krueger, he was seeking the responsibility chiefly among a group of Polish, Russian, and Serbian newcomers who were employed in the cannon foundry; they and countless others had been questioned without interruption since midnight. Among the thirteen dead and eighty-nine injured, victims of the explosions and fires, there was not one Czech, Pole, Russian, or Serb. So far all arrests had been made. Reports kept coming in to the managing director. He had not even had time to change his clothes, but was in the dinner jacket he had worn to yesterday's concert.

"Well, Mumelter!" he said. "A fine how-do-you-do! Lucky that nothing happened to your model. Nothing wrong, I hope?"

"No, Director. Nothing at all."

"Look here—when do you think you'll be finished? You know I haven't hurried you so far, and have got you deferred from military service on the ground that it was necessary to give you time for uninterrupted work. But now we've got to consider two facts: in the first place, the English bombings, which according to our information will now become considerably more violent; in the second place, this business yesterday. I can't possibly admit, either outside or inside, that Skoda has lost even one per cent of its capacity. We've got to forestall the fantastic exaggerations that that ridiculous Nazdar Station and—of course—the Jewish democratic press will spread in a voice of triumph. I know how to do it too: as soon as the wrecking and repair operations permit, I shall invite the foreign press correspondents for a tour of inspection. We'll show them what's undamaged, and claim that the destroyed parts—boarded from sight—are the site of new construction, just as we have done in all the bombed industrial centers. The foreign journalists are so highly honored anyway if you invite them to be eyewitnesses that they'll believe and write anything you tell them. This time they're to let the world know that at a period of alleged reduction in capacity we have turned out our most important new product. I mean your invention. We'll make great play with its completion—a solemn tryout before the government, the Party, and the army. If possible—I hope it will be possible—I shall ask the Führer to attend in person. That would give a resounding answer not only to the subversive criminals, who aren't going to amount to *that* with their tortoise sabotage and their handful of explosions, but also to the English, who, of course, are behind the whole thing. Have I made myself clear? Can you be finished, say, in not more than six weeks?"

"I shall try, Director."

"Good. Meanwhile, you shall have anything that seems desirable. I want you to spare neither expense nor labor. Is there anything you want?"

"No."

"One other thing, Mumelter. If the Führer should honor us, I should think that for the above-mentioned reasons it would be more appropriate to emphasize Skoda, so to speak, rather than individuals, don't you think? I mean, in the world's eyes the honor of the day ought to belong to Skoda, whose prestige as a German arsenal has, after all, suffered from yesterday's occurrences. You agree with me, I take it?"

"I don't quite understand."

"Don't you? Then I'll make myself still plainer. It really is hard to get anywhere with you and your father-in-law! Speaking of your father-in-law, I have requested you several times to do something in that direction, and you've always evaded it. Since—well, I'd rather not say since when. I'm beginning to feel like Schuschnigg, who was always demanding things and never insisting on them! The man has been due to design the new U truck for us. Instead he goes on making the old S type. That isn't what I need him for! I brought him here for the new U's, and he begs off because he can't infringe an American patent. Hell's bells! We're at war, and we can't stop to think about sentimentalities. Please make him see that, for goodness' sake!"

"In what capacity, Director?"

"As his son-in-law, I suppose."

"In the course of time you have repeatedly requested me to exert influence on members of the Hoffman family. It seems to me it has been shown that I never have any success."

This allusion to the ritual-murder trial made the corners of Schultheiss' mouth twitch.

"People succeed when they want to. Not when they shuffle ambiguously. I say ambiguously. Do you hear?"

"I do."

"And now I no longer request you, as you choose to put it, but order you. You are going to be successful with your father-in-law. Do you understand?"

"I do."

"Well, then. And about your invention, I was going to say: there is such a thing as a spirit of fellowship. There is even such a thing as a principle, all for one, one for all. You're from the land of Andreas Hofer, so I suppose that must be second nature to you."

In the brief pause allowed by the speaker, who was growing more and more nervous, Andreas said slowly and loudly: "Yes. I come from there."

"Every answer you make presents a fresh problem. If a person has a great deal of time and more than a great deal of nervous energy, that may be quite amusing. But when a person has very little of either, it's more likely to be provoking. Was that your purpose?"

"No."

"Glad to hear it. And now, to be absolutely plain: I want your invention to appear, in accordance with our National Socialist conception of the nature of the national fellowship, not as an individual accomplishment, but as an accomplishment of the fellowship. In other words, as an accomplishment of the Skoda Works. National Socialism requires that the individual should step into the background, becoming part of the community, and surrendering to it the glory where there is glory, and the honor where there is honor. Now do you understand?"

"Yes."

"You say that as if you had some objection."

"I thought the Führer did it the other way around. Where there is glory, it is surrendered to him."

"Man! I hope you aren't comparing yourself to the Führer! We average, unexceptional people, we who have no higher mission, constitute no more than a hundred millionth of the national fellowship. Don't think I underestimate your engineering abilities, Mumelter. But don't think either that I don't know the feelings you and your family cherish toward our movement. There's a lot on the debit side of your account. By surrendering your invention to the plant you may —perhaps—just balance it. If you want some advice, don't overdraw it! It wouldn't be honored. Thank you."

Andreas was a realist. Going out, he told himself: *Two years ago they stole my country from me. Now they've stolen my invention. Sooner or later they'll steal my life.* His intoxicating sense of jubilation was gone. They were stealing his invention, the first property he had ever lost in his life. And even he, much as he knew of the new Germany, had never known before what it felt like to be robbed by the Third Reich. It was only at this moment that he began to feel what the millions before him had felt when one fine day they were deprived of what they had created and worked for. Why? For reasons of national fellowship. He did not telephone Gwen, but called in his assistants; he would urge them to hurry, and hurry desperately, so that his property could be solemnly stolen from him as soon as possible in the presence of the Führer and the Party and the government and the army. *Go to it!* he thought, *that's what one of us fellows needs if he's going to play in the quartet—to play the tune that will make them dance when we whistle!* His hatred went deeper. *Isn't it pitiful,* he thought, *that you always have to be party to something yourself before you do the right thing?* He had not finished thinking the words "the right thing" when he caught his breath and turned his eyes from the young man to whom he was dictating the table of ranges, focusing on something that he alone saw; he was forced to stop and catch his breath. Then he went on, that the height at which the shells inserted into the bell-mouthed fuse-setter would explode might be calculated at a maximum of fifteen thousand feet, instead of the usual ten thousand. And he knew he had found out "the right thing."

He had to summon all the self-control of a nature accustomed to not giving itself away in order to repress a wild gleam of triumph that flashed for a moment in his eyes, and to impose upon his voice the steady, deep tone that was his wont. He had hit upon the right thing, thanks to that footpad Schultheiss, who was about to rob him, and whom he felt like thanking fervently for it now. Yes! He had hit upon the right thing! *Quiet,* he told himself. *Keep cool. The plan I've had so far is mere child's play by comparison with this.* The blood rushed to his head; he was dizzy.

Keep calm, he said, and forced himself to do so. *You had a very promising plan that might or might not succeed; now you have a superb plan that is bound to succeed, the best that anyone has ever had since the Third Reich has existed. Because it is absolutely* the *solution, and the moment it succeeds, all these haunting specters, all the shame and agony will vanish into nothingness. Our Father which art in Heaven,* he prayed, dictating estimated projectile altitudes and telling the three assistant engineers, one from Danzig, one from Königsberg, and one from Prague, to shift the elevation by 90 degrees, *don't let me go mad—it's in my hands, mine, Andreas Mumelter's, from Bozen! I have good news for you, Herr Powondra from Prague, and bad, disastrous news for you, Herren Werner and Muehlhof of Danzig and Königsberg. If instead of asking me: "How many degrees of correction for the elevation, Herr Mumelter?" you had asked me:*

"When, Herr Mumelter?" I would have told you: "It depends on you, gentlemen. On you, Pane Powondra—preposterous, this business of the tortoise and the P! What's quickly in Czech? Kindly write the first letter of quickly *on your brain, and if there's a Czech word for* like lightning, *so much the better. You see we've got to work like lightning, gentlemen, because our future depends on the finishing of this model. I wouldn't give tuppence for your future, meine Herren Werner and Muehlhof. But I would for yours, Pane Powondra, and for mine and Gwen's!"*

And in fact, yielding to an irresistible, almost diabolical urge, he said, "It will depend more or less on this model and the time when it is put in operation, gentlemen, what the future of all of us will be like." *More! Entirely!* the diabolical voice whispered to him, and he yielded, correcting himself: "In fact, it will depend entirely on that." This was the first time the man with the Tirolean accent, who weighed what he said and was never heard to exaggerate, had ever spoken such grand words. They did not fail of their effect, and both Herr Werner and Herr Muehlhof replied: "Yes sir, very well, sir!" The Czech said nothing, presumably disapproving of such boasting. *You're the very one who ought to open his mouth,* Andreas thought, *because in your case it's true!*

His thoughts raced. His brain was so crowded that he could no longer manage to keep up the mask, but dismissed the three young men early. He must tell her—he could not wait another second.

"You're in fine fettle today!" said the Czech as he went out of the laboratory after the other two; and when the two Germans were out of earshot he admitted: "So am I!" As he spoke he turned over the lapel of his coat, as the Gestapo men do; there was a tortoise under it.

"Yes," replied Andreas. "I am in fine fettle. My work is progressing. So far as the tortoise goes, we shall see. In our case it's better to hurry." Then he telephoned to Gwen and asked her to bring him a ham sandwich sometime, because (this for the benefit of wire-tappers) he had to work at top speed, and meant to use even his lunch hour—every day from now on.

The ham sandwich was brought; Gwen came not sometime, but almost at once. For five days she had gone through the same thing with him that her mother had been going through with her father ever since they had been here: she was afraid for him every living second. From the moment he left her in the morning she never stirred from the telephone, waiting for word from him, which came horribly late. But now he bit into the sandwich she gave him like a schoolboy at recess; he seemed to enjoy it tremendously. Her fear began to fade.

She rediscovered it instantly, and could scarcely bear it, when he told her in English what he had to tell, rather breathing than whispering. Every single drop of blood froze in her veins as she listened; she smiled at him, and tried to look like a fascinated audience.

"I told you everything before," he began, looking for some sort of introduction, because what he had to say seemed too monstrous. "You were terribly enthusiastic, and it was wonderful of you, because it gave me courage. What I'm going to tell you now will excite you even more. Don't say anything, just listen. I had to tell someone, or I'd have choked. You must forget it again right away. I think I asked you to do that before, too, and it brought us luck. Tremendous luck. All right. In six weeks, or in five—I don't know, more likely in five, because I'm going to work night and day—Hitler will be dead. Don't move. I'm going to assassinate him. In connection with the finishing of my invention—for propaganda reasons—there's going to be a big celebration here, which he will attend. He and other Party members, probably Goering; and his staff, which means Himmler. They'll all die at once. You look so blank! If the elevation of my model, which is going to be tried out on the proving grounds at this celebration, is lowered by some 90 degrees, the shells will blanket the spectators. There can be no escape."

She was still listening. But he was finished. His eyes blazed.

"And where are you going to be?" That was all she asked.

"I?" he replied, explaining something that was taken for granted. "With the model. I shall be working it. I'll change the elevation. That'll assure results."

She repeated: "That'll assure results." Then, after an unsuccessful smile, she asked: "And will that—I mean—how about you?"

Funny what things women think of! This had not even occurred to him before. He had been too full of one fantastic idea: In all the time that Hitler had been making public appearances, this would be the first one where there was gunfire. With real shells. Firing was, so to speak, an indispensable and required item on the program. The shooting was what he was coming for. You could shoot as often as you pleased and as long as you needed to. It was a shooting trial, that was what it was. And it was he who would direct it. Here he would be given fully and officially, so to speak, the opportunity that had been frantically and officially cut off for seven years. Hitler was being stood before his gun. And she asked: "What about you?"

"It's marvelous for me," he answered. "And for you. And for everyone. It's the greatest happiness there is. Don't you see?"

Of course she saw. "Forgive me," she said, "I'm so stupid." It was the greatest happiness that could happen to anyone. Naturally. And with her most fascinated expression, and her heart like a lump of lead, she got up, brushed a crumb off his jacket, and went. "So long!" she said gaily.

At the gate she showed the pass that allowed her to enter the works by day (not by night), got into her car, and drove back. They were still living at the Hotel Waldeck. But they had decided, or rather Gwen had decided early that morning, to look for an apartment. *If today comes out right,* she had thought, *I shall take an apartment.* She had even known what neighborhood it would be in. Now she changed her mind. Her hand was so icy that she could scarcely hold the wheel. *In six weeks, or in five,* she thought. *More likely in five. If he works day and night. I shall have him that long. Even that isn't true. If he works day and night I shan't have him ever again. It's the greatest happiness there is.*

Though she had reached the hotel she did not get out, but drove on at random along the Pragergasse, the Šafařík Promenade, the Otokar Promenade, the Radbuza. Mist was rising from the river. They had stood there on the bridge, and then gone over to the chapel. It was the greatest happiness there was. In six weeks, or in five, or in four weeks and four days, Hitler would be dead. And Andreas would be dead. You couldn't be delighted enough. It was a gain of six weeks, or less. And this morning she had thought it would be a gain for life if the day came to a good end. The day had not come to a good end, for it had brought the summit of all happiness. How ungrateful one is. Until yesterday she had counted on only four days. Well, then! The time was longer, a period of grace. This morning, when she woke up, it was true that she had thanked God on her knees as he lay there, healthy, somehow protected. And, listening with closed eyes to his calm breathing, she had thought of the apartment that she meant to take, three rooms or four, perhaps better four, because someday they might need another. Was she insane to have thought such things? What is it about human nature that makes it so easily believe the good? Had she made plans at five this morning because Andreas had not yet been arrested and executed? Patience!

In six weeks, or less, he would be arrested and executed. He himself had set the date, and was in great haste to keep it. *Am I so tiny or so bad,* she thought, driving aimlessly along the strange, misty river, *that I'm not "excited" as he expected? Hitler will be dead in six weeks. And what will follow from that? Andreas will be dead—that's what will follow from that.* She drove on and on, deeper and deeper into an impenetrability that she could not pierce. She tried, but she could not. *The Czech captain that called me noble ought to see me now,* she thought. "I don't believe in nobility," he had said. He was right. *People aren't noble. But they're impartial. I'm not taking my own part, that much I know. I'm not taking anyone's part. Possibly his.* With almost frozen hands she turned the wheel to go back, for no road led on from where she was. *Isn't the woman who loves a man allowed to take the man's part?* she asked herself. *Is it forbidden to consider his life more important than Hitler's death?* She was driving faster now. *I ought to be proud of him!* she thought, *but I'm proud of him if he merely says "Good morning," with that boyish smile that you so seldom see him wear. Oh, I'd be proud of him, immensely, as if he were the greatest hero of all time, if he sat with me in a living room that was our living room, just reading the paper or peeling an apple. We shall never have had a living room. We shall never have lived.* As she hurried back, not knowing where, tears streamed down her face, and she shed them without feeling it.

Where am I? she asked herself. *Where do I belong?* She was so completely aimless, and her bewilderment was growing so swiftly, that she set herself an objective and drove to Riccarda's apartment. She wanted to talk to someone. She wanted to ask someone who knew him better than she did, someone of his own blood, "How can this be borne? Please tell me, and I shall try to do everything you say. You're his sister—you think as he does. And you're a woman; you feel as I do."

But when she went into the ugly little three-room apartment in the Karl Hermann Frankgasse, the question seemed absurd.

Riccarda was in the middle room, giving the little boy something in a spoon. He was fourteen months old, with white-blond hair and a tiny mouth, and was named Laurenz, after his great-grandfather. The stuff in the spoon was unsweetened boiled rice in milk, for he had been a bit sickly for a few days owing to the watered milk; but now he was well again, and enjoying the rice. One of the three-wave-length boxes was on the table, hidden behind the photograph of old Mumelter.

"Has something happened?" asked Riccarda, the invariable first question that citizens of the New Order ask each other; it is always safe to assume that something dreadful has occurred.

"No," said Gwen, and meant to say more. But she did not. She had one secret to keep, and one secret to discover. "How can you stand it?" she asked her sister-in-law.

"As you see," replied Riccarda. "I feed the child. Take a seat."

"Are you afraid, Riccarda?" Gwen asked again, for she wanted to discover the secret; and she smiled at the child, who was afraid of her.

"We're in the same boat," replied Andreas' sister. "Are you afraid?"

"Terribly."

"Has anything come to your ears—I mean aside from what we know?"

"Nothing concrete. No."

"What are you afraid of?"

"Of everything. That——"

"Something will happen to Andreas?"

"Yes."

"Gwen," said Andreas' sister, wiping the boy's tiny mouth, "I thought you were brave."

"I'm a coward."

"I thought you understood and approved of what was going on now?"

No answer.

"You are brave. And you know what's involved. I don't like you very much, but you're brave."

"Why don't you like me?"

"Must I say?"

"Go ahead. I don't like myself either."

"I don't like you because you don't know anything about us. You're fond of Andreas, but you don't know anything of us. And it's only because you're fond of Andreas that you care about any of it."

"What don't I know about you?"

"Nothing. Who we are. Why Grandfather had to die. Why Andreas will have to die. And Jaro. The youngster over there won't have any father. No, you don't know anything."

"And why don't I know anything?"

"Because I don't know anything about America. You tell this and that about Boston and New York. But I can't imagine it. When you say Boston, I don't see anything, and when you say America, I can't form any conception of it; to you over there I'm a stranger. You can't form any conception of us; to us here you're a stranger."

"But I was in Bozen, and I know what it's like."

"You don't know anything. You're a traveler. When you're here, you're on your travels. When we're here, we're in exile. You can get away from here; we can't. We're outcasts. That's what you don't know."

"Riccarda! I'm in exile too. Whatever Andreas is, I am."

"Wrong. You're on your travels. Do you think America will ever not be America? But South Tirol isn't South Tirol any more. Sometime, say when Andreas is dead, you can stop traveling, and then you'll be at home again. We can't. If we don't die of the Gestapo, then we'll die of that. Grandfather died of that."

"But I know that! Don't act as if you were telling me something new."

"I'm telling you something you haven't even any idea of. You don't know what it is to be an outcast. You don't know that people can't live in exile. They say you get used to it. You don't say it, you only expect us to do it. But people don't get used to it. That's everything you don't know. No one ever knows anything that hasn't happened to himself. I've never lived with a man I loved. Not even for five days. So I don't know what that's like. And I don't want to know!"

The wife of five days said to the other: "Don't be so hard!"

"Am I hard?" she asked. "I'm truthful. I hate lies. Do you know what you seem like to me? Like the people in Germany of whom you hear it said: 'But it must be admitted in favor of the Germans that many of them are against the Nazis.' How so? What do these many do? Do they fight the Nazis? Do they balk? No. They give some vegetables or milk to a few Jews. They murmur against the Gestapo. They whisper doubts of Hitler's infallibility, or annoyance at contributions and rationing. Those who think that such people are a credit to the Germans are perfectly satisfied, because they ask: 'What else are they to do?' I'll tell you what they ought to do: not be afraid!"

"You just said I wasn't. You're contradicting yourself."

"No. You've got courage, but you pretend to yourself that you've done enough. And you pretend to Andreas that he does too much. Not because you're a coward, but because you want to be happy. Oh yes, people can say of you, 'It must be admitted to her credit that she's against the Nazis.' How so? What has she done? She brought an accusation, and didn't sustain it. Then she married."

"Are you reproaching me for that, Riccarda?"

"Yes. You influence Andreas. It's bad enough that he can be influenced. But how can you influence a man you don't know?"

"That's crazy! I know him better than I do myself."

"Then you don't know yourself very well. I know him. If he had a choice between our country and you, he wouldn't even turn to look at you! He'd choose our country."

Gwen was silent. Then she asked: "Why are you trying to hurt me?"

The other fixed her likewise enormous dark eyes on her sister-in-law with an angry look. "You're a stranger to us," she replied, "and we are to you. You needn't think anything else. You're a stranger to Andreas too—maybe not today, but soon. Do you know what sometimes seems to me the most hostile thing there is? Being a stranger! You know us, you say? How do we feel as we walk around here? I'll tell you. Just inside our eyes is our town. We sometimes close them, or just open them a little, to pretend to ourselves that we're at home. Around that corner is not the Karl Hermann Frankgasse but the Silbergasse, and that red in the sky isn't the rain of sparks from the Skoda plant, it's the Rosengarten. That's how we walk around here, day after day, week after week, month after month, year after year. It doesn't change, it doesn't get any better; it gets worse the longer it goes on. Do you know that? No! Not long ago you said, 'The new borders of Germany'—as if it were something altogether taken for granted. Have you any idea what a monstrous thing you said, you tourist? People sat down around a table somewhere with a map, and made a line, and said: 'From here to here the country is German as of tomorrow, and the people that lived there before, the Hottentots or Fiji Islanders or South Tiroleans, will have to leave there, and Germans must go in in their place.' Do you know that these border-makers are the most dangerous madmen since the creation of the world? Because when they make a new order like that on paper, they forget that the Old Order was not made of paper, but of eyes and ears and hearts and flesh and blood. And that those eyes are suddenly supposed to see differently, those ears to hear differently, those hearts to beat differently. And that's out of the question. Because you can change the borders of countries, but not the borders of human nature."

She nodded and looked at the baby. Not at the other woman. It was the longest speech the short-spoken girl had ever made. She could feel it, and it embarrassed her.

Gwen, too, allowed a moment to pass before countering: "You underestimate my imagination."

Now Riccarda looked at her. "Didn't you come here to ask me if I was afraid?"

"What do you mean?"

"Since you're afraid, you're afraid that something might happen that would render those boundary-makers harmless. You think it's safer, and a person doesn't have to be so much afraid, and gets more good out of the man she loves, you think, if he doesn't do things that endanger his life. Yes or no?"

"Yes."

"At least you don't tell lies. Then you'd rather things stayed as they were—provided you could prolong your honeymoon, or honey-years?"

Gwen might have said, "I'm not terribly strong, Riccarda. I'm not counting in years. It was only this morning that I did." Or she might have said: "*You're* a stranger, Riccarda. You don't love your husband." She preferred to say: "Sometimes I think so. Sometimes I don't."

"And Andreas sometimes thinks as you do! Jaro tells me that he never thinks of anything whatever except you! That's a compliment—congratulations. The ideal young marriage. Only this isn't the time for it. Hitler has abolished private life. At least for outcasts that have lost their home. But you haven't done that."

The wife of five days could feel in the other woman's words all the bitterness and jealousy of one cheated of love. Was she really not thinking of herself—this mother who rocked her child unsmiling back to the sleep from which loud voices had awakened it? *Is she a heroine and I an egotist?* Gwen asked herself. She might have said: "Wait six weeks, Riccarda, or less." But all she said was: "I realize that one mustn't think of oneself now." She had learned the secret.

Her sister-in-law put the baby in his crib, where he began to cry. "Then you know what you wanted to know?"

Yes. This wife who would never have a child knew now, and had known since she had first become a witness. Only the heavenly awakening this morning had allowed her to forget it for a moment. Happiness makes you forget so easily. So does unhappiness.

"Thank you, Riccarda," she said, and went. Her second dream also, far too short, was dreamed out.

Chapter 22

Reprisal measures began with a savagery that put anything previously perpetrated in the shade. Starting from the altogether unproved assumption that the foreign Slavic workers were the ones carrying out the acts of sabotage, which had not yet been halted, and that university students directed from England had incited them, the Gestapo machine unloosed all its fury on those two groups. Whether it was Herr Krueger's own theory or a catchword from Berlin, no one knew; at any rate, he began, and Prague followed his example, a movement that the Gestapo called "Anti-intellectual defense in the Protectorate." An edict of the Reich Protector was published, saying: "There is too large a class of educated people in the country. The Czechs have no destiny except to work and produce children." The intention was obvious. With the usual Gestapo tendency to generalize and schematize everything, it was supposed that workingmen everywhere instinctively hated the educated class. So by turning against the intellectuals the favor of the workingmen would be won at a blow. This blow was struck.

Mass dismissals of teachers in colleges, secondary and elementary schools began. At the Czech university in Prague the rector posted a proclamation: "Students! On behalf of the Reich Protector I have to address the following warning to you. Minority or misinterpretation of the concept of academic freedom will afford you no protection. Czech students brought before military courts will be either acquitted or sentenced to death." Thereupon Jan Němeček, a law student, shouted four times from the balcony of the university: *"Nedáme se* [We won't surrender]!"

These shouts were the signal for battle. The students hurled down on the Gestapo men volleys of files, laboratory equipment, desks, cupboards, plaster busts. The Czech police refused to move against their own people, and so the machine guns of the Gestapo armored cars came into play.

By evening the students of Prague were overpowered, seven of them were dead, and the following morning nine were court-martialed and shot before the eyes of all the rest. The sister of one of the victims, Anna Richawy, also a student, took the cap and red-and-gold ribbon of the Moldava student fraternity, to which her brother belonged, and which he was wearing when shot, to the tomb of the Unknown Soldier. More than 1,500 students followed her in procession. The Czech police tried vainly to disperse them; three Waffen S.S. battalions in battle equipment were then marched forward. The soldiers clubbed the students back to the university with the butts of their guns. In the process thirty of both sexes were killed, and a hundred and thirty arrested; of those arrested, eighty-seven were shot that evening in the stadium of the Slavia Sports Club. During the night a shipment of over 1,200 students departed for the German concentration camps of Buchenwald and Oranienburg. Parents, relatives, and others who tried to learn the fate of those removed were handed a printed form: "You are instructed not to institute inquiries concerning the student ——, as they are futile. German military police in the Protectorate of Bohemia and Moravia."

Within a week all the Czech technical schools, clinics, high schools, *Realschulen,* laboratories, and libraries of the Protectorate were permanently closed. All books borrowed by students or instructors were to be returned immediately on pain of imprisonment up to twenty years. It was thus made impossible for Czechs in the Protectorate to pursue higher studies.

On the day when the high schools were closed, however, a bomb exploded in the Beneš High School at Pilsen, doing no damage. Herr Krueger, who assumed that a pupil was the culprit, had all four hundred and forty-nine pupils of the school arrested, and gave them ten hours to report the criminal. This the children did not do. When the time was up, it was threatened that "in case they did not decide to tell the truth" a number of them would be shot in the school yard, in their parents' presence. The threat, officially broadcast by the Prague German station, and printed in the papers, read: "As the criminal bomb outrage at the Beneš High School in Pilsen, which has been closed since the day before yesterday, has not yet been entirely cleared up, the Secret State Police, in concert with the German military police of Pilsen, finds itself compelled to make an example. Unless the culprit is apprehended by 6 P.M. tomorrow, six representatives of each class will, in accordance with the Reich Protector's decree of May 24, 1941, be shot under military law tomorrow, May 28, 1941, at 6:30 P.M." The decree of the Reich Protector here referred to applied to college students, not to children; to those legally sentenced, not to hostages.

The Beneš High School at Pilsen, until its closing, had had eight classes, the lowest four of which had been double, making twelve altogether. Before the eyes of their fathers and mothers, seventy-two children were stood up against the wall of the gymnasium in the school yard on May 28, 1941, at 6:30 P.M., and shot. The oldest, Josef Mokrý, was sixteen; the youngest, František Vlk, ten.

With this "child-murder of Pilsen," as the Nazdar Station called the atrocity, Pilsen became the city of Europe where hatred for the oppressor burned most passionately and insatiably. From that day forward hatred was the guiding theme of every act and thought.

Hatred was the leitmotiv of the chamber-music amateurs, at whose meetings a certain Milan Vojtich, an optician of Serbian origin, now took the place of gentle Monsieur Roux; for some reason or other, all four were spared. After the revolts in Austria and Norway, Serbia began to be a hotbed of constant disturbance; the blue-eyed

Olaf Herdal, returning from a second trip to Essen, had tales o
Dutch preparations; Paumgartner saw progress in his campaign fo
the decimation of Austrian, Bohemian, and Moravian food supplie
Jaroslav Uliř had won a steadily increasing popularity for the Nazda
Station, and thus provided the Czechs with their daily timetable o
sabotage and slowdown, while the frantic efforts of the Gestapo t
localize the transmitter remained fruitless. (It had not one locatio
but seven, all interconnected.) Paumgartner found Andreas harde
to understand as each day went by, despite his own diagnostic gift
and was beginning to think he had considerably overestimated th
Tirolean's value to the movement. If the young husband had not bee
so much in love, he, too, should have been much farther along, an
the arming of his men should have been a matter not of months bu
of days.

But Andreas had traveled a long way. Now it was he who wa
living in a dream. The nights were intoxication, for he shared then
with Gwen, who had never seemed gayer or happier to him; th
working days were intoxication, now that Schultheiss had summone
him again to announce: "The Führer has accepted the invitation fo
Corpus Christi Day!" This accordingly established Corpus Christi Da
as the time by which Andreas must be finished "under all circum
stances," as Schultheiss said. He was also allowed to see the lette
from Secretary of State Meissner, dated at Berlin and addressed to
Schultheiss, expressing the Führer's great satisfaction at the undi
minished capacity of the Skoda Works, and promising his appearanc
"at the initial trial of the new anti-aircraft gun, Skoda 9."

When this was assured, Andreas applied for an audience with th
Czech Prime Minister, General Eliáš; thanks to Jaro Uliř it wa
granted him. Schultheiss himself, attaching some importance to th
personal attendance of the Czech general (who was staying for rea
sons of health, it was asserted, at a Karlsbad sanatorium), gave his
approval for Andreas' half-hour plane trip to Karlsbad. He saw in this
trip what Andreas meant him to see, or at least pretended to—an
invitation to the head of the government to join in the factory celebration on June 29. He saw also the wounded vanity of an inventor who,
being unable to find a Nazi for the purpose, went looking for some
Czech in authority to show himself off as the inventor, and presumably to complain of the Nazis. Herr Schultheiss and Herr Krueger,

who had become inseparable, decided that this cheap gratification might be allowed Andreas. If he succeeded in dragging this peculiar prime minister, who was never seen any more, out into the spotlight just at the moment when the Führer in person eclipsed all else, the Skoda celebration would be so much the more complete. And so far as the subversive conversations that the two would probably conduct on this occasion went, that, said Herr Krueger, could safely be left to him.

So it was that Andreas went on his little trip by special permission of his superior and the Gestapo. Gwen did not know about it, nor would she find out, for the entire round trip would scarcely require a morning; no one else had any idea why Herr Mumelter was playing truant from a morning's work. Jaro was an exception; he found himself agreeing for the first time with Herr Schultheiss, and for the first time in a good while with his brother-in-law; he, too, approved of the audience, and sent Andreas off with careful instructions how to behave at it.

Two weeks before Corpus Christi Day Andreas arrived at the Karlsbad airport; upon being announced at the Palace Sanatorium, he was received without delay by the Czech Prime Minister. One would never have known that the general was a patient—neither by his looks nor by his speech. This was the hour of the morning when he invariably drank the waters, and he invited his caller to walk with him from the "English Quarter," where the sanatorium was situated, down to the Sprudel Colonnade. Followed at some distance by two men in civilian dress, to whom Andreas was not introduced, and who did not introduce themselves, the two went down the steps to the Market Fountain and turned right. Karlsbad, ordinarily swarming with guests taking the cure at this season, looked as it once had in late October; everyone you saw on the street was a convalescent German officer or soldier. "People don't do so much for their health nowadays," remarked the general (he, too, was in mufti) as they passed a number of closed hotels and cafés. "I hardly suppose it's any different in Bozen and Meran?" He spoke German fluently.

"Unfortunately I can't tell you from personal observation. And we hardly have any news at all," replied Andreas, not yet over his astonishment that this guest at the watering place should be so much more concerned to drink Sprudel water than to discuss in his apartment upstairs the more important things upon which Andreas had called on him.

"Oh," said the Czech, "I expect it's the same everywhere. Splendid city, Bozen. There are few more beautiful ones in the world. What's the name of that glacier, with the Alpine sunset almost redder than on the Jungfrau?"

"The Rosengarten, Your Excellency," replied Andreas, noticing by the electric clock on the Sprudel Colonnade that it was eight-fifty. His plane left at eleven-ten, and it was half an hour's drive to the airport.

"Right you are, the Rosengarten," agreed His Excellency, who had followed Andreas' glance. "And what was the name of the little lookout that you get to by the cable railway?—I have spent some delightful hours there. Yes, those were the days when one was younger! And the world was more beautiful." He was obviously not waiting for Andreas to answer, "Virgl Lookout," but went with him into the great glass-roofed hall where the boiling hot springs bubbled from the depths into two marble basins. The steam condensed on the glass, and the continuous rush of the water drowned out all else.

"Now you can talk," said the general, accepting a full cup from one of the fountain attendants, who greeted him with a "Good morning, Your Excellency!" "Not here, over there." He chose the spot where they were to stand for the next fifteen minutes, close together, and so near the fountain that the moist steam enshrouded them. "The more briefly the better. Those two are Gestapo men, of course—honorary duty," he added with a knowing smile that could make his face very attractive.

"I have come to ask Your Excellency for help," said Andreas.

"Army? Police?" asked the other, sucking the hot water through a glass straw.

"Army."

"In connection with your armament list, I take it. The list is valuable. But I'm afraid you overestimate the importance of arms, and, on the other hand, underestimate what I might briefly call active operations. We can arm them, of course—that's no problem now that Mladá Boleslav is working for us. But we can't operate actively, neither strategically nor tactically. To be exact, not yet. I've always been surprised that you consulted so little with army men. Your plan is a typical civilian's plan. We need an area to assemble it. What are you going to do with the men? Much too big for a police army. Not prepared to serve as an operating army. In your thinking you make the mistake of setting up an army without giving it any terrain. And I regard it as my chief task to create this terrain for it."

The two civilians had come to the opposite side of the fountain basin.

"I just wanted to explain to you why I'm not such a passionate admirer of your plan, and why I have left you without an answer so far," said the general in mufti. "Weapons distributed in quantity go off at random. You can't distribute them until you are ready to march."

"This is about something else," replied Andreas impatiently. "Your Excellency will use my list and our stores, or else you won't. The point is that Hitler is coming to Skoda at Pilsen on Corpus Christi Day."

"I know that," said the other.

"And that I shall kill him," finished the visitor. "I need our factory gun-proving grounds segregated. They mustn't be segregated by Nazi troops."

The resort guest's cup was empty. "Stand still," he instructed. "Right where you are. I'll get another."

He did so. He came back with the refilled cup, steaming in his hand and trembling slightly. "Details," he said. He began once more to drink through the glass straw.

"We're testing my anti-aircraft gun, as Your Excellency knows."

The two men looked at each other.

"You intend to change the elevation?"

"Yes, Your Excellency."

"How many degrees?"

"Ninety to a hundred and twenty."

"Charge?"

"Shrapnel."

"Dispersion radius?"

"A spread of a hundred and twenty feet at a distance of seven hundred and fifty."

"Who's to do the aiming?"

"I. Your Excellency knows the grounds. There is no escape."

The glass straw in the cup, still three fourths full, made a shrill sound. "If it's done correctly, scarcely," replied the general, and his face, an average citizen's face, changed abruptly. He noticed this himself, went on drinking, and said more to himself than to Andreas: "It won't be easy to convince the city command that we ought to patrol the place instead of them."

"The Nazi garrison will be out for the Corpus Christi parade."

"Go get yourself a cup. I'll wait."

Andreas, too, was now given a porcelain cup of steaming Sprudel. With this he returned to the other, who was sipping very, very slowly. "You drink," he said. "You haven't got a glass straw; look out—it's very hot!"

The two patrons of the waters leaned over the brass rail around the basin. Their two watchers did the same on the other side. "Virgl Lookout!" cried the general in mufti. "Now I remember! And the beef goulash they served up there—a regular poem, I tell you! By the way, Herr Mumelter, how do you like our Pilsner? Better than the Sprudel?"

This was a warning, and Andreas drank some of the salty water.

"I'll talk to Ježek, the Minister of the Interior," said Eliáš in a low voice.

"Is that advisable, if you'll forgive me?" Andreas objected.

"I thought you were better informed than that."

"I hear that General Ježek enjoys Himmler's confidence."

"You've probably heard that I have Goering's confidence too. You people hear too much. And you believe too much. You even think you're the ones it depends on. That's childish—excuse my speaking so plainly, but now I owe you complete frankness. Everything that happens originates with the Beseda, and the Beseda is every decent Czech, every one without exception. Please tell that to your brother-in-law, who has been going too far on the air recently. It's very laudable for individuals to pass on their ideas to the Beseda. But without the Beseda the best idea is useless. And we control the Beseda, not he. If none of you were there, the Beseda would still exist."

This was the outpouring of an injured feeling that the general in mufti had apparently been nursing for some time.

"I ask your pardon," said Andreas.

"That would be the world turned upside down," the other protested. "We ought to thank you. It's just that the, shall we say, head of a government feels queer when he sees himself with a subordinate government that takes itself for the main government—although it's the main government that shuffles the cards in such a way as to deal the trumps into the subordinate government's hand. But never mind that. Are you finished with your glass? Let's go, then. We mustn't underestimate the curiosity of those two gentlemen yonder."

Leaving the pump room, they took the path across the Old Meadow. On the right was the Carrier Pigeon book and stationery store, which had once belonged to the now Secretary of State, K. H. Frank. As they passed Goethe's house, the Czech premier remarked: "I keep expecting them to call it the 'Hitler House.' Please keep your answers as monosyllabic as my questions. And don't be surprised at the way I jump around. Hereabouts not only the walls but the very trees have ears. Day before yesterday one of my people discovered a microphone in this linden here."

They went in silence through the front garden of the Hotel Pupp. Few of the tables were occupied; at one of them somebody got up, greeted the Prime Minister with a deep bow, and sat down again.

"He means he's against Hitler," the person thus worshipfully saluted excused the worship.

A few paces farther on, leaving the Kaiser Bath behind them, and starting down the magnificent avenue of elms that led to the Freundschaftssaal and Kaiserpark cafés, the Czech (first making sure that the two civilians had not reduced their customary distance of twenty paces) asked: "You give him another two weeks?"

"Yes."

"And yourself?"

"The same. If it goes wrong."

A marble tablet on the cliff to their right bore an inscription written here by a visitor named Goethe, valuing wisdom above life.

"It can't go wrong," the general corrected.

"Of course," Andreas agreed, trying to excuse himself in turn for having thought of Gwen.

"Are you single?"

"Married."

"Children?"

"None."

"Is there anything you want—aside from the patrols? The patrols you shall have."

"No. That is——"

"What do you want?"

"If it goes wrong—I mean——"

"Then what?"

"Would Your Excellency look after my wife?"

"Of course, naturally. Though only for a limited time—up to the twenty-ninth of September. Still, that's two months more. And the more one reads him, the more incomparable he is. There is no question which he did not think about and find the answer to. Whenever I'm baffled, I turn to *Faust*."

The footsteps of the two civilians had suddenly been audible; now they were no longer heard.

"You see on September 29, the second anniversary of Munich, the Beseda is going to strike. If you succeed in a fortnight, that may not be necessary. But if things don't go on Corpus Christi Day as you hope and as the whole world must hope, then on the twenty-ninth of September they will go that way. I promise you that. That will be the beginning of the armed, marching, fighting Czech revolution. For by then, Herr Mumelter, I shall have the terrain I need. You have considered your compatriots from South Tirol in your plan, but only as a numerical unit. I'm thinking of the territory where they will be settled by then, the strip between Moravia and Slovakia, the main rail route from Poland to Austria. You know better than anyone else that your compatriots are to be depended on. And I know that we can depend on this territory that the Nazis are now clearing for the South Tiroleans. For our purpose of invading Austria and Poland it is positively made to order. I was going to say, whatever I may be able to do for your wife will have to be done by then. I'm allowing myself two months."

Andreas gave him a sidelong look.

"Don't apologize, Herr Mumelter. And don't even give me your word. You'll keep what I've confided to you to yourself even without a word of honor. Won't you?"

"Yes, Your Excellency."

"What were you going to say?"

"I was going to say that I'm very grateful."

"For what?"
"For your confidence."
"I have it in you. And you in me?"
"I admire Your Excellency."
"The world will admire you."
"If I succeed."
"The world never admires anything but success. How long did you say he still had to live?"
"Two weeks."
"I'd like to ask you that a hundred times and hear you answer a hundred times." They went on in silence. Then the general in mufti stopped where the road branched off to the Hotel Imperial. "There. That's your bus to the airport. I shall pray for your success and help you however I can. May God protect you."
"And Your Excellency."
"Your courage is fine. Give me your hand."
"I love my fatherland as you do yours. My hand on it."
They shook hands. They looked like two guests at the watering place, who had chanced to strike up an acquaintance on the promenade, had strolled a little way together, and were parting now, never to meet again.
The last part was the truth.

Chapter 23

IN THE CATHOLIC EMPIRE OF AUSTRIA processions were held on Corpus Christi Day in every city and village. An open altar decorated with birch foliage, pictures of the saints, and burning candles was set up in the streets, and the procession marched to it. It was an immemorial custom, and in every one of the sixty-eight years of his reign Emperor Francis Joseph marched bareheaded with all his ministers behind the cardinal's canopy, to show the devotion of the State to the Church. The Nazis showed their scorn for the Church, but in the former territory of the Austrian Empire they continued the Corpus Christi celebration, and even the habit of having a company of soldiers fire a salute before each altar. This was perhaps the only custom they took over unchanged, and people who showed surprise at its being a Church custom were told: "Why, Party Comrade, how shortsighted of you! Don't they accuse us of being hostile to the Church? Well, then! Once a year we show our respect for the Church, thus conciliating not only the clergy but our incorrigibly bigoted army!"

On this twenty-ninth of June 1941, a Sunday, the Corpus Christi procession was to be solemnly held as always, and as early as eight in the morning the loud-speakers, after reporting the latest victories in Russia, announced in German and Czech: "The populace of Pilsen is instructed to refrain from any demonstration during the procession, particularly from shouts unbefitting the dignity of the ecclesiastical ceremony. The scattering or throwing of flowers is also strictly forbidden." Whether this was meant for or against the Nazis was anyone's guess. Most people saw in it a proof of Hitler's personal appearance, which had been whispered about a good deal among insiders in the last few days; it was said that he would join the procession and afterward make a great political speech at the Skoda Works about the reason for his Russian campaign, to which the Czechs had reacted with especial bitterness; many saw this as the political purpose of his visit. These rumors were also nourished by the fact that the so-called royal suite at the Hotel Waldeck was being got ready, and that for days important party members had been arriving from Berlin and Munich. Official Pilsen, indeed, maintained silence, but had made not the slightest objection when *Die Neue Zeit* of yesterday evening, Saturday, had characterized June 29 as a sort of "Nürnberg Party Congress," and had hinted at a "sensational event at the Skoda Works."

The procession had been moving since nine o'clock. Since eight Andreas had been busy setting up the perfected model of Skoda 9, and putting it in position on the gun-proving grounds of Plant 9. His three engineers and a number of picked workmen whom Jaroslav Uliř had suggested one by one, and whom Herr Schultheiss had approved one by one after a conference with Herr Krueger, lent a hand in the process. The terrain had been segregated entirely from three sides by three companies of the "Praha" Czech infantry regiment from Prague (the new army of 7,000 men possessed a total of four regiments), and the side where the entrance was had been shut off except for a passageway a yard or two wide, well guarded by troops. For those who were to enjoy that privilege of attending there were two stands. One was small, with room for about twenty-five persons, with a raised center draped in red, and a speakers' desk before it, also draped in red, with a monstrous swastika; to the left of this was a larger stand, for at least two hundred spectators. The smaller, protected from the sun by a sloping canvas awning, bore Hitler's standard; the larger, uncovered one flew a huge swastika on a red ground, flanked by the standard of the Reich Protector and the new Czech state flag.

It was the sight of these stands, as yet unoccupied, which excited Andreas so much that he kept interrupting his almost completed work to stare at them. There in the clear, bright sun, under a sky that was blue (for the Skoda Works), lay the spot he would aim at to hit the most evil thing that the world of humankind had ever produced. The thought of the man who was to stand there had no terrors for Andreas—nothing but fascination. His hand would not tremble. His heart would not beat faster. He promised himself this as the sun climbed higher, making the white boards of the stands glare more harshly.

One could see so plainly that a mended tear in the Reich Protector's standard was visible. *I can't allow myself to be excited,* Andreas told himself in his excitement. *It's ridiculous to think that, but the fate of the world depends on my being as cold as that steel barrel there, which I'm putting my hand on, and which the sun cannot warm. I must be as rigid and unerring as that. I've got to be a machine. I shall be a machine.*

The idea that he would die had no terrors for him now, indeed not even any probability. If he handled the machine like a machine, and he would, then the hits would go where they would not endanger him. With all attention fixed on the chief spectator, his swift maneuver would go unnoticed. It was an example in mathematics, carefully calculated beforehand; every decimal figure counted.

As the morning wore on, and the gun he had designed and helped build came closer and closer to the exact position he had prescribed for it, he found himself growing more accustomed to the idea of being a machine. The concentrated resolution that comes before great decisions took possession of him. His will became so strong, his passion for carrying it out, allowing not even the tiniest fraction of error, so overpowering, that he felt himself growing colder from moment to moment.

Not even the thought of Gwen, which had shattered his night, terrified him now. What he had prayed for in the morning was vouchsafed him: Utter cold-bloodedness. Even more than that: the Tirolean fierceness that had sometimes flared up like flashes of lightning both in him and in his grandfather. And it was his grandfather whom he thought of now, if he thought of people at all; everything else was wiped away. He even talked to him as he checked the final operations. "Good morning," he said to him. "Isn't this a fine morning for Pilsen? And talking about fine, what an afternoon it's going to be! We're starting at nine-thirty sharp, just after the procession, and at ten-thirty sharp, just five minutes after he's finished talking, we shall be finished, and your last will is going to be carried out."

"Christ Almighty!" he shouted at Vlk, the Czech foreman, who was turning the front wheels too far to the right. "What are you doing there, Vlk?"

And the man, who, like all the Czech workmen at Skoda, had worshiped this German-speaking engineer for some time now, touched his cap and said in horrified tones: "I do beg your pardon, sir! I'll have it in a second!" The millimeter's divergence was corrected to Andreas' satisfaction, and he made sure everything was right to a hair.

Meanwhile the loud-speakers set up on the gun-proving grounds were describing the procession. It was approaching St. Bartholomew's Cathedral on the Adolf Hitler Platz. First came little girls dressed in white, with forget-me-not wreaths in their hair, scattering grass and flowers on the pavement from little baskets. ("In order to give this innocent pleasure to the children," the announcer had the face to say, "adults were forbidden to scatter flowers.") The mayor and vice-mayor of Pilsen followed. Behind them marched the town band, which could be heard playing the hymn to Mary, *"Mater Divina"*; then, according to the announcer, a "goose-stepping" guard of honor from the King Frederick of Prussia Grenadier regiment, personally commanded by Lieutenant General von Herrdegen; then the members of the Czech government, Havelka and General Ježek; deputations from the Czech National Unity party, the Orel and Vlajka parties. "Now," said the announcer's voice, taking on a more solemn note, "the purple canopy is coming in sight under which His Eminence, the Archbishop of Prague, Cardinal Kaspar, is proceeding with the holy of holies. He is garbed in the ritually gold-embroidered white satin vestments of his office, and covered with the historic miter of Prague, which St. Wenceslaus wore; he never takes his eyes off the monstrance that he holds high in both hands. The canons of St. Bartholomew and of Sts. Cyril and Methodius walk by his side; the chaplains of Jan Nepomuk, St. Bethlehem, St. Wenceslaus, and St. Matthew are carrying the canopy; choir boys swing silver censers. The nuns of Svatá Anna are singing, 'O Lord, look upon our world!'

"And now"—the announcer made a pause during which Andreas' heart stood still—"a few paces' interval. Alone, erect, tanned by the wind and weather of the battlefields, his uncovered face downcast in thought, wearing the uniform of a simple front soldier, the Iron Cross on his breast, comes our Führer, Adolf Hitler. The multitude, numbering thousands, is moved beyond expression. Many of them are falling to their knees and crossing themselves. But with his utter modesty the leader of the German nation, of Europe, and ere long of the whole civilized world, deprecates this only-too-justified homage by keeping his eyes downcast, apparently indicating to the devout that their devotion today should be for the religious ceremony. At some distance follow, in that order, Reich Marshal Hermann Goering, Reich Leader Heinrich Himmler, Reich Protector Baron Konstantin von Neurath, and deputy Reich Protector Dr. K. H. Frank. Two companies of the Führer's S.S. bodyguard standard follow." The names of a number of German and Czech dignitaries were less solemnly mentioned. When the announcer reached the end of the procession—the German regiments of the Pilsen garrison and the formation of Hitler Youth, District of Pilsen ("fresh oak leaves on helmets and caps")—a volley was fired, signifying that the cardinal had said Mass before the altar outside the cathedral and pronounced the blessing.

Punctually to the moment, fifteen minutes before the guests of honor, who were to have the small stand, those invited to occupy the large stand arrived on the gun-proving grounds of the Skoda Works. The printed program, handed to each person as he came in, read: "1. Party Comrade Rudolf Paul Schultheiss, Address of Welcome. 2. The Führer will speak. 3. Demonstration of the new anti-aircraft gun, Skoda 9, and Tour of inspection through the plant." A note at the foot of the program said: "The audience is requested to occupy the seats assigned by the plant authorities, and not to leave them without instructions."

"Všechno hotovy?" asked Jaro, who, as head of the experimental division, not only had access to everything but was in duty bound to be just here at the moment. "All set?"

Andreas said he was. From where he stood he could see the stands filling up. First the larger one: in a matter of seconds it was full to the last seat; the uniforms, black frock coats, cutaways, top hats, and black bowlers underlined the solemnity of the occasion. No women were present. Schultheiss himself, silk hat in hand, hands kid-gloved, came across the open field to Andreas, and said with his nervous twitch: "Good luck, now!"

Andreas had his eyes everywhere. He noticed that the managing director spoke in a very low voice for a moment with the two engineers from Danzig and Königsberg. *Can they have been given to me as spies the whole time I've been working here?* he thought. Then there was no time left to think.

Things happened with mad speed.

Schultheiss was back among the guests. He now stepped up to the speakers' desk on the still-vacant small stand, and began to speak. *The others won't come until after his address,* Andreas told himself. Nothing escaped him—neither the workmen and engineers immediately around, whose eyes were fixed on him, nor the stand, where all eyes were on the speaker. Andreas even heard what the speaker was saying. But he did not follow the words. He was staring at the entrance.

Everything took place at immense speed. Herr Schultheiss was through with his speech, and uniforms appeared at the entrance, the violet robes of the cardinal and the black soutanes of some priests. They turned toward the small stand. The entire audience in the big stand rose, lifting right arms in the Hitler salute. There was a pause, lasting no more than a quarter minute, but to Andreas it seemed like a lifetime. A man in uniform stepped up to the desk, and everyone sat down.

It was not Hitler.

He said, and the loud-speaker made his words crash out brazenly: "Your Eminence! Your Excellencies! Mr. Mayor of Pilsen! Fellow Germans! I am to bring you the greetings of the Führer. Affairs of state of an imperative nature recalled him and his companions unexpectedly—or rather expectedly—to the front but a few moments ago. The first weeks of operations against Russia have brought results of a magnitude unequaled in world history. Two large Russian armies are now inextricably surrounded in the region east of Bialystok. Only today the Russians near Minsk lost 520,000 prisoners, 370 tanks, more than 2,000 guns, and innumerable quantities of other war matériel. Thus their defeat is assuming the dimensions of a collapse. The genius of our Führer has practically eliminated the Russian colossus as an adversary within a week's time, making the abject and unconditional capitulation of this world enemy a mere matter of days. To assure this tremendous goal and make the necessary decisions in person, he has been obliged to return to the front. To his great regret, therefore, he could neither be present at the initial operation of the important new invention of the Skoda Works nor accept the toast of welcome so kindly planned for him by you, Mr. Mayor, at the venerable Municipal Brewery. He has, however, commissioned me to . . ."

The brazen words resounded.

It was not Hitler.

Simultaneously with the beginning of this speech, S.S. Elite Guards had marched in through the yard-wide passageway. They paid no attention to the Czech troops standing guard, but shut off the whole place themselves in double ranks. One rank faced the Czech troops, the other the stands and the gun emplacement.

The orator spoke. The engineer from Danzig said to Andreas: "That's a shame! But this man is a first-rate speaker too. Don't you know him? It's Konstantin Hoess, the Prague Gauleiter."

"Yes. It's a shame," Andreas answered. Was that his voice speaking? He could hear that someone had said it. He could see that someone was standing over there at the red-draped speakers' stand, someone who was a first-rate speaker too. What was his name? Hoess. It was not Hitler.

Andreas' body was as rigid as if it had been carved of wood. He had difficulty in moving. He could not feel his own arms and legs; he *could* feel a disappointment so overpowering that it paralyzed him. The man at the desk was still talking. If Andreas had not been so completely paralyzed, he would have noticed the nervousness of the brazen words, and seen that the first-rate speaker was repeatedly turning in every direction to watch how far the S.S. guards had got with their human barricade. It became evident that he was supposed to speak exactly as long as this operation required, for his address now consisted of nothing but random party phrases having nothing to do with the occasion.

When he finished with *"Heil* Hitler!" both stands applauded. It was disappointed applause.

Once more Herr Schultheiss stepped forward. "We now show you our new anti-aircraft gun, Skoda 9, in action," he announced. If the previous speaker's voice had been brazen, his, despite the loudspeakers, was now toneless. Hurrying from the stand to the gun emplacement, he said to Andreas, the corners of his mouth twitching: "Isn't that the damnedest luck! Just at the very last moment!" As he spoke he looked at him with eyes that freed the Tirolean from his rigidity. *What do those eyes mean?* he thought, and his blood began to circulate again. He saw black and then red; a terrific disappointment became terrific bitterness.

"I'm ready," he said, facing those ambiguous eyes, and he could hear himself speak.

"Go ahead!" the managing director ordered.

Again everything went swiftly. Herr Muehlhof stepped to the microphone. "We are assuming," he explained, in words carefully rehearsed beforehand, "that enemy planes are approaching from the north, heading for the Skoda Works. There are five bombers, which have succeeded in evading the interceptors and thus threatening the works. They are flying at a level of 15,000 feet. Please remain perfectly calm. The planes employed by us are experimental machines, which of course will drop no missiles of any kind, and their crews will escape by parachute at the proper moment. The safety of the spectators and those carrying out the tests is fully assured. Sir, I report that we are ready to fire."

"Thank you," replied Andreas. Now it was his voice that the loudspeakers magnified.

The distant hum of invisible planes was heard. Beside the new antiaircraft gun there was a command: "Stand by!" In an actual emergency the gun would have been protected by walls of sandbags; in case of emergency, also, it would be guarded by machine guns against strafing. But this was not an emergency.

Andreas stood by the barrel, a telephone headset connecting him with the engineers and the crew. He spoke into the microphone like a tutor: "All is in readiness. We are in constant communication with our observer post, which reports to us the momentary position of the approaching planes. Accordingly, we calculate the speed, angle, and elevation, making allowances for wind speed and direction, barometric pressure, and temperature. The next few seconds will be decisive."

As he said this, in a real emergency he would have fixed the aim of the deadly projectiles by a lightning-like correction of the elevation. As it was, he went on, like a tutor: "But during these seconds the bombers above us must be on an even keel and flying in a straight line, without dodging or acrobatics, so that the bombardier can operate his bombsight and release his bombs. During this period, which lasts from ten to forty-five seconds, depending on the weather and the skill of the bombardier, the planes are at their most vulnerable. Our shells require approximately twenty seconds to reach 15,000 feet." He stopped to listen to a report.

"It is reported to me," he continued, his voice now carrying again, so that it scarcely required amplification, "that the five bombers will be occupying within the next forty seconds the position I have just spoken of." He pulled out a stop watch. "Ready?"

"Ready," the three engineers replied with one voice.

Long, deadly-looking shells had been broken out. A workman, Vlk, held one—it weighed forty pounds—so that the brass shell case rested on the ground just beside the gun.

"Target?" Andreas asked.

"On target," came the three answers.

"Commence firing!" Andreas ordered.

This was the moment that would have counted in case of real emergency. Perfect silence reigned over the broad expanse, broken only by the roar of the bombers, invisibly maneuvering high in the haze above. Occasionally a sparkling dot flashed high up, like a diamond

All eyes in the stand were staring upward; the men at the gun would have had every opportunity to do what would have been done if the man at the speakers' desk had been named Hitler. Detail after detail came about exactly as it had been planned. Only one detail did not.

Vlk, the foreman, had inserted the nose of the shell into the bell-mouthed fuse setter. The cap was turned. A second man took the shell and hurled it into the breech of the gun. A second shell had already been passed to Vlk at the fuse cutter.

The breechblock snapped shut. There were four earsplitting smacks as the shells began their journey into the sky. The empty shell case hurtled backward, away from the gun into the bare field, and another shell was rammed home. Another, and another; the gun-pointing crew kept moving the wheels to hold the gun on its target.

Up in the air there were little puffs of light as the shells exploded. One. Two. Three. Four. Five. Six. Seven. Eight. Nine.

In case of real emergency only two, or three at the most would have been needed.

Herr Werner, the engineer from Danzig, made a report.

"Cease firing!" Andreas ordered. And announced, in the accents of a tutor: "Three bombers knocked out. Two bombers hit. You will immediately see and hear the fall of the experimental machines."

When these hypotheses were verified before their eyes, the spectators in the stands burst into frantic applause. While they were still applauding, and the Hitler Youth began to file before the new gun, a faint crack like a whip was heard, to which no one paid any attention.

"All absolutely according to schedule," Herr Schultheiss had said yonder beside the small stand, accepting congratulations, and in an obviously better humor since the splendid result of the trial. The five severely damaged planes, sacrificed by Skoda for this great day, had come down, quite useless, and were open to inspection by the guests in groups of ten at a time. The crews of the three that had been destroyed actually landed by parachute; those of the two that had been damaged came down with their machines.

Yes, everything had gone off according to schedule.

Except perhaps for the faint whiplike crack, not provided for in the schedule, which had claimed one victim. When the Pilsen Hitler

Youth, coming from the gun emplacement, had filed past the stands, the leader, Kuno Schultheiss, collapsed before the eyes of his father. Dying, the son cried: *"Sieg, Heil!"* The father, seeing him die, replied: *"Sieg, Heil!"*

This was the only thing, in the opinion of some of the guests, that marred the festivities. Others, on the contrary, felt that this very thing had been the climax, and called it a Spartan spectacle. The morning was generally spoken of as elevating, and Herr Schultheiss, who joined the tour of press inspection despite the accident, received enthusiastic congratulations along with the condolences. Skoda 9 and the death of his son had doubled his prestige. Half an hour later accounts of both were racing across the world. "Skoda 9 revolutionizes anti-aircraft defense. Spartan death of a Hitler Youth. Heroism of the managing director of Skoda," were a few of the D. N. B. headlines.

Before the tour of inspection was over, Herr Krueger was personally questioning every individual who had been on the proving grounds, holding for examination all the workmen who had manned the gun, and arresting the foreman Vlk, who was discovered to have a revolver of the same caliber that had inflicted the mortal wound on Kuno Schultheiss. The man found time to whisper to Andreas: "At least it wasn't quite for nothing, sir! My boy was the youngest at the Beneš High School. I had to look on then too!"

The Tirolean was neither questioned nor arrested. He, with the engineers from Danzig, Königsberg, and Prague, supervised the removal of the new model to his laboratory. As he explained to the three, he had discovered a "trifling flaw"; he asked them to bring him whatever material they had bearing on Skoda 9; and, this done, requested them to leave him alone so that he might locate the trouble. The engineers, for their part, had noticed no such flaw. Nevertheless, the inventor, whose name had not been mentioned during that elevating morning, insisted that the "trifling flaw" existed, and demanded to be left alone.

The trifling flaw consisted in the fact that his gun had not hit Hitler, for which he could never forgive it. Nor, on the other hand, could he allow it to "make Germany's anti-aircraft defense impregnable from this day forward." When he had come here in September of 1939 to work on this gun, he had given himself a promise on his word of honor: to break the word of honor he had given Gauleiter Udacher in Bozen. Today for the last time he summoned all his energy, his coolness, his Tirolean fierceness, and broke his word of honor, which he had been breaking daily since September of 1939, for the last time. At the regular hour he left his job. No earlier, no later. At one o'clock that night a time bomb would go off, blowing Skoda 9 and all the designs for it sky-high and preventing the trifling flaw from recurring.

Before this, however, as was proper on a day that had gone off according to schedule, he spent the evening at home, that is to say in the hotel room that was still home. When Gwen enfolded him in her arms, incapable of speech, saying nothing but, "Thank God!" he stopped on the threshold. These words were every bit as unexpected as it was to finish the day by coming into a room where Easter roses and flowering jasmine were standing on the table and someone enfolded him in her arms.

"Did you know?" he asked.

She knew. She had spent the day by the radio.

"And you still say thank God?"

Yes.

The yes was not on her lips, for she could not speak, but only looked at him and held him to her. But it was in her eyes, in her arms, in everything that was herself.

"Gwen," he said. "The chance is gone, once and for all. And you still say thank God?"

Now they were sitting together. Her face rested upon his breast; the refuge she felt there and her happiness because this refuge was there gleamed from her face like silent, everlasting beacons.

"You know," she managed to say after a while, "I wrote to you once when things were just as they are now, and I said I was perfectly happy, and it was shameful. But I am. I know it's shameful, but still I'm not ashamed. Don't say anything. What you're going to say will be true. And still it isn't true. Today I haven't prayed for anything except for what happened. I didn't pray that you would kill Hitler, but that you would come home. You did come."

He held her closer, and all he said was: "Gwen, I'm afraid that will always be our problem." He said "always," and when he said it he believed it.

"The problem is insoluble," she answered in his arms. "You want me not to think of the moment, not to think of you or me. There are more important things than we are. There is no private life now, your sister says. I know she's right. But I can't do it. I do think of you. It is the most important thing. A million times more important than anything! And your sister says for that reason you won't want anything to do with me. Is she right?"

"But Gwen," he answered, "you've already proved the very opposite. You fought against everyone in the ritual-murder case. Even against yourself. Even against me!"

"I didn't prove anything. What did I fight for? Tell me that!"

"For the truth. Or for justice. Not for yourself, in any case."

"Yes, I did! For myself! Because I couldn't stand it otherwise. One always thinks of oneself!"

"Why do you belittle yourself?"

"Because I am little. When you haven't anything to risk, it's easy to gamble. I didn't have you then. Now I have you."

"You should have seen Father Schultheiss! When the mortally wounded boy marched past him with one last effort, the way he bore watching him die, without stirring a muscle—I'm sorry to say it, but it was magnificent. Perhaps that's why they're winning."

"Maybe he didn't love his son. I love you. I'd have died."

They kissed each other.

"You must promise me something, Gwen."

"Anything."

"It's a hard promise to keep."

"Tell me what it is."

"If anything should happen to me—sometime—forty years from now——"

"Or eighty——"

"Or eighty, you're to——"

"Be sensible?" she broke in, gripping his hand. "That's what you want to say! That's what you kept wanting to say in the four days after our wedding, and never did say!"

"I want to say, you're to be brave. You are brave, Gwen. I don't want—let me finish; it flashed through my head when Schultheiss gave me that queer look this morning—I don't want everything to be over along with me! They've just been waiting until my job was done. That's why they didn't want my name to be mentioned. It's easier to remove someone if you don't owe him public thanks. Don't look that way. It isn't necessarily true, of course. But if it should be true, Gwen, I want someone to be there who can go on thinking it through. All of it. Promise me!"

"I won't promise."

"But you said 'anything' before!"

"Your sister knows I'd only take it back. Don't you know it?"

"Aside from our love, there's this world too!"

"That's your mistake. My love for you is greater than this world."

They kissed.

"Gwen," he begged. "Promise me what I asked. It's my only request to you."

They were silent; he could feel the infinity of this love and the happiness that it was. Easter roses and jasmine were blossoming red and white, smelling sweet. The world outside was mute.

"It's the one thing I want of you, Gwen."

"I'm sorry, Andreas. I can't promise you anything. I love you too much!"

Then the telephone rang very briefly; Gwen started, ran over, answered, and heard a voice: "Is that you, Gwen? Is your husband at home? Don't call him. Tell him he's got to go at once!"

She felt she was dying.

"Oh," she said, making her voice sound casual, "it's you, Dr. Paumgartner. Yes, I did call you, and it's nothing. I feel perfectly all right again now."

"What was wrong with you?" asked Andreas, who had kept his seat, and to whom sickness was an unknown mystery.

Shaking her head at him from the telephone, she indicated: *Nothing*. Into the instrument she said: "Yes. He came home very well satisfied." Then the voice at the other end said something that seemed to amuse her. She smiled.

The voice at the other end said: "The order for his arrest was telephoned from Berlin a moment ago. It's obvious now that they were only sparing him till his invention was ready. Can you hear me? At the corner of the Salzgasse and the Dominikanergasse there will be a sedan waiting not more than five minutes from now, license number P 5578—don't repeat it. Tell him to get in and not stop to bother about anything. And for God's sake hurry!"

"Thank you, Doctor," she said. "Awfully nice of you to call." She hung up and went back across the room. "Andreas," she said, "we've got to go. Come on."

"Was that what he wanted?" he asked, turning pale.

"Yes. There's no time. Only for this." She kissed him. And he could feel how cold her lips were. "Let's go," she said.

"Not you!" he objected.

"You and I. Come on."

"I won't run away!" he decided. "I wouldn't dream of it!"

"Haven't you often told me that Schuschnigg said that too?"

"Because he's a Tirolean!"

"And you said he was crazy! Haven't you proved to me over and over that he could have served his country a hundred times better at liberty?"

"Liberty! Where is it?"

"I don't know. We'll go together."

"I won't run away!" he persisted obstinately.

Again the telephone. She pushed him away. It was Riccarda, saying the same thing Paumgartner had said. She even said: "Gwen, I'm making you personally responsible for his going. If you keep him, it's all your fault!" Her voice was as hard as rock. Gwen did not let him speak to his sister, but cut off the conversation. "Darling," she said to him, "here's my hand. I'll promise you what you wanted. But I only want one thing, too, now, just one: come on!"

"One doesn't run away," he repeated. "One stands up to it. Who was that just then?"

Two of the five minutes were gone.

"Andreas," she cried, with utter determination, yanking open the window, "if you don't come with me now, I shall throw myself out of here. You let another girl do it. Don't do it again!"

He took a deep breath, looked around him, and saw. In front of him were the Easter roses and the jasmine. They were blossoming and smelling sweet, in the same colors, with the same scent that they had had for centuries. Centuries from today they would blossom and smell sweet just as they did now. Nothing about them would show that there had been a today. This he saw.

"Come on," he said.
"Come on," she answered.
"Don't you want to say a word to your parents?"
"No. I promised you I'd see them again."
She did not let him take anything with him, not even his hat. All he took was a book, the one old Mumelter had so often been reading. She, too, went as she was, hatless. Two young people, leaving the house for a moment to buy cigarettes next door or eat ice cream across the street, walked past the doorman and through the revolving door. At the corner stood a limousine, license number P 5578. They got in. The man at the wheel was the Serb in the quartet who played the violin in Monsieur Roux's stead. He said nothing, and drove. The day that had gone off exactly according to schedule was at an end.

Chapter 24

Before dawn broke, birds sang. Just a few at first, here and there. As if they were trying their voices. A brief, soft twittering, then silence. When the stars went out and the sky brightened, others sang, more loudly. A fluting note mingled with the twitter of the sparrows—thrushes. Then the goldfinches began their little song, the same thing over and over again, to be tirelessly repeated until late in the evening; it consisted of six short warbling notes and three longer, inquiring ones; the Czech country people have set words to it: *"Jak se ty babičky pékné zivi* [How do these pretty wenches live]?"
As soon as dawn came birds sang. It was an infinitely sweet, peaceful sound, heavenly if you had not heard it for a long time. Andreas listened, his head on his arms. It was a long time since birds had sung when he awoke. They sang in the yard at the Silbergasse; that was two years ago. Two bitter years. Two useless years. Perhaps, before they were quite finished, they would be of some use. After September 29, perhaps?
The singing of the birds came from the forest, a glorious forest. Even the mere fact that there was such a thing as forests and singing birds, and the air coming pure, smokeless, cool, and resinous through the tiny attic window—all this was something he had been deprived of for a long time. It was a different air from that in which

Rosengarten and Schlern had mingled their snowy breath and the pungent scent of gentian, alpine roses, new-mown upland meadows; this was the perfume of the tall, silent, ancient spruces and firs of the Böhmerwald.

The hamlet was called Klein-Kubitzen, quite near the Bohemian-Moravian frontier and not far from the Austrian. It was a typical Czech hamlet, where a few peasants lived in low, whitewashed, thatched cottages; there was a schoolhouse, a town hall, and a white-washed church at the end of the village street, across which fat geese waddled all day, and where there were puddles even on dry days, and manure heaps year in and year out. A few paces beyond the village the forest rose like a sheltering wall, and before it and on both sides were fields of Indian corn, potatoes, and oats. Andreas and Gwen had already spent a whole day in Klein-Kubitzen, getting acquainted with the fat geese and the church and the cool woods. And old Babka, who was putting them up. No—who was sheltering them. Today would be their second day here; the first night was just over, for they had arrived early yesterday morning.

Gwen was still asleep. Andreas looked at her. He had done this every morning since their wedding, and although that was not so very many mornings, he found it hard to imagine that there had been mornings when that face, growing ever more transparent, was not turned toward him in sleep. The transparency was now so perfect that one seemed to see the dreams through the forehead. Two use-less years? *I have found a person who has nothing to hide, sleeping or waking. Life can give one no more than that,* he thought.

Life had never been tender to him, and he had never been tender to life. He could feel this monstrous omission of tenderness now that he had leisure, on his holiday, so to speak, to look at this face that was thinking of him as it slept. He wanted to stroke it, but did not—his hand was awkward at caresses. He wanted to tell her in her sleep words that fall easily from other people's lips. For him they were hard; his mouth was awkward at flattery. So all he whispered was: "I love you," and she did not hear it.

Then the morning grew more radiant; the thin veils that had been draped over reality were gone, and Andreas, lying on a bed of straw in the thatched attic of old Babka, the peasant woman, began to think about the day.

They could not stay here; the place was too tiny, and although it was a wholly Czech village, there was no way to hide. Its only advantage (for which Jaro and Paumgartner had chosen it) was that it lay close to the frontier, so that with a trifling bit of luck they might get through the woods to Austria; there Paumgartner would take care of the subsequent steps.

The plan was to let grass grow over their escape for a few days, and then, when the outcry had died down, to flee systematically. Systematic flight: the idea had a bitter taste as Andreas stared into the air. But every time his eye fell upon the sleeping girl, he said to himself: *All right. Systematic flight.*

Old Babka, the peasant woman, who had always lived here in Klein-Kubitzen, without making very generous use of the school on the village street, had got a letter from Jaro; first she had kept it for a long time in the pocket of her blue-and-red striped calico skirt; then she had read it much longer still, and finally she had said: *"Anō, milostpane. Anō, milostpani.* Yes, sir. Yes, lady." She had offered them the thatched attic room where gourds and ears of Indian corn were ordinarily dried; she had, against the law, killed one of the fat geese, and brought it on the table with dumplings—*husu s knedlikem,* the national dish. Before going to sleep she had fiddled with a little box, and listened to what the Nazdar Station told her as devoutly as she would have to a sermon; for whenever the little box spoke she felt that it was addressing her personally; it was for her, Babka, the seventy-four-year-old childless widow, owner of the tiniest cottage in the world, a flock of geese, two cows, a potato patch, and a cornfield. At that she was by no means mistaken in feeling herself thus personally addressed, for she was one of the hundreds of thousands of members of the Beseda, far too insignificant, impoverished, and illiterate to be suspected by the Gestapo. But this was the very thing that the Beseda relied on, that made it undiscoverable and unconquerable; it was the countless hosts of those like herself that did it, Widow Babka knew, and she was very proud of it.

She was about to begin her day's work, which today would consist of sealing up a letter that had come with Pan Uliř's letter, ready stamped and in an envelope, dropping it into the ridiculous rusty mailbox (who in Klein-Kubitzen would correspond with the outside world?), and then picking the ripe Indian corn and hanging it up to dry for goose fodder, with the ears downward. But first she knocked at the door of the attic room. Andreas opened it, finger to his lips, for Gwen was still asleep. This pleased old Babka; it showed that the grand city lady had not found her poor bed too rough for her. Curling a face that looked like parchment into a silent laugh, she communicated with her guest in a barbarous mixture of Czech and German, which was nevertheless plain enough, being explained with many gestures: Breakfast was on the stove downstairs, only wanting to be warmed up; old Babka would cook nothing, *nic kuřit,* because she would be out in the field, and the gentleman and the lady would have to make do with cold roast goose, *studená husa,* fresh bread, and cucumbers; she would be back by coffee time, because she would be through hanging up the Indian corn. And she would get supper as befitted the gentry. If the gentleman and lady would go up the wood road behind the cottage, past the big woodpile, they would come to Fuerth Outlook, where you could see as far as Fuerth in Germany, and even further than that.

Holidays!

Gwen awoke; her look of horror turned to a smile as she remembered that they had escaped. They washed, using a water pitcher meant for dwarfs; then they warmed up their breakfast downstairs in the earth-floored kitchen, which was really the only habitable room in the house. Enjoying it, they resisted the temptation to turn on the little box, whose hiding place old Babka had shown them yesterday.

Holidays.

The first they had ever had together. They had never been in the country together.

They took lunch with them, just what old Babka had provided for them—cold roast goose, cucumbers, and bread—and went past the old woodpile, up the wood road that led to an outlook. They walked hand in hand under the old evergreens, feeling the cool shadow and their own passion. The sun tossed its light on the ground like bright, swift coins, and the ground was roots that you stumbled over, moss soft as velvet, and blueberries, thousands of them, that blackened your lips. They picked and ate them, and stumbled over the long, woody roots, and thought neither of yesterday nor of tomorrow. They had so much to tell each other—they knew so little of each other; it is not easy to catch up with twenty-seven years and twenty-two years in one day. Gwen told him how she had been eating sandwiches at a drugstore in Poughkeepsie (when she was at Vassar), and had had her first compliment from a man. He had said to her, and she mimicked him—but Andreas, matter of fact as always, wanted to know first how it happened that a person would be eating sandwiches at a chemist's.

"The drugstore," she said, "is a national institution of ours—it's something you've got to know about if you go over with me sometime."

He saw no obstacle whatever to his going over with her sometime, but doubted that people ate at chemists', and they argued about this a little.

And when he in turn told her about old Veronika, Foxy, the bitch, and the green school bus that he had envied his fellow pupils, she got back her own, saying: "I hardly believe anyone could envy anyone a green omnibus, could they?"

Although it was not funny at all, they could not help laughing and laughing. And then they had their hands very full with picking blueberries, and they kissed each other with black lips, and looked even more ridiculous afterward, and could not help laughing again, and were passionately happy.

Yes, they both felt, this was what one lived for! That's what the toil and terror and agony are for, so that one can have this! They took it as a reward that was their due, that so far had been withheld from them; they even demanded usurious interest. For they did not come back for coffee as old Babka had instructed them—old Babka was the only authority whom they still recognized. Long live old Babka with her hundred wrinkles and her stiff blue-and-red striped calico skirt. She had given them the loveliest day of their lives.

But when they saw her again (having first conspired not to tell her for anything in the world that they were lazy holiday trippers, and had not got as far as the outlook she had recommended to them, because they had had to lie in the moss and be passionately happy), she was making signs to them from afar. She had apparently been waiting for them; now, in her barbarous word-and-sign language, she let them know that there had been a telephone call to the village head man, Pan Doležal—he was over yonder in his cornfield. Would the gentleman be kind enough to go over there?

So Andreas went the short distance over to Pan Doležal's cornfield; he was busily at work cutting the ripe ears. There are always interruptions, he complained—a peasant ought not to be a mayor, sir, but what's the use! They write letters from Prague, and even telephone from there, and you can't get any help, because everyone has been called in for compulsory labor. These Nazis, the *potvory,* send the young people to God knows where, to Saxony and Silesia and Poland, anywhere except where they belong, on their own Czech soil. And so far as the long-distance telephone was concerned, somebody from Prague, Pan Doležal didn't know who, had inquired whether a gentleman and lady had passed through or been seen yesterday or today. The person had described them, and they had looked thus and so, something like the gentleman and lady. And that's why the mayor, who had been called away from his corn-cutting, had said no. Because of course he knew from Babka that the gentleman and lady were on a little wedding trip, and so why disturb them? Even so, he had thought it might be a good idea to tell them. And he did beg their pardon for disturbing them, and also sent his profound respects, and went on cutting his ears of corn.

Meanwhile, Gwen had been waiting with old Babka, and when Andreas came back he was laughing all over his face, and he said in his deep voice: "Absolutely nothing! That mayor's a character!"

But Gwen knew very well what you did when you looked amused at something that was tearing you apart; she took him aside and said: "Shall we go on pretending to ourselves even now? We've pretended we were happy for a whole day. Tell me the truth."

He stuck to it that the telephone call meant nothing at all, because it had simply repeated their description, which the radio had presumably been broadcasting incessantly since day before yesterday evening. Mere routine, nothing more. And anyway, they hadn't pretended to be happy, they'd been happy! And still were. Weren't they?

She started to turn on the little box.

"What for?" he figured. "Do you insist on having this loveliest day of my life come to an unlovely end?"

"It was my loveliest too. But if you think the telephone call was so unimportant, why don't you want to hear the news?"

"What logic!" he said. But he turned it on.

There was a report of some act of sabotage in Moravia. She prevented him from turning it off at once. Then they heard the statistics of harvest destruction in the districts of Kladno, Budweis, and Komotau, and a list of the hostages who would be shot at 5 P.M. tomorrow, July 1, 1941, unless by that time the fugitives, Andreas Mumelter, engineer at the Skoda Works, a South Tirolean, and his wife, Gwen Mumelter, maiden name Hoffman, an American, had been surrendered, or information given leading to their apprehension. The names of the hostages were: Antonín Powondra, engineer at the Skoda Works, Pilsen; Josef Zerzavy, laborer at the Skoda Works, Pilsen; Jan Sedláček and Pavel Klapka, workmen at the Skoda Works, Pilsen; Ferdinand Svátek, apothecary in Pilsen; Antonia Krejčí, chambermaid at the Hotel Waldeck, Pilsen; Bedřich Soukup, doorman at the Hotel Waldeck, Pilsen; Karel Rudník, proprietor of the Stříbrné Střechy Inn on the road between Pilsen and Eger; Karel and Ludmilla Travniček, tobacco retailers at Eger; Marie Babka, peasant at Klein-Kubitzen; Vladislav Doležal, peasant and village headman at Klein-Kubitzen. Twelve all told.

The voice of the Nazdar Station (it was not Jaro's voice) warned: "Don't be intimidated! The two fugitives are important to our cause. Do not surrender them under any circumstances. Shelter them, care for them, and make sure that they are not found. Nazdar!" He did not address the twelve hostages, which was the reason old Babka was listening to him so disdainfully. On this day of all days, when her name was solemnly proclaimed over the air, he put her in the company of perfect strangers (except for stupid old Doležal) instead of saying: "Czech men and women! Our valued comrade Babka at Klein-Kubitzen is the one who is sheltering the gentleman and lady. That is why she is being shot tomorrow." That would have been right and proper. Not just all in one lump with Krethi and Plethi!

She had known that she was going to be shot at five tomorrow afternoon since early this morning, when idiotic old Doležal had come running out to her in the fields to tell her what he had just heard over the telephone. He wanted her to run after the honeymooners in the woods and advise them not to come back, but to escape into the Fuerth region—the blockhead! What good would that have done? Whether they came back or not, if the Nazis took a person as a hostage, they would shoot him one way or another. And since they had taken a person as a hostage, they knew where the young gentleman and lady were, and nothing was any use. Wasn't it just the same with Jan Smutek, who had shot a couple of Gestapo people at Taus—and very right he was!—and who even had a price of 120,000 Czech crowns on his head? They had caught Smutek, the yellow dogs, and the hostages they had taken for him were shot anyway. Then why run after the gentleman and lady, who seem to be so fond of each other, and this at the very moment when the Indian corn had to be cut? There wouldn't be anyone left to cut it tomorrow anyhow, and although her sister, who was a cook at Eger, would unfortunately inherit all she had, she would never touch the Indian corn, the lazy thing.

This was how old Babka looked at the matter, and how she discussed it with her guests. Meanwhile, she was picking out the chickens she intended for the gentleman's and lady's supper tonight, which she would bake brown, garnish with parsley, and serve with cucumber salad.

But now that the names of the hostages had reached Andreas' ears, he could hear and see nothing else.

The twelve names belonged to twelve perfectly innocent people; *just as innocent as old Babka here,* he thought, *or the old man in the cornfield who begged my pardon because they were going to shoot him on my account.* Twelve, half of whom he did not know at all, and the others only slightly.

Confronted with this thought, he ceased to think, for his thoughts could not approach the unimaginability of the radio news.

"What do you say?" he asked Gwen helplessly.

She said nothing. She knew what was coming.

"Speak!" he demanded. "Is this thinkable? Is it thinkable in our day, in the year 1941, that twelve innocent people are picked out and told: 'You're hostages'? What kind of word is hostages for 1941? 'I'm giving you until five tomorrow afternoon,' they say to these hostages, 'and if by then you haven't changed something you're innocent of and have no power over, you're going to die at five sharp tomorrow afternoon.' What is this? Imagine these people! And those that belong to them! How are they spending the hours until five tomorrow afternoon?"

And Gwen answered, with the hoarse catch in her voice: "Like us, Andreas. Just the same."

Thereupon, instead of asking further questions, he went back to the cornfield to ask the old peasant to telephone Prague, or wherever it would do any good, and say: "The people you want are here." But it was not easy work, with the village headman of Klein-Kubitzen.

"Well, you see, sir," he said, cutting away busily, for his stint must be finished, "pardon me for contradicting you. I'm only an uneducated farmer, and you're a trained engineer, and important for the Beseda. Life is nothing to me" (he used a much stronger phrase), "and if they shoot me, why not? So much the better! My wife is dead. They've taken away my three boys; two of them are in Poland building roads, the third's in a concentration camp, I don't know which one, because he spat on a picture of Hitler, and I don't even know if he's alive. And I'm here. They take your harvest away, and cart off your milk and your eggs. They haven't left a person anything. I'm seventy-five now, a year or two older than Babka. We're the eldest in the village, although she claims to be younger, the silly goose. And if I'd known what was coming when I was thirty—— Good God, even though it is a mortal sin, sir, I'd have killed myself. That's why I said to the official gentleman on the telephone: 'You don't need to arrest us here—Babka nor me neither. We won't run away from you. We're as glad as anything to have it over with.' You know, sir, when you're as young as you are, it's a very different matter. There's some sense in it, then, because then you can still do some damage to these hounds. But old people like us! Don't be unreasonable, if I may make bold to give you some advice. Don't listen to old Babka—she's a silly, vain woman. You take your lady, and get clear away. You won't be doing us any kindness if you give yourself up. Nor to your lady either, I'm sure. Nor to the millions of Czechs that think as I do. You stay alive and fight against those mad dogs! That's a thousand times better."

Although Andreas had never been more determined, he regarded the man in the cornfield for some time with silent amazement. He remembered having heard another old man say very much the same things. *Isn't it utterly astonishing,* he thought, *what the man whom I missed has made of human beings? Before long people will stop using the term human beings. They'll simply say "unhappy ones."*

Then he persisted in his request.

"If those are your orders, sir," the old peasant yielded with a mournful sigh. And he accompanied Andreas from his cornfield to the ridiculous little town hall (which was only a plank shed with a bare table made of boards, some dried-up ink, a few announcements on the walls, and an antediluvian long brown telephone box), and put through the call. It was some time before he started speaking Czech to someone. Andreas understood nothing but his own name, and had a chance to discover a brand-new "wanted" with his picture among those posted on the wall. "You see," the headman at Klein-Kubitzen said to Andreas when he had finished, smiling embarrassedly, "our village is small. We haven't even a jail." Then they shook hands; each went back to his proper destiny: the peasant to harvest the corn, Andreas to wait for arrest.

Gwen was sitting with old Babka at the kitchen table, peeling cucumbers. She did not ask him, and he said nothing. He sat down with them and waited. Before long, just as the fried chickens were about to be spread with bread crumbs dipped in white of egg—it was strictly forbidden to make them as it was strictly forbidden to kill chickens and geese—orders, the tramp of feet, and a command were heard from the village street. All this came much too soon, for even by plane the surprise detail whose approach could be seen through the kitchen window would never have got here by this time. But it was soon explained. The surprise detail was not coming in response to the village headman's telephone call, but in response to the report of someone else. This someone else now appeared in the kitchen door, and, speaking to men outside who did not come in, said: "Here they are."

The someone else was Sepp, Andreas' brother, and he had his reasons for being here. The post of leader of the Hitler Youth, District of Pilsen, had become vacant through Kuno Schultheiss' death, and Sepp was a candidate for it. But in order to secure the post one had to be able to show an "accomplishment of decisive importance for the Party"; Sepp wanted to produce such an accomplishment. More than this, however, he wanted to wipe out the shame that had come upon the name of Mumelter, suddenly dragged into all the broadcasts, hounded through all the newspapers, posted in all the police stations. He had promised that girl of good blood, Adelheid Walpurga Schimetschek, that the name should be not that of an outlawed fugitive and enemy of the national community, but that of a dependable fellow German, devoted with blood and property to the cause. This was why, having wormed the plan of flight out of Riccarda with a guile that he made no small boast of in talking to Adelheid Walpurga, he felt the moment had arrived for an accomplishment of decisive importance. He went and reported his brother's route. For that reason old Babka and old Doležal had been chosen as hostages, and even left at large for a time, so that they might the more certainly give themselves and the others away.

And now the informer stood in Babka's kitchen, for he had almost been made commander of the surprise detail (almost, the actual commander being Standard Leader Ruppert) and said to the Standard: "There they are." And thus he played, on the evening of June 30, 1941, in Klein-Kubitzen on the Bohemian frontier, the part of a man who had lived just 1,913 years before him, in Judea.

And Andreas looked at his own brother, whom his grandfather before him had died of, with eyes in which utter lack of understanding was the dominant emotion. They understood less and less, the easier the young fellow's conscience appeared to be. "Sepp," he asked, just as Gwen had asked the judges at Pilsen, "aren't you ashamed?"

If his grandfather had been alive, he would have said: "The New Order!" But Grandfather was dead, and the New Order revealed itself only to the wide eyes of the brother who found himself facing his brother and hearing him reply with firm lips and quivering eyes: "*You* ought to be ashamed! You've brought shame upon our name!" He spoke with such conviction and such fanaticism that the elder gave up the idea of arguing or invoking the name of the man who had done the same thing 1,913 years before. That man had been ashamed, though, and this man was unashamed. Andreas could not help thinking of the moment in the sealed train when it had occurred to him that they might separate families. They *had* separated families.

Gwen's self-control, however, gave way in the face of those flashing eyes. "How can you dare to insult your brother!" she flared up. "What do you know about shame? You set these people on him! You're no——"

"Quiet!" Sepp broke in, and the anger that so frequently carried him away began to swell in the veins at his temples. "You're to be quiet! It's you that brought my brother so low! You and your Jewish stock-market ideas!"

Even then Andreas did not speak the word Judas, but cried out with the last tumultuous fury of his life: "Shut up! You parrot! All you do is chatter and ape those that have made the name *human being* unnecessary, by putting *unhappy ones* and *criminals* in its place!" And with an unconfined yell, discharging all the grudges at once, all the contempt, all the hatred that had been stored up in him since the sealed train, with a cry that made the plates on the kitchen table tremble, he ordered: "Get out of here! I want to be with human beings as long as I'm still alive!" Foaming at the mouth, he sat down to his place. And for the third time since he had turned against his family Sepp gave way and went out.

In his place Standard Leader Ruppert came in. "Andreas Mumelter!" he said to the Tirolean, who was still quaking with anger and contempt. And he read from a paper: "The court-martial at Pilsen, under the presidency of Lieutenant General von Herrdegen, has condemned you to death in absentia upon charges brought by Judge Advocate Koetzschen, for attempted murder of our Führer, treason to the national community, malicious mischief, and incitement to armed rebellion. I am directed to inform you of the sentence and execute it upon you."

"The sentence isn't valid! My husband hasn't even had a hearing!" declared Gwen, fighting the hopeless fight nevertheless.

"The sentence is valid in accordance with the legal authority which I have just cited. In case of flight the court-martial hands down its sentences in absentia. You may thank your kind stars, Frau Mumelter, that hitherto no charge was brought against you for complicity!" replied the standard leader, also a young fellow, with the same flashing eyes as the other young fellow who had just left the room.

"Yes. The sentence is valid. I accept it," said Andreas, mortally terrified at the threat to Gwen. "Excuse me, Gwen. Nothing else has any meaning. At least now let's try to give things some meaning."

Badly as old Babka understood German, she had watched everything intently, and she was anything but satisfied with what her angry gentleman was saying. Just before this, when they were peeling cucumbers, the little box had spoken to her and promised her that the hour of liberation was closer than she thought. Why didn't her angry gentleman wait until then? Must he absolutely tell them the sentence was valid? Nothing they did could be valid!

"Anything else would be quite futile in any case," replied the standard leader. Anyone who had eyes for such things would have been amazed at the enmity he was displaying toward a man under sentence of death and his wife, both of whom he was now seeing for the first time. "I am under orders to inform you of the legally——"

"Legally!" ejaculated Gwen, still fighting.

"—established period of twelve hours' grace between the announcement of a death sentence pronounced by a court-martial in absentia and its execution. You may express wishes in regard to your food. You are also entitled, if you insist, to clerical attendance. Express your wishes. The execution will take place," he said, looking at his wrist watch, "twelve hours from now, that is, at four fifty-five tomorrow morning."

Old Babka made signs to Gwen to do something. But even her lady disappointed her now. She sat down slowly, very slowly, in the seat in front of her plate, shut her eyes for a moment, and then opened them.

"I wish my wife to stay with me," said Andreas. "And when the time comes, I want to see the pastor. My brother is to go away from here. I don't want him anywhere near me!" Again the deep voice swelled menacingly.

"These wishes are granted," the standard leader declared curtly. "What do you wish to eat?"

At this Gwen's face reddened, then instantly turned deathly pale.

"Thank you," said Andreas. "We have sufficient to eat. If you would leave us alone now!"

The standard leader nodded. He bowed, just barely, before Gwen, and went outdoors. Those whom he had brought with him were posted around the cottage. They could be heard talking. The footsteps of two people could also be heard departing, and looking out of the window one saw the standard leader accompanying Sepp to a car that waited by the church; Sepp got in and drove off. The standard leader came back to Babka's cottage.

Andreas now had twelve hours, less five minutes, to live. And Gwen had as long to see him living. So far as he was concerned, after his supreme agitation the reaction followed; he was exhausted, almost relieved. The tension of the last few months had been too fierce. It relaxed, and the same vast craving for peace came over him that had overpowered him two years before when they were waiting in the empty house at Bozen for the school bus. In this state he found it neither surprising nor alarming that he was sitting at a half-set table in a foreign land, and was to be shot tomorrow at five minutes before five. On the contrary, it seemed to him the natural thing.

The table was completely set, with Gwen's help; looking at her was the only thing that hurt him unspeakably. *Should I have given up having her stay with me?* he asked himself, and discarded the idea. That, too, had to be the way it was. That, too, was the natural thing.

Of death he was not afraid. He was not looking forward to it, as his grandfather had done, for he would have liked to live in order to love Gwen and kill Hitler. But he realized that there was only the one or the other, not both together, and that he wanted to live only for both together. One had been taken from him. So the other would have to be taken from him also.

They started eating the forbidden food. Old Babka was a good cook; she considered herself a better one than her sister, who was cooking for a grand household in Eger; and certainly no one could have fried chickens more crisply. In the midst of the meal Gwen began to cry.

He said: "All right, Gwen. Let go. Frau Babka forgot the salt anyway." This was the way he would talk to her in the hours that remained. When something natural happened, it ought not to be made unnatural.

They finished eating, the table was cleared, and they said good night to old Babka, although it was scarcely evening, and the birds were still singing and the sun still shining. But upstairs in the room under the thatch they would be alone, and there was nothing else that they wanted now.

They climbed the ridiculously steep chicken ladder. "Watch your step!" he said to her now, as he had last night when they went up for the first time, and they reached their tiny refuge in safety. There was really no room for anything but the straw tick, the dwarfs' water pitcher, the tin washbasin standing on a chair, and a rickety table on which lay two things the like of which had lain on it never before: a lipstick and a German book.

Going in, they fell into each other's arms almost at the door. A sob went through Gwen's body, shaking her, and he let it die away; he held her tightly, as tightly as he could, tenderly, as tenderly as he could, and with her he felt the sob traveling from her eyes into her throat and deeper down into her breast and her heart. Her transparent face was washed with tears, and when she was able to kiss him he tasted the tears, as salty as an ocean of love. He drank them, and plunged into the ocean; the waves closed over the two of them, burying them, releasing them, overwhelming them again. They had not let each other go from the moment they came into the tiny room, and each felt the other's joy, suffering, fear, and tranquillity. Darkness fell outside the tiny window, the moon shone in, and a clock ticked death. But even as they heard it tick, they did not let each other go; into that one night they compressed the nights that the clock withheld from them. They said nothing, only the three most important words in life: "I love you." They could feel that these were also the three most important words in death. They repeated them now and then, not too often, for even in this last night he did not want to be a flatterer, and she did not want to talk grand words; and they both knew that "I love you" were the grandest of all words.

It grew later and later; exhaustion came over Gwen, and she fell asleep in his arms. He held her, rejoicing at the full moon that allowed him to see her so clearly, giving him the finest thing his eyes had seen in life—that transparent face.

She sobbed in her sleep and cried: "Andreas!" He answered: "I'm here!" and, with profound release, blissfully beyond compare, she fell more deeply asleep again.

He had not forgotten for a second since the sentence had been read to him that he was to die. He thought it was proper to prepare for death, and for this, he thought, the time had come. The stars were still sparkling, the full moon still shone, and he reached over to the table with one hand, took the German book, opened it, and began to read in the moonlight what his grandfather had so often read, at the passage where he had left his spectacles before he died. Gwen was sleeping deeply; her dreams were fine. And Andreas, settling her more comfortably in his lap, with one arm around her shoulder, at which she smiled in her dreams, held the book in his other hand, and read the letter that Andreas Hofer had written, before being shot, to his friend Pühler at Neumarkt:

DEAREST COMRADE!

It is God's will that I should exchange the temporal for the eternal here in Mantua. But, God be thanked for this Divine Mercy, to me it seems as if I were being consigned to something else, further on. God will continue His grace to me down to the last moment, that through it I may go to that place where my soul shall everlastingly rejoice with all His elect, and where in God's presence I may pray for all—especially those for whom I am bound so to pray, as for yourself and your dear wife. May all good friends pray also for me, thus helping me through the flames of fire if I must yet atone in Purgatory.

Let my dear one arrange the Mass for the Dead at St. Martin's, where all our relatives are to have soup and meat together with a measure of wine at the inn. The good wife must make out her reckoning with all honesty, that I may have no cause for regret; the money that I had on me I have already distributed to the poor.

Farewell all, until we meet in Heaven, there to live without end.

May all those of Passeier and all my acquaintance remember me in their prayers, and let not the hostess of the *Sand* grieve overmuch. I shall pray for all before God.

Adieu, vile world, death to me seems so light a thing that I shed not a single tear.

Written at five o'clock in the morning. At nine, with the help of all the Saints, I journey to God.

Mantua, February 20, 1810.

ANDRE HOFER, who loved thee in life, of Sand in Passeier.

In the name of the Lord will I undertake the journey.

The stars paled.

And still Andreas held love in one hand, and in the other the epitome of trust and faith in God. Then the heavens grew wan, and the birds began to sing.

Just a few at first, here and there. As if they were trying their voices. A brief, soft twittering, then silence. When the stars went out and the sky brightened, others sang, more loudly. Andreas shut the book.

He was not afraid. He was filled with the confidence of that man who had come from the same land where he was born. And again old Babka knocked gently at the door, as she had yesterday morning, and he opened it on tiptoe, his finger to his lips, because of the sleeping girl. But old Babka was whispering anyway. She had told her beads all night, listening to the little box as she did so. And just now, a few moments ago, it had addressed her quite particularly. For it had said: "The man with whom Herr Mumelter, the engineer, drank water sends word to him that not much water will flow down the rivers before everything is as he would wish. And even if it should be later than the autumn rainfall, the Moldava and the Danube and the Drina and the Vistula and the Volga have water enough, and they are flowing in the right direction." She had carefully written down the names of the rivers in her awkward, childish hand, for she supposed each individual river was important; she had remembered the rest, knowing that it was addressed to her, and she reported it verbatim. Then she tiptoed back to the kitchen, for she must make hot soup for her gentleman before he went out there.

Outside, the standard leader had already drawn up his men in rank and file. There were nine of them, standing along the front of the tiny cottage, which was too narrow for them. *Nine to one,* old Babka thought—*that's too much.*

At that moment Andreas was not thinking of the message he had just had, which reminded him of the twenty-ninth of September. He was thinking of the message of Andreas Hofer, his countryman, and he wrote in the book under the printed letter: "That's the way it is! Farewell! Farewell!" And he left the book open.

Downstairs a voice could be heard answering another voice; a moment later old Babka reappeared, again on tiptoe, and asked the gentleman whether he cared to see the chaplain. Andreas did. He went down. He knelt in the kitchen, where old Babka was standing by the fire, getting breakfast, before a strange man who understood German and death. While the stranger's hand rested lightly upon his head, he confessed to him his deadly sins and his venial sins. He received absolution for both and the consecrated wafer.

"Have you any wish, my son?" asked the chaplain, who was scarcely older than Andreas, and whose eyes flashed as the standard leader's and the Hitler Youth's had, but more deeply and luminously.

Andreas pointed upward to the tiny room where Gwen was sleeping.

The kitchen clock pointed to ten minutes before five, and the sun over the Böhmerwald was beginning to hint at its splendor with gold-edged clouds.

The standard leader flung the kitchen door wide open. "Prisoner Mumelter!" he said. "Step forward!"

The Tirolean nodded to the old Czech woman, who had not had time to pour the soup she had made; but she did have time to kneel down before him and kiss his hand.

"Why, Frau Babka!" he admonished, rejecting flattery even to the last.

Then he went outdoors.

"Dear God, let her sleep!" was his prayer. And God granted him the illusion that she was asleep.

But the voice of the chaplain had awakened her from her deep slumber, and a little later she had got up, gone to the tiny window, looked out, still drugged with sleep, and seen a man with his back to her, who took the few steps to the side of the barn opposite old Babka's cottage. There the man stopped, shook his head in response to a question, turned around, and it was her husband Andreas. A second later, after an excessively loud bang, he fell on his face. She staggered down the ridiculously steep steps, out of the kitchen door, over to the barn. There the man lay, and he was dead. His eyes were open; nothing about his face was injured, not the defiant mouth that she had loved so when it was thrust forward, not the eyes, not the open forehead over which fell the refractory hair that he had been accustomed to tame with two motions of his fingers. The face was as she had known it. But it was not breathing; it was growing cold. And the breast was bleeding.

Now fully awakened from sleep, she did not fall. Her heartbeat did not stop. She survived it. Human beings can survive anything.

She knelt beside the dead man who had been her husband and her life, and closed his eyes, into which the new sun was beginning to shine. The detail obeyed the command: "Shoulder arms!" The chaplain prayed. The birds sang louder. A fluting note mingled with the twitter of the sparrows—thrushes. Then the goldfinches warbled over and over again their question: "How do these pretty wenches live?"

Nature proceeded to the order of the day.

Chapter 25

A LADY GOT OFF THE TRAIN at the station in Bozen. She was dressed in black. An elderly woman who was expecting her recognized her by the black dress, for she had never seen her before. The elderly woman was Vroni, the Mumelters' servant; Gwen was the lady arriving.

It was not easy to carry on a conversation with the new arrival, and the Bozen woman, accustomed through twenty-seven years to the taciturnity of the Mumelter household, did not attempt it. She welcomed the lady, took her suitcase, and started to take the little bag she had in her left hand, or rather under her left arm. But this Gwen would not allow.

Then the two went out through the platform gate, and outside the station the hotel runners were shouting: "*Albergo Griffone! Albergo Luna! Albergo Laurin!*"

These offers they declined, because Gwen was going to live in a private home here, at number 7 Silbergasse; nor did they take a taxi, but walked the few steps through the public park, across the Waltherplatz, and down the Laubengasse. There were very few people to be seen, and those few were speaking Italian.

As they went, Vroni said: "Did you have a good trip, madam?"

Yes.

Before they turned into the Silbergasse she asked: "And Fräulein Riccarda—I mean is Frau Riccarda well?" She could not get used to all the changes in the family so quickly. The old gentleman dead. The young master dead. The young lady married, with a little son named after the old gentleman. All in two years! "And Sepp? I mean to say young Herr Sepp—because I suppose by now he's a young Herr? How's he? Is he still as good-looking as ever?"

He was well. And still as good-looking as ever. Thank you.

The lady in black looked quite thin, Vroni thought. And, she decided, *She'll gain weight all right if I'm cooking for her! I hope she'll stay long enough*. Like old Babka, who had no opinion of her sister's cookery, Vroni was thinking: *Who knows what kind of a mess they stew together in Pilsen!* People think the same thoughts.

As they were now outside number 7 Silbergasse, which they entered not from the garden but from the front, it was time for the old servant to apologize for the state of affairs that the newcomer might find.

The day before yesterday, when the telegram arrived (Vroni had never known that you could send such long telegrams): "Arriving Tuesday 4 P.M. Please meet me at station and try to get me a room at Mumelter house for a few days. Best regards. GWEN MUMELTER," she had come over and spoken to the new owner of the house, Signor Udacher. Signor Udacher, who lived alone in the house, and had left the wood-carving shop, with the same old sign "Christoph Mumelter's Heirs," undisturbed on the ground floor, was immediately willing to vacate one or two rooms for the widow. He said "widow," and that she was from America; it was only then that Vroni had found out Andreas had been married, had died, and that Gwen Mumelter was his widow. Signor Udacher did not tell her how he had died, but she had not even cared to know that, because the news was bad enough anyway. She had it told over and over again all evening to Foxy, the bitch, whose hearing was no longer what it had been, in the furnished room that she now occupied, where she had nothing to do day in and day out but think of the past. For the few old people and those incapable of bearing arms had been temporarily left in the almost deserted city, and not sent to Moravia. "For old people like the old gentleman to die, there's nothing wrong with that," she had explained to Foxy. "But young ones like our young master!" Foxy could not understand this either, and had barked long and loud.

Now she prepared Gwen to realize that she had been in no way responsible for the house Gwen was about to enter since the day a year and a half before when Signor Udacher, functioning as the prefect's deputy ("sub-prefect entrusted with the liquidation of the German minority," was his full title), had moved into the first floor. She had never written this to the family in Pilsen, because they were on bad terms with him, and would only have been annoyed. Very likely the rooms weren't even aired, and surely they would be dusty. She hadn't cleaned them in ever and ever so long! And she didn't even know which rooms they would be.

On the little table next to the front door, where the old gentleman had always put his Loden hat, however, they found a note with the compliments of the sub-prefect, indicating two rooms on the second floor as guest rooms—the ones where Andreas and Sepp had lived, the "boys' rooms." Riccarda had lived on the ground floor, the old man on the third. The windows of the boys' rooms were open, not a speck of dust was on the furniture, and everything was so clean that Vroni stopped being ashamed. Only the wallpaper in Sepp's old room was damaged, as if someone had amused himself by tearing it off.

As she unpacked, Vroni ventured to ask: "Was the poor young master sick long?"

"No," said Gwen. "Was this his room?" She was standing by the window. The glacier on the Rosengarten shimmered in the afternoon light, and the jagged crest of the Schlern was white. Vroni gave an eager affirmative.

"Did he live here when he was small?" Gwen asked, facing suddenly about.

What a chance for Vroni! He was born downstairs on the ground floor. And he had lived up here since he was three, in the "boys' room." First the bed was a crib, no bigger than that. Then the old gentleman bought him this iron bed here—the old gentleman was a trial, he was that close. How much more suitable a wooden bed would have been, or, more fashionable still, a brass one! But no! The old gentleman had only gone as far as an iron bed, and it was true enough, the young master had slept well even in the cheap bed, so soundly that she had often had to shake him in the morning. And then he'd go to school on the dot, first to the primary school yonder behind the fruit market, then to the Realschule, then to the Polytechnicum, and finally he was three years abroad, and had gone far there. But of course Madam knew about that?

That she knew. He had gone far abroad. With glances that frightened Vroni a little because they were so fixed, Gwen looked around the room carefully, attentively, as if to see and never to forget every tiny point in it, even the splashes of ink on the desk that would never come out after all those years.

And the young gentleman had died suddenly? Fräulein—pardon, Frau Riccarda's last letter hadn't said anything about his being sick, had it?

Yes, very quickly.

Then Vroni, having finished unpacking the suitcase, asked for the other little bag that the lady still clutched firmly under her left arm. Perhaps she wasn't quite right in her head after all the terrible things that had happened?

Gwen made a violent gesture of refusal to the servant. "Don't!" she said. "It's the ashes." Every word seemed to cause her indescribable difficulty; she took a breath before each one, and her voice was hoarse.

Vroni did not understand right away. So Gwen had to explain. One day, eleven days after his death, she got a package by mail, wrapped in brown paper. The mailman brought it and said: "Frau Mumelter? A collect package for you. Two crowns fifty." She paid the charges and opened the wrappings. There was an urn in it, with a label like the one on school copybooks, white with a blue border, and on it was typewritten, "Ashes of Andreas Mumelter." Here. This was the urn with the label.

She took it out of the little bag, which was full of jasmine and Easter roses, and overpoweringly fragrant. The flowers had withered. While Vroni looked at the clay vessel with eyes that grew moist, Gwen lifted a second urn out of the flowers. There was no label on it. But the servant was told the story of this second urn as well. When Gwen had realized that it was Andreas' ashes, because of which she had not died at old Babka's attic window and against the side of the barn, but had gone on living, and when, after efforts that she chose not to describe, she had got permission "for a stay of not more than four weeks in Bozen because of a recurrence of a lung ailment," signed, "Krueger, director of the Pilsen Secret State Police," she had managed also to get the body of Andreas' grandfather exhumed and cremated. His ashes were in the unlabeled urn. And Gwen was here to bury the two. Her continuing to live must have some meaning. This was the meaning she had discovered. Or perhaps even this was meaningless.

She did not say it in so many words, for her voice would not let her; besides, she felt that when the ultimate has been said, words begin to sound unbearably gratuitous. So she mentioned the facts, was silent again, and looked at each point in the room where a boyhood, a youth, and a manhood had been spent of which she knew nothing—so many years missed. Her eyes traveled from the wall to the desk, from bed to window, and across the floor his feet had trodden.

Then, after some little time of the speechlessness that was necessary for Vroni to understand that the young master had not died, but been shot, Gwen heard her voice: "God reward you for that, Frau Mumelter. So they did come home after all."

She was so unaccustomed to answering to the name of "Frau Mumelter" that she glanced up. As she did, she saw that the servant was also looking up at her, as if she had done something truly great.

"You know, Frau Mumelter," said Vroni, trying to rub out the ink spots, already a hundred times scrubbed in vain, because otherwise she would have had to cry, which was not suitable, "before the young master had to go away with the others, I brought him a special-delivery post card in this room. He was sitting over here by the desk, and I asked him: 'What do you think, young master, will you ever be coming back?' And he told me: 'Of course, Vroni.' I didn't believe him then, but he was right." Then she exchanged the obstinate daub of ink for the arm of a chair, which she kept dusting although there was no dust on it, and added: "Our poor gentlemen will be better off soon now." She said it perfectly seriously.

And Gwen looked at her again, and saw that she meant it. Then, for the first time since she had opened her eyes at Babka's tiny window, she began to see something like a meaning. Almost something like joy. She had thought so, too, although she had not dared give that reason for her journey, since it was not among the legally permissible "urgent reasons for travel in the territory of the Third Reich." But she had Vroni's feeling that the men would be better off then. So she had gone.

"How long did you know the gentlemen?" she asked Vroni. A quarter century longer than she herself had known them. This, too, pleased her, for it meant that she was right.

Then it was three days before the interment of the ashes could take place in the Mumelter family vault, and Pastor Gemaassmer was the one who finally secured permission for her to do it. As she had not known him before, she could not see how he had aged in the interval; but she felt that it was good to talk to him. He, too, knew so much about the two at whose funeral he was to preach, and he knew so much about the country here, and even about the world, although he had scarcely been outside the Tirol. He, too, gave her the pleasure Vroni had given her by saying to her: "What you've done is the finest thing that has come to my ears in these times, when one scarcely hears any but ugly things."

She replied: "There couldn't be anything more perfectly natural."

And he said: "Haven't you realized that in the world of today the perfectly natural has become a miracle, the best thing that can befall us?"

In the Bozen parish church, very early on the morning of July 23, 1941, at an hour that no one was allowed to know except himself and Gwen and Vroni, he said the first blessing over the ashes. Gwen was sitting in one of the hereditary seats of the Mumelter family; the brass plate with the name was still there. The church was empty. The hard wood of the benches told her nothing of the devout who had once knelt in them. The air in the cathedral had retained nothing of their joys and sorrows. Nevertheless, Gwen at that moment could see them sitting on the empty benches, hereditary seat after hereditary seat, men, women, children, graybeards, all with the same expression, the same face. Andreas' expression. Andreas' face. They had all come home.

Afterward the pastor stood outside with the women by the open vault where the two urns were to be placed. Instead of Cemetery Superintendent Hoermann, who was somewhere between Moravia and Slovakia, waiting for the revolution, another man performed the duty of lowering them into the earth. But it was Pastor Gemaassmer who spoke the blessing upon the earth in which Laurenz Mumelter, who had confessed to him, and Andreas Mumelter, whom he had baptized, would henceforth rest with their forefathers:

"You return to the earth from which you came. Welcome to the Tirol. Did they think they could tear you from your homeland? Did they think they could plant you in some other place? Yes, so they thought, and so they think. But that is their great mistake, the one that will be most fearfully avenged upon them. Blind men that they are! They make their plans to uproot human beings here, everywhere in the world, by the hundred thousand, by the million. They dig them up where they grow, and plant them where they cannot grow. And they call it the New Order. But it is only the root of disorder, of the ruin that the transplanters will bring upon themselves. For just as rivers cannot flow backward, but only from source to mouth forever, men can fulfill themselves only where they grow out of their own roots, from birth to death. Nature will not be compelled! 'Woe unto them that injure the roots,' says Jeremiah, the prophet, 'for it shall be avenged upon them a thousand fold! By every root that they pluck up shall their field diminish, and by the roots that they plant in strange earth shall their own fields dry up!' You know it, you two —you are the blood witnesses, the martyrs to it. You proved it by your living and dying: Nature will not be compelled. Return now to the earth that the power of the mighty would have taken from you, and that the power of love has opened to you. Welcome. In the name of the Father, of the Son, and of the Holy Ghost. Amen!" He made over the vault the same great sign of the cross that he had sent after them as the singing train took them away in the dark of night. Now dawn was breaking.

Gwen said: "Thank you, Pastor." Vroni said: "That was a beautiful sermon, Your Reverence." And the vault was closed.

Someone remarked ominously: "That *was* a beautiful sermon, Pastor!" To Gwen he volunteered: "I have not yet had an opportunity to offer you my condolences. Please accept my sympathy." It was Signor Udacher, the sub-prefect, entrusted with the liquidation of the German minority. And as Gwen did not answer him, he asked with emphasis: "How long may I offer you my hospitality?"

Looking not at him but at the Rosengarten, which rose from the twilight like a monument of purity, she answered: "Not too long, I hope." The high functionary took this as a snub, which he could not pocket in the presence of the others, and therefore, beside the grave that had scarcely been closed, he continued the conversation in a casual, offhand tone: "You have had interesting experiences abroad, I take it?"

Her eyes lost their tears and grew cold. "Yes," she said, making conversation by the scarcely closed grave with the man on whose account it had been opened and closed, "I met some interesting people."

He meant it to be he, rather than she, who broke off the conversation, and so he did his best to keep the upper hand. "Who, for instance? I know quite a lot of people in Pilsen," he inquired, with extreme indifference.

"Oh—their names are Babka and Doležal and that sort of thing—I hardly believe you'd know them."

"No," he admitted reluctantly. "They can hardly be very prominent people. Czechs?"

"Some of them. I have come to know them, and I know they can be depended on. Absolutely."

Her tone, which struck him as scornful, challenged him. "You mean to say they are good friends?" he corrected, looking at his watch and preparing for an effective termination to the talk.

"And good enemies."

He frowned. "I beg your pardon?"

"I mean to say they are all people who mean well by me. I shall hear from them. I shall be here until then."

"That hardly depends altogether on you. Your stay is limited. Am I mistaken?"

"If it should be necessary, I shall get an extension."

"From whom?"

"From my lungs."

"Do you think you're as sick as that?"

"I shall be well by the time I hear from my friends."

The sun touched the peaks of the mountains.

"You're hoping for some special news? May I ask what it is?"

"I don't hope. I know. And I want to be the first to bring my husband the news. Good morning, Signor Sub-prefect."

She left the man in the black shirt standing there. So it was she, after all, who broke off the conversation! *Now, now, black lady,* he thought peevishly, *this isn't Pilsen, it's Bozen. I'll find out soon enough what this means! What was that name again? Babka?*

Meanwhile, with the pastor and the old servant, without a second's hesitation, or a backward look, she was going along the cemetery wall, up the ever brighter walk into the dawn.

Acknowledgments

I am greatly indebted to:

Mr. Guido Zernatto, former Austrian Secretary of State and leader of the Austrian Fatherland Front, for allowing me to use his documents and studies bearing on the South Tirolean problem.

The Czechoslovak Legation in Washington for valuable material on Pilsen.

Mr. Robert J. Kerner, Professor of Modern History at the University of California, for allowing me to reprint parts of Karel Čapek's "A Prayer for Tonight," from the book about Czechoslovakia edited by him.

Messrs. Roscoe Drummond and Glen Perry for allowing me to use their study, "How Our Cities Are Protected from Axis Bombs," in the *Saturday Evening Post* of June 13, 1942.

The editors of *Free World* for allowing me to use an article on the "Go Slow Campaign," published in Vol. 1, No. 3.

Dr. Eduard Reut-Nicolussi, former deputy from the South Tirol in the Vienna Parliament, for allowing me to reprint Andreas Hofer's farewell letter, translated by K. L. Montgomery, from his book, *Tirol Under the Axe of Italian Fascism* (London, George Allen & Unwin, Ltd.).

Miss Louise F. Kampf, librarian of Colorado College, and Miss Maxine J. Cromwell, her assistant, for their tireless efforts in securing inaccessible sources and documents.

To them all I offer my heartiest thanks.

E. L.

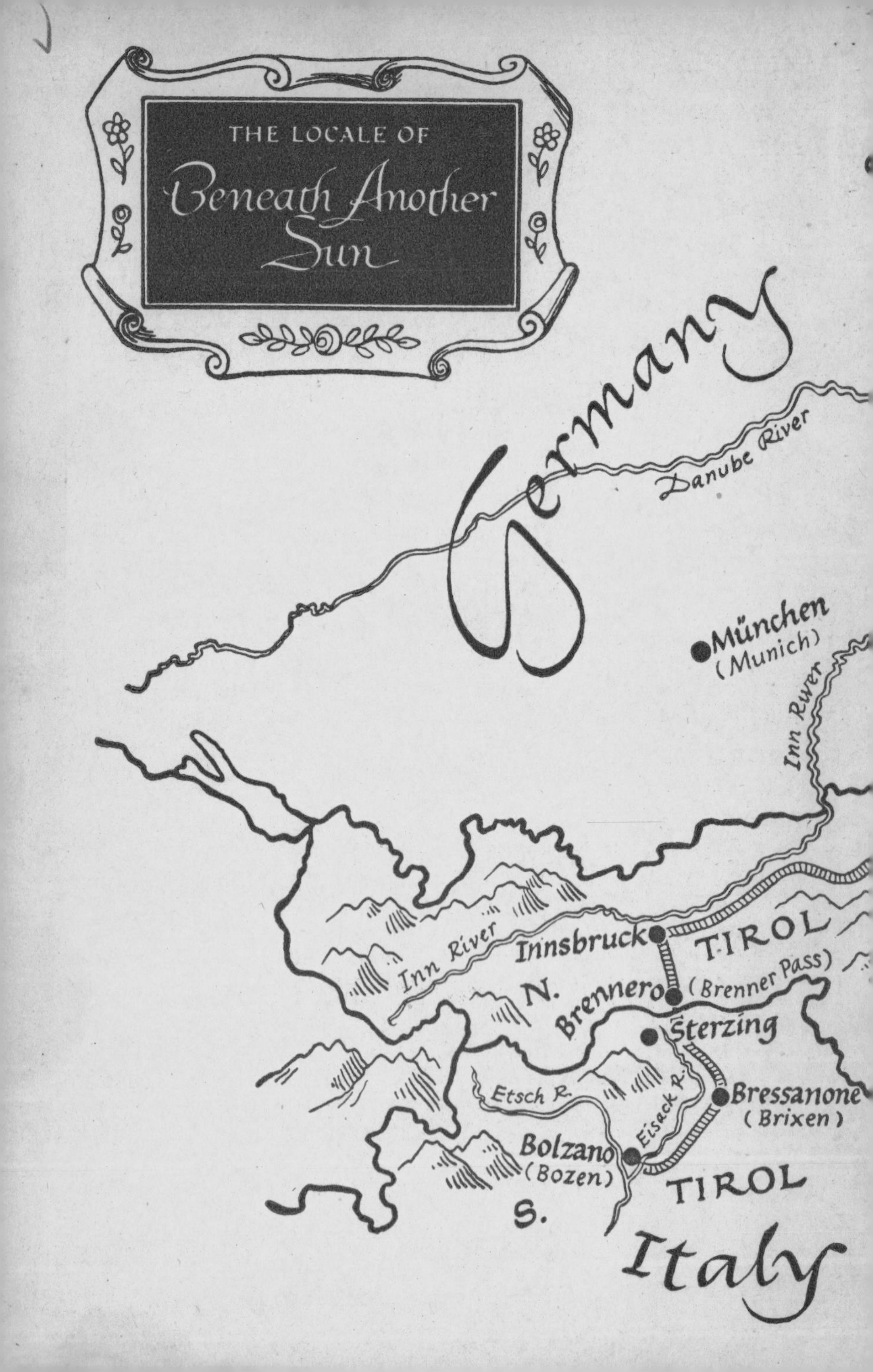
THE LOCALE OF
Beneath Another Sun
Germany
Danube River
München
(Munich)
Inn River
Inn River
Innsbruck
TIROL
N.
Brennero
(Brenner Pass)
Sterzing
Etsch R.
Eisack R.
Bressanone
(Brixen)
Bolzano
(Bozen)
TIROL
S.
Italy